Frederick William Hawkins

The Life of Edmund Kean - From Published and Original Sources

Vol. 1

Frederick William Hawkins

The Life of Edmund Kean - From Published and Original Sources
Vol. 1

ISBN/EAN: 9783337095574

Printed in Europe, USA, Canada, Australia, Japan

Cover: Foto ©Raphael Reischuk / pixelio.de

More available books at **www.hansebooks.com**

THE LIFE

OF

EDMUND KEAN.

From Published and Original Sources.

BY

F. W. HAWKINS.

"In all romance, in all literature, there is nothing more melancholy, nothing more utterly tragic, than the story of the career of Edmund Kean. So bitter and weary a struggle for a chance, so splendid and bewildering a success, so sad a waste of genius and fortune, so lamentable a fall, can hardly be found among all the records of the follies and sins and misfortunes of genius."—*Morning Star.*

IN TWO VOLUMES.

VOL. I.

LONDON:

TINSLEY BROTHERS, 18, CATHERINE STREET, STRAND.

1869.

LONDON :
SAVILL, EDWARDS AND CO., PRINTERS, CHANDOS STREET,
COVENT GARDEN.

TO

JOHN OXENFORD, Esq.,

IN GRATEFUL REMEMBRANCE

OF NEVER FAILING KINDNESS AND ENCOURAGEMENT,

THESE VOLUMES

ARE

Inscribed.

(*UNKNOWN*.)

"*To* Edmund Kean, Esq.
From Noel Byron."

Thou art the sun's bright child !

The genius which irradiates thy mind

Caught all its purity and light from heaven.

Thine is the task, with mastery most perfect,

To bind the passions captive in thy train.

Each crystal tear that slumbers in the depth

Of Feeling's fountain doth obey thy call.

There's not a joy or sorrow mortals prove,

A passion to humanity allied,

But tribute of allegiance owes to thee.

The shrine thou worshippest is Nature's self—

The only altar genius deigns to seek ;

Thine offering—a bold and burning mind,

Whose impulse guides thee to the realms of fame,

Where, crownèd with well-earned laurels, all thine own,

I herald thee to immortality !

PREFACE.

THE objects with which these volumes have been written may be briefly enumerated. To compose an impartial and satisfactory biography of our greatest actor; to avail myself of some original sources of information which have fallen into my hands; to prove that the fine comprehension of Shakspeare's tragic characters which now prevails is in great measure to be attributed to Kean's strong conceptive power and intuitive grasp of his author's sense; to connect him closely with the history of the stage by showing how great was the revolution in the art of acting which his appearance at Drury-lane in 1814 served to effect; above all, to clear his memory from the stains and dirt which envy, hatred, and all uncharitableness have cast upon it; and, by removing from the story of his extraordinary career all those anecdotes with which the appetites of the scandal-loving community have been satiated, but any authentication of which it is absolutely impossible to discover, to present a faithful and reliable portrait of him who, four-and-fifty years ago, thrilled our souls, fired our imaginations, stirred us to enthusiasm, moved us to pity, to admiration, to tears,—a portrait which, without being invested with undue attractiveness, or without throwing a veil over unquestionable blemishes, shall delineate Edmund Kean as he appeared amongst us during his brief mundane existence, a man to love, to admire, and to esteem. Such has been the purpose of the author of these pages.

Long plausible prefaces are altogether out of date. I will not trespass on the patience of my readers further than to refer in a few words to the disadvantages under which I laboured in bringing these volumes to a termination, to say something in anticipation of an accusation that will in all probability be brought against me, and to make all necessary acknowledgments of the assistance I have received.

As this *Life of Edmund Kean* bears internal evidence

of an inexperienced pen, I hope that my deficiencies in literary art will be ascribed to their actual source. But, subscribing as I do implicitly to Goethe's maxim, what have I to fear? As one servant cannot serve two masters, so my readers cannot condemn this book and share the opinion of the great German poet at one time, for I have performed my task *con amore*, and has not Goethe said that " enthusiasm is the *one* thing necessary to history?"

The great disadvantage attendant upon the publication of a work of this kind is the perishable and transitory nature of dramatic fame. The actor is but the hero of the hour. He passes like a splendid meteor across the horizon of his own age, sends forth a train of scintillation brief, brilliant, and sublime, and then sinks into all but oblivion, " leaving the world no copy." He cannot, like the poet or the painter, bequeath to posterity an imperishable monument of his genius ; his excellences virtually live no longer than the feeble breath by which they are presented, dying with the evanescent applause which greets them, and leaving nothing to convey an adequate idea of their rarity and brilliance. This obstacle I have not endeavoured to surmount, because it would be in vain to do so, but I have left it out of my calculations.

The accusation which I have referred to as likely to be brought against me is this :—there will be some who, cherishing the axiom that "no human work is perfect," will charge me with having praised Kean's acting with too much liberality, and also with having paid too little attention to his defects. My reply is very simple. His beauties were above all praise ; his faults arose exclusively from the fulness of his wealth. The sorry distinction of excelling in the discovery of excrescences which thus originated I have not been anxious to acquire ; I have not hesitated to notice them where truth and sincerity required them to be noticed ; but I have striven all along not to degenerate into hypercriticism, consoling myself with the reflection, " let who will search for the bad, and—much good may it do them when they have found it !"

It is with great pleasure that I hasten to acknowledge the assistance I have received from Mr. Procter's *Life;* Mr. Leman Rede's *Recollections* of Edmund Kean (published in the *New Monthly Magazine*); the memoir of Kean in the *Annual Biography and Obituary* for 1834; Dr. Doran's *Their Majesties' Servants;* and Mr. Walter Donaldson's *Reminiscences of an Actor.* In describing Kean's performances I have been frequently assisted by references to files of *The Times,* the *Examiner,* the *Morning Post,* and the *Champion,* especial importance being attached to the criticisms of the two former; and for orally-communicated information I am indebted to Mr. John Oxenford, Mr. John Hurlstone (of Hampstead), Dr. James Smith (of Richmond), and other gentlemen.

F. W. H.

54, ARUNDEL-SQUARE, N.,
March 1, 1869.

CONTENTS

OF

THE FIRST VOLUME.

BOOK I.

Rise.

PAGE

CHAPTER I.

1787–1803.

PAGE

Ancestry of Edmund Kean . . 1
Henry Carey 2
George Saville Carey 2
Ann Carey 3
Birth and birthplace of Edmund
    Kean 4
Miss Tidswell's narrative . . 4
Inhumanity of Ann Carey . . 5
Deserted 5
With a poor couple in Frith-
    street 6
First appearance on the stage . 7
Michael Kelly's reminiscence . 7
Edmund's great personal beauty . 7
In the Drury-lane pantomime as
    a " demon " 7
Distortion of limbs prevented . 8
Short stature accounted for . 8
At Drury-lane as an imp in
    Macbeth 9
Untoward result of John Kemble's
    interpolation 9
Edmund's mischievousness . . 9

Fills the parts of pages in *Love*
    Makes a Man and *The Merry*
    Wives of Windsor 11
Leaves Drury-lane 11
His first education 11
Orange-court, Leicester-square . 12
Holcroft and Opie 12
Evil influences of unchecked
    childhood 12
Edmund's quickness at learning . 12
At a school in Chapel-street,
    Soho 12
Determined to go to sea . . . 13
The house in Ewer-street, South-
    wark 13
Phœbe Carey 13
Edmund goes to Portsmouth . 13
At sea as a cabin boy 14
Rigorous servitude 14
Resolves to escape 14
Strategy adopted 14
His secretiveness 15
At Madeira 15
Baffles the doctor's skill . . . 15
Returns to England 15
An unexpected evolution . . . 15
Again in London 16

	PAGE
" What shall I do ?"	16
Moses Kean—his dress, vocation, and history	17
An advertisement from *The Times*	18
A hearty reception	18
Moses's admiration of *King Lear*	19
Edmund studies Hamlet . . .	19
His intelligence and originality .	20
Conventionalities set aside . .	20
A solemn junto in Lisle-street .	20
Miss Tidswell	21
Mrs. Price	21
At a school in Green-street . . .	21
Receives instruction for the stage	21
D'Egville	21
Angelo	21
Incledon	21
Edmund's early proficiency in swordsmanship	22
An anecdote related	23
Edmund's magnanimity . . .	23
Wild as the quagga	23
Tavern performances	24
Found tarred and feathered at a public-house in St. George's Fields	24
Dragged home by Miss Tidswell	24
Escape	24
Return	25
The brass collar	25
Engaged to represent child's part at Drury-lane	25
Mrs. Charles Kemble's reminiscence	26
Plays Arthur in *King John* . .	26
Miss Tidswell's instruction . .	26
Plays the Lady-killer in *Blue Beard*	27
Death of Moses Kean	27
Impression upon the boy . . .	28
His early comprehension of Shakspeare	28
Studies in *Hamlet, Othello, Macbeth,* and *King Lear*	28
	PAGE
His excellence in Richard III. .	29
Unintermittent rehearsals of the character	30
Roach, the bookseller's, garret .	30
Who played Lady Anne . . .	30
Master Rae	30
What happened in Mrs. Price's back parlour	30
Denman, the musician	31
Mrs. Clarke of Guildford-street .	32
Interrogatories	33
Acting in a drawing-room . .	34
Extraordinary impression produced	34
Adopted by Mrs. Clarke . . .	35
Refinement	35
Intellectual pursuits	35
Insult	36
Edmund's quickness of temper .	36
Thrown back upon Miss Tidswell	36
Bitterness of spirit	37
At Bartholomew Fair	38
George Alexander Steevens' description of the "sports" . .	38
Booth performances	39
Boldness in equestrianism . .	39
Fractures his legs	40
Recovers	40
Davies's reminiscence	40
Return to Lisle-street . . .	41
Studies of Shaksperian character renewed	41
Study of Hamlet	41
" Alas, poor Yorick !"	41
Dislike to Romeo and Cato . .	42
His voice	42
At Portsmouth in search of his mother	42
Disappointed	43
Self-reliance	43
Returns to London	44
At Sadler's Wells Theatre . . .	44
Belzoni	44
Recites Rolla's address . . .	44

	PAGE
Studies Shylock	45
Original conception of the character	45
At the Rolls' Rooms	46
At York	47
His remarkable volition	47
The fate of juvenile "wonders"	47
Plays Hamlet, Hastings, and Cato	47
Precocious talent	48
His deficiencies	48
A strolling player	48
Meets with Ann Carey	49
Separation	49
With Richardson's troupe	50
At Sheerness	50
Plays Norval, George Barnwell, &c.	50
At Windsor	51
The King's message	51
Richardson's embarrassment	51
A metamorphosis effected	51
Conducted before the King	51
Recites from various plays	52
Remuneration	52
Consequent attractiveness	53

CHAPTER II.

THE STROLLING PLAYER.—THE
STUDENT.—1803-14.

	PAGE
Kean's education at Eton	54
Evidence adduced	55
An extract from the *European Magazine*	56
At Dumfries	57
Arduous study	57
Manager Moss—his career	58
In Butler's troupe at Northallerton	59
Old George	59
Butler's liberality	60
Kean's return to London	60

	PAGE
In "little business" at the Haymarket	61
Waits on John Kemble	62
A silent rebuff	62
Miss Maria Germain	63
Kean's inconstancy	63
Again a strolling player	63
Vicissitudes of such a life	64
The contempt experienced by the strolling player	65
What Captain Marryat and Washington Irving thought of the strolling player	66
The artificial "gentleman" *versus* nature's gentleman	66
Kean's indomitable perseverance	67
At Tunbridge Wells	68
At Hoddesdon	68
Studies Greek	68
Becomes assistant in the Hoddesdon seminary	68
Studies physiology	68
At Birmingham and Edinburgh	68
Self-denial	68
At Belfast	69
Plays with Mrs. Siddons in *The Mourning Bride*	69
Mrs. Siddons' Zara	69
Kean's Osmyn, Jaffier, and Norval	70
His Lord Townley and Tancred	71
Departure from Belfast	72
A maturing genius	73
His observance of nature	73
Instances recorded	74
Studying Sir Giles Overreach	74
At Sheerness	75
His Sir John Brute	75
A happy retort	76
Swims over the Thames	76
Faints away on the Braintree stage	77
Illness and recovery	77
In Beverley's troupe at Gloucester	77
Jack Hughes	77

	PAGE
First meeting with Miss Chambers	78
Mutual recrimination	78
Kean's Job Thornberry . . .	79
Watson's opinion thereof . . .	79
Kean's Tekeli and Harlequin .	80
Gladiatorial excellence . . .	80
At Stroud	80
His Archer and Hastings . . .	80
Master Betty engaged	80
Kean's disappearance	81
Returns	81
His intense application . . .	81
Marries Miss Chambers . . .	82
Dismissed from the company .	82
Privations endured	83
Increasing perseverance . . .	83
At Warwick	84
Plays Lothaire in *Adelgitha* . .	84
In Watson's company at Walsall	84
Adverse criticism	84
At Birmingham	85
Stephen Kemble's opinion of Kean's Hotspur	85
Kean's Octavian	86
Stephen's offer declined . . .	86
At Swansea	87
Plays Rolla to Mrs. Kean's Cora	87
Bengough	87
Birth of Howard Kean . . .	87
At Waterford	88
Sheridan Knowles	88
Leo the Gipsy	89
Mr. Grattan	90
Kean in the fencing scene in *Hamlet*	91
His benefit	93
Birth of Charles Kean	93
At Dumfries	94
A tavern performance and one auditor	94
At Carlisle and York	94
A playbill	95
Energies weakened by reverses .	97
Mrs. Nokes's timely generosity .	98

	PAGE
A long and weary journey to London on foot	99
Kean sees Kemble and Mrs. Siddons in Wolsey and Catharine at Covent-garden	99
A determination	99
At Weymouth	100
Asked to play second to Master Betty	100
Takes to the woods	100
His Zanga	101
At Exeter	101
Miss Hakes's china-shop . . .	101
A midnight prank	102
Accumulating adversities . . .	103
Popularity of his Harlequin . .	103
What he did for an old Latin dictionary	104
Mrs. Jordan	105
Kean plays Don Felix and Frank Heartall	105
Sunshine and shadow	105
Lord and Lady Cork	105
At Guernsey	106
Adverse criticism	106
Popular derision	107
His courageous defiance . . .	108
Invidiousness of the press . . .	109
Sir John Doyle's interposition .	109
At St. Pierre	110
Mr. Savory Brock	110
Return to England	110
A *ruse*	110
Brightening prospects	111
Interest of Dr. Drury	111
Kean engages with Elliston . .	112
What the Drury-lane Committee did	112
Arnold at Dorchester	113
Kean's account of their meeting	113
Engaged for Drury-lane . . .	114
Death of Howard Kean . . .	115
Edmund's letter to Dr. Drury .	116
Departure for London	117

	PAGE
Introduced to the Committee	117
Mutual disappointment	117
Kean's firmness and independence	118
An obstacle	119
Elliston waives his claim	120
Sneered at by the actors	121
More obstacles	121

	PAGE
The spite of the Committee	121
Stephen Kemble's Shylock	121
Tokely's appearance	121
Huddart's Shylock	121
Kean's " *début* " announced	122
Reckless and miserable	122
Absence of all puff	123
Termination of an itinerant life	123

BOOK II.

At the Zenith.

1814–1825.

CHAPTER I.

THE IDOL OF THE PEOPLE.— THE
THEME OF POETS AND CRITICS.—
1813-14.

	PAGE
The 26th January, 1814	124
The one morning rehearsal	124
Startling effect of his originality	125
Having a dinner	125
Despondency	125
On his way to the theatre	125
The black wig	126
Oxberry and Bannister's kindness	126
Sorry condition of the house	127
Kean quite undaunted	127
Before the audience	127
A favourable impression	127
A vague expectation excited	128
The first applause	129
In the third act	130
A thunder of acclamation	130
Success placed beyond doubt	131
The trial scene	131
The performance concluded	132

	PAGE
The goal won!	132
Ecstatic joy	132
What occurred in the Cecil-street garret	133
William Hazlitt	134
His criticism on Kean	135
The Committee's suggestion	137
Kean and Byron	138
Their resemblance	138
The poet's intercession	139
Kean's second appearance	139
Extraordinary impression made	140
All obstacles surmounted	141
The criticism	142
The scene changing rapidly	143
Lordly patronage	144
Biographical sketches in the newspapers	144
The house filled to repletion	144
Kean liberally remunerated	145
Numerous presents	145
Bannister's wit	146
The character of Shylock	147
How it had been previously represented	148

	PAGE
Kean's Shylock described. . .	149
Appears as Richard III. . . .	153
Great success	153
His excellence analysed . . .	153
The fulness of his riches . . .	155
Originality of the conception. .	156
Mrs. R. Trench on his Richard .	157
The 12th of February, 1814 . .	158
A dense and expectant audience.	158
Kean suffering from the effect of a cold	158
His opening soliloquy	159
The scene with Lady Anne . .	160
His " Chop off his head !" . .	161
Mind unceasingly at work . .	162
His "The Tower?—*aye*, the Tower".	163
Beauties thickly scattered . .	164
His caustic vigour	164
The reverie and the "Good night"	165
The tent scene	167
Noble poetry of the death scene	169
The audience beside themselves.	170
Criticism upon his Richard III.	171
Kean's illness	174
Letter to Arnold	175
Byron on his Richard	176
Kean at Holland House . . .	176
Appears as Hamlet.	177
Truth of the conception and brilliancy of the execution . . .	178
His Hamlet described	180
Original treatment of the ghost scene	182
The death soliloquy	184
The kissing of Ophelia's hand	185
The play scene	187
Physiological accuracy of the death scene	190
New readings	191
The classic and the romantic schools of acting	193
The Kemble school swept from the stage by Kean	197
	PAGE
Nature re-established	198
Kemble's Hamlet	200
Criticism upon Kean's performance	201
A struggle for supremacy . . .	204
What the actor of originality and power has to contend with .	205
Mrs. Garrick	206
Her admiration of Kean . . .	207
Garrick's arm-chair.	208
Indiscriminating criticism. . .	208
Impulsive character of Kean's acting	209
Garrick's Hamlet	210
Kean's hatred of "polished society "	210
The Coal Hole in Fountain-court	210
Rank and talent frequenting the Drury-lane green-room . . .	211
President West	212
His opinion of Kean's Richard .	212
James Northcote—Richard Brinsley Sheridan	212
Samuel Taylor Coleridge . . .	213
His opinion of Kean's acting .	213
Lord Byron	213
The *Ode to Napoleon Buonaparte*	213
Passage suggested by Kean's Richard III.	213
Lines in the *Corsair* applied by its author to Kean	214
Reappearance of Ann Carey . .	214
Edmund Darnley	214
Kean's paternity in question . .	215
The Earl of Essex and the Duke of Norfolk	215
Kean's gratitude to Miss Tidswell	215
A contrast	215
Appears as Othello	216
General description of the performance	217
The character of the Moor . .	220
Is Othello a black ?	221
Kean's Othello described . . .	222

	PAGE
His senate scene	222
His rebuke to and dismissal of Cassio	223
Marvellous performance of the third act	224
The "Farewell"	226
Accumulating triumphs	227
The fourth act	228
The last scene	229
Criticism	233
Hazlitt's, Leigh Hunt's, and Barry Cornwall's eulogies of his Othello	233
Byron's recommendation	241
John Kemble's jealousy of Kean	242
Mrs. F. Kemble thereon	242
Dowton's envy	243
Kean's appearance in Iago	243
Brilliancy of the performance	244
New aspect given to the character	245
Kean's conception justified	245
Authorities quoted	248
His Iago described	249
Denationalization	250
Iago's song	251
Splendour of the third act	252
The watching of Roderigo's body	253
Lord Byron's opinion of Kean's Iago	255
First benefit at Drury-lane	256
Appears as Luke	256
Byron and Moore present	256
Massinger's *City Madam*	257
Sir John Burgess's alteration of the play	257
The character of Luke	258
Kean's performance described	258
Anecdote connected therewith	259
Conclusion of the season	259
Profit to the theatre	260
A dividend of five per cent. declared	260
Mr. Whitbread's eulogy of Kean	261
The actor's lofty position	262

	PAGE
Commencement of his splendid race	263
"On the ocean of Shakspeare's genius"	263
A noble voyage and an unprosperous termination	263

CHAPTER II.

SECOND SEASON.—1814–1815.

	PAGE
Kean in Dublin	264
Great success	264
Repute as a "jolly good fellow"	264
Return to London	265
Variation of his original conception of the dying scene in *Richard III.*	265
Hazlitt's criticism	265
Kean's "pauses" explained	265
His alleged want of dignity	266
Appears as Macbeth	267
Previous representatives of the character	268
Kean's pre-eminence	268
Remarks on the character	269
Kean's Macbeth described	270
The vision of the dagger	272
Great effect of the murder scene	273
Banquo's ghost an anomaly	275
The final combat with Macduff	276
Kean's individualization of his performances	277
Hazlitt on the murder scene	279
Mrs. R. Trench on his Macbeth	279
The witches	280
Improvements in costume	281
Miss O'Neill's "*début*"	282
Her acting described	283
Miss Walstein	285
Kean appears as Romeo	286
His wilful negligence in the balcony scene	286
Great effect of the banishment and death scenes	288

PAGE

Garrick's version of *Romeo and Juliet* 289
His Reuben Glenroy 290
Production of *Richard II.* . . 291
Kean's performance 293
Moore and Byron in the pit . . 294
Mrs. Wilmot's tragedy of *Ina* . 295
Kean's Penruddock 297
Revival of *The Revenge* . . . 298
Remarks on the character of Zanga 298
Dramatic history of the play . . 299
Hazlitt's criticism 300
Kean's Zanga described . . . 301
Great effect of the last scene . . 302
Barry Cornwall and Southey thereon 302
Kean's Abel Drugger 303
His comic versatility 303
Hazlitt's and Mrs. Garrick's opinions of his Abel 304
Formation of the Wolf Club . . 305
Kean's inaugural speech . . . 305
The members 308
The Coal Hole in Fountain-court 309
A jeu d'esprit 310
Kean's Leon 314
Leigh Hunt's liberation from prison 315
His opinion of Kean's acting . . 316
Presents 316
The American lion 317
Kean's resentment of Raymond's servility 317
Kean's Octavian 3⅟
Retirement of Jack Bannister . 319
Sir George Rose's epigram . . 321

CHAPTER III.

THIRD SEASON.—1815-16.

Rebukes the Portsmouth innkeeper 322
Kean's generosity 324

PAGE

His freedom from false pride . 325
His sensitiveness to insult . . 331
Takes Lady Rycroft's house in Clarges-street, Piccadilly . . 332
Mrs. Kean's tastes and those of her husband 332
Edmund's indefatigable study . 332
His erratic habits 333
Studies music 334
Opening of his third season . . 335
His dying speech in *Richard III.* (written by Cibber) 335
Revival of Rowe's *Tamerlane* . 335
Kean's Bajazet 336
His Aranza 337
Equivocal success 337
Revival of some old plays resolved upon 338
The *Merchant of Bruges* . . . 340
Kean's Goswin 341
Dowton's Shylock 342
Kean appears as Sir Giles Overreach 343
The performance described . . 344
Overwhelming effect of the last scene 345
Mrs. Glover fainting on the stage 347
Effect upon Lord Byron . . . 347
Mrs. Kean informed by Kean of his success 347
Hazlitt's criticism upon Kean's Sir Giles 348
Critique from *Blackwood* . . . 350
Softer beauties in the performance 353
Kean's acting disrelished by the upper circles 355
Effect of his Sir Giles on the Kemble school 357
John Kemble hissed in Sir Giles 358
Hazlitt's criticism 358
Revival of the *Duke of Milan* . 361
Kean's Sforza 362
A "serious accident" 364
Reappearance 367

PAGE

Production of *Bertram* . . . 369
Byron as a member of the Drury-
lane Committee 370
Rise of melodrama in England . 370
Maturin's play 371
Kean's Bertram 372
His "God bless the child !" . . 373
Revival of *Every Man in his
Humour* 374
Kean's Kitely 375
His own opinion of it 376
Rebuking sycophants 377
Miss O'Neill 377
Presentation to Kean of a silver
cup by the Drury-lane company 378
The inscription 379
Kean's reply 380
At Bath 381
At Edinburgh 383
The criticism in the *Courant* . 383
Departure of Lord Byron from
England 388
His regard for Kean 388
Kean's hatred of rank 389
Evenings at the Kinnairds' . . 389
An anecdote 391
Kean at Cribbs's 392
His friendship for Incledon . . 392
An interview with Lord Essex . 394
Kean's refusal to recite before
the Duke of Wellington . . 394

CHAPTER IV.

FOURTH SEASON.—1816-17.

Opening 398
Revival of *Timon of Athens* . . 398
Kean's performance 397

PAGE

Leigh Hunt's description of the
Encounter with Alcibiades . 398
"*Début*" of Mr. Macready . . 399
Mr. Macready's Orestes, Men-
tevole, and Othello 400
Revival of *The Iron Chest* . . 401
Kean's Sir Edward Mortimer . 403
Excellence of the performance . 404
Hazlitt and Barry Cornwall
thereon 406
Enthusiasm of the audience . . 406
Kean's readiness to undertake
any of his characters at a
moment's notice 407
Revival of *The African Prince* . 407
The character of Oroonoko . . 408
Kean's performance 409
A letter from poet Gray respect-
ing Southerne 410
"*Début*" of Junius Brutus Booth 411
A skilful imitation of Kean . . 412
Booth at Drury-lane 412
Plays Iago to Kean's Othello . 413
Great effect of Kean's Othello
on this occasion 413
Fall of Booth 414
Bannister's opinion 415
Booth's return to Covent-garden 416
A tumult 416
Invidiousness of the Covent-
garden proprietors 417
A false statement respecting the
Wolf Club 418
Why the Club was broken up . 418
The letter in the *Examiner* . . 418
The Covent-garden proprietors
caught in a trap 420

LIFE OF EDMUND KEAN.

BOOK I.
𝔕𝔦𝔰𝔢.

CHAPTER I.

" I T is perhaps not generally known," writes
Macaulay, when closing his narrative of the
death, in 1695, of George Saville, Marquis of Halifax,
"that some adventurers who, without advantages of
fortune or position, made themselves conspicuous by
the mere force of ability, inherited the blood of
Halifax.   He left a natural son, Henry Carey, whose
dramas once drew crowded audiences to the theatres,
and some of whose gay and spirited verses live still
in the memory of hundreds of thousands.   From
Henry Carey descended that Edmund Kean who, in
our own time, transformed himself so marvellously
into Shylock, Iago, and Othello."   From this it

appears that Edmund Kean might have indulged in a pardonable pride of birth, inasmuch as the celebrated Lord Halifax belonged to a family which originated in this country with Drogo de Monte-acuto, a prominent member of the Conqueror's retinue at the battle of Hastings, and ancestor of the Dukes of Manchester and the Earls of Salisbury and Montague.

Of Henry Carey, the reputed author of the National Anthem, something is to be said. His sorrowful career brings before us in vivid colours the contrast occasionally exhibited between the delights imparted by men of genius and their own feelings and worldly condition. Of popular admiration he experienced no want; the genius, wit, humour, and refined tenderness displayed in his lyrical and dramatic works obtained a wide recognition; but for some reason that remains unexplained he was always involved in difficulties. These difficulties, joined to his constitutional sadness and melancholy, at last affected his reason; and on the 4th of October, 1743, he destroyed himself at his house in Warner-street, Coldbath-fields.

George Saville Carey inherited his father's genius—and his misfortunes. He was originally intended for a printer, but having conceived a *penchant* for the stage, he threw aside the " composing-stick" and came out at Covent-garden.   Notwithstanding his talent for mimicry, he produced no effect, and did not remain on the boards more than one season.   The scanty records of his life during the subsequent forty years exhibit a painful instance of genius incessantly striving for bare subsistence.   At one time he would appear with success before the public as an anatomical lecturer; at another as the author of lyric, satirical, dramatic, and pastoral fragments.   Towards the close of his life the infirmities of age gathered quickly upon him, and he suddenly expired on the 14th of July, 1807. To charity he was indebted for a respectable funeral.

George Saville Carey was cursed in a worthless, inhuman daughter.   Ann Carey had, at the age of fifteen, ran away from home to join a company of strolling players ; and when itinerant business was at a standstill, she figured in the streets of London as a hawker.   It was in the latter capacity that her not unprepossessing face attracted the attention of Aaron Kean, an architect, who took her under his protection, but subsequently abandoned her.   Shortly afterwards she became the mother of Edmund Kean, the circumstances attending whose birth were, as the reader will see, hardly of a nature suggestive of the extraordinary future which awaited him.

Notwithstanding certain plausibilities to the contrary, the parentage and birth-place of Edmund
Kean are not involved in the slightest uncertainty.
He was born on the 4th of November, 1787,
in a deserted, solitary, and otherwise unoccupied
chamber in the neighbourhood of Gray's Inn.
"About half-past three in the morning," writes
Miss Tidswell, the actress, "Aaron Kean, the
father, came to me and said 'Nance Carey is with
child, and begs you to go to her at her lodgings
in Chancery-lane.' Accordingly my aunt and I went
with him and found Nance Carey near her time. We
asked her if she had proper necessaries, and she replied 'No, nothing;' whereupon Mrs. Byrne begged
the loan of some baby clothes, and Nance Carey was
removed to the chambers in Gray's Inn, which her
father then occupied, and it was there that the future
tragedian was born." That Edmund Kean was a
natural son of Miss Tidswell was at one time
a favourite belief; but in addition to the above-
quoted statement, indubitable evidence has come to
light showing beyond all doubt that Ann Carey was
the mother of the greatest of English actors, and that
his father was one Aaron Kean, differently described
as a tailor, an architect, and a stage carpenter.

From the moment of his birth, so to speak, Edmund Kean entered into that dark and fœtid atmosphere of sorrow and depravity which, surrounding him during a period when the character is formed and moulded according to the nature of external influences, probably served to inculcate that established independence and uncontrollable self-will which retarded his advancement to prosperity, darkened the otherwise unclouded sky of his after career, and rendered him inaccessible to the healthy counsel of those who would have guided his steps away from that abyss into which he fell at the comparatively early age of forty-six. Probably in that lonely and deserted Gray's Inn apartment, faintly illumined by the flickering and uncertain flame of a rush-light, there was no one who greeted him with the welcome usually accorded to the little stranger. Certainly, the last person who would hail the advent of the child was the mother, who appears to have been so destitute of natural and gentle affections that, after supporting the child for about three months, she abandoned him to the caprice—to the charity of strangers, and thereafter denied to her hapless boy the exercise of any maternal consideration whatsoever. She passed into the country to resume her wanderings, and a veil

of obscurity descends over the first three years
of Edmund's life. At the expiration of that
time the mist clears up, and the pitiable, repulsive selfishness of his mother is again laid open
to view. Revisiting London, that estimable lady
discovered her infant son under the care of a poor
couple in Frith Street, Soho, who, attracted by
his engaging, winsome manners, had lately taken him
under their protection. One November night in 1789
they had found the child left in a dark doorway, cold,
hungry, and desolate. How it came there was never
known. . Relieved from all the cares and anxieties
incident to the nurture of an infant, Ann Carey was
not long in formally demanding the surrender of her
" property," and having obtained possession of the
boy from the liberal-minded couple, whose means
were too limited to conveniently admit of his support,
the mother, with no consideration for his tender
years, set herself to devise the means whereby she
could turn the intelligence which he had manifested even at that early age to account. Miss
Carey, with a true eye to business, decided that
he should be initiated, into the mysteries of the
stage, in order. that he might be of service to
her in subsequent' " strolling." With this view she

succeeded in obtaining him, first a position as the Cupid recumbent at the feet of Sylvia and Cymon in one of Noverre's ballets at the Opera House, and afterwards in the lower department of the Drury Lane pantomime. This was towards the close of 1790. He owed his elevation to the dignity of Cupid less to the influence of his mother than to the rare personal beauty for which he was already distinguished. "Before the piece was brought out," writes Michael Kelly, in his *Reminiscences*, "I had a number of children brought to me that I might choose a Cupid. One struck me, with a fine pair of black eyes, who seemed by his looks and little gestures most anxious to be chosen as the little God of Love. I chose him, and little did I then imagine that my little Cupid would eventually become a great actor : the then little urchin was nothing more nor less than Edmund Kean." His first appearance on the stage was accordingly made, and the impression created by his personal beauty was so deep, that an old lady, "in the fulness of her dotage," inquired, "Is that really a living child?" The impression went for nothing when, a few months later, he was appointed to personate one of the demons in the Drury Lane pantomime. Under the tuition of the posture master his limbs acquired a flexibility so extraordinary as to be capable, by the time he had attained his fourth year, of instantaneous adaptation to the most surprising attitudes and contortions. The rapidity of his progress in this branch of pantomimic art was contemplated by his mother with a selfish satisfaction soon converted into dismay as the exercises to which he was constantly subjected produced a distortion of the limbs; and for the purpose of averting a result so ruinous to Miss Carey's interests as the permanent disfigurement of his body, irons were resorted to as a means of restoring the bones to their natural form. The antidote operated with the most happy results; his figure reassumed that symmetry which never afterwards deserted it; but his shortness of stature in after years appears to have been caused by his mother's persistence that he should continue his work at the theatre, the irons being at the same time attached to his body in order that distortion might be prevented.

Three years passed, and we now arrive at an incident which curiously illustrates the inexplicable manner in which Fortune sometimes shuffles her cards. On the 12th of March, 1794, Drury Lane Theatre, then under the management of John Philip

Kemble, opened with Shakspeare's tragedy of *Macbeth*. With the view of heightening the weird solemnity and impressive grandeur of the cauldron scene, the manager, adopting a course scarcely illustrative of the good taste with which he is usually credited, decided upon introducing the goblin troupe *in propria personâ;* and among the children engaged to personate these fantastic creations was Edmund Kean, in whom originated the disaster which led to the abandonment of what Kemble is reported to have termed the finest commentary on and illustration of Shakspeare ever attempted on the stage. All promised a complete representation when the act drop rose, discovering the cauldron (a new one) and the attendant witches; but at the moment when Kemble, as Macbeth, entered the cavern, little Edmund, who appears to have entertained a shrewd suspicion as to the absurdity of the whole affair, mischievously contrived what seemed to be an unlucky step, from which, owing to the incumbrance of his irons, he was apparently unable to recover himself; he upset his neighbour, who in turn dislodged another, and the impulse having communicated itself to the whole troop, the stage immediately exhibited a scene of confusion altogether indescribable. " I tripped the goblins up,"

said the tragedian, when some years later he laugh-
ingly related the incident; "they fell like a pack of
cards." The unbounded merriment which followed
this untoward result of the manager's interpolation
was still less in unison with the feelings of its
originator, who stood quietly at the mouth of the
cavern surveying the struggling mass of humanity
with emotions to be better imagined than described.
His reverence for solemnity of stage effect received a
shock too rude to permit the experiment to be repeated; and his resolution having been strengthened
by a quietly satirical notice in the *Oracle*, which
recommended the expulsion of

> "Black spirits and white,
> Red spirits and grey,"

with the muck-fork unless they could produce an
effect less ludicrous, the finest commentary on and
illustration of Shakspeare ever attempted on the stage
was forthwith abandoned. The cause of all the mischief, however, "smiled in the storm," and in reply
to the manager's thumps and reproaches demurely
directed his attention to the fact that it was "the first
time he had performed in tragedy,"—an excuse which
appears to have soothed the managerial resentment,
inasmuch as we find the little fellow subsequently

filling the unimportant part of page in *Love Makes a Man* and the *Merry Wives of Windsor.* Shortly afterwards he left the theatre, and in the handsome and intelligent boy who had converted the interpolation in *Macbeth* into a burlesque Kemble probably did not recognise the genius who, twenty years later, deposed him from his pre-eminence on the stage, subjected him on almost every hand to a comparison so unfavourable that positive sibilation marked the distinction between the respective antagonists, and whose powers shone forth with a meridian splendour in which the brilliance of the elder actor faded and turned pale.

In a locality already distinguished as the lowly abode of genius, as the birthplace of Holcroft,* the dwelling-place of Opie — Orange-court, Leicester-square—Edmund Kean drew his first draught from the fountain of learning. The complete ignorance in which Ann Carey had permitted her son to remain established within him an amount of independence and self-will that at an early age awoke the dormant

---

* "Till I was six years old," writes the author of the *Road to Ruin*, "my father kept a shoemaker's shop in Orange-court; and I have a faint recollection that my mother dealt in greens and oysters."

energies too often deadened by academical restraint, but it nevertheless formed the groundwork of a series of evil influences which, unchecked and unrestrained by a wise and gentle training, increased in power until they acquired the form of a predominating cha- racteristic. A philanthropic and liberal-minded few, attracted to the boy by his singular personal beauty and intelligence, entered into an agreement to defray between them the slender expenses of his rudimentary education,—an indispensable requisite, they wisely argued, to the fulfilment of his early promise. This proposition encountered the sturdy opposition of Ann Carey, who, appalled at the pros- pect of losing the pitiful emolument derived from his exertions, and unable from her own deficiencies to recognise the benefits of instruction, combated it with all the resolution in her power; but the sturdy oppo- sition of the mother was eventually overruled, and in a dirty school-room in the dirty locality referred to Ed- mund Kean mastered the common rudiments of learn- ing with surprising readiness and facility. After leaving Orange-court he went to a somewhat cleaner school, in Chapel-street, Soho, kept by a Mr. King. The for- tunes of Ann Carey were now at the lowest ebb, and mother and son occupied in common a humble tenement at 61, Ewer-street, Southwark. There is also a sister spoken of—a Phœbe Carey—who, together with her mother, was at this time a member of Richardson's troupe. With the removal of the family from Castle-street, Leicester-square, to Southwark, a change had come over the spirit of the boy. He longed for the freedom of action which he had hitherto enjoyed ; attached to his books he was, but he hated the disciplinary restraints enforced in Chapel-street, Soho ; and with imagination captivated by the marvellous and romantic adventures of that wayward Scot, Alexander Selkirk, he arrived at a determination to go to sea. Not quite eight years of age, he had the temerity to announce such determination to his mother, who in reply gave him a lusty application of the stick. This, instead of deterring, decided him. In the dead of night, with a few necessaries tied up in a bundle and slung over his shoulder on a stout stick, he left the house in Ewer-street, passed out of London, and made direct for the coast. As the sun rose he might have been seen trudging manfully along the road; and arrived at Portsmouth, he shipped himself as cabin boy on board a ship bound to Madeira.

The vessel had barely gone beyond sight of his native shores when the little sailor discovered that he

had widely miscalculated the amount of labour to
which he should be subjected in his new capacity.
His tender years naturally rendered him unequal to
the rigorous duties he had undertaken to discharge,
and, disgusted and impatient with the servitude upon
which he had voluntarily entered, he determined to
effect his escape.   The charm of "Robinson Crusoe"
was destroyed, and for a time his seafaring predilec-
tions were cured.   The uncertainty of his return to
England alone deterred him from abandoning the
ship as it stopped at different ports on the way, and
in the strategic means he ultimately adopted to
emancipate himself from his unpleasant situation he
showed that secretiveness was with him an inborn
faculty.   He represented that a cold contracted on
board had produced a total deafness, and so well was
the deception supported by every look and gesture,
that captain and crew were alike deceived ; but fearing
that this infirmity might be deemed insufficient to
preclude the performance of his duties, he further
pretended that the aforesaid cold had settled in his
extremities, producing a lameness that rendered him
unable to leave his berth.   The success of the last
ruse was as unequivocal as its predecessor ; he was
permitted to keep his bed, and his wants were

administered to.   On the arrival of the ship at Madeira, he was removed to the hospital in that town, where, determined to maintain his assumed character to the last, he practised the deception for two months with so much care that all investigations into the nature of the malady were pronounced to be at fault.   Cure was finally pronounced impossible, but as a kind of forlorn hope, the doctors, unconsciously playing into the hands of the interesting patient, prescribed his return to England.   He was accordingly removed on board a homeward bound ship, and so firmly maintained his deceptive exterior throughout the voyage that not even the horrors of a tempest, which threatened every moment to engulph the ship in the surging waters, could induce him to turn otherwise than a *deaf* ear to the surrounding roar, or, in the endeavour to avert the destruction of the vessel, to participate in the bustle which prevails on a ship's deck during a storm.

Arrived on shore, he tendered his gratitude to those who carried him from the ship by a sudden and vigorous execution of the college hornpipe, and disappeared amongst the ramifications of Portsmouth before his custodians recovered from the stupefying amazement into which they had been thrown by this unexpected evolution. Hungry, weary, and footsore, he eventually reached the metropolis, and found himself homeless, destitute, and without any visible means of support. The humble tenement at the house in Ewer-street, formerly inhabited by his mother, was now occupied by strangers; Ann Carey, accompanied by Phœbe, had gone into the country with Richardson's troupe. In this emergency two alternatives presented themselves; one, that he should solicit a renewal of the kindness he had already experienced at the hands of those who had sent him to school, and the other that he should seek a shelter beneath the roof of his paternal uncle, Moses Kean, who had invariably treated him with the greatest kindness. The latter alternative was immediately adopted; and proceeding to Lisle-street, Leicester-square, he knocked at his uncle's door.

Mr. Moses Kean, mimic, ventriloquist, and general " entertainer," was emphatically " a character." With his stout-built frame, black bushy hair, and wooden leg; his imposing dress, which usually consisted of a bright scarlet coat, white satin waistcoat, black satin smallclothes, a Scot's liquid dye blue silk stocking, and ruffled shirt; his cocked hat, long-quartered shoe with a large buckle; and a switch or cane which

appeared to have never left him;—Moses exhibited
an exterior that might have charmed the eye and
inspired the pencil of Hogarth himself. Mr. Kean
was a very popular man. The numerous scrapes and
turmoils in which he became involved through a
want of scrupulousness and caution in the exercise of
his dangerous talents only served to render him a
greater favourite with the amusement-seeking public;
and, as an instance of the respect in which they held
him, it may be stated that when an actor named Rees
ridiculed his wooden leg in an interlude appropriately
entitled *Thimble's Flight from the Shop Board* (Moses
was bred a tailor), produced at the Haymarket for
the benefit of Charles Bannister, the audience marked
their sense of the unsympathetic caricature by driving
Mr. Rees from the stage with an energetic shower of
hisses. Visiting Paris in company with La Porte,
the artist, and Ryan, a bookseller of Oxford-street, his
success in the French capital was unequivocal. Ryan
employed to good effect his talent in the delineation
of Irish character; Moses made the Parisians laugh by
excellent caricatures of the most celebrated statesmen
and artists; and La Porte turned his artistic acquirements to account by reproducing with the pencil, under
the form of an advertisement, the mirth depicted on the

faces of the audience.   The following is an announcement of one of Moses's entertainments, copied from
a file of *The Times* for 1791 :—

"L Y C E U M,   S T R A N D.

" This evening, April 19.

" Mr. Kean, impressed with the most lively sensations of gratitude for the multitude of favours which it has been his good fortune
to experience at the hands of the nobility, gentry, &c., begs leave
again to present himself to that patronage with which he has been
so liberally countenanced on former occasions.

" At the pressing solicitation of many persons of distinction, and
under the sanction of those illustrious characters whose approbation
gave an additional energy to his past exertions, Mr. Kean again
submits himself a candidate for public favour, and humbly hopes
the public expectation will be gratified by the several novelties
in his

E V E N I N G   L O U N G E,

In which will be delineated with perspicuity the voices, gestures,
and manners of the most conspicuous characters of the senate, the
stage, &c.   In the course of the evening many original and eccentric anecdotes will be introduced.

" Doors to be opened at 7 o'clock, to begin exactly at 8.   Boxes,
5*s.*; saloon, 3*s.*; gallery, 2*s.*   Places for the boxes to be taken of
Mr. Tilleard, at the Lyceum."

Even at this length of time, we seem to hear the
hearty roar of satisfaction with which Moses Kean
welcomed his nephew to the house in Lisle-street.
For a day or two, he alternately felicitated the runaway on his return and rated him soundly for going

to sea; decided to include among "the original and eccentric anecdotes" in his next "lounge" a short and graphic account of the deception maintained by the youthful sailor; and then, detecting the bent of the boy's inclination, proceeded to initiate him into the mysteries of the dramatic art. Although the powers of Moses Kean lay in a walk of the drama diametrically opposite to the "legitimate," he was by no means insensible to the beauties of Shakspeare, for whose tragedy of *King Lear* he is reported to have entertained an especial admiration. Anxious to indoctrinate his nephew's mind with views akin to his own, he caused him to enter upon the study of Hamlet as a character conformable in some respects to juvenile instincts and powers; and although in his attachment to pantomimic pursuits the pupil exhibited a tendency which scarcely promised to lead him into the path which he subsequently followed up with such brilliant results, he nevertheless conquered intuitively all the difficulties of an art which, after all, cannot be taught, and made amends for an imperfect comprehension of the deep philosophy pertaining to the part by the inimitable grace and earnestness infused into the ghost scene, in which Moses impersonated the buried Majesty of Denmark with all due solemnity. Edmund was also

instructed by his uncle to recite Shaksperian
soliloquies in the manner of the most popular performers of the day; but his characteristic originality
of thought refused to be restricted by the bonds of
tradition and convention, and he not unfrequently
astonished his tutor with innovations evidently resulting from the most careful study and laborious research.
From the first he manifested a remarkable freedom
from the measured enunciation and formal, studied demeanour then in vogue, and an instinctive disposition
to re-model accepted conceptions upon his own (as yet
necessarily imperfect) observation of human nature
and character. Avoiding an imitation of individual
masters, he surveyed their performances in union with
natural truth, and, like the intelligent and industrious
bee, sipped from every flower that caught his eye in
her wide domain. Under the auspices of Moses Kean
he made constant visits to the sacred quarters of
Drury-lane Theatre, and as, a rapt and attentive
listener, he drank at the fountain of Shaksperian lore,
a fine idea of sublimity and grandeur dawned upon his
nascent, brightening intellect.

Shortly afterwards, a solemn conclave was convened
in Lisle-street, to determine the future career of little
Edmund. Moses Kean, good-naturedly disposed to

countenance any scheme likely to advance his nephew's interests; Mrs. Price, sister to Ann Carey, and mantua-maker, carrying on business in Green-street, Leicester-square; Miss Tidswell, the actress, interested in the boy from his relationship to her old professional associate Ann Carey, attracted to him by his personal beauty and early intelligence, and sympathizing with him in the vivid impression which the beauties of dramatic poetry had produced on his mind—these were the individuals who constituted the junto which assembled on the occasion referred to. The result of their deliberations was, that Edmund became a pupil at a day-school in Green-street. Neither Moses Kean, Mrs. Price, nor Miss Tidswell appears to have entertained any particular presentiment of the brilliant future which awaited their protégé, and in facilitating the development of his intellectual and histrionic powers they were probably actuated by views no more ambitious than that he might achieve a respectable rank in the profession. When away from school, Aunt " Tid" instructed him in the mechanical principles of the art; D'Egville so far initiated him into the mysteries of dancing as to enable him to combine in himself the duties of ballet-master with those of the sock and buskin; Angelo rendered him

" cunning of fence ;" and Incledon, who treated him
with the utmost kindness, and for whom Edmund
ever cherished the warmest regard, imparted to him
all the skill that he himself possessed as a vocalist.
The rapid acquirement of these valuable auxiliaries
indicated the conscious power of a mind endowed with
qualities of the highest order. Never losing an
opportunity of getting behind the scenes, he was ever
on the alert to pick up every hint that could be
turned to advantage. His dancing became singularly
graceful ; his voice, clear, full, and sweet to a degree
of tenderness, became capable of imitating Incledon's
with such facility that scarcely any dissonance could
be detected between the copy and the original; while
of his early skill as a swordsman an anecdote must be
recorded, as marking not only his quickness of eye
and dexterity of hand, but also his firmness, intre-
pidity, and self-command. On one occasion he
opposed in the academy a black man, who, celebrated
as he was for the rapidity of his passes and the certainty of his hits, was unable to beat down the
boy's guard, or prevent him obtaining the mastery
in several passes. Enraged by his ill success,
the black, determined to inflict summary vengeance
on his conqueror, struck his foil on the ground so as

to break off the button; but Edmund, detecting the movement, composedly awaited the assault, disarmed his assailant, caught the foil as it sprang from his hand, presented it to his treacherous antagonist, " unbated " as it was, bade him keep his own secret, and left the room. With a consideration of which the black was altogether unworthy, the boy never mentioned the fact until the death of his opponent removed all scruple as to its disclosure.

His application was assiduous, but his wayward mischievousness was as great as ever. A wild, generous, and ungovernable boy he is reported to have been, and no doubt was, delighting in all kinds of mischief and danger, but withal tender, affectionate, and sincere. Forming a high but not mistaken estimate of his powers, he would sometimes remain absent from the hospitable roofs of Moses Kean and Miss Tidswell for weeks together, and having gone through his acrobatic evolutions at a series of road-side inns, he would be brought back by some burly honest farmer, with an account of having found the young runaway in a barn, where, having lost his way, and overcome with fatigue, he had sought shelter. Sometimes poor Moses's regard for appearances sustained a shock on finding that his scapegrace nephew had

turned head-over-heels and given imitations of monkeys and knife-grinders at taverns in the immediate
neighbourhood of Lisle-street, picking up the halfpence
bestowed on him in return with no unwilling hand.
On one occasion, after an anxious search, he was found
actually tarred and feathered at a public-house in St.
George's Fields, collecting a few pence as largess for
the amusement he had afforded the company in the
"tap" by reciting, tumbling, and singing. Evincing
a strong disinclination to close the entertainment,
Miss Tidswell tied a rope round his waist and dragged
him, tarred and feathered as he was, to Lisle-street,
amidst the shouts and laughter of a motley and unruly crowd. Bolts and bars could not always keep
him indoors. On the following evening, while Miss
Tidswell, as the *Gentlewoman*, was, as in duty bound,
expressing her surprise at the unearthly appearance of
Mrs. Siddons in the sleep-walking scene of *Macbeth*,
the window of the room in which Master Edmund
had been locked was triumphantly opened, descent
was made at the risk of his neck, and he was once
more free. During the ensuing three months he acquired at various fairs some notoriety as a pretty
singer, a skilful and energetic acrobat, and as a young
gentleman of remarkable self-possession. He lived

frugally, slept in barns when opportunity permitted, and brought home his gains to uncle Moses. But the old actor wanted not the money. He was angry that his nephew did not stay at home, and, with imagination uncaptivated by the glitter of pantomimic pursuits, give his undivided attention to the precepts of Miss Tidswell and himself. With the wish came the suggestion of a remedy. Restoring the barbarities of the Anglo-Saxon period, described by Sir Walter Scott in his portrait of Gurth the swineherd, a brass collar was placed round his neck inscribed with, "This boy belongs to 9, Lisle-street, Leicester-square ; please bring him home." But the expedient proved of no avail. A handkerchief tied round his neck concealed the obnoxious circlet from view, and Miss Tidswell was eventually compelled to lock him up during her absence, and in a room from which there was no possibility of escaping.

An engagement at Drury-lane as the representative of child's parts corrected to some extent the quagga-like wildness of Edmund Kean. The progress he made in his studies from Shakspeare may be gathered from the following anecdote, related by Mrs. C. Kemble :—"One morning, before the rehearsal commenced, I was crossing the stage when my attention was attracted to the sounds of loud applause issuing from the direction of the green-room. I inquired the cause, and was told that it was 'only little Kean reciting *Richard III.* in the green-room.' My informant said that he was very clever. I went into the green-room and saw the little fellow facing an admiring group and reciting lustily. I listened, and in my opinion he *was* very clever." A few nights later he played Arthur with a spirit so judicious, and a conception so clear, that his efforts called down a thunder of applause. Kemble that night played King John to the Constance of Mrs. Siddons, and it was no slight evidence of the boy's great natural abilities that he shone forth to advantage on such a canvas. He had been cast for Arthur at the instance of Miss Tidswell, who, naturally anxious that his performance should justify her intercession on his behalf, caused him to recite the scene with Hubert over and over again at home, in addition to the rehearsals at the theatre. A system devised by herself —that of getting him into the habit of rehearsing his parts before a portrait, and inducing him to suppose for a time that it represented the other characters in the scene—may be referred to as one of the reasons for the freedom from all statuesque inflexibility and

formal enunciation which distinguished his performance on this occasion. Replete with grace and tenderness, it exhibited a perception of poetic beauty,
the force of diction, and the graces of eloquence, more
vivid than those of men who then enjoyed dramatic
celebrity. When the holiday pageant of *Blue Beard*
was produced, Edmund was appointed to represent
the unloveable lady-killer in the palanquin borne
down the mountains by the wicker-work elephant,
and so earnestly is he said to have entered into the
absolute self-will of the great bashaw that, accoutred
as he was in the trappings of the minor bashaw, with
a short scimitar by his side, he was about to surrep-
titiously leave the theatre to let "Aunt Tid see
how fine he looked," when his progress was somewhat unceremoniously arrested by the doorkeeper,
who removed him in triumph to the wardrobe, and,
heedless of the young gentleman's brandished sword
or threats of vengeance, disrobed and disarmed
him.

The death of Moses Kean threw Edmund entirely
upon the bounty of Miss Tidswell, who thereupon
gave him a home, instruction for the stage, and—the
stick. The little actor appears to have cherished a
sincere attachment to his uncle, and the sudden and

unexpected demise of the latter introduced into his
manner a shade of gravity which contrasted oddly
enough with the impulsive spirit he had previously
displayed. Hastening to improve the opportunity
afforded by this temporary check upon his characteristic wildness, Miss Tidswell endeavoured to withdraw his attention from acrobatic pursuits, and
to awaken in his youthful mind a refined susceptibility to the numberless beauties of the great
poet of nature. Owing to an early though undetected
development of his powers of reflection and abstraction, the latter endeavour was attended with complete success; his eyes begun to open wider than
ever to the rarity and value of what Shakspeare wrote;
his conceptive power so increased and strengthened
as to enable him to comprehend and elucidate the
spirit of his author with remarkable facility; and he
saw that a fruitful harvest might be reaped by a
studious and diligent exploration of that wonderful, half-explored mine. He studied respectively
Hamlet, Othello, Macbeth, and King Lear, each of
which, both in conception and execution, opposed a
direct contrast to Kemble's manner of doing them.
Being a constant visitor behind the scenes at Drury-
lane Theatre while the performance was going on, it

was not difficult for him to detect the adventitious
artifice resorted to by Kemble in his representations,
and in the general dissonance of that actor's subordi-
nation to critical propriety with the unrestrained, un-
forced, and impulsive aspect of nature, arose that strict
fidelity to truth and flexibility of conduct which displayed so beautiful a harmony with the fiery and
glowing idea for which he was subsequently distinguished. From this time the imperfect records of
his early life exhibit a rare instance of industry and
genius directed to the attainment of a specific end
—the restoration of nature to the stage. A conception of his future greatness now dawned on his
mind, and as he contemplated the distant prospect
with a fascinated gaze, the ethereal spark, fanned by
a warm and enthusiastic temperament, burst into a
flame of a brilliance and intensity which no reverses
could diminish or destroy, and sustained in more
trying moments a native energy which no peril could
disturb, no obstacle, however great and apparently
insuperable, bend or turn aside.

Of all the Shaksperian characters which Edmund
studied at this time, no one appears to have engaged
so large a share of his attention as Richard III.
Upon the very spirit and essence of this character his

already strong conceptive power fastened from the
very first with swift, sure, and unerring instinct; and,
if we receive the testimony of Miss Tidswell, there is
no doubt that even at thirteen years of age he had
arrived at a fine comprehension and brilliant realization of the crook-back king. His rehearsals were
almost unintermittent. At one time he might have
been found practising the courtship scene in a garret
in the house of a bookseller named Roach, situate in
a court running from Brydges-street to Drury-lane,
Lady Anne being represented by a "Scotch lassie,"
who subsequently acquired some distinction as the
successor to Mrs. Davenport in the line of characters
which belonged to the latter at a theatre in Scotland
—Mrs. Robertson; at another we find him rehearsing the combat scene in Mrs. Price's back parlour in
Green-street, to the Richmond of Master Rae, the son
of the matron at St. George's Hospital, the mantua-
maker's yard measures serving for the swords of the
furious antagonists on the agitated field of Bosworth.
Master Rae, inoculated with the dramatic mania by
his companion, had recently arrived at a determination
to become an actor; within four years he will have
achieved a very respectable share of success; after
two years more he will lead the business of the Hay-

market Theatre, Edmund supporting him in *fifth-rate*
characters; in seven years after that he will have
become so proud as to decline to recognise his old
companion, as the latter, a pale, restless, dark-eyed
little man, enveloped in a capacious cape, and the
butt of general ridicule, waited in the lobby of Drury-
lane Theatre for an audience of the manager; and
two months later he will play Richmond to the
Richard of Kean to an audience which included in
its overflowing numbers the actress and the mantua-
maker who had smiled with approbation on the boyish
efforts of each.   Contemporary with Edmund's early
studies of Richard III., is a highly interesting anecdote. A fine taste for music formed one of the
qualities which Kean possessed for the profession
which fate as well as inclination seems to have
marked out for his pursuit, and in proportion as it
recommended him to the notice of the musicians connected with the theatre, it led him to profit by the
instruction which they, charmed with his aptitude
and taste, felt themselves by no means disinclined
to impart. Among those for whom he appears to
have conceived a warm attachment, was one whose
undeniable genius was degraded and eventually
destroyed by its abuse—Denman.   One morning

Kean was passing through Deptford, when he observed Denman stretched at full length on a form
in front of a tap-room, and as Kean approached
it became evident that the musician, rising superior
to the effects of the previous night's excess, was engaged in the mental composition of a piece of music.
Ascertaining that Edmund had a few pence in his
pocket, he despatched him for a sheet of paper, and a
pen, ink, and ruler having been obtained from the
worthy Boniface, Denman's eloquent setting to the
Lord's Prayer—a comparatively unknown yet impressive piece of sacred harmony—was placed upon paper.
Acting upon the musician's instructions, Kean carried
the manuscript to Williams's in Paternoster-row,
and the stained and blotted paper was upon the point
of being rejected, when its excellence was detected by
a professor, who purchased it for a guinea. The sum
was carried by Edmund to the bemused musician,
who appears only to have attached value to his talents
as the means of administering to his unfortunate propensity to drink.

Among those who in private circles came to detect
the dawnings of that genius which was to restore its
waning splendour to the drama was a Mrs. Clarke,
of Guildford-street, Russell-square, to whom Ann

Carey had in years gone by been introduced as a dealer in perfumery and Mareschalle powder " genuine and cheap." At that time Mrs. Clarke had, much to Miss Carey's astonishment, expressed considerable interest in the pale, handsome, and brilliant-eyed little fellow who, laden with the perfumery and Mareschalles powder, wearily trudged by the side of his mother; nor did that interest appear incapable of revival when, accidentally meeting with the representative of child's parts at Drury-lane, the lady recognised in him the Master Carey of seven years ago. " You are the little boy who can act so well ?" she said to Edmund a few days later. A bow of assent and a heightening colour constituted the reply. " What can you act ?" " Richard III.—*Speed the Plough*—Hamlet—Harlequin." " I should very much like to see you perform." " I should be proud to act to you," returned the boy, promptly. An introduction to Mr. Clarke, who was much struck with the contrast exhibited between the poverty of his clothes and his delicate, expressive face, led to an arrangement that he should revisit Guildford-street that evening, to give them a specimen of his powers; and precisely at the appointed time a knock at the door heralded the arrival of the boy, who was found on examination to have a clean face, his brown curly hair neatly adjusted, and a frilled handkerchief stuck into his coat as a collar.   An audience consisting of about a dozen of Mrs. Clarke's friends had been brought together, and that lady, not forgetting that some scepticism had been expressed by her visitors relative to the talents of the "wonder," carried him off in triumph to her dressing-room, and equipped him in an old black riding hat with feathers, and a real sword and belt. He surveyed himself in the glass, and felt convinced, as he himself expressed it some years later to a friend of the writer, that "he had never looked so fine before." Introduced to the audience, he rushed on to a platform which had been erected at the end of the room ; ceremony was dispensed with ; the platform became a stage ; and as he embodied the tent scene in *Richard III.*, the play scene in *Hamlet*, the third act of *Othello*, and the murder scene in *Macbeth* with impassioned fervour, the feelings of the visitors changed from distrust to attention, from attention to approval, from approval to silent wonder, from silent wonder to absolute enthusiasm.   As he descended from the platform, the "audience" could only find relief for their pent up feelings in earnest applause ; and a shower of shillings and sixpences fell at his

feet.   He expressed a wish not to receive them, but
Mrs. Clarke eventually overcame his objections, and
he placed them in his pocket with a determination
that " Aunt Tid should have the lot "—a determination which he carried out.   With her admiration of
his talents Mrs. Clarke blended a sincere attachment
to the boy; having withdrawn him from the school
in Green-street, she adopted him; and the recognition
of his abilities becoming wider among her friends
with each successive performance, Mrs. Clarke's carriage was frequently in requisition to convey the
little actor and his " properties "—viz., a sword, white
gloves, and a hat and feathers—to evening parties for
the purpose of giving them the tent scene in
Richard III.   In the day Mrs. Clarke instructed him
in various branches of knowledge; and in his leisure
hours he taught himself to play upon the pianoforte, to
compose music, and to construct little plays on incidents in Spenser's *Faërie Queen.*   Under this wise
and gentle culture his manners became wholly di-
vested of all colouring indicative of lowly associations; this was the care which, for his future welfare,
ought to have surrounded him during the remainder
of his boyhood; and it is impossible to contemplate
without regret the unhappy circumstance which de-

prived him of Mrs. Clarke's interest and protection.
Some visitors at the house in Guildford-street were
arranging to go to the theatre, and on Edmund's
name being included in the list of the playgoers,
a gentleman, with more bad taste than good sense,
inquired " What! Does *he* sit in the box with us?"
" Certainly," was the reply. The doubt implied in
the question as to his fitness for the company of his
friend's visitors was too much for the sensitive nature
of the boy. Night though it was, he rushed almost distracted out of the house, and it was not until three
weeks after, during which time all inquiries as to his
whereabouts had been of no avail, that he was found
asleep on a dust-heap near Mrs. Clarke's house,
ragged, squalid, and footsore. In answer to Mrs.
Clarke's inquiries, he stated that he had tramped to
Bristol with the intention of shipping himself to
America, but that as none of the seafaring men to
whom he had applied would take him in consequence
of his apparent weakness, he bent his steps back
again to London, and after enduring almost every
variety of wretchedness on the way, he had fallen
exhausted on the spot where they had found him.
Mrs. Clarke's interest in the player-boy ceased, and a
benefit having been made up in order that his de-

parture might not wear a look of dismissal, he was again thrown on the charity of Miss Tidswell.

This undeserved repulse stirred up all that was bitter, all that was antagonistic, in the boy's temperament.   At the house in Guildford-street a new world had opened before him; conversant throughout his childhood with human nature in its most sorrowful aspects, he there saw refinement, order, and gentility for the first time; he appreciated the advantages with which he had been surrounded by Mrs. Clarke; and having desired to turn those advantages to account by separating himself from the old life, to raise himself above the vulgar associations to which he had hitherto been connected, the blow told heavily. From the effects of that repulse, which may be regarded as one of the principal turning-points of his life, he never recovered.   His inherent gentleness of disposition had quickly aroused him to a consciousness of the superiority of the new life over that of the old one; and now, finding that his cherished hopes of permanently clearing himself from all trace of his former associations were destroyed, that he was again reduced to the level of a street Arab, and that he should be forced for his bread, to say nothing of pursuing the goal he had determined to win, to

mingle again with the lowest of the low, he became
filled with bitterness against the (to him) illusory
sweets of the new life,—a bitterness which eventually
resolved itself into an implacable aversion to rank,
wealth, and refinement.

Bartholomew Fair! Irresolute, unsettled, and careless, he became a member of Saunders's company.
From George Alexander Stevens's graphic description
of the " Sports of the City Jubilee," the reader may
form some idea as to the atmosphere which Edmund
was now breathing :—

> " Here was, first of all, crowds against other crowds driving,
> Like wind and tide meeting, each contrary striving ;
> Shrill fiddling, sharp fighting, and shouting and shrieking,
> Fifes, trumpets, drums, bagpipes, and barrow-girls squeaking,
> Come ! my rare round-and-sound, here's choice of fine ware,
> Though *all* was not sound sold at Bartelmy Fair ;
> There was drolls, hornpipe-dancing, and showing of postures,
> With frying black puddings and opening of oysters ;
> With salt-boxes solos, and gallery folks squalling,
> The tap-house guests roaring and mouth-pieces bawling ;
> Pimps, pawnbrokers, strollers, fat landladies, sailors,
> Bawds, bailies, jilts, jockies, thieves, *tumblers*, and tailors :
> Here's Punch's whole play of the Gunpowder Plot,
> Wild beasts all alive, and peas-pudding all hot ;
> Fine sausages fried, and the Black on the wire ;
> The whole Court of France, and nice pig at the fire :
> Here's the up-and-downs, Who'll take a seat in the chair ?
> Though there's more up-and-downs than at Bartelmy Fair.
> Here's Whittington's cat, and the tall dromedary,
> The chaise without horses, and Queen of Hungary ;

Here's the merry-go-rounds,—Come! who rides? come! who
    rides, Sir?
Wine, beer, ale, and cakes, fire-eating besides, Sir;
The fam'd learned dog, that can tell all his letters,
And some men, as scholars, are not much his betters."

When the contrast exhibited between the features of
Bartholomew Fair and the house in Guildford-street
is pictured to the mind it does not occasion any surprise that the boy should have taken Mrs. Clarke's
repulse so much to heart.   The daily instruction, the
learning to play on the piano, and the constructing of
plays on incidents in Spenser's *Faërie Queen*, were
things of the past; he now belonged to the class
referred to in the noble lines I have quoted—the
tumblers.   At one time he gives imitations of a
monkey and a nightingale—the former of which
serves to display his remarkable flexibility of body,
the latter a voice of great fertility and sweetness; at
another he climbs with squirrel-like agility a ladder
balanced on a man's chin, surveys the spectators from
the top with a countenance expressive of anything
but a sense of the insecurity of his position, and on
reaching the ground assumes with wonderful accuracy
the form and movements of a snake ; at another he
plays Tom Thumb to the Queen Dollalolla of a Mrs.
H. Carey, to whom he is no wise related.   In his

heedlessness of danger he seems to have sought
relief from the thoughts which oppressed him; in
equestrianism his boldness was equally conspicuous
with his grace and skill. On one occasion he was
attempting some extraordinary exploit in the circus
with a reckless determination to carry off the palm of
superiority, when, losing his equipoise, he fractured
both his legs by falling on to the sharp boards which
formed the ring. From the effects of this accident his
legs never entirely recovered their original beauty, an
enlargement of the bone in front of the instep (not
observable except upon a close survey) arising as if to
warn him against any subsequent disregard of life or
limb. When he regained the use of the fractured
members, his hardihood, energy, and resource were
once more brought into conspicuous play. Davies,
once the manager of Astley's Amphitheatre, describes
the occasion on which he first saw Kean in the following choice specimen of the Houyhnhnm dialect:—
"I was passing down Great Surrey-street one morning, when, just as I had comed to the place where
the Riding House now stands, at the corner of the
'Syleum, or Mag-dallen, as they calls it, I seed
Master Saunders a packing up his traps. His booth,
you see, had been there standing for three or four

days, or thereabouts; and on the boards in front of
the painting—the *prossenium*, as the painters says—I
seed a slim young chap with marks of paint—and
bad paint it was, for all the world like raddle on the
jaw of a sheep—on his face, a tying up some of the
canwass wot the wonderfullest carakters and curosties
of that 'ere exhibition was painted upon. And so
when I had shook hands with Master Saunders, and
all that 'ere, he turns him right round to the young
chap, wot had just throwed a summerset behind his
back, and says, 'I say, you —— Mister King Dick,
if you don't mind what you're arter, and pack up
that 'ere wan pretty tight and nimble, we shan't be
off before to-morrow, that we shan't, and so you mind
your eye, my lad.'   That 'ere —— Mister King
Dick, as Master Saunders called him, was young
Kean, wot's now your great Mister Kean."

This unthankful toil and drudgery did not, however, last very long. When Saunders left London
for the country with his band, Kean returned to Lisle-
street and resumed his studies of Shaksperian literature. His spirits had now recovered from the depression caused by the death of Moses Kean and the
repulse of Mrs. Clarke, and finding that his ungovernable animation was altogether at variance with the

pensive gravity of the philosophic prince as he stood by
the grave of Ophelia, Miss Tidswell, with the view of
having the apostrophe " Alas ! poor Yorick" rendered
in its true spirit, first made him say " Alas ! *poor
uncle*" in order that a reference to the lamented decease
of Moses Kean might impart to his utterance the
requisite combination of pathos, tenderness, and
regret.   This object was so thoroughly accomplished
that the boy himself was moved by the sad and
touching melody of his voice as he gave out the
words.   Subsequently he studied Hastings, Jaffier,
Romeo, and Cato, but the Veronese lover and the
Roman stoic had few charms for him. ·Meanwhile,
he endeavoured without success to remove the harsh-
ness of his voice in its upper register ; in its lower
register it was distinguished by a sweet melodiousness,
but in the upper the energy of the moment deprived
him of the musical intonation which, under favourable
circumstances, exhibited a capability of adaptation to
the tenderness which any particular situation required.

Information reached the young actor that his
mother was performing at Portsmouth, and he arrived
at a determination to seek his fortunes in the band to
which she was attached.   Anomalous in the history
of the female heart as Ann Carey had proved herself

by the manner in which she had fulfilled her maternal duties, the boy's decision could scarcely have resulted from a pure impulse of filial affection, but it would perhaps be going too far to say that the fine under-current which leads the child in spite of everything to the parent, was dried up in his heart. He repaired to Portsmouth—a town with which he was by no means unacquainted; but on arriving at his destination he found that he had been misinformed—the band which included Ann Carey in its numbers had not been seen there for several months. So implicitly does he appear to have relied upon the accuracy of the intelligence which brought him to Portsmouth that he had omitted to provide himself with any more money out of Miss Tidswell's slender store than was absolutely necessary for a bare subsistence on the journey; and in consequence he found himself in a distant seaport town homeless and destitute. Too proud to beg, too active-minded to despair, his prolific ingenuity soon pointed out the means of extricating himself from the difficulty in which he was involved. It was a bold and hazardous experiment, an experiment which, in the absence of success, would have served to surround him with additional difficulties. Fourteen years of age, with nothing beyond intelligent looks for a recommendation, he hired on credit a room in one of the Portsmouth inns for the purpose of giving an entertainment, and in a performance consisting of selections from *Hamlet, Richard III.*, and *Jane Shore*, interspersed with a series of acrobatic evolutions and some exquisite singing, "by Master Carey, of the Theatre Royal, Drury Lane," he achieved a success so unequivocal that it was repeated on the following day, and, the expenses incidental to the undertaking defrayed, he found himself 3*l.* in pocket by the venture. Nothing further was needed to confirm his determination to adopt the stage as his profession.

That Miss Tidswell was earnestly gratified at this substantial recognition of her pupil's talents there can be no doubt. Stimulated to the assiduous cultivation of every acquirement that could strengthen and mature his already considerable powers, nearly the whole of his time was exclusively devoted to study; and shortly after his return from Portsmouth he appeared before an audience at Sadler's Wells Theatre,— then the scene of the displays in mountebankism with which Belzoni prefaced his celebrated explorations of the buried wonders of Egypt,—to give a recitation of Rolla's address to the Peruvians. The rapturous

applause which rewarded Edmund for his pains was
for the most part due, perhaps, to the application of
Sheridan's grandiloquent sentences to contemporary
events in those days of war, but the eloquence and
discrimination exhibited by the boy were quite sufficient to satisfy one of the auditors—the manager of a
small country theatre in Yorkshire—that the representative of the aboriginal chief was an actor of more
than ordinary abilities.   He went behind the scenes,
held a short conversation with Master Carey, accompanied him home to Lisle-street, and, with Miss
Tidswell's consent, engaged him to play leading
characters. for twenty nights at the York Theatre.
During the interval which elapsed between the entering into and fulfilment of the compact, Edmund was
intent upon a study of Shylock.   He penetrated the
author's subtle conception of this character with a
sagacity really wonderful in a boy of his years.   At
this time the Jew was represented by Kemble, and a
few months later by George Frederick Cooke, as a " decrepit old man, bent with age, warped with passion, and
grinning deadly malice ;" but Edmund instinctively
arrived at a finer comprehension of the character :
his conception of Shylock included from the very first
those minor but nice considerations which constitute

the human element thrown around the portrait, and which, from their fidelity to natural truth, cause us to sympathize with the revenge which rankled in his heart rather than hate him for indulging in so dark a passion. " The devil is not so black as he's painted," he said to Miss Tidswell a few days after he had entered upon his study of the Jew ; " and Shylock is not such a devil as black-looking Mr. Kemble would make us believe." In this simple remark, which is here set down as I received it from a friend to whom Miss Tidswell reported it twenty years later, is to be found the germs of that fine original conception which, on the 26th of January, 1814, satisfied Hazlitt that he had hitherto misunderstood the character, and which convinced the slender audience assembled on that occasion that a master-spirit had suddenly, and without any warning, risen before them. Shortly after that conception had been formed he read the whole of the *Merchant of Venice* at the Rolls Rooms, Chancery-lane, and this was followed by a series of readings and recitations at the little Sans Souci Theatre, in Leicester-place. Several years afterwards, Mrs. Plumtre, speaking to the great tragedian (of whose identity she was unaware) of the Leicester-place entertainments, said, " I used to be very pleased

with a little boy who spoke poetry at the Sans Souci."
"Should you like to know who that little boy was?"
inquired the tragedian. The lady answered in the
affirmative. "Well," rejoined Kean, turning over
head-and-heels in his drawing-room at the house
in Clarges-street, and bringing himself up in the
famous attitude in Zanga, "Know, then, 'twas I !"

The steady improvement of Edmund Kean encountered no impediment in the shape of vanity
arising from the success which attended his appearances at the York Theatre. He sought rather to
impress upon himself an idea of the great difficulties
he had yet to overcome than to feed himself on too
great an opinion of what he had already accomplished.
By this effort of volition he strengthened his power of
resistance to the stern tide of adversity by which he
was thenceforth assailed; and saved himself from the
regretful fate of Master Betty as an actor—a
discovery that when grown up to manhood his at-
tainments were valued by himself more than by the
public—like a tree in a forcing-house, to be cherished
while he put forth his early blossoms and fruit, to
be neglected and thrown aside when his young task
was performed.

His engagement at the York Theatre was inaugu-

rated by a representation of Hamlet, followed by
Hastings and Cato on the two succeeding nights.
Graceful as was his courtier, earnest as was his stoic,
both yielded in attractiveness to his Hamlet, in
which he exhibited a fervour and impressiveness that
operated perceptibly on the audience. Free from all
unpleasant assumption, yet surprising his audiences
with the existence of such undoubted talents in one
so young, the originality of his conception, the
readiness of his comprehension, the brilliancy of his
execution, and the general tone of truth which
pervaded the performance, elicited warm and unqualified admiration. *Ogni medaglio ha il suo reverso.*
His action, eventually free, varied, and appropriate,
was stiff, awkward, and ungraceful; his facial expression and deportment had not yet fully acquired
that quiet ease consonant with the solemn impressiveness of tragedy; his conception, free as it was
from the bonds of tradition and convention, had not
yet attained a complete and thorough unity; but the
audience seemed scarcely conscious of such shortcomings when involved in so large a preponderation
of excellence. With his engagement at York the
foundation was laid.

A strolling player! He is now at the commence-

ment of his wearisome race, plodding along the dis-
roads, picking up a scanty subsistence by working'ity
country fairs, and reciting soliloquies in gentlemen's
houses. Engaged thus, he encountered Richardson
and his celebrated troupe, and, having given the
worthy manager a taste of his quality, was readily
enrolled in the ranks. The first person on whom he
set eyes after the arrangement with Richardson was
his mother! Ann Carey quickly recognised her son
—and the talents which he possessed; improving the
opportunity, she prevailed upon him to become her
pack-horse, to join her in her wanderings, and to co-
operate with her in the disposal of her pomatums,
hairbrushes, &c. Moreover, all money earned by
him by acting, he, like a good boy, was to deliver up
to her. This motherly project fell through. A very
brief experience of the new duties which had devolved
upon him convinced the boy that no alternative
remained but to give an emphatic refusal to perform
them any longer, and this he gave, adding that her
rapacity and heartlessness had wholly obliterated
every trace of filial gratitude and respect. Ann Carey
stormed, threatened, and coaxed in vain; his resolution, once taken, was impregnable; and with a
motherly curse upon what she was pleased to term

rate;,stubborn obstinacy," she went away, never to
гэ him again until she turned up to exact 50*l.* a year
from the not over-delighted tragedian in February,
1814. Edmund now devoted himself with renewed
assiduity to his labours; he worked zealously and
studied hard; and the results of his industry were
exhibited in the unequivocal success which attended
his performance of young Norval and Harlequin at
Sheerness, on Easter Monday, 1803.* He also appeared in this town as George Barnwell, together
with a variety of characters in all walks of the drama.
His song of " Watty Cockney and Risk" is spoken of
as excellent. His salary at this time was fifteen
shillings a week. Remaining in Richardson's troupe,
conscious that he was here picking up hints that
would prove infinitely serviceable to him in the
pursuit of dramatic celebrity, he accompanied the
band to Windsor, and the booth having been erected
without loss of time, the campaign was opened in that
town by a performance of *Tom Thumb and the Magic
Oak*, in which Edmund, still known as Master Carey,
appeared with considerable success as the diminutive
hero. This pantomimic *rôle* was succeeded by a series

---

* Not 1804, as erroneously stated by Douglas Jerrold.

of Shaksperian recitations, and the intelligence he displayed—exhibiting a propriety of emphasis, a facility
of happy pausing, an appropriate grace of action,
and a conception conformable in great measure to the
spirit of the different selections—led to that gratifying
recognition of his powers which must have confirmed
his resolution, if indeed it ever wavered, to devote
himself to the stage.   I refer to his memorable
performance at Windsor Castle before King George
the Third, who, having heard of the versatile young
actor in Richardson's Company, caused a note to be
conveyed to the manager, intimating his desire that
Master Carey should be brought to recite before him.
The message was delivered on the Saturday as the
campaign opened on the Friday.   Between the excitement produced by this unexpected summons and
the scantiness of Edmund's wardrobe, Richardson was
almost at his wits' end, and to add to the dilemma,
the Jews' shops were closed, and the manager's purse
in a most sorry condition.   The funds, however, on
the strength of the honour about to be conferred,
were ultimately raised, and the Israelites not proving
over scrupulous with regard to the observance of their
Sabbath, Edmund Kean was eventually conducted
into the royal presence in all the bravery of a clean

shirt, a smart suit of clothes, and a personal appearance considerably enhanced by the skilful hands of
the village barber. Exhibited to this advantage, even
the callous heart of Ann Carey could scarcely have
repressed a throb of pride in the consciousness that
the handsome and intelligent boy before the king was
her son. Attracted by the report of the boy's clever-
ness, an audience comprising the flower of the Court
assembled to witness the performance; but Edmund
did not lose his self-possession, neither in maintaining
it did he make the slightest approach to assumption.
"He was not a bit abashed when the king spoke to
him," says Richardson, in his peculiar vernacular,
"and went to work—like a man. He spouted some
of *Richard, Hamlet, Macbeth*, and speeches from other
plays. The king and the whole tribe of people who
were there applauded very much. For this we had
two guineas given us. I did not care for the money,
the honour was the thing." How that honour had
been conferred was speedily made known by the
astute manager to the peaceful townspeople of
Windsor; considerable curiosity was excited relative
to Master Carey, whose talents, as Richardson took
infinite pains to announce, " had elicited his majesty's
unbounded approval ;" and with sound managerial tact

the presiding genius of the troupe engaged the market-hall for three nights in order that Master Carey might extend the recognition which his "extraordinary genius," as Richardson termed it, had recently obtained. The boy's recitations, as might be expected, were numerously attended, and, stimulated by the applause which rewarded his exertions, his spirit shone out brilliantly from within him. The temple was rearing itself aloft in unrivalled magnificence and beauty.

CHAPTER II.

THE STROLLING PLAYER.—THE STUDENT.

BUT, if reliance is to be placed upon a tradition that relates to the early history of Edmund Kean, the advantages which resulted from the royal encouragement of his talent were scarcely confined to the consequent increase of fame and emolument. If the tradition referred to has a foundation in truth it appears that one of the auditors of Edmund's recitations before the king was Dr. Drury, the head master of Harrow; that the learned doctor was deeply impressed by the intellectual sparkles which Master Carey glanced forth on that occasion; that, ascertaining the humble extraction and imperfect culture of the boy, he, with the view of impelling Master Carey's mental energy to a sound development, withdrew him from Richardson's troupe and sent him to Eton; that during the two and a half years he remained there he imbibed a lasting taste for the images of beauty, tenderness, and grace with which classic

literature abounds; and that the acuteness of understanding and craving for knowledge which he here
displayed were such as to more than realize the expectations indulged in by his liberal-minded benefactor.
The tradition informs us, moreover, that he thoroughly
mastered Virgil, Sallust, and Cicero ; that he devoted
himself with especial attention to the precepts and
examples of the latter; and that his authorship and
recitation of a Latin ode commanded the approbation
of his preceptors.   It is now necessary to determine
the reliability of that tradition.   Mr. Procter, Kean's
biographer, discredits the story of the Etonian education altogether; Mr. Leman Rede, in his *Recollections,*
characterises it as " a fiction."   Both writers, however,
—and the fact is notable—base their conclusions on
the occasional imperfectness of the tragedian's Latin;
the former, without endeavouring to render himself
master of the intricacies of the Gordian knot, has recourse to the royal expedient of cutting it.   This
occasional imperfectness of Kean's Latin, which does
not after all militate against the authority of the tradition, constitutes the sum total of the evidence on
which its reliability has been impugned.   On the other
hand, we have the following reasons to form an
opposite conclusion :—1. That a week after the boy's

performance before the king he was withdrawn from Richardson's troupe.   2. That during the interval which elapsed between August, 1803, and March, 1806,—an interval which represents the exact length of time that Edmund is said to have remained at Eton —we lose all trace of him.   3. That in after years Kean was as familiar with Cicero, Virgil, and Sallust as with Shakspeare.   4. That the materials for a biographical sketch in the *European Magazine* for March, 1814, in which it is distinctly stated that the tragedian had been educated at Eton, were derived from Dr. Drury himself.*   Having stated these facts, it remains to be contended that the remarkable interest exhibited by Dr. Drury in the professional success of Kean at Drury-lane in 1814 arose from that expressed in the boy's intellectual culture in 1803, and

---

* Extract from the biographical sketch in the *European Maga-zine* referred to :—" Of this very excellent performer we should have been glad to have given a more copious account than is now in our power, but on his being applied to for some materials of his life, he declared that he considered himself too unimportant a sub-ject for public attention on paper, and that his utmost ambition was to experience the public favour in his profession.   With this answer we are obliged to acquiesce, and therefore are under the necessity of *seeking information through other channels.*"   That other channel, as I am given distinctly to understand, was Dr. Drury.

that the classical acquirements displayed by the tragedian subsequent to his appearance in London could not by any means have been attained at the schools in Orange - court, Chapel - street, Green - street, or during his sorrowful career as a strolling player. These facts and probabilities go far to establish the authority of the tradition in question; and when it is remembered that this strong circumstantial evidence is opposed by nothing more conclusive than the occasional imperfectness of the tragedian's Latin, we are justified, I think, in arriving at a conclusion that Edmund Kean, the greatest actor of modern times, imbibed his fine taste for classical literature at Eton.

In March, 1806, we alight from these somewhat aerial discursions upon firm, tenable ground. Eighteen years of age, he is at Dumfries, low comedian in the company managed by the celebrated Moss— a bright name associated with the most melancholy history. Kean is earnestly addressing himself to the task of overcoming the difficulties of his art; he is giving himself up with no restraint to the prosecution of his ambitious views; following up the path which he had marked out for his pursuit many years before, he deviates neither to the right nor to

the left ; awake while others were sleeping, he makes
himself *au fait* in everything necessary to his profession ; and if it was the merest chance that eventually
recalled him from the obscurity of rural shades, it was
his own indomitable firmness and perseverance which
brought him under the notice of those who guided
him into the tide that wafted him to fame and fortune.   The regard which Edmund entertained for his
manager was thoroughly reciprocated.   Indeed Moss's
attachment to his low comedian was so marked that
it exposed the latter to the ill-will of his colleagues,
who burst into a peal of derisive laughter when the
youth, stirred to enthusiasm by one great effort of
his master in the *Merchant of Venice*, exclaimed, " If
ever I play Shylock, it shall be after the style of Mr.
Moss."   One of these jealous deriders was Maywood,
the actor who, in 1817, made an abortive attempt to
divide the popular applause with Edmund Kean in
the interpretation of the Jew.   Manager Moss, in
his early days, was a pupil of Charles Macklin, who
bequeathed to him a conception of Shylock which he
realized with a physical and mental energy that
closely trod upon the footsteps of his master.   When
the Haymarket was under the management of George
Colman the younger, Moss appeared with great suc-

cess as Lovegold, in an English version of Molière's
L'Avare, but the insolence with which he was treated
by the subsequent deputy-licenser of plays led to his
secession, and after a series of unavailing struggles
with fortune, both as an actor and as a manager, he
was found in 1814 at Stirling. This was shortly after
Kean's first appearance at Drury-lane; and it is re-
freshing to remember that when the powers of Moss
had been reduced by age and decay to a mere reflection of their former impressiveness, the pupil of old,
but now the greatest dramatic luminary of the day,
stepped in to his relief with a munificence liberally
yet delicately rendered.

Leaving Dumfries, Kean proceeded to Northallerton,
and on the way replaced a jockey who had been dis-
abled, mounted the thorough-bred racer with alacrity,
and—lost the race with extraordinary spirit. In
Butler's company at Northallerton he did the walking
gentleman, harlequin, and comic singing for fifteen
shillings a week. There was an aged actor in this
company known as "Old George," who slept on the
same truckle bed with Kean, and who entertained a
strong presentiment of the brilliant career which
awaited the low comedian. During the period of his
stay in Butler's troupe, Kean appeared for the first

time in the character of Octavian, and the matchless
skill with which he represented the desolate mountaineer attracted the attention of a gentleman connected with the Haymarket in London, who forthwith
expressed considerable interest in Edmund's professional welfare, and undertook to secure him an
engagement provided he reached London within a
specified time. He departed from Northallerton,
however, without assisting the youth in any pecu-
niary way ; and Kean, unprovided with the means of
reaching the metropolis by any other means than on
foot, would have been compelled to abandon all hopes
of presenting himself before a London audience had
it not been for the liberality of the old manager, who
defrayed the expenses of travelling by the stage coach
in order that the young gentleman might reach
London with the expedition required. A tear started
to Kean's eye when he learned Butler's intention.
" If ever fortune smiles upon my efforts," he said at
parting, " I will not forget you." The records of the
actor's life show that he kept his promise.

Arrived in London, he found to his intense mortification that so far from leading in *The Mountaineers*,
as he had fondly anticipated, the principal character
had been cast to Rae, Ganem being the part entrusted

to " Mr. Kean, his first appearance at this theatre,"
as stated at the fag end of the programme. He
entered, however, upon his fifth-rate characters with
apparent earnestness, and although secretly disgusted
at the unprofitable work that lay before him, he
mentally resolved to do ample justice to the simple
material, or, in technical phraseology, " to make a
part." The season opened on the 28th of June, 1806,
the company consisting of Rae, Winston, Mathews,
Liston, Wewitzer, Mrs. Glover, Mrs. Gibbs, and
above all the incomparable Fawcett, to whose Caleb
Quotem in the *Review* Kean played the most pro-
fitable character he obtained during that uneventful
season—the somewhat insignificant part of Dubbs.
His other characters were Peter in *The Iron Chest*,
Simon in *John Bull*, Carney in *Ways and Means*,
Waiter in *Mrs. Wiggins*, Landlord in *The Prisoner at
Large*, Servant in the *Heir-at-Law*, an Alguazil in
She Would and She Would Not, the Fiddler in *Speed
the Plough*, Rosencrantz in *Hamlet*, Fifer in the *Battle
of Hexham*, and Ganem in *The Mountaineers*. How
strange appears this allotment when compared with
subsequent events! When he played Carney, a
looker-on at the wings said in derision, " Look at the
little man—he's trying to act ; he's trying to make a

part of Carney ;" but he did not succeed in awakening
the audience to a sense of his merit until he played
Ganem, when, by his touching delivery of some half
dozen words uttered in the act of kneeling to Bul-
cazim Muley, the sympathies of the house, aroused
by the unlooked-for burst of energy and feeling, were
indicated by three distinct rounds of applause. The
increase of consideration which resulted from this
special mark of favour, however, did not operate to
deter Kean from availing himself of a letter of recommendation to John Kemble, to whom it was presented
by Edmund one night behind the scenes at Covent-
garden Theatre, just as the elder tragedian was recovering from the reverie which he was wont to
indulge in on the stage before the public were admitted. Kean's own account of his reception was
that it was so cold, haughty, and repulsive that,
predisposed as he was to throw up his duties at the
Haymarket, he mentally resolved to resume his career
as a strolling player rather than submit to the managerial authority of John Philip. The Haymarket
season closed on the 15th of September, and Kean
was once more thrown with imperfect prospects on
the world.

During his engagement at the Haymarket he resided at one time with Miss Tidswell and at another with Mrs. Price. While playing with Moss at Dumfries he formed an attachment to a young girl of his own age, and had, in fact, engaged to marry her. "The bonnie Highland lassie" was not, however, destined to monopolize a heart that a glance from another would at any time set on fire with a new flame. Miss Maria Germain, an apprentice to Mrs. Price, was the next object of his affections; but although Mrs. Price fomented the love fever between her nephew and her apprentice, and " heaps of letters" passed between the lovers during the time Kean remained in London, the proposed match was finally broken off, and when the young tragedian returned to the country, he certainly carried with him more durable impressions than Miss Maria Germain's beauty, intelligence, &c., imprinted on his brain.

The obstacles which sprang up in his path were innumerable. It is seldom that genius is appreciated at its true worth. In the different companies of which he successively became a member, it was in vain that his fine talents exerted themselves to attract the attention of the solitary few who now and then assembled to witness his performances; ignorant of or inattentive to the rarity of the intellectual energy which he displayed, they regarded him with less consideration than the illiterate rustic. If at another time a philanthropic few, rising superior to the illiberal prejudices against the strolling player, exerted themselves to obtain for him a reward worthy of the noble resources which he had laid under contribution, a natural torpor spread over the minds of the many, or a paucity in their numbers, not unfrequently defeated the good intentions which had been entertained in his favour. If he performed on his own account, his age led people to distrust the possibility of adequate attraction; if he joined a company of strolling players, he was left to repose in secondary characters, "the lead" being taken by old men between fifty and sixty years of age, with furrowed cheeks and quavering voices, who exhibited their folly to the greatest possible advantage by appearing in Romeo and Hamlet. Unthankful and unimportant parts fell to Kean's lot; it is not surprising that he was frequently careless and inattentive; quarrels with managers followed; his sensitive pride rendered him hasty to take offence; and acting, as he always did, on the impulse of the moment, he rushed away, and became immersed in a vortex of misery and privation from which he eventually issued, his energy and perseverance undiminished, but involved in the toils of the insidious tempter, drink.

The contempt for his calling which the strolling player encountered almost at every step was not the least of the multiplied adversities to which he was exposed. In most ages the dramatic profession, more especially its humbler ranks, has been held in a lower degree of estimation than any other; and for the prevalence of this illiberal sentiment it would be difficult to assign a reason. The variety of mental qualifications which constitute the true master of the stage,—the sound understanding, the plastic imagination, the susceptible passion, the sensitive temper,— these ought to protect the actor from the illiberality of the indiscriminating, and to rank the profession to which Shakspeare belonged amongst the liberal and imitative arts. Provincial audiences of those days, however, were not very philanthropic; neither had they the will to recognise intellectual energy when united to the humble, unpretending exterior of a strolling player. As an illustration of this I may refer to the opinions entertained by Washington Irving and Captain Marryat with respect to the votaries of the country stage. The former, who is stated by one of his critics to have possessed a fine

taste and "manly, generous sentiments," stigma-
tized the strolling player as a "worthless vagabond;"
Marryat was of opinion that the man is degraded in
the actor, and that the latter is beneath the dignity of
a gentleman. That the man is *not* degraded in the
actor I do most strenuously contend; very likely he
does not come up to the standard of what "society"
terms a gentleman. If a black-hearted scoundrel
possesses wealth, high lineage, and influence, with the
estimable accomplishment of talking with as much
vapidness as possible, well-bred indifference to the
most natural sensibilities, refinement and elegance of
manners, and an undeviating compliance with the
usages of the upper circles, he will be cordially welcomed into polished society as "a perfect gentleman;"
but a true nature's gentleman—the nature's gentleman which the author of *John Halifax* so completely
delineates in the character of the hero of that work
—is treated, if he is poor and rough in his manner,
with supercilious contempt by the very circles who
recognise in the black-hearted scoundrel a perfect
gentleman, but who, if he possessed the advantages
of wealth and influence, would overwhelm him with
servile adulation. Perhaps the "perfect gentleman"
represents the class of individuals the dignity of whom

the accomplished writer of fiction regards the strolling player as beneath.

As these reverses impeded the progress of the young actor, they nevertheless contributed not a little to stimulate his resolution, and his powers of endurance seemed as it were to augment in proportion to the trials they had to encounter. The charm constituted by the applause awarded to his boyish efforts was destroyed, and stern experience, casting aside the tinsel mask of beauty, disclosed a deformed and wrinkled hag, which for seven years pursued her enthusiastic but unfortunate votary with rags and starvation. The more his adversities seemed likely to damp and depress his spirits the more valuable in his eyes became the goal to which he aspired. Shortly after the close of his Haymarket engagement he appeared at Tunbridge Wells, where it was announced that " Mr. Kean, from the Theatre Royal, Haymarket, would appear as Lord Hastings and Peeping Tom." From an anecdote which occurred some years afterwards, I conjecture that on leaving Tunbridge Wells he proceeded to Portsmouth. Insult struck deeply into his heart, and his fine rebuke of the Portsmouth innkeeper who treated him with contempt as a strolling player, but overwhelmed him with servile respect as the great Mr. Kean, will be presently recorded in detail. As a member of Humphreys's company he appeared a few months later at Hoddesdon, in Hertfordshire, where he devoted what little leisure he obtained to the study of a Greek Lexicon kindly lent to him by Miss Sams, the proprietress of the library in that town. At this period he temporarily withdrew from the stage to become the assistant in the Hoddesdon seminary, and here he acquired that knowledge of physiology which proved of such infinite service to him in after years by regulating the expression of his countenance in accordance with natural truth. At Birmingham his talents were underrated; at Edinburgh he was received with considerable favour. Exhibitions at fairs and taverns then mark his way to the western coast, and by dint of the most rigid self-denial he saved a sum which enabled him to cross from Great Britain to the sister isle.

Soon afterwards, in the summer of 1807, he obtained an engagement at the Belfast Theatre, and here, in Congreve's descriptive tragedy of *The Mourning Bride*, he and Mrs. Siddons met and played together for the first time since, in 1800, he had performed Arthur to her Lady Constance at Drury-lane. The tragedy of *The Mourning Bride,*

although embellished with poetical flowers of the
highest beauty and picturesqueness, is so decked out
with pantomimic tricks, and so much arrayed in all
the idle pomp of redundant verbosity, that those who
form an opinion on it with candour will experience
little difficulty in assenting to the judgment of Dr.
Johnson, "that we are rather amused by noise and
stratagem, than entertained by any true delineation
of natural truth." The interest which the revival of
The Mourning Bride excited at Belfast was amply
satisfied by the support it received from the combined
talents of Sarah Siddons and Edmund Kean. The
former was now sinking into the vale of years; the
leaf was slowly exchanging its freshness for decay;
in five more years she will take her farewell of the
stage. But her Zara on this occasion was as noble
as ever. With a power and grandeur all her own,
she depicted the various passions which assail the
captive queen. There is a constitutional weakness
and want of energy in the character of Osmyn, which
rendered its delineation far from striking in the hands
of Kean, who, moreover, had been compelled to study
the part in a hurry; but all that could be done was
accomplished not only in the outline but in the detail.
Siddons, failing to detect the real cause of its repre-

sentative's occasional imperfectness, and attributing
it to another reason, haughtily asked Manager Atkins
who that "horrid little man was?" A few nights
later, *Venice Preserved* was announced, and Siddons,
to her unbounded consternation, was informed that
the horrid little man was to play Jaffier. "He is
very clever," Atkins assured her, "he will play the
part finely." The result did not falsify the prediction. The powers restricted by the narrow limits of
Osmyn had now alighted on a favourable scope for
their display, and as he stood prominently forth on a
canvas dignified by one of the tragedienne's finest
and most finished impersonations, he showed that he
was no studied ape of the passions, but a man of
genius, in whom all the finer touches of manner, the
flashes of the eye, and the untaught and varying
gesture, sprang directly from the soul. Mrs. Siddons
was surprised into admiration, and expressed her unqualified approbation of his efforts to *illustrate* the
text rather than seek to invest it with the turgid and
measured declamation then in vogue. The tragedienne's good opinion of Kean's talents was confirmed
by his representation of Norval to her Lady Randolph.
Graceful and affecting, all that he uttered was given
in the pure unsophisticated accents of human nature,

and from first to last he maintained an irresistible sway over the hearts of his audience. "Douglas, enthusiastic, romantic, desirous of honour, careless of life and every other advantage when glory lay in the balance," was, in the hands of Edmund Kean, the *beau ideal* of the author's conception.

Mrs. Siddons departed from Belfast, and the bright intellectual sparkles which the coalition had served to elicit from Kean decided Manager Atkins to prolong his engagement. He achieved a moderate success in the character of Lord Townley, in which the native dignity of the old nobleman was finely depicted. In the scene where he arrived at the determination to separate himself from the unhappy victim to a passion for gambling, I have heard it stated that he was highly impressive, and that when he pardoned her indiscretions, and restored her to her former place in his affections, his emotions were expressed with a fidelity to nature which operated perceptibly on the audience. He also appeared as Tancred, in *Tancred and Sigismunda*, and if he did not succeed in creating any powerful effect in the character, the cause is to be sought for rather in the heaviness of the play than any inability of the performer. That vague feeling of restlessness which so often takes possession of the

minds of men reserved for great destinies, now came
over him. Satisfied that no actor improves with
rapidity whilst performing continually before one
audience, he determined to change the scene of his
exertions as often as possible, and accordingly bade
Manager Atkins good-bye. The old adage that a
rolling stone gathers no moss does not hold good when
applied to the actor in his probationership.

The Belfast engagement marks an epoch in the
steady advancement of Edmund Kean to the position
he subsequently attained. His little, well-wrought
figure had emancipated itself from much of that
uneasy and embarrassed stiffness which had hitherto
hampered the grace and freedom of his action, and
the dawnings of a master-spirit cast light and beauty
upon all that engaged his attention. Considerations as to how a work was to be accomplished were
subordinated to the object aimed at, and its intended
effect on the mind; careless whether it was with or
without this or that requisite, he sought only to
elevate the imagination and deeply absorb the feelings. In Jaffier and Norval this endeavour was
attended with complete success; and Mrs. Siddons
could only have had an eye to those few respects in
which his powers had as yet only passed adolescence,

when, speaking of his performance of Jaffier, she said, " He plays the part very, very well, but there is *too little* of him wherewith to make a great actor." The tragedienne's perception was at fault. His figure was not adapted for dramatic effect, it was true ; but the "mind is the standard of the man," and he could redeem all physical deficiencies by the power of his understanding. And if that power of understanding was destined to elevate him at one stroke to fame, let it be said that one of the firmest pillars of his reputation originated in his attentive observation of nature. A fine physiognomist, he studied the human face wherever he met it, and the tempers and passions of those around him. By these means he discovered new beauties in his author, new ideas combined in his head, new chords struck in his heart ; and he expressed them all accordingly, because, while he studied the feelings of mankind, he studied the glass in which they were reflected and displayed. Like a painter and a philosopher, he let nothing escape him. He obtained conception and execution by the same means by which Michael Angelo became a great painter— by the continual exercise of his mind and his eye.

In illustration of this statement, two instances of the manner in which Kean's performance was regulated by his observation of nature may be cited. On one occasion he, and a brother actor named Giles, had unintentionally trespassed upon some forbidden ground, when they were confronted by the enraged owner, who, on learning that they were players, wrathfully threatened to have the "vagabonds" put in the stocks. Giles resented the opprobrious epithet, challenged the farmer to a fight, charged his companion not to interfere, and Kean, sorely against his inclination, was compelled to remain a passive spectator of the encounter. The muscular prowess of the farmer soon decided the contest in his favour, but Giles, though physically overpowered, remained unsubdued in spirit, and in a paroxysm of defeated wrath, which convulsed his whole frame and seemed all but to suffocate him, he dragged open his shirt-collar, and tore it to ribands. This incident was not lost upon Kean, who subsequently reproduced it in the last scene of *A New Way to Pay Old Debts* when he appeared as Overreach in London; and no one who saw him in that character can ever forget the appalling sensations produced by his manner as, with face livid, eyes distended, lips swollen and parted at the corners, teeth set, and visage quivering, he dragged open his shirt-collar and tore it to ribands.

His falling on his back in the last scene of *Othello* was suggested by a similar incident in nature. He was giving a young officer some instruction in fencing, when he accidentally received an alarming wound in the breast, from the effect of which, becoming insensible, he fell to the ground on his back. When he recovered his senses, he asked, "How did I fall?"

A few weeks after the close of his Belfast engagement we find him at Sheerness. Here he appeared in a series of standard comedy characters. Parts of the Archer class had no atmosphere for Kean; but in one character of the group referred to — Sir John Brute — he achieved a complete and unequivocal success. I am informed by a friend who has long since passed the scriptural confines of life that Kean frequently appeared in this character previous to his London career, and that, judging from one representation at which he was fortunate enough to be present, the actor was capable of embodying Vanbrugh's whimsical yet fine conception with wonderful effect. It was in Sheerness that, "by one of the happiest retorts on dramatic record, he indicated a consciousness of his own powers, and triumphantly repelled the ignorant and invidious attack of the 'cant of criticism.'" One night he appeared as

Alexander the Great, and as he passed over the stage in the triumphal car drawn in mimic procession, a supercilious coxcomb in the stage-box exclaimed with a sneer, "Alexander *the Great*—Alexander *the little.*" With great presence of mind, Kean turned his head deliberately round, without altering his position, and darting a look of withering scorn at the self-sufficient sneerer, replied, "Yes, but with a great soul!" The promptitude and sufficiency of the retort quickly aroused the audience to a sense of the insult which had been offered, and the assailant "hid his diminished head" as a shower of applause marked the direction in which the sympathy lay. His engagement at Sheerness concluded, Kean visited Rochester, Dover, and other towns in that part of the country. About this time he was engaged to act for one night at Braintree, but on the day of the performance he found himself separated from Essex by the Thames, and with no money in his pocket. The only alternative was immediately adopted, and, stripping himself of his clothes, he tied them up in a pocket handkerchief, seized the bundle with his teeth, and swam over the river as readily as an Indian would have done. The frequent submergence of the bundle on the way rendered its contents far from comfortable when reassumed, and wet, hungry, and worn out with fatigue, he contrived to reach Braintree in time for the performance. But nature reasserted her sway. He was going through the part of Rolla when he fainted outright on the stage, and a combination of ague and fever supervened. Having, after some weeks' confinement, recovered his health he tramped to Swansea, and with his engagement at that city he completed his twentieth year. He was now five feet four inches in height, thick set, with raven black hair, a somewhat sallow complexion, a wonderfully expressive eye, and a countenance capable of every variety and intensity of expression. Leaving Swansea he proceeded to Gloucester, and in March, 1808, became a member of Beverley's troupe. A prominent member of the company was Hughes, familiarly known as Jack Hughes, who afterwards achieved so great and so deserved a celebrity. The fortunes of the company were at this time at the lowest possible ebb, and in the hope of in some measure recruiting their exhausted finances, *A Cure for the Heart Ache* was announced, Kean appearing on the occasion as Young Rapid. The bills were distributed with extraordinary diligence, the lamps were lighted, the doors opened, the curtain drawn up, and

—two auditors found to represent the playgoing
community of the good city of Gloucester. A council
of war having been held, the lamps were unceremoniously extinguished, and the eighteenpence which
lay at the bottom of the money-taker's box was restored
to the playgoers with heartfelt reluctance. *Laugh
When You Can* was produced a few nights later, Kean
appearing as Sambo, and a member of a highly respectable Waterford family, Miss Chambers, who had
forsaken the scholastic profession for that of the
stage, as Mrs. Mortimer. The play had been got
up in a hurry, and Kean was so imperfect that he
not only spoiled the part of Sambo, but that of Mrs.
Mortimer also. The lady was greatly incensed,
and asked the manager with some asperity, "Who
that shabby little man with the brilliant eyes was?"
Kean overheard the remark, and coolly walking
up to the manager, asked "Who the devil is
she?" He had his revenge, however, on the following night, when, in a representation of *John Bull* he
proved letter perfect as Job Thornberry, and Miss
Chambers exceedingly forgetful as Mary. To the
credit of Kean be it said, that he did not avail himself
of the opportunity of retorting his fair antagonist's
discontent, but received her overabounding apologies

when the play was over with infinite good humour. From that moment all acrimony between the pair gave place to a friendship which rapidly ripened into a more tender feeling.   The character of Job Thornberry, burnished out with such extraordinary lustre in the hands of Kean, its rough and unaffected pathos was so forcibly expressed, and the mingled satire and humour towards the close given with such unfailing effect, that Watson, the veteran actor and proprietor of the Gloucester Theatre, said to Beverley, "That young man who played Job is a capital actor, and some day or other will be a great man."   The master spirit displayed in the honest brazier, however, did not obtain such a wide recognition as to draw the discriminating people of Gloucester to the theatre; and another effort was made to redeem recent losses by introducing *Tekeli* and *Mother Goose*, in the preparation of which Kean superintended everything, taught the troupe to fight, march, dance, and Miss Chambers how to play Columbine.   And when all was done he himself represented Tekeli and Harlequin. His dance as Harlequin in *Mother Goose*, Beverley playing the clown, stirred even apathetic Gloucester to enthusiasm.   But the effect of the harlequinade was poor in comparison to that created by the combat (arranged by himself) in Tekeli. It was a fine and even marvellous exhibition of gladiatorial excellence. To employ the words of an eyewitness, " The fight in Tekeli was splendid. It called down thunders of applause. The effect is even now quite fresh in my mind. I never saw anything like it." How this grace and energy foreshadowed the brilliant results which he achieved in the final encounters of Richard and Macbeth remains to be seen.

After a stay of three months in Gloucester, the company migrated to Stroud, where Kean appeared as Archer in the *Beaux' Stratagem*, and Hastings in *Jane Shore*. In the former he was imperfect, but all shortcomings were more than redeemed by the excellence of the latter. Stroud proved as indifferent to dramatic excellence as Gloucester, and Beverley, finding that the nightly average of 7*l.* to 10*l.* was insufficient to meet the expenses, invited Master Betty to display his talents to the inhabitants of Stroud in Gloucestershire. An engagement was entered into, the coming star announced for Hamlet and Norval, and Kean, to his unbounded mortification, found himself cast for Laertes in *Hamlet* and Glenalvon in *Douglas*. He play secondary characters to a boy ! His mind was soon made up on the subject, and, leaving the Young Roscius and the worthy manager to extricate themselves from all difficulties in the best way they could, for three days and three nights he was not to be found. Miss Chambers was debating with her sister as to the advisability of dragging the neighbouring ponds, when the runaway turned up, and in answer to the young lady's solicitous inquiries, he said, "I have been in the fields—in the woods; I am starved; I have eaten nothing but turnips and cabbages since I've been out; but I'll go again—and as often as I see myself put in such characters. Damme, I wont play second to any man living except to John Kemble." The industry and talent exhibited in his performances ought to have protected him from such a slight. In after years Mrs. Kean, speaking of this period of her husband's life, said, " He used to mope about for hours, walking miles and miles alone, with his hands in his pockets, thinking intensely on his characters. No one could get a word from him. He studied and slaved beyond any actor I ever knew." And here Mrs. Kean revealed one great secret of his subsequent success.

In the month of July, 1808, Edmund Kean and Mary Chambers were united in the bonds of holy wedlock at Stroud, the bridegroom being in his twentieth and the bride in her twenty-ninth year. Miss Chambers had repeatedly declared that she should not be happy except she was married to Mr. Kean, and the ceremony which sealed an attachment which sprang from the healthy impulse of disinterested affection and not from any sordid considerations on the part of Kean, as has been insinuated, took place, as we have already seen, at Stroud, a coach and four, paid for by the sister, conveying them to and from the hymeneal altar.   Neither appears to have entertained any presentiment of the unhappy influences which, many years later, caused man and wife to separate; at present all was happiness, felicitation, and hopefulness; and the only cloud that came across the otherwise undarkened sky was Manager Beverley's intimation that their services were no longer required, alleging as his reason for their dismissal that, the attraction of Kean, little as it was, would wane when it was discovered that he was no longer an unmarried tragedian, and that the lady, so far from being an acquisition, was an incumbrance.

The vicissitudes, privations, and multiplied varieties of wretchedness which the young couple suffered during the interval that elapsed between March, 1808, and January, 1814, find no parallel either in history or romance. The sister of Mrs. Kean remained in Beverley's troupe; deprived of a source upon which she had exclusively depended for support, and united to a man who was now thrown penniless on the world, the young wife saw nothing before her but the worst miseries incident to the strolling player's career. Unhappily, her fears proved to be but too well founded. The obstacle which had now sprung up in his path served, however, to invigorate rather than relax the energies to be devoted to its removal, and the conscientiousness, industry, and painstaking care hitherto exhibited in his acting underwent no diminution. But the genius, the labour, the research expended upon his performances obtained no recognition at the hands of his audiences; fame and emolument, like the grapes which hung so alluringly over the head of mythological Tantalus, flew out of his reach when all but within his grasp. The soothing and grateful balsam, applause—a return that would have rendered his incessant study a delight rather than a task, and compensated for the many hours " stolen from sleep " which were devoted to an anxious consideration of his characters, was withheld with an apathy less calculated to strengthen his resolutions than to replace the hope which had hitherto girded up

his energies for bitter despair.   To the end which he
constantly kept before his eyes—to be a great actor—
no reverses daunted him.   Cheered by his wife, who
shared his sufferings with an uncomplainingness ap-
proximating to heroism, and readily stirred to enthusiasm by the ethereal spark within him, his fortitude
was no sooner lost than regained, and as he indulged
in the contemplation of a bright and happy future,
he would murmur " *If I succeed I shall go mad.*"

At Warwick, whither he proceeded on leaving
Gloucester, Kean played, amongst other characters,
that of Lothaire to the Guiscard of Chatterley.   Subsequently he became a member of Watson's company,
then performing at Walsall; and it was here that he
first experienced the ill-effects of hostile criticism.
The gaberdine of Shylock and the deformities of
Richard did not prevent the sagacious and observant
critic of the *Staffordshire Advertiser* from finding out
that the figure of the new actor was "insignificant;"
and on the strength of this insignificant figure he,
speaking of Edmund's representation of Gloster, insisted that Mr. Kean was most misplaced, that he had
never seen a man less gifted as a tragedian, and that
"*without energy*, dignity, or the advantages of a
voice, he dragged through the heroic scenes with a

dull monotony oppressive to himself and doubly so
to the audience." Probably our discriminating critic
forgot that Edmund was

"To be measured by his soul;"

and also that Richard, having a crooked back, must of
necessity have been of short stature; but it affords us
some satisfaction to learn that his strictures did not
have the effect of putting it out of Kean's power to
realize 12*l.* by his benefit. With a hopeful heart
Kean, having paid his debts with the 12*l.*, made
his way to Lichfield. He next appeared at Birmingham, and with professional pride no longer nourished
now that a double responsibility rested upon him, he
accepted engagements for his wife and himself to play
secondary characters at a salary of a guinea a week to
each—a stipend which seemed to represent comparative wealth to the strollers. Stephen Kemble was
then leading the business, and to his King Lear
Kean played Edgar. When Edmund played Hotspur,
the physically qualified representative of Sir John
Falstaff, delighted with the spirit and effect which
Kean imparted to his character, said, "You have
played Hotspur, sir, as well as Mr. John Kemble."
Such praise was not without its effect upon the
manager's mind; and one evening Kean was per-

mitted to play Octavian. The matchless beauty with which the character was sustained on this occasion convinced Mr. Stephen Kemble, in common with the audience, that Mr. Kean's Octavian was superior to that of Mr. Elliston, and that it was second only to that of Mr. John Kemble. Stephen offered him an engagement in London, but Kean, with sound judgment, replied that his powers had not yet arrived at maturity, and that it would not do to perfect himself beneath the critical eye of a London audience. It cost him an effort to decline the offer, but the temptation was resisted. Entertaining the highest confidence in his powers, he was repeatedly heard to predict his eventual rise to the summit of his profession.

Two years later the powers of Edmund Kean had arrived at full maturity; but no such opportunity was presented then, and five years of toil and privation crept by before the goal was won. At four o'clock one fine July morning Kean set out from Birmingham, having closed with an offer from Manager Cherry, of Swansea. Two hundred miles to be travelled over on foot, and Mrs. Kean likely to become a mother before the journey is half accomplished! Kean would fain have left her in Birmingham, but there was a furious pack of unsatisfied creditors in that town, and the unfortunate lady was compelled to accompany her husband. Travelling twelve miles a day, and eking out their scanty funds by giving recitations in gentlemen's houses, they arrived in a fortnight at Bristol, and crossed in a boat to Newport. Passing through Cardiff, Cowbridge, and other towns, they eventually reached Swansea, where they obtained a little tiled parlour and bed-room for eight shillings a week. A few days later Cherry announced *Pizarro* in the bills, Rolla being cast to Edmund, and Cora, the Virgin of the Sun, to Mrs. Kean, who was then within a short time of her confinement. Kean took the lead until Bengough came; and during the ascendancy of this "elephantine simpleton," as he has been not inaptly termed, Edmund was reduced to secondary characters. In these, contrary to his wont, he exerted himself to the utmost; but no applause followed, and he would return home, dispirited, furious, and unsober. "I played the part finely, and yet they would not applaud me."

The threatened danger was passed with safety, and with their first son, whom he named Howard, Kean and his wife accompanied Cherry's troupe from

Swansea to Carmarthen, from Carmarthen to Haverfordwest, and from Haverfordwest to Waterford.
Here they were joined by Sheridan Knowles, and the
two strolling players, then to fortune and to fame
unknown, contracted a friendship which subsisted
between them when each had attained the summit of
their respective ambitions,—the one as the greatest
tragedian, and the other as the greatest dramatic poet
of the day. Born in 1784, and awakening at an early
age to an instinctive consciousness of the mental
energy which he subsequently displayed, Sheridan
Knowles, assisted by the precepts of Hazlitt in
dramatic studies, proceeded to Dublin in 1798, and
made an unsuccessful " *début* " at the old Crow-street
theatre. His joviality, good nature, and inexhaustible fund of anecdote and reminiscence, however, rendered him an acceptable, although not very
talented, member of the company to which he was
attached, and enabled him to acquire that practical
knowledge of the stage which proved of such infinite
service to him in his literary pursuits. Following
up the path which inclination as well as the guidance
of Hazlitt seems to have marked out for his pursuit,
he obtained respectable " business" in Montague
Talbot's company, at that time performing at the

Belfast Theatre. His engagement closely followed
upon that of Edmund Kean and Mrs. Siddons. In
Cherry's troupe he met with the energetic, impulsive,
and dark-eyed stranger who played Richard III. and
Harlequin on the same night for a stipend of twenty-
five shillings a week. Although a marked dissimi-
larity of character was exhibited in the two strollers,
caused in some measure by the careful training of
the one, and the imperfect culture of the other,
the friendship formed between the two was firm,
steady, and indissoluble; and for him, Edmund Kean,
Knowles wrote a melodramatic play, entitled *Leo the
Gipsy*, fragments of which have been preserved by
Mr. Procter. The success achieved by Kean in the
representation of the principal character was so unequivocal and complete that in his impulsive enthusiasm he seized the author's hand and vowed that
his first appearance at Drury-lane, if ever he did
succeed in getting before the floats of that theatre,
should be signalized by the production in London of
Leo the Gipsy. If he seriously entertained such an
intention, it was a lucky circumstance for him that
he mislaid his copy of the play; for although the
fragments which Mr. Procter has transmitted to
posterity preluded and gave promise of the eloquence

and poetry expended upon Knowles's plays in after
years, they, nevertheless, show that *Leo the Gipsy*
was wanting in that ready and felicitous construction
of scene and plot which lend so great a charm to
Virginius and the *Hunchback.*

In a regiment stationed at Waterford at this time,
there was a young subaltern whose love for fencing
led to an acquaintance with Kean under somewhat
singular circumstances. The subaltern never lost an
opportunity of encountering amateurs and professors
of the noble science of defence, and frequently took
up the foils with a little lieutenant of a troop of
artillery which formed part of the Waterford garrison.
One evening the lieutenant and the subaltern were
sauntering along the Mall, when their attention was
attracted to Cherry's programme, which announced
Hamlet to be the play; Hamlet, Mr. Kean. They
went into the theatre as the curtain drew up on the
fifth act, and in a stage-box turned their attention to
the chief actors of the scene. "The young man who
played Laertes was extremely handsome and very
tall; and a pair of high-heeled boots added so much
to his natural stature, that the little, pale, thin man
who represented Hamlet appeared a mere pigmy
beside him. Laertes commenced (after slurring ' for

better for worse' through the salute) to push carte and tierce, which might, as far as the scientific use of the small sword was concerned, have been as correctly termed cart and horse.   The lieutenant, who had by no means a poor opinion of his own skill, and who was rather unmerciful towards the awkwardness of others, laughed outright, and in a manner sufficient to disconcert even an adroit performer.   He proposed to leave the place, calling out theatrically, 'Hold, enough!' and I might have agreed had I not thought I perceived in the Hamlet a quiet gracefulness of manner while he parried the cut and thrust attacks of his adversary, as well as a quick glance of haughty resentment at the uncivil laugh by which they were noticed.   When he begun to return the lunges, *secundum artem*, we were quite taken by surprise to see the carriage and action of a practised swordsman, and as he went through the whole play we were satisfied that we had, in the phrase of Osric, made

'A hit, a very palpable hit.'

We immediately inquired of the woman who filled the nearly sinecure place of money-taker as to the gentleman whose 'excellence for his weapon' had so pleasantly surprised us.   She told us that his name was Kean; that he was an actor of first-rate talent; chief tragic hero (for they were all honourable men in the company), and also the principal singer, stage manager, getter-up of pantomimes, and one of the best harlequins in Wales or the West of England."

The subaltern was Mr. Grattan, and the above is an account of his first meeting with Kean, contributed to the *New Monthly Magazine.* After detailing his introduction to Kean, and the favourable impression which the latter created upon him, he goes on to say, " Nothing could exceed Kean's good conduct or un-presuming manners during some weeks that I knew him in this way. Several of the officers of the gar-rison met him with us on these occasions, and a strong interest was excited for him. He owed to this cause, I believe, rather than to any just appreciation of his professional merit, a good benefit and some private kindnesses."

The performance for the benefit referred to consisted of Hannah More's tragedy of *Percy*, a musical interlude, and a melodramatic pantomime founded on the story of *La Perouse.* Mr. Grattan is continuing his narra-tive :—" The last thing I remember of Kean in Water-ford was the performance for his benefit. The play was Hannah More's tragedy of *Percy*, in which he of course played the hero.   Edwina was played by Mrs. Kean, who was applauded to her heart's content. Kean was so popular, both as an actor and from the excellent character he bore, that the audience thought less of the actor's demerits than the husband's feelings; and besides this the *débutante* had many personal friends in her native city and among the gentry of the neighbourhood, for she had been governess to a lady of good fortune, who used all her influence at this benefit.   After the tragedy Kean gave a specimen of tight-rope dancing, and another of sparring with a professional pugilist.   He then played the leading part in a musical interlude, and finished with Chimpanzee the Monkey in the melodramatic pantomime of *La Perouse*, and in this character he showed agility scarcely since surpassed by Mazurier or Gouffe, and touches of deep tragedy in the monkey's death-scene which made the audience shed tears."   Kean in one of his mischievous pranks carried the monkey into private life—that is to say, he went home in the dress of the ill-favoured animal, threw himself on the bed, and went to sleep as he was!

The late Mr. Charles Kean was born at Waterford on the 18th of January, 1811.   With the additional

son Kean proceeded to Clonmel, where he endeavoured
without success to procure an engagement at the
hands of Frederick Jones, the manager of the Dublin
Theatre, who does not appear to have been visited with
a presentiment that three years later he would be offering *carte blanche* to the very man whose proposals he
was now coldly rejecting.   By the time Kean reached
Dumfries, the little money produced by the Waterford
benefit had been completely exhausted.   The town so
much endeared to us by its associations with the memory of Burns does not appear to have been infected
at this time with a love for dramatic representation ;
at a tavern entertainment, on the receipts of which
the food and shelter of the family depended, there was
one auditor, an honest cobbler, who paid sixpence for
admission !   From Dumfries he proceeded to Annan,
and from Annan to Carlisle.   Here Kean addressed a
letter to the barristers practising at the assizes, pro-
posing to get up an entertainment consisting of recitations, and leaving the reward to their own generosity.
The men of law, however, declined to entertain the
proposition ; and Kean, finding it in vain to hope for
any succour from Carlisle, made his way to York,
where, in October, 1811, he and his family arrived,
worn, weary, and footsore.   The following programme,

drawn up in Kean's handwriting for the printer, has been recalled from a "dread repose" by Dr. Doran :—

UNDER PATRONAGE.

BALL ROOM, MINSTER YARD.

Thursday Evening, Oct. 10, 1811,

MR. KEAN

(Late of the Theatres Royal, Haymarket and Edinburgh, and author of the *Cottage Foundling*; *or, Robbers of Ancona,* now preparing for immediate representation at the Theatre Lyceum)

AND

MRS. KEAN

(Late of the Theatres Cheltenham and Birmingham)

Respectfully inform the inhabitants of York and its vicinity that they will stop,

FOR ONE NIGHT ONLY,

On their way to London, and present such entertainments that have never failed of giving satisfaction, humbly requesting the support of the public.

PART I.

A Scene from the celebrated Comedy of

THE HONEYMOON;

OR,

HOW TO RULE A WIFE.

Duke Aranza . . . MR. KEAN.   *Juliana* . . . MRS. KEAN.

Favourite comic song of "Beggars and Ballad Singers," in which Mr. Kean will display his powers of mimicry in the well-known characters of London Beggars.

IMITATIONS OF THE LONDON PERFORMERS;

VIZ.,

Kemble, Cook, Braham, Incledon, Munden, Fawcett, and the Young Roscius.

PART II.

THE AFRICAN SLAVE'S APPEAL TO LIBERTY.

Scenes from the laughable Farce of

THE WATERMAN;

OR,

THE FIRST OF AUGUST.

Tom Tug (with the song of "Did you not hear of a Jolly Young Waterman," and the pathetic ballad of "Then farewell, my Trim-built Wherry"). . . . . MR. KEAN.
Miss Wilhelmina . . . . MRS. KEAN.

After which Mr. Kean will sing in character George Alexander Stevens's description of a

S T O R M.

PART III.

Scenes from the Popular Drama of

T H E   C A S T L E   S P E C T R E.

Earl Osmond . . . . MR. KEAN.   *Angelina* . . . . MRS. KEAN.

Favourite comic song of the "Cosmetic Doctor."

To conclude with the laughable farce of

S Y L V E S T E R   D A G G E R W O O D;

OR,

THE DUNSTABLE ACTOR.

Female Author . . . . - . . . MRS. KEAN.

Sylvester Daggerwood, MR. KEAN (in which character he will read the celebrated Play Bill written by Geo. Colman, Esq., originally sung by him at the Theatre Royal, Haymarket.)

Each character to be personated in their appropriate dresses, made by the principal theatrical dressmakers of London—viz., Brooks & Heath, Martin, &c.

First Seats, 2s. 6d.   Back Seats, 1s.

Doors to be open at six, and commence at seven precisely.

Tickets to be had of the Printer.

A poor response was made to this invitation, which expresses only too eloquently the humiliating straits to which the strollers were reduced.

Privation and repeated disappointment were doing their work. His indomitable energy was slowly weakening. As hope gradually gives place to despair in the breast of the shipwrecked mariner, who is left at the mercy of the heaving ocean with nothing but a few planks interposing between him and death, and who watches in vain for the sail which shall speak of rescue, so the spirit of Edmund Kean was yielding in its contest with the combined adversities of hope destroyed and expectation disappointed. If his wife could impart by her apparent cheerfulness a transient impulse to his powers of endurance, she failed to repossess him of the ambrosial expectancy of success which sustained him so tenaciously under his early trials. Hope seemed dead within him. If some wayward circumstance rekindled it, it was like the candle in the socket, to burn up brightly for a moment, and then go out. Charity frequently interposed between him and absolute starvation; but charity is terminable, and a relapse into their former penury followed. On one occasion, when a strain of more than usual severity was applied to his fortitude, it gave way, and a bitter curse upon his perverse destiny broke almost savagely from his lips. For a moment the heroic courage with which Mrs. Kean had borne up against the adverse tide abandoned her also, and sinking down upon her knees, she looked upon her children, and offered up a heartfelt prayer that He might see fit to terminate their sufferings and her own by death. The husband and father recovered himself, kissed away the tears from his wife's pale and careworn face, and murmured something about all being well yet. "I will go on; I will hope against hope."

Acting upon that resolution, the weary pilgrimage was pursued. A Mrs. Nokes, the wife of a dancing-master at York, very kindly came forward to relieve the necessities of the suffering family, and found no difficulty in inducing her husband, who appears to have been as liberal-minded as his wife, to place the room in which he received his pupils at Edmund's disposal for one night. Spite of the objections raised by the landlord, a clergyman, who protested against Mr. Nokes "letting the room to theatrical people," an entertainment was got up with some success. A long and weary journey, with its tedium and fatigue occasionally relieved by a friendly "lift" on the road, brought the travellers to Highgate Hill in a waggon. Dismounting, and sending the children forward under the care of some person who promised to look after them, Kean and his wife accomplished the remainder of the journey on foot. They sought out Aunt Price, who, kindly disposed as she was towards her nephew, did not appear to relish the idea of housing a wife and two children in addition to himself. She gave in, however, to the force of circumstances, and Kean, after remaining beneath her roof a week, endeavoured, with a view of relieving her of her burden for a time, to procure the hospitality of Miss Tidswell, who then resided at 39, Tavistock-street, Covent-garden. The prospect of sheltering a whole family did not find favour in the actress's eyes; and Kean returned to Mrs. Price's house. In this dependent condition he did not long remain. "Jack" Hughes, his former associate in Beverley's troupe, was at this time manager of Sadler's Wells Theatre and of the Exeter company, and for the latter Edmund was engaged to "do everything" for the magnificent stipend of 2*l.* a week. Before leaving London he went to see John Kemble and Mrs. Siddons in Wolsey and Catharine. On arriving at home he gave a fine imitation of Kemble's manner of doing the Cardinal's " farewell" apostrophe; but he was not insensible to the merits of the performances, especially that of Mrs. Siddons. "He's a great actor, and she's a noble actress; and *I'll* be here a great actor too." He kept his word.

Kean, accompanied by his wife and children, joined the Exeter company at Weymouth, and opened the campaign in a part which, above all in the Shakesperian group, he most disliked to play—Romeo. On one occasion he was heard to heretically denounce the son of Montague as a "mawkish lover;" intentionally unimpressive in the tender scenes, those of the banishment and the death alone revealed the strength and maturity of his powers when he appeared in the character. He performed first characters until Master Betty came to Weymouth as "a star;" and he was then pressed to play second to the Young Roscius. He returned a decisive refusal, and finding the manager inexorable on the point, he, pursuing the same course which he adopted at Gloucester in 1808, took to the woods until Master Betty had departed. He was first seen on his return walking at a quick pace up and down the pavement in front of the theatre; his brow was stormy, his hands were thrust in an angry manner into his pockets, and bitter upbraidings at his unpropitious fortune escaped his lips. A friend reasoned with him, but his indignation was not to be appeased. "I must feel deeply, sir. *He* commands overflowing houses; *I* play to empty benches. I know my powers are superior to his." At the instance

of a few friends he signalized his benefit by appearing
as Zanga in the *Revenge,* and was rewarded with tremendous acclamation; even in apparently insignificant
passages he created surprising effect, and his utterance of the three words, "Then lose her!" was re-
sponded to by applause such as is awarded to no one
but a master spirit in dramatic art.

From Weymouth Kean proceeded to Exeter, where
he took up his quarters at a china-shop kept by Miss
Hake, to whose anxious inquiries as to whether he
was sober, well-conducted, and in fact a model of
propriety, he returned an unhesitating answer in the
affirmative. Miss Hake's ideas as to the unimpeachable respectability of her lodger were somewhat
rudely upset. About two o'clock one morning an
altercation took place between Edmund and a man
who made some offensive comments upon his acting;
and the actor, dressed as he was for Harlequin, rushed
home for his Richard and Macbeth swords, determined to have that satisfaction which is the due of
"wounded honour." Acting upon an impulse of a
moment, he disappeared, harlequin-like, through a
glass door with a tremendous crash! The sequel to
this anecdote is so agreeably and so facetiously related by Barry Cornwall that I shall venture to

borrow a page from him. "Mrs. Kean, who was
sitting up for him, was alarmed; Mr. Cawsey, a
lodger, was alarmed; both the little Misses Hake
were very much alarmed. Kean recovered himself
just as Mr. Cawsey in his night-cap came out of
his bed-room door. In another instant Mrs. Kean
appeared, and shortly after, scarcely visible in the
imperfect light, peeped forth the two little Misses
Hake in their night-dresses, trembling with all their
might. Fronting them all, and gazing steadfastly at
Mr. Cawsey, who cautiously advanced, was the cause
of all this disturbance. That personage now drew
himself into a position, set his arms a-kimbo, began
rolling his black head round and round—quick—
quicker—quicker still—they thought it would never
stop. At last, making a sudden spring towards Mr.
Cawsey, he cleared the solicitor (night-cap and all) at
a bound, and disappeared like a ghost! It is no
wonder that the little Misses Hake, unacquainted as
they were with the pranks of Harlequin, should have
imagined that he had gone off in a flash of sulphur;
and what Cawsey, with his extinguished candle, must
have surmised touching the character of his black-
visaged visitor, we do not presume to guess. After a
magnificent struggle with his wife, he seized the

swords with the air of a conqueror, but on getting back to the Red Lion he found that his adversary had judiciously beaten a retreat."

It is more than probable that in pranks of this description the actor sought relief from the depression caused by his repeated disappointments. His Shylock, Richard, and Othello were being played to empty benches; his Harlequin filled the house! Although the tragic department included Vandenhoff and Tokely, who were then as obscure as Edmund himself, Melpomene's charms were disregarded. Kean's Harlequin proved so attractive to the multitude that when an accident laid him up for a few days, the disappointment caused by his non-appearance was very great; and on his recovery the manager proudly distributed notices announcing that " Mr. Kean will resume the part of Harlequin this evening." The meagre applause awarded to his Shylock, Richard, and Othello did not, however, cause him to diminish the fine conscientious exertions which he had hitherto made in those characters; and as an illustration of this, and also of the self-denial to which he subjected himself at this time, it may be stated that on one occasion he would have broken down at the close of the third act of *Othello* for the want of a draught of porter, had not the dramatic barber, learning that the actor had no money wherewith to purchase it, supplied it at his own expense. This was not the only instance of consideration which he met with in Exeter. A bookseller in the town, impressed with Edmund's Terpsichorean excellence, and aware of the necessitous circumstances to which the actor had been reduced (for the salary of 2*l.* a week had been lessened one half), counselled him as a promising speculation to set up as a professor of dancing and fencing. The suggestion, however, was not adopted; but Kean, having caught sight of an old Latin dictionary in the shop, offered in return for it to teach the bookseller's boys to dance. The bargain was struck, and Kean carried off the book. *Argent reçu, le bras rompu.* The boys became adepts in dancing, it is true, but their rapid acquirement of the art was due rather to their own perseverance than to any particular diligence on the part of the preceptor.

Fair prospects, negatived by the result, occasionally dawned upon him. Mrs. Jordan came down to Exeter, and to her Violante and Widow Cheerly Kean played Don Felix and Frank Heartall. The incomparable daughter of Thalia, who in two years and a half will be sleeping in the cemetery of St. Cloud, saw nothing in Kean but a little man with brilliant eyes; and somewhat unceremoniously informed the manager that "she had never played to so bad a Don Felix in her life." Whether his performance merited this stricture or not I cannot say; but, judging from the favourable impression which he subsequently produced in the character at Drury-lane, I am inclined to think that when he played it at Exeter he must have undertaken it at a very short notice. This was not the only occasion when some high expectations were cruelly disappointed. "My fortune is made," he exclaimed in an ecstatic manner to a friend; "Lord and Lady Cork are coming to see my Othello to-morrow night, and Lord Cork is esteemed a very good judge of acting, as you know." The discrimination exhibited by my Lord Cork on the night referred to scarcely justified his repute as "a very good judge of acting." "Well, Kean, what success?" asked his friend on the following day. "Oh, sir," returned the tragedian, "don't mention it; I am miserable. While I was playing the finest parts of Othello in my best style, Lord and Lady Cork's children were playing at hot cockles in front of the box, and my Lord and Lady Cork laughing at them."

From Exeter, Kean proceeded to Guernsey, where, in March, 1813, he appeared as Hamlet. The following report of his " *début* " appeared in one of the Guernsey papers, and it merits a place in these pages, if only as a warning to those malicious and incompetent " critics " who disgrace the press to which they belong.

"Last night a young man, whose name the bills said was Kean, made his first appearance as Hamlet, and truly his performance of the character made us wish that we had been indulged with the country system of excluding it and playing all the other characters. This person has, we understand, a high character in several parts of England, and his vanity has repeatedly prompted him to endeavour to procure an engagement at one of the theatres in the metropolis : the difficulties he has met with have, however, proved insurmountable, and the managers of Drury-lane and Covent-garden have saved themselves the disgrace to which they would be subject by countenancing such impudence and incompetency. Even his performance of the inferior characters of the drama would be objectionable, if there was nothing to render him ridiculous by one of the vilest figures that has been seen either on or off the stage, and if his mind was half so qualified for the representation of Richard III., which he is shortly to appear in, as his person is suited to the deformities with which the tyrant is supposed to have been distinguished from his fellows, his success would be most unequivocal. As to his Hamlet, it is one of the most terrible misrepresentations to which Shakspeare has ever been subjected. Without grace or dignity he comes forward; he shows an unconsciousness that anybody is before him; and is often so forgetful of the respect due to an audience, that he turns his back upon them in some of those scenes in which contemplation is to be indulged, as if for the purpose of showing his abstractedness from all ordinary subjects. His voice is harsh and monotonous, but, as it is deep, answers well enough the idea he entertains of impressing terror by a tone which seems to proceed from a charnel-house."

The effect of this stricture upon the unruly and indiscriminating rabble which usually graced the interior of the Guernsey theatre may be readily conceived. Too courageous to bow before the inevitable tempest, Kean made his appearance in Richard III. Shouts of derisive laughter, followed by a storm of sibilation, broke from all parts of the house as he

came on the ·stage. For a time his patience was
proof against an opposition which he hoped to subdue
by the merits of his acting, but as no sign of abate-
ment appeared, he boldly advanced to the front, and
with an eye that seemed to emit bright and deadly
flashes, applied to them with tremendous emphasis
the words of his part—

"Unmannered dogs, stand ye when I command."

For a moment the audience were taken aback by
this unexpected resistance; all became as noiseless as
the gathering storm before the tempest, and the
clamour only revived when a stalwart fellow in his
shirt-sleeves yelled out from the back of the pit a demand for an " apology." "Apology !" cried the little
man—and his form dilated with excitement—"take it
from this remark : The only proof of intelligence you
have yet given is in the proper application of the
words I have just uttered." The uproar which succeeded this retort rendered the interference of the
manager imperative. Kean was hurried off the stage,
and the part given to an outsider immeasurably less
talented than his predecessor, but who stood high in
favour with the discerning and enlightened audience
in front.

But the persecution did not stay here. The paper in which the disgraceful stricture on the actor's Hamlet appeared venomously reprobated his conduct as a piece of "impudent effrontery," and sought to reduce his proud spirit to unconditional submission. The fact that their intended victim was poor, and that a wife and two children depended upon him for bread, seemed to add to rather than mitigate the furiousness of their attack. Strolling companies in the island were warned that the slightest disposition to shield "the fellow Kean" from the consequences of his "audacious insult" to the intelligent audience would certainly bring upon them a large share of public disfavour; private people were solemnly enjoined, for the sake of their own credit, not to assist in any way "the ignorant, incompetent blackguard." Sir John Doyle, the governor of the island, now interposed. He generously interested himself on Kean's behalf, and sought by his influence to protect the actor from the persecution to which he had been exposed.   The favour of the governor, though it produced a remarkable alteration in the tone of the press, was altogether unable to extinguish the flame which had been stirred up; and an entertainment given for his benefit, under the auspices of Sir John, at the St.

Pierre Assembly Rooms, was far from well attended. On this occasion Kean enacted Chiron, and his son Howard the infant Achilles. The governor, angered at the unjust reception which his protégé had met with in Guernsey, finely rebuked those who had been concerned in the malicious attack by introducing him to his friends, and amongst many others to Mr. Savory Brock, the brother of the General Brock who fell in the American war of 1814. At the house of Mr. Brock Kean became a constant visitor until he terminated his Guernsey experiences by embarking for England. For Sir John Doyle he ever cherished a warm and sincere gratitude.

On his arrival in England, he advertised his eldest son and himself in a new pantomime, and turning to account the prevailing topic of the day—the vindication of the Princess of Wales from the unfounded aspersions of Lady Douglas—he industriously circulated a report that the latter was to be present on the occasion. The crowd which assembled to gratify curiosity by a sight of her ladyship was so great that the temporarily erected seats gave way, and the major part of the audience suddenly found themselves deposited in unstudied attitudes on the floor. Fortunately no serious accident occurred, and the activity of Kean having speedily prepared another room for their reception, an apology was made for the absence of the expected visitor, and the performance proceeded with. At Weymouth he resented the discourtesy extended to him in the previous March by refusing to play to benches which since his departure had been abandoned even by the scanty audiences who used to witness performances which a few months later were pronounced the greatest dramatic efforts of the time. At Dorchester he was caught in the impetuous tide which carried him on to fame, fortune, and a premature grave. Here he encountered his old patron, Dr. Drury, who immediately conceived so high an opinion of the talents of his former *protégé*, that he at once proceeded to actively interest himself on Kean's behalf with the Drury-lane Committee. The learned doctor, however, did not communicate to the actor either the fact that he was a member of that important body, or that he had recommended him to their notice as one who was alone likely to sustain the declining fortunes of Drury-lane Theatre; and Kean, with prospects gloomily overcast, and cherishing faint hopes of ever attaining the goal he had so determinately pursued for the last thirteen years, made up his mind to close with an offer which

Elliston had recently made him,—viz., to play melodramatic characters at the London Olympic for 4*l.* a
week,—and so compensate himself for the toil and
endless drudgery of a minor theatre with the certainty of a regular salary.

A few hours after Kean had written to Elliston,
notifying his acceptance of the proffered engagement,
Dr. Drury's representations on his behalf were
answered in a manner that showed the termination of
the young tragedian's ill-requited labours to be close
at hand.   The Committee, expressing themselves perfectly satisfied with the doctor's recommendation,
commissioned Arnold, their stage manager, to proceed at once to Dorchester, and, if satisfied that the
actor's performances were of the genuine stamp, to
engage him there and then.   Arnold accordingly set
out, and on the 14th of November witnessed Kean's
performance from a private box at the Dorchester
theatre.   The characters in which Kean appeared on
that eventful evening were Octavian, in *The Mountaineers*, and Kankou the Savage, in a pantomime
written by himself, and founded on the story of
Perouse, the French navigator.   The occurrence
may be told as he himself related it to his wife
with ecstatic joy on arriving home.   " When the

curtain drew up, I saw a wretched house: a few people in the pit and gallery, and three persons in the boxes, showed the quality of attraction we possessed. In the stage-box, however, there was a gentleman who appeared to understand acting—he was very attentive to the performance. Seeing this, I was determined to play my best. The strange man did not applaud, but his looks told me that he was pleased. After the play I went to my dressing-room under the stage, to change my dress for the savage, so that I could hear every word that was said overhead. I heard the gentleman of the stage-box ask Lee, who was the manager, the name of the performer who played Octavian. 'Oh,' answered Lee, 'his name is Kean—a wonderful clever fellow. He's going to London: a great man, sir. Mr. Whitbread, the head man at Drury-lane, has engaged him.'* 'Indeed!' said the gentleman. 'He is certainly very clever, but he is very small.' 'His mind is large; no matter for his height,' said Lee. By this time I was dressed for the savage, and I therefore mounted the stage. The gentleman bowed to me, and complimented me slightly

---

* It is here necessary to explain that Kean gave out that he was going to Drury-lane instead of the Olympic, in order to increase his attraction.

upon my playing, observing, ' Your manager says that you are engaged for London.' ' I am offered a trial,' said I ; ' and if I succeed, I understand I am to be engaged.' ' Well,' said the gentleman, ' will you breakfast with me to-morrow ? I shall be glad to have some conversation with you. My name is Arnold; I am the manager of Drury-lane Theatre.' I staggered as if I had been shot. My acting the savage was done for. I, however, stumbled through the part." On catching sight of his eldest son, who was suffering from water on the brain, he checked his delight, and closed his narrative with the touching comment, "If Howard gets well, we shall all be happy yet."

Kean attended upon Arnold the following morning, and two propositions were made to him by the Drury-lane manager ; firstly, that he (Arnold) would engage him, successful or unsuccessful, for three seasons, at eight guineas a week the first, ten the second, and twelve the third ; or secondly, that his expenses to and in London should be paid, leaving him to make his terms with the Committee on the event of a success, or that his expenses back to Dorchester should be defrayed. Kean unhesitatingly closed with the first proposition, and the specific object to the attainment of which his energies had all along been directed—an engagement to take the lead at Drury-lane Theatre — was at last accomplished!

Howard died.   Over the gentle mound which indicated the last resting-place of his favourite son, the father often wept in uncontrollable anguish.   He never recovered from the shock.   The image of the pale, attenuated, loving child, suffering privation without a murmur, and ever ready to soothe his father's worn-out spirit with an affectionate caress, was one which indelibly impressed itself on the heart of the tragedian to his dying day, and one which mingled with his very last thoughts and reflections.   Howard had at the time of his death just entered his fifth year; and I have heard it stated that a finer, more intelligent, or handsome boy never gladdened the heart of a parent.   "There was a singular beauty and expression in every feature of his fair face; an intellectual joyousness and spirit in his bright eyes; his finely-formed head seemed wreathed all over with clusters of flaxen ringlets; and his figure, which was perfectly symmetrical, was thrown at will, and without an effort, into the most graceful attitudes."   How touching are the simple sentences with which Kean announced the sad event to Dr. Drury.

Nov. 23, 1813.

"SIR,

"The joy I felt three days since at my flattering prospects of future prosperity is now obliterated by the unexpected loss of my child. Howard, sir, died on Monday morning last. You will conceive my feelings, and pardon the brevity of my letter.

"Mr. Arnold has seen me play Alexander and Octavian. This heartrending event must delay me longer in Dorchester than I intended. Immediately I reach London I will again, and I hope with more fortitude, address you. In the midst of my affliction I remember your kindness, and with the greatest respect sign myself,

" Yours &c.,

" Dr. Drury."   " E. KEAN.

From Dorchester, Kean proceeded to Exeter to fulfil a short engagement he had entered into prior to that with Arnold. The news of his approaching appearance in London had preceded him, and he acted Cato for his benefit to a crowded house. Leaving his wife and Charles at Exeter, he set out for London; and on arriving in the metropolis, secured for his lodgings a dismantled comfortless garret in Cecil-street, Strand. On the following morning Arnold introduced him to the Drury-lane Committee. Had the manager participated in the notions entertained by those sage guardians of dramatic interests as to the qualities which constitute an actor's claims to distinction, Kean's recall from the obscurity of provincial shades in 1813 would have been, to say the least, problematical, inasmuch that, calling in vulgar personality to their aid, they expressed themselves disappointed in not finding in the new candidate that Apollo-like symmetry of figure which, as a member of the Committee grandiloquently observed, "could alone furnish a passport to the footlights of the national stage." On the contrary, they only saw a little, self-possessed man, the native pallor of whose face was heightened by the contrast it exhibited to the penetrating brilliancy of his eyes, and the shabby-genteel mourning he wore in memory of his lost son. To the massive intellectuality of his countenance the committee were as blind as they were to the fact that, although deprived by nature of a noble presence, he might yet possess genius sufficient to "set up a corps of regular

stagers."   " Bless me !"   " What a puny looking
man !"   " He would help to destroy the property !"
An angry flush swept over the stroller's face as they
crowned their insults by demanding to hear him
recite.   Faithful to his established notions of independence, he returned a blank and emphatic refusal
to comply with the request.   " I am engaged at the
instance of Dr. Drury," he said, firmly; "and he
will see that my engagement is fulfilled.   You are
not to judge of my capabilities, but the public, by
whose verdict I shall abide."   The Committee were
rebuked, but not vanquished.   After some desultory
conversation, it was suggested that Mr. Kean should
" try the pulse " of the public in a secondary character ;
but Mr. Kean walked deliberately up to the table,
looked the chairman steadfastly in the face, and replied, " *Aut Cæsar aut nullus* is my text."   When at
length it was decided that his " *début*" was to be made
in *Richard III.*, he was as prompt in his refusal as in
the suggestion to open in a second-rate character.
He was afraid of the littleness of his figure being
exhibited in the trunks of Gloster on his first appearance.   The gaberdine of Shylock would conceal his
physical deficiencies.   " Shylock or nothing" was his
courageous answer.   The point was carried ; and the

Committee closed the meeting with a severe lecture to Arnold for precipitancy of judgment—the same Committee who, six months later, applauded his judgment, &c., in having secured Mr. Kean, "the brightest star which had adorned the dramatic hemisphere for some years."

An obstacle now arose. Elliston wrote to Arnold stating that, holding a prior claim to the services of Kean, the latter must abandon all hopes of making a "*début*" on the boards of Drury-lane, and at once enter upon the duties he had undertaken to discharge in consideration of 4*l.* a week. Kean's allowance from the Drury-lane treasury was accordingly stopped, and when, after numerous repulses, he succeeded in obtaining an audience of Arnold, the latter said, "Young man, you have acted a strange part in engaging with me when you were already bound to Mr. Elliston." The young man declared he was not so engaged; but without carrying the desired conviction to the stage manager's mind. He was determined, at all hazards, not to relax what hold he had got of Drury-lane. He wrote to Elliston, swearing in round terms that he would not act at the renowned Olympic; he wrote to Mr. Whitbread, but that gentleman "knew nothing of the matter. If Mr.

Kean had talent he would show it on his appearance;
if not, he would return to the country." A delay,
highly distressing to Kean, whose family (having
come up from Exeter, and taken up their abode in the
Cecil-street garret) were living upon air, was at
length terminated by the intercession of Dr. Drury,
at whose instance the Committee declined to avail
themselves of the opportunity of ridding themselves
of a man so little likely, in their opinion, to repair the
fallen fortunes of the theatre. If Elliston had entertained the slightest idea of the talent of a man who
in a dozen nights redeemed the theatre from bank-
ruptcy, he would have been the last to yield—he would
have had his bond; but he, as well as all members of
the dramatic profession then in London, was ignorant of Kean's transcendant abilities. He therefore
waived his claim with a grace that seemed to wish the
Drury-lane Committee luck of their bargain. During
the time in which this question was pending Kean was
treated by the Committee and by the performers with
the greatest indignity. Rae, who then belonged to the
company, declined to recognise the sometime companion of his boyish days; and the pale, restless little
man was daily to be found standing in the hall,
clothed in the frock with small capes then in fashion.

" Who is that little man in the capes ?"   " I wonder when he'll return to the country."   " He'll be smothered in those capes."

One obstacle had scarcely been removed when another sprung up in its place.   The Committee, in whose eyes Kean had become hateful through the firmness with which he stood upon his rights, deter-mined to subject him to the last indignity in their power to inflict by ordering his appearance to stand last on the list of " features" by which it was hoped to retrieve, in some measure, their recent deficiencies. Stephen Kemble was brought on in Shylock ; and the experiment proved, as might be expected, a palpable mistake ;   drunken Tokely, like Edmund himself, from Exeter, made a poor impression; and a Mr. Huddart, from the Dublin Theatre, undertook Shylock as if for the sole purpose of showing that his powers were absolutely unequal to even a respectable por-traiture of the complex and difficult part he had undertaken.   Huddart's appearance preceded that of Edmund Kean by one month, and he winged his way to oblivion, never to be heard of again.   There was now no alternative but to order the " *début* " of the apparently unpromising actor from Exeter.

On Saturday the 22nd of January, 1814, the first

intimation to the public of Kean's appearance was made in *The Times*.

THEATRE ROYAL, DRURY LANE.

This Evening, ILLUSION.

After which TWO STRINGS TO YOUR BOW.

To which will be added the new splendid comic pantomime, called

HARLEQUIN HARPER; OR, A JUMP FROM JAPAN.

On Monday, OTHELLO, with the Pantomime. On Tuesday THE CASTLE OF ANDALUSIA, with the Pantomime. On Wednesday, Mr. KEAN, from the Theatre Royal, Exeter, will make his first appearance at this Theatre as *Shylock* in the MERCHANT OF VENICE.

This was the only channel through which the public were informed of the approaching "*début*," and the actor was so unprepared for the announcement, that on the morning when the above advertisement appeared he, dispirited, furious, and rendered desperate by the wretched condition to which the malice of the Committee had reduced him, sallied forth from Cecil-street with a half-formed determination to commit suicide. Fortunately, however, he was met by a friend who acquainted him with the welcome news; and the announcement in *The Times*, as I have before stated, was the only channel though which the public were informed of the approaching "*début*." Boaden's statement, in his *Life of John Kemble*, that " Mr.

Kean's way was well prepared for him by his friends in London," and that " the press commented on the resemblance of the new actor's name to that of Le Kain," is a total misrepresentation. No paragraphs heralding the advent of Edmund were copied from the provincial into the London papers; there was no puffing of any sort, no expectation sought to be excited, save by Dr. Drury, whose laudations of his protégé's talent were confined to the hearing of his own private circle. And so, on that memorable night of the 26th of January, 1814, the actor stood on his merits alone.

His itinerant and strolling life had now terminated and his brilliant career commenced—a sorrowful and disturbed one, spite of that dazzling and meteoric splendour which shed a halo of lustre around him as he passed on—to fame, to riches, to sorrow, to an early tomb. The march had been long, toilsome, dispiriting; with lacerated feet he had often been on the point of falling exhausted on the thorny road; but a vigorous intellect, sustained by an indomitable will, enabled him to achieve a noble victory over the difficulties which beset him, and a great and ample position crowned the miseries of years of unrequited toil, sorrow, and wretchedness.

BOOK II.

At the Zenith.

1814—1825.

CHAPTER I.

THE IDOL OF THE PEOPLE—THE THEME OF POETS AND
CRITICS.

THE 26th of January at length arrived. Morning
dawned upon a dreary, miserable aspect ; a heavy
fall of snow which had taken place a few days previous
was melting away before a sudden and unexpected
thaw ; a drizzling rain kept falling the whole day ; and
a cloudy atmosphere, hiding the sun from view, pro-
jected a melancholy gloom over the whole metropolis.
The *one* morning rehearsal of the *Merchant of Venice*
had been fixed for 12 o'clock, and precisely at the appointed time Kean made his appearance at the theatre.
The rehearsal was proceeded with. A bombshell
exploding in the midst of the slender company could
not have startled them more than the thoroughly

original interpretation which Kean gave to each line of his part. Raymond, the acting manager, protested against the "innovation," as he termed it. "Sir," returned Kean, proudly, " I wish it to be an innovation." " It will never do, depend upon it," remarked the stage manager, with a patronizing air that was excessively galling. "Well, sir," rejoined Kean, "perhaps I may be wrong; but, if so, the public will set me right." Notwithstanding the bold originality in question, his rehearsal was remarkably ineffective ; and the performers, taking his intentional tameness as a criterion of what the public performance would be, predicted his failure with energetic liberality. The rehearsal concluded, Kean returned home to enjoy with his wife the unusual luxury of a dinner. He remained at home until six o'clock, when the striking of the church clocks warned him that it was time to depart. Snatching up a small bundle containing the few necessaries with which he was bound to provide himself, he kissed his wife and infant son, and hurriedly left the house. " I wish," he muttered, " that I was going to be shot." With his well-worn boots soaked with the thickly encumbered slush, he slunk in at the stage door as if desirous of escaping observation, and then proceeded to a small, dilapidated dressing-room in the remotest part of the house, occupying it in common with three or four of the secondary actors.   He quickly exchanged his dripping, threadbare apparel for the more comfortable gaberdine of Shylock, slipped his feet into the tradi- tional Venetian slippers, and, taking a *black* wig from his little bundle, adjusted it to his head, heedless of or inattentive to the astonishment depicted on the faces of his companions.   Nevertheless, they did not attempt to expostulate with him; the reserved manner he had invariably maintained rendered *that* out of the question; but the news spread like wild-fire that the little man in the capes had rejected the conventional red wig.   In Burbage's epitaph we are told of

> " The *red-haired* Jew
> That sought the bankrupt merchant's pound of flesh."

Arnold lamented such extraordinary conduct; Raymond tapped his forehead significantly when he heard of the " black wig."   Both kept aloof.   Not so Bannister and Oxberry.   The former, with his characteristic good nature, came to give him an encouraging word; Oxberry, with a closer eye to business, to give him a glass of brandy-and-water. Gratefully accepting both, he issued from the dressing-

room, and proud in the consciousness of the approaching triumph, walked slowly to the wings, where he
was heartily greeted by Dr. Drury. Peeping through
the eyelet hole in the curtain, he surveyed a dreary,
hopeless aspect. The announcement of " Mr. Kean
from Exeter" carried with it no charm; another
addition to the list of failures for which the public
were indebted to the discrimination of the managers
was anticipated; and " there was that sense of previous
damnation which a thin house inspires." The boxes
were empty; there were about fifty people in the pit,
" some quantity of barren spectators and idle renters
being thinly scattered to make up a show." Un-
daunted by the discouraging aspect of affairs, he
awaited the decisive moment.

The cherished hope of twenty years is realized. He
is before the floats of Drury-lane, and is going to
show them what an obscure strolling player can do.
His fine Italian countenance, the lightness of his step,
the piercing brilliancy of his eye, the expressiveness
of his gesture, and the buoyancy and perfect self-
possession of his manner, impress the scanty audience
in his favour. His personal disadvantages are so great
that it is at once evident that a success can only be
achieved by sheer excellence, exposed to the discrimi-

nating test of the understanding. But there can be no
doubt that he will pass triumphantly through the
rigid severity of the ordeal. There is an animating
soul perceptible in all he says and does which at once
gives a high interest to his acting, and excites those
emotions which are always felt in the presence of
genius—a union of power with a fine sensibility.
It is giving fire to his eye, energy to his tones, such a
variety and expressiveness to all his gestures, that you
might have said "his body thinks."

The scene begins. The manner in which he acknowledges the applause usually accorded to a stranger
is a study for a painter. There is nothing of the
sullen gaol delivery common to the traditional Shy-
locks of the stage—a vague expectation is excited.
He takes up his position, leans across his cane, and
looks askance at Bassanio as he refers to the three
thousand ducats—"He is safe," cried Dr. Drury.
The scene goes on. "I will be assured I may" is
given with such truth, such significance, such beauty,
that the audience burst into a shower of applause :
then !—as he himself expressed it, "then, indeed, I
felt, I knew, I had them with me !"

In that part where, leaning on his stick, he told the
tale of Jacob and his flock with the garrulous ease of

old age and animation of spirit that seems borne back to the olden time, and the privileged example in which he exults, he shows them that a man of genius has lighted on the stage. His acting here is all a study. There is one present who notes with delight " the flexibility and indefiniteness of outline about it, like a figure with a landscape background : Shylock is in Venice with his money-bags, his daughter, and his injuries ; but his thoughts take wing to the east ; his voice swells and deepens at the mention of his sacred tribe and ancient law, and he dwells with joy on any digression to distant times and places as a relief to his rooted and vindictive purposes." The audience is then stirred to enthusiasm by the epigrammatic point and distinctness with which he gives the lines :

> " Hath a *dog* money ? is it possible
>   A *cur* can lend three thousand ducats ?"

and then—

> " Fair sir, you spat on me on Wednesday last,
>   You spurned me such a day ; another
>   You called me—*dog ;* and for these *courtesies,*
>   I'll lend you thus much monies."

The act drop falls ; all doubts as to a splendid success have been removed. In the interval between this and his appearance in the fifth scene of the second

act there was an obvious disposition on the part of
those who had previously contemned him to offer
their congratulations; but, as if divining their intention, he shrank from observation, and only emerged
from his concealment as the scene came on between
Shylock and Jessica, in his very calling to whom,
" Why, Jessica, I say," there was a charm as of
music. I shall close the record of this memorable
night in the words of Dr. Doran: " The whole scene
(that between Shylock and Jessica), was played with
rare merit; but the absolute triumph was not won
until the scene (which was marvellous in his hands)
in the third act between Shylock, Solanio, and Salarino, ending with the dialogue between the first and
Tubal. Shylock's anguish at his daughter's flight, his
wrath at the two Christians who made sport of his
suffering, his hatred of all Christians generally, and
of Antonio in particular, and his alternations of rage,
grief, and ecstasy as Tubal enumerated the losses in-
curred in the search of Jessica—her extravagances,
and then the ill-luck that had fallen on Antonio; in
all this there was such originality, such terrible force,
such assurance of a new and mighty master, that the
house burst forth into a very whirlwind of approbation. ' What now ?' was the cry in the green-room.

The answer was that the presence and power of the genius were acknowledged with an enthusiasm that shook the very roof. 'How the devil so few of them kicked up such a row,' said Oxberry, 'was something marvellous.' As before, Kean remained reserved and solitary, but he was now sought after. Raymond, the acting manager, who had haughtily told him that his innovations would not do, came to offer him oranges. Arnold, the stage manager, who had 'young manned' him, came to present him—'Sir'—with some negus. Kean cared for nothing more now than his fourth act, and in that his triumph culminated. His calm demeanour at first, his confident appeal to justice, his deafness to the appeal made to him for mercy, his steady joyousness when the validity of the bond is recognised, his burst of exultation when his right is acknowledged, the fiendish eagerness with which he whetted the knife—and then the sudden collapse of disappointment in the words, 'Is that the law?'—in all was made manifest that a noble successor to the noblest actors of old had arisen. Then his trembling anxiety to recover what he had before refused, his sordid abjectness as he found himself foiled at every turn, his subdued fury, and at the last (and it was always the crowning glory of his acting in this character) the withering sneer, hardly concealing the crushed heart, with which he replied to the jibes of Gratiano as he left the court ; all raised a new sensa-tion in the audience, who acknowledged it in a perfect tumult of acclamation. As he passed to the sorry and almost roofless dressing-room, Raymond saluted him with the confession that he had made a hit; Pope, more generous, avowed that he had saved the house from ruin."

With every limb trembling from excitement the hero of the night returned to his damp and threadbare ap-parel, and having received with a hurried carelessness the congratulations offered to him, he waited on Arnold in the manager's room. He was formally informed that their expectations had been exceeded, and that the play would be repeated on the following Wednes-day. To Kean the announcement was quite super-fluous. In an almost frenzied ecstasy he rushed through the wet to his humble lodging, sprang up the stairs and threw open the door. His wife ran to meet him ; no words were required ; his radiant coun-tenance told all ; and they mingled together the first tears of true happiness they had as yet experienced. He told her of his proud achievement, and in a burst of exultation exclaimed, " Mary, you shall ride in your carriage, and Charley, my boy"—taking the child from the cradle and kissing him—"you shall go to Eton, and"—a sad reminiscence crossed his mind, his joy was overshadowed, and he murmured in broken accents, "Oh, that Howard had lived to see it!—but he is better where he is."

The goal was won. The aspirations of years—aspirations which had enabled him to rise superior to all the apparently insuperable impediments which obstructed his way—were realized. He had got before the floats of Drury-lane; he had "had them with him!" His spring into fame was so sudden, so startling, so brilliant, that the scanty few assembled in the theatre on that memorable night might have imagined the shooting of a meteor, with all its attendant splendour. By a strong effort of volition he had declined to avail himself of opportunities which had offered years before to secure a footing in London; but now his powers were matured by practice, fertilized by study, and enriched by observation.

There was yet an obstacle, however, that remained to be swept away. So many first appearances had been made of late, and so much disappointment to all parties had been the result, that the edge of expectation became blunted, and the announcement of a new

tragedian carried with it no charm. Declining to
adopt a walk in the drama conformable to their peculiar instincts and powers, no new performers were
content with a less ambitious onset than a performance of the most prominent characters ; the consequence was that the public, distrusting the possibility
of adequate attraction, held aloof from the theatre,
and the journalists, disinclined to tire their readers by
announcing a constant repetition of failures, stayed
away also. Two critics, however, came on the night
of the 26th of January — those representing the
Morning Post and the *Morning Chronicle;* and having
the spirit and candour (for his mind was not yet
warped and soured) to hail the lucky omen, the recollection of that moment of startling yet welcome surprise was always a proud and satisfactory one to
William Hazlitt. The dramatic critic of the *Morning
Chronicle,* he freely bestows praise where he conscien-
tiously believes it to be due; but he is irremediably
captious and almost incorrigibly dogmatic.   "From
the first scene in which Mr. Kean came on," he writes
in his *View of the English Stage,* when describing his
first impressions of the tragedian, " my apprehensions
were set at rest. I had been told to give as favourable
an account as I could : I gave a true one. I am not

one of those who, when they see the sun breaking from
behind a cloud, stop to ask others whether it is the
moon.　Mr. Kean's appearance was the first gleam of
genius breaking athwart the gloom of the stage, and
the public have gladly basked in its ray, spite of actors,
managers, and critics." In the course of his account of
the "*début*" in the *Morning Chronicle* he writes:—"Notwithstanding the complete success of Mr. Kean in
Shylock, we question whether he will not become a
greater favourite in other parts.　There was a
lightness and vigour in his tread, a buoyancy and
elasticity of spirit, a fire and animation, which would
accord better with almost any other character than
with the morose, sullen, inward, inveterate, inflexible
malignity of Shylock.　The character of Shylock is
that of a man brooding over one idea, that of his
wrongs ; and bent on an unalterable purpose, that of
revenge.　In conveying a profound impression of this
feeling, or in embodying the general conception of
rigid and uncontrollable self-will, equally proof against
every sentiment of humanity or prejudice of opinion,
we have seen actors more successful than Mr. Kean ;
but in giving effect to the conflict of passions arising
out of the contrast of situation, in varied vehemence
of declamation, in keenness of sarcasm, in the rapidity

of his transitions from one tone or feeling to another, in propriety and novelty of action, presenting a succession of striking pictures, and giving perpetually fresh shocks of delight and surprise, it would be difficult to single out a competitor. The fault of his acting was (if we may hazard an objection) an over-display of the resources of his art, which gave too much relief to the hard, impenetrable, dark ground-work of Shylock. It would be needless to point out individual beauties, where almost every passage was received with equal and deserved applause. His style of acting is, if we may use the expression, more significant, more pregnant with meaning, more varied and alive in every part, than any we have almost ever witnessed. The character never stands still; there is no vacant pause in the action : the eye is never silent. It is not saying too much of Mr. Kean, though it is saying a great deal, that he is all that Mr. Kemble *wants* of perfection."

The objection maintained in the above critique— viz. that Kean's over-display of the resources of his art gave too much relief to the " hard, impenetrable dark ground of the character," was subsequently with-drawn. Never having studied the fine Jewish figure in the *Merchant of Venice*, Hazlitt's notions of the character had been exclusively founded upon its conventional stage treatment; but a thoughtful reading of the original quickly convinced him of his error, and enabled him to arrive at the conclusion that Shylock was anything but a compound of morose, sullen, inward, inflexible, inveterate malignity. "My idea of the gloomy groundwork was overstrained," he writes two years later; "Shakspeare could not easily divest his characters of their entire humanity; his Jew is more than half a Christian; and Mr. Kean's manner is much nearer the mark." This was no less ingenuous than just; and as all his objections to the performance depend upon this issue, Kean's Shylock obtained an unqualified eulogium at his hands.

Whether the Committee were intimidated or short-sighted, or whether they estimated the value of the new actor in proportion to the number of critiques written upon him, or whether they were malevolently desirous of making as little as possible of the applause which Edmund had elicited in the theatre, does not clearly appear; but it is certain that they expressed doubts as to whether his success was genuine, and even went so far as to suggest that for the present his name should be removed from the bills. Possibly such suggestion might have been adopted had not a member of their body interposed, and prevented the contemplated suicide. This was the author of *Childe Harold.*

Between Byron and Kean there existed many reasons for sympathy. Interest in the pale, dark-eyed, restless little man who was so liberally sneered at drew his lordship in the first instance towards the actor—an interest that increased and intensified until it assumed the form of a steady and lasting friendship. The similitude in one sense of their early culture served to strengthen the ties that bound one to the other; both were comparatively neglected in their boyhood, uninfluenced by a wise and gentle training, left " lords of themselves—that heritage of woe," at the time they most required restraint; and the future career of each was strongly tinted with the colouring of their early experiences and associations. Moreover, they had many faults and foibles and excellences in common. Both were obedient to strong impulses; both were visited with a settled melancholy, to relieve which they resorted to excitement, no matter in what shape; both were destined to be overtaken by a heavy disaster, which deprived them of many endearing qualities; both were intoxicated with success and general praise in the morn of their manhood.   It was in this mutuality that their friendship took rise.

His lordship by no means felt inclined to allow such a man as Kean to slip through the fingers of the non-observant Committee. " You have got a great genius amongst you," he said, "and you don't know it.   But he will fall through, like many others, unless we lift him, and force the town to come and see him. There is enough in Kean to bear out any extent of panegyric, and it will not do to trust an opportunity like this to the mere routine of the ordinary chances. We must go in a body, call upon the proprietors and editors of the leading papers, ask them to attend in person, and write the articles themselves."

After a little hesitation the suggestion was adopted, and an expedient that would have been at once fatal to anything short of the highest order of superiority, established at one stroke the young tragedian upon the most exalted pinnacle of dramatic fame. The 2nd of February was appointed for the second display of those brilliant powers which had secured emolument and attention to one who had hitherto been an unknown wanderer, unheeded, unprotected, unpatronized ; and the expectation excited by the solitary critiques in the *Morning Chronicle* and the

Morning Post exhibited itself in the attendance of an audience about twice as large as that to which he played on the 26th of January. On the former occasion the money paid at the doors amounted to 164*l.*; on the second performance the receipts went up to 340*l.* A jury of critics were empannelled, too, and at their hands the young actor's talent was to be estimated with every prejudice which a reference to departed merit must necessarily excite. Cooke had died; and represented as the character was by Kemble, it was at once evident that Shylock had died with him; while Macklin's interpretation of the Jew had hitherto ranked as one of the most cherished traditions of the stage. To a comparison and contrast with these great masters of their art Edmund was subjected with all the rigid severity of such an ordeal; and the brilliance with which he underwent the test at once stamped him as the most extraordinary representative of the part at any period. The fact that, after he had made a graceful acknowledgment of the welcoming applause, he took about as much notice of those in front as Napoleon is said to have done of his Parisian audiences, at once impressed the spectators in his favour. This, by the way, always constituted one of the greatest charms of his acting. He never sought or

seemed to think that he deserved the plaudits which
he invariably commanded; attentive to the scene, and
unmindful of the audience, he yet imparted to the one
a charm which insensibly subdued the other. His
representation of the opening scene with Bassanio
was as vigorous and as comprehensive as in the impassioned brilliancy of his performance in the third
act he was superior to himself; and as, with knitted
figure, he gave with tremendous energy that unan-
swerable interrogation, " Has not a Jew eyes?" &c.,
he towered above himself and reached the noblest
heights of grandeur. The energy of the moment,
however, deprived him of the clear and not unmusical
articulation which had charmed the audience in the
previous parts; the defects of his voice in its upper
register, which had on the first night been attributed to
hoarseness, were now observable ; but if his somewhat
harsh and grating tones came upon the ear strangely,
the unpleasantness of the impression was but momentary. The master-touches which adorned his
representation of the trial scene revealed a discrimination so noble that a thunder of applause attended
each passage where a more noticeable separation of
his acting from precedent indicated the strength and
originality of his conceptive power; and at the close,

as, with a tribute commensurate with the fine powers
he had exerted still ringing in his ears, he made his
way to the dressing-room, he must have felt that the
cherished belief in the indissoluble identification of
Macklin's name with the interpretation of the character had at last given way before the resistless
force of a young, powerful, and vigorous comprehension.

The criticism—for the most part admirably and
impartially written—appeared. There were a few, it
is true, who evinced a disposition to infer that, as
Kemble and his followers had made statuesqueness
and magniloquence the order of the day, rapidity,
energy, and intensity were altogether out of date, and
consequently indulged in the unphilosophical vulgarity
of estimating a production of genius by a standard
formed exclusively on the prevalent taste of the
passing hour. In this they presented a direct contrast to the more influential critics, who, so far from
being swayed by so misdirected a prejudice, steadily
opposed the injustice encountered by Kean in his disposition to escape the predominant train of associations in regard to the school of acting now in vogue.
Hazlitt screwed the courage of the *Morning Chronicle*
to the sticking-place, nor did he ever regret having

done so; and *The Times*, though exhibiting a reluctance to abjure the Kemble religion, rendered a discriminating and handsome tribute to the genius of
the new actor. Kean's Shylock impressed the *Examiner*
with an idea that he had risen by his representation
of this character alone to the very summit of his profession; and that paper adverted in terms of the most
eloquent praise to the fact that the stranger saw the
very essence of grace resided in the management of
the arms; instruments which with Kean were rendered
almost as eloquent as the tongue or eye; which were
the noble machinery fabricated to perform all those
works of beauty and of power that distinguish man
from the brute; which, to the mind of Socrates, formed
one of the strongest proofs of the Deity's providential
wisdom.   One critic applauded the absence of all common or contradictory expression in the tragedian's
countenance through the importance attached to the
lower part of the face as a medium of expression; and
another was reminded by Kean's success of the
observation made upon Sir John Denham on the
publication of *Cooper's Hill*—that he broke out at
once on the town twenty thousand strong.

The scene now changed with magic rapidity. The
intellectual world hastened to do honour to the genius

which but a few weeks before had been expending its
purest rays to no purpose in the obscurity of rural
shades; Lord Holland and Mr. Grenfell enrolled
themselves on the list of his patrons; portraits and
biographical sketches* of the new actor enjoyed an
extensive circulation; and the long-expected tide of
fame and fortune set in with an impetuosity before
which no prejudice arising from long-established principles could hope to maintain a stand.   On the 10th
and 12th of February he faced audiences so brilliant
and replete that we cannot experience any surprise at
the wonderment and almost incredulity of a member
of the Committee, who, on looking through the eyelet-
hole of the curtain, rubbed his eyes and declared that
it was like a dream !   Such acting and such applause
had not been seen or heard in Old Drury for many
years; and as the feelings of the audience accompanied the actor in his progress, he gained glory after
glory, and shout after shout, until the curtain fell.
The favour and admiration of the public, exerting a
correspondent effect upon the minds of the committee,
rapidly veered their opinions round to that point of

---

* The biographical sketches were necessarily somewhat meagre
and incorrect, for Kean modestly declined to entertain any application for materials.   See foot-note on page 56.

the compass, which looked in the direction of their
interest; and having made a partially veiled apology
for the indifference with which they had treated him
before his appearance, they made him a present of
fifty guineas in addition to his salary.   Nor did their
endeavours to atone for the past stop here; Mr. Whitbread, acting as the chairman, honourably cancelled
the agreement entered into by Kean with Arnold; and
20*l.* a week rewarded efforts far superior to those for
which he subsequently received one hundred guineas
a night.   A dressing-room on a scale of luxury and
completeness before unknown was provided; and
after his performance of Richard the Committee presented him with a hundred pounds as a further mark
that his industry and talents were justly appreciated.
In other circles the recognition of his genius was no
less gratifying.   Lord Jersey sent him anonymously
a bank-note for 100*l.*; Mr. Whitbread called one
morning, took Charles on his knee, and put a draft
for 50*l.* into the child's hand; the same sum was
tendered by the Duchess of St. Alban's; Lord Essex,
Mr. Ellice, Mr. Chandos Leigh, and Mr. Scrope
Davis gave him each a share in the theatre; and to
crown all, only a week after they had presented him
with the 100*l.* the Committee gave him another

500*l.* Kean did not prize these marks of favour
half so much as honest John Bannister's memorable
piece of wit. On the night of Edmund's first appearance as Richard, a group of idle actors in the
green-room were discussing his merits in anything
but a liberal spirit. "I understand," said one,
with an elaborate sneer, "that he is an admirable
harlequin." Bannister entered at that moment, overheard the remark, and retorted, *impromptu*, "I am
certain of that, for he has jumped over all our
heads."

Among the varied characters on which Shakspeare
has expended the results of his rich and fruitful invention, few are so striking or so admirably finished
as that of Shylock. Although its displays are confined to two or three scenes, it is, from his entrance
to his final exit, so masterly an exhibition of dramatic
skill that nothing could be added with profit or removed with advantage. Though the dark passion
of revenge and worldly, or rather usurious thrift,
constitute the principal features of the character,
there is in it nevertheless a variety of secondary
considerations, a series of delicate shades and differences which the greatest actors have found it impossible to comprehend, and, in many instances, impossible

to express. Many have, no doubt, been fully competent to depict in broad and legitimate colouring the
greedy thrift and the "lodged hate and certain
loathing" which the Jew bears towards the merchant;
but it has fallen to the lot of few, if we consult the
best records of our acting drama, to interpret with
due completeness those minor but nice discriminations
which constitute the fine human element that pervades
the character, and a thorough mastery of which is
indispensable to the illustration of the grand object
of this noble composition—the redemption of Shylock
from the detestation which an unrelieved exhibition of
his more prominent features would be calculated to
produce. Garrick, deterred from undertaking the
character in consequence of these difficulties, offered
no opposition to the pre-eminence of Macklin; and
on the death of the latter, George Frederick Cooke
sprang forward, grasped the mantle which John
Kemble had failed to make his own, and stamped
himself the most forcible, energetic, and magnificent
representative of the character with which the stage
had up to his time been adorned. In the Shylock of
Cooke, however, the subtle intricacy referred to was lost
to view in a broad and massive, yet exclusive delineation of what he erroneously regarded as the governing

principle of the character—the malignant spirit of
insatiable revenge ; and in his performance this spirit
took entire possession of his heart, absorbed every
faculty responsive to other and more tender calls, and
accompanied him in all his bargains, thrifts, and
transactions. This was a misconception. To introduce Shylock as a "decrepit old man, bent with
passion, warped with prejudice, and grinning deadly
malice " is an obvious inconformity with the spirit of
the part ; and it was reserved for Kean to withdraw
the portrait from the conventional errors of its representation, to apply his clear, sound, and vigorous
understanding to a new and original conception of the
character, and to exhibit Shylock from a point of view
which, from its scrupulous adherence to the author's
design, gave rise to the fine comprehension of the Jew
that prevails at the present time. Let us remember
with admiration that this view dawned upon him when
only thirteen years of age.

The Shylock of Edmund Kean was one of those
emanations of genius which, once seen, can never be
forgotten. Fulfilling with energy the highest de-
mands of dramatic art, and working up every shade
and phase of the character into a whole of surpassing
splendour and magnificence, the performance could

only have been produced by a mind profoundly conversant with human nature and character, its thoughts, instincts, and prejudices. Shylock ranks the fourth of Kean's performances, giving precedence to Othello, Lear, and Richard III. Byron, Hazlitt, and Sheridan, held it to be a portrait perfect both in principle and detail. Those who had the good fortune to witness the Shylock of Edmund Kean, and in a situation sufficiently near the stage not to lose the more refined delicacies and beauties of his performance—his low, quiet, milder tones, the minute fillings up of the character he was identifying, and above all, the effect of the finer lights and shades of his expressive and ever-varying features,—can well remember and appreciate the eloquent, and it may be said religious scorn with which he rejected Bassanio's invitation to dine :—" Yes, to smell pork—to eat of the habitation which *your* prophet, *the Nazarite*, conjured the devil into ;" the full force of an old untainted religious aristocracy which came upon the mind when, speaking of Launcelot, he said, " What says that fool of Hagar's offspring ?" and with what subtlety of expression he gave Shylock's answer to Salarino's inquiry as to what the pound of flesh is good for : " *To bait fish* withal ! If it will feed nothing else it will feed my revenge. He

hath disgraced me, and hindered me of half a million;
laughed at my losses, mocked at my gains, scorned my
nation, thwarted my bargains, cooled my friends,
heated mine enemies; and what's his reason?—*I am
a Jew.*" How beautifully did Kean express these last
four words! A slight approach to deprecation on
account of his unmitigated injuries passed away in a
moment when he reflected that the dignity of his race
must not be hurt by his exciting commiseration in a
Christian. In this single speech he was worth, Hazlitt states, "a wilderness of the monkeys that have
aped humanity." The scene with Tubal, where he is
alternately depressed by the announcement of Jessica's
extravagances, and savagely ecstatic at the tidings of
Antonio's misfortune (how terrifically impressive was
his interrogatory, "Is it true? Is it true?") has
been so faithfully described in the page which I have
borrowed from *Their Majesties' Servants,* that any
further comment is unnecessary. In the trial scene
his touches declared the master-spirit. The cool
and triumphant look of assured revenge which
he fixed upon Antonio from the moment of his
entrance into the court; his unfaltering determination and imperturbable devotion to his purpose;
his smile at heart upon every reference he made

to his bond; his self-satisfied answer to Gratiano's abuse :

> " Till thou canst rail the seal from off my bond,
> Thou but offend'st thy lungs to speak so loud.
> Repair thy wit, good youth, or it will fall
> To careless ruin"—

in all this his acting was irreproachable. In the reply to Portia's several appeals, the originality of his conception disclosed itself with startling effect. The pretended doctor of laws having explained the legal enactment in a way which the Jew considered entirely in his favour, his heart warmed towards the friendly interpreter, and after having handed to him the bond, confident that all was technically correct, he gazed upon the face of the supposed lawyer as the latter read the instrument with an eye that fairly reeled with exultation. In—

> " An oath ! an oath ! I have an oath in heaven.
> Shall I lay perjury on my soul ?
> No ! not for Venice !"—

where he was advised to close with Bassanio's offer, he replaced the conventional solemn severity of manner with a tone of humour bordering on the ludicrous ; it was the bitter ironical joke of a man who saw no obstacle standing between him and the

consummation of his cherished purpose. In his reply
to Portia's entreaty to procure a surgeon for charity's
sake—

> " I cannot find it; 'tis not in the bond"—

he substituted a chuckle of transport for the savage
sneer with which the line had been rendered in the
hands of Cooke and Macklin. This was a fine touch
of nature. " The most ferocious and deadly passions,"
writes one of the critics in justification of this innovation, " relapse into an almost paroxysm of joy
when the victims are placed in their power; as the
poet has made death grin horribly a ghastly smile at
the prospect of an abundant food for his savage
appetite." The sudden change of his whole appearance when the cause turned against him; the happy
pause in " I am—content," as if it almost choked
him to bring out the word; the partial bowing down
of his inflexible will when he said—

> " I pray you give me leave to go from hence,
> *I am not well* ;"

the horror of his countenance when told that his con-
version to Christianity was conditional on his pardon;
and to crown all, the fine mixture of scorn and pity
with which he turned and surveyed the ribald

Gratiano; all exhibited a succession of studies of passion to which words would fail to do justice. He retired, as the author intended he should do, with the audience prepossessed in his favour.

Having in the general memory displaced Macklin from his supremacy in Shylock, Kean was now called upon to dissolve the association of Garrick's name with the interpretation of Richard III. In this object, according to honest John Bannister, who somewhat reluctantly admitted that in the brilliance of Kean's Richard he almost forgot his old master David, he was completely successful; and the masterly manner in which he represented the last of the Plantagenets achieved a triumph second only to that which he subsequently won in Othello and Lear. In this second effort, which was immeasurably more difficult than the first, the fertility and ready application of his resource were in every respect equal to the manifold requirements of the part; his performance gave full expression to all those fine, delicate touches of dramatic art which Shakspeare has expended upon the character; it exhibited all those distinctive forms of expression and peculiar collocations which result from originality of conception and brilliance of execution; it realized his comprehensive views of the character

with an energy and completeness which wrung from
press and public an unfeigned acknowledgment that his
Richard III. formed the grandest flight into the
tragic atmosphere that had within their memory been
achieved; and the unsurpassable excellence of his
representation, so far from attained to by fitful and
meteoric bursts of his genius, was found to lie in
an unabated, fervid, and pervading radiance which
extended itself to every passage, however slight and
apparently insignificant, in the part.   The plenitude
of power exhibited in this last mentioned feature of
the performance exposed him to the one charge
brought against his Richard III.   Hazlitt contended
that this perfect *articulation* of every part tended to
dissipate the impression of the character by the
variety of Mr. Kean's resources: "The extreme
elaboration of the parts," writes the critic, "is in-
jurious to the broad and massy effect; the general
impulse of the machine is retarded by the variety
and intricacy of its movements."   Ingenious, but not
convincing.   An inattention to the minutiæ of the
part would have rendered the actor amenable to a
charge of wishing thereby to invest the more obvious
features with more prominence and strikingness; and
when Hazlitt subsequently objected to Kean's King

Lear as exhibiting the bright points of the character instead of the whole, he forgot that he was charging the actor with a fault which he had done his best to introduce. Kean had his faults, it is true ; but all his faults arose out of the fulness of his riches. In themselves they begot an interest, for power, the true characteristic of genius, was visible in all that he did ; and the spectator felt all hypercritical objections silenced when he referred to the axiom that faults are imitated and admired because they are more or less always united to the great exemplars of genius. It is the gift of genius to attract in spite of its rules, and not unfrequently to secure most applause from its very aberrations. *Abundat dulcibus vitiis.*

All the diversified traits in the character of Richard III. were included in Kean's conception. The villain moving onward to his purpose with an utter disregard of ordinary duties and ordinary feelings ; the daring and comprehensive intelligence, seizing its objects with the grasp of a giant ; the immovably fearless spirit, exulting in his immeasurable superiority over all others ; the profound acquaintance with the human soul, enabling him to appreciate and search out motives at a glance ; all the multiplied varieties of the character (scantily enumerated above)

were, to borrow a line from one of the actor's bio-
graphers, "played upon by Kean as though they
were so many keys of an instrument; while every
difficult passage was mastered with a hand which only
genius could stretch forth." One of the greatest of
his merits in this performance was his substitution of
a kingly for the conventional vulgar assassin of the
stage. He never lost sight of the fact that Richard
was a Plantagenet—a man whose deeds, however
repulsive, indicated an enormous strength of will and
understanding; he brought the strong relief of his fine
irony, caustic sarcasm, and occasional touches of an
almost devilish gaiety into the portrait; and, by the
tone of natural truth and fine comprehension of the
character exhibited throughout, "he showed," writes
Mrs. Richard Trench, in her *Correspondence*, "that
Gloster possessed a mine of humour and pleasantry,
with all the grace of high breeding grafted on strong
and brilliant intellect." "He carries one's views
backwards and forwards as to the character," continues that gifted lady, "instead of confining them,
like other actors, within the limits of the present hour;
and he gives a breadth of colouring to the part which
strongly excites the imagination. He gave probability
to the drama by throwing the favourable light of

Richard's higher qualities on the character, particularly in the scene with Lady Anne, and he made it more consistent with the varied lot of poor humanity. He reminded me constantly of Buonaparte — that restless quickness, that Catiline inquietude, that fearful somewhat resembling the impatience of a lion in his cage. I would willingly have heard him repeat his part that same evening." In the originality, breadth, and terrible force of his Shylock he was beyond all comparison, but in Richard—

> " The fiery soul which working out its way,
> Fretted the pigmy body to decay,
> And o'er-informed its tenement of clay,"—

his genius shone out with a more resistless effect. To close this general description; in every part he showed himself to be an adequate representative of this the most buoyant portrait of intellectual villany in the universal drama,—a portrait which almost makes mind triumph over morals even in the estimation of the spectator, who, called upon by every human sympathy to abominate, is almost involuntarily disposed to admire. The voice of execration is lost in the awe and wonder with which we follow the crookback in his march ; he belongs to a class above mankind, and we admire him in spite of ourselves.

The announcement of the first appearance of
Edmund Kean as Richard III. caused a stir in all
circles, and the most exalted anticipations of dramatic excellence were never raised in greater strength
or satisfied with so much completeness as on this
occasion. As the doors opened the rush and influx
were terrific, and about five minutes afterwards the
theatre was crowded to repletion with the most expec-
tant, brilliant, and overflowing audience it was ever
known to have contained. The receipts amounted to
720*l.*—how different to the condition of the treasury
on the 26th of January, when 164*l.* graced its interior ! Kean, dispirited and almost afraid to appear,
sat in an easy-chair in his dressing-room, very apprehensive lest a cold, from the effects of which he was
suffering, should render his voice unequal to the
strain about to be applied to it—and on the momen-
tous occasion, too, that was to " make him or mar him
quite !" " I am afraid most of it will be dumb show
to-night ; do you," he said to Wroughton, " tell them
that I've got a cold." This was done ; Kean determined to go on, and to do what he could. And now,
if the reader will accompany me in imagination
before the curtain, I will try to let him see what a
noble, brilliant, and eminently effectual performance

Edmund Kean's Richard III. was.   No doubt a large
majority of that dense audience in front, not having
seen any of his few previous performances of Shylock,
expected to witness a good conventional representation of Richard; but those who had been present
when he appeared as the Jew, and marked the fine
original conception which he realized with such wonderful vigour and effect, expected what they subsequently found—a novel, brilliant, and characteristic
piece of acting.   He came out from behind the scenes
with a step so natural and so appropriate that the audience, accustomed to a fine, picturesque and heroic
stride, were absolutely startled; and as, conscious of
nothing but his own reflections, and communing with
his own gigantic thought, he silently rubbed his
hands—what a daring innovation !—they saw that
no common man was before them.   The soliloquy
proceeded; there was no ferocious and studied declamation, all was easy, natural, and unlaboured; and
as, with a beautifully expressive action, he gave out
the line, " The dogs bark at me as I halt by them !"
the first applause elicited that night broke out in fervent enthusiasm.   The soliloquy went on; the audience saw that the actor had become Richard himself—
there was the devilish but calm calculation, as if solely

occupied with means, and not wasting a reflection on
qualities; the terrible jocundity, sure of his purpose,
seeming to hug himself in his very heart on assassi-
nation, enjoying it almost as a joke, and exulting in
it as an advantage. And then came the scene with
Lady Anne, the nauseousness of which had been
much increased by Kemble and Cooke; the former
whined it in a way not at all attractive to the ear,
the latter was harsh, coarse, and unkingly. Not so
Kean. An enchanting smile played upon his lips;
a courteous humility bowed his head; his voice,
though hoarse with cold, was yet modulated to a
tone which no common female mind ever did or ever
could resist. Gentle, yet self-respected, insinuating
yet determined, humble yet over-awing, he presented
an exterior by which the mere human senses must,
from their very constitution, be subjected and en-
thralled. Cooke in this scene was anxious, hurried,
and uncertain; but Kean's love-making was confident, easy, and unaffected, earnest and expressive,
and managed with such exquisite skill that a close
observer might have distinguished it from real
tenderness, however well calculated to have imposed
on the credulity of Lady Anne. His attitude in
leaning against the side of the stage before coming

forward in this scene was so graceful, so striking, and so picturesque, "that"—writes Hazlitt, enthusiastically—"it would have done for Titian to paint." Speaking of Kean's representation of the courtship scene, he continues: "It was an admirable exhibition of smooth and smiling villany. The progress of wily adulation, of encroaching humility, was finely marked throughout by action, voice, and eye. He seemed like the first tempter to approach his prey, certain of the event, and as if success had smoothed the way before him." This praise was confirmed by his brother critics; not so his objection to the quickness of familiar utterance with which the actor said of Hastings, "Chop off his head!" In this quickness of familiar utterance, which revealed a courageous adoption of the simplicities of the commonest everyday life, Kean exhibited his superior understanding, his noble disdain of what was little, and his thorough comprehension of the part; but Hazlitt, who up to this time appears to have derived his conceptions of Shaksperian characters exclusively from their conventional stage treatment, and who had been spoilt for natural truth by the pompous and ferocious utterance with which the "Chop off his head!" had hitherto been dispensed, failed to see that the immovably fearless

Richard, conscious of his towering superiority over those by whom he is surrounded, could feel nothing but contempt for the wavering, pusillanimous Hastings, and would consequently deliver the order as Kean did —in a manner which showed that he despised his victim equally from the consequences that might ensue from his execution. Moreover the king was addressing himself to a friend in confidential conversation, and on a subject that necessarily supposed a perfect familiarity with murder :—would the formal and the pompous have been appropriate here? A similar absence of all theatrical flourish marked his acting when, on being taunted by the little Duke of York, the expression of his countenance formed a fine picture of stifled rage and affected composure—here the delicacy of the performance constituted its strength. The interest of the audience was growing more intense every moment. Why was this? Because the actor was showing that his activity of mind was unceasingly at work; because he was showing that thought followed thought through the immediate operation of the mind, instead of indicating by his delivery of the first line of a passage that he accurately knew the tenour of the last; and because this was keeping his countenance in a perpetual and a picturesque animation, chequered according to the diversifications of the character, and his entire frame and hands and legs in appropriate and symbolical action. Nothing could have been more happy, nothing more electric in its effect than the soliloquy where he debated what course to take with the young princes. His apprehensive mind kindled at his casual mention of *the Tower;* it communicated itself in a blaze to his ardent and fiery spirit, and in the fatal lightning of his eye and the energy of his gesture the audience saw that the remorseless deed he contemplated was already done! In the sudden variation of his manner to the messenger who arrives with the tidings of Edward's death; his interview with the princes, where his eye indicated a fearful restlessness to crush the obnoxious "spiders;" the scene in which he taunted Lady Anne with the savage avowal of his hatred—quite equal in spirit and force to that in which he wooed and won her; his interview with Buckingham, in which, entirely separating himself from the usual solemn pedantry of the stage, he placed his hands carelessly and gracefully behind him as the Duke described his reception by the citizens; and, above all, the scene with the Lord Mayor, in which the scarcely subdued triumph which glittered in his eyes as he refused the crown, the

M 2

accession to the pleas of his confederates with "Call
him in again," his acceptation of the crown, and the
triumphant burst of exultation after he had dismissed
the petitioners—all exhibited an originality, vigour,
and transcendant talent altogether new to the surprised and delighted audience. A new man appeared
to be revealed to them when he descended from the
throne with that fine assumption of condescending
familiarity, "Stand all apart—Cousin of Buckingham;" his expostulation with Lord Stanley was
managed with infinite spirit; and in his exultation
at the death of Buckingham his acting exhibited a
rare combination of energy and skill. Who that
heard can ever forget the blighting sarcasm which
broke out in part of this performance; first in
"Well, as you guess," secondly in his taunt to
Stanley "Where be your forces, then, to beat them
back?" and thirdly in that withering interrogatory,

> " What do they in the *north*,
> When they should serve their sovereign in the west ?"

More variety, more depth, more intensity of expression were thrown into these words than were ever
brought together in the same space; rage, hatred,
sarcasm, suspicion, and contempt were all expressed
in the single word *north*. In short, the whole per-

formance was an uninterrupted succession of beauties ; but it was reserved for the closing scenes to convey anything like an adequate idea of the depth and fulness of his riches. His embodiment of the intense and feverish glow which pervades the character through- out the tumultuous and vivid interest of those scenes was a diamond on the breast of genius, and elevated him to the front rank of nobility and vigour of mind. In the parting with his friends before the battle, and in the treatment of the paper sent to Norfolk, his acting was pregnant with truth and energy; and "nothing could have expressed in a deeper manner the intentness of Richard's mind on the approaching contest, or have quitted the scene with an abruptness more self-recollecting, pithy, and familiar, than by the reverie in which he stood fixed, drawing figures on the sand with the point of his sword, before retiring to his tent, and his sudden recovery of himself with a 'Good night.'"* And as, surrounded by his generals, and lost to everything else but his own thoughts, he adopted that attitude— an attitude which was so beautiful that it might have adorned the palæstra where the Grecians cultivated

---

* Leigh Hunt.

health and elegance, and where their sculptors obtained vital impressions of form and motion—he stood
more like a grand picture by one of the old masters
than anything living in this commonplace nineteenth
century.   His eye, so dark, and wild, and piercing,
fixed, but on no visible object, and seeming to live
upon things past or to come, appeared to hold the
concentrated rays of the mind, and to have a deep and
desolate feeling of its own; his eyebrows, so marked
and flexible, came down edgy and contracted; his
face, so fine and changeful and charged with meaning,
was pale and full of loneliness; his lips, the slightest
movement of which was always so expressive and significant, were compressed with immense feeling; and
the effect of all was perfected by a fine massive flow
of hair, which fell round his face on his shoulders, and
lay there in rich black curls.   The adopting of this
attitude, and the drawing figures on the sand were
most expressive and original ideas—the touches of a
master justly confident in the certain effect of his
judgment.   The audience, after looking on in silent
admiration, gave vent to earnest applause; and thus it
survived a very decisive test, for only a man who held
the hearts of his audience in his hand could have
ventured on an illustration which, involving as it did

a stoppage of the performance, would not in an inferior actor have been tolerated for a moment. They were now to be stirred to uncontrollable enthusiasm, for to the heroic part he lent the greatest animation and effect; and when he gave Richard's proud boast that "a thousand hearts were swelling in his bosom," he imparted to every spectator a portion of the enthusiasm which dilated his form as if it would rival the stature of Lucifer himself, and cause his voice to rush forth like the bursting of a water-spout. His tent-scene was filled with a radiance altogether new to the stage, and as he recovered from the dream he burst forth upon the audience with a meridian splendour which would have shed additional glory on Garrick's representation even as handed down to posterity by Hogarth. The power of Kean's understanding was nobly proved in the variety of phase and world of thought and significance comprised in the speech which followed. With "Give me another horse!" he was the courageous and valiant warrior, oblivious to all but the carnage before him; his voice, energetic and fearless a moment before, sank into a plaintive murmur of physical distress as he feebly cried, "Bind up my wounds. Have mercy, Heaven." With the order for the horse he was the usurper, tossing in the

tumult and conflict of imaginary battle, infuriated
with the danger in which he found himself involved;
but with the supplication to Heaven the actor denoted
with the rarest skill that a different succession of
thought had suddenly revolved in his mind, and
ceasing for a moment to be the warrior infuriated
with pain and the prospect of instant death, the fever
of his brain was diverted into another channel, and the
consequent depression of the assassin, enervated by the
predictions of the spirits which had hovered over his
couch, prompted an invocation to a power which he
had before neglected and despised. The accuracy and
power and subtle force with which this interpretation
was effected showed a man fit to exposit the finest
touches of Shakspeare. The words "Soft, soft, 'twas
but a dream," marked the emancipation of his fiery
and unconquerable soul from the trammels in which
for a time it had been confined; and the gradual recovery of reason, the proud resumption of faculties
lately subservient to terror, and the lofty and sarcastic
contempt with which a daring spirit reviled itself for
yielding to the influence of a dream, wound up the
display, and shed additional lustre round the actor
who could sustain and embody an illusion so trying
and so noble. " Who's there?" An indefinable terror

seized him, and, snatching up a sword, he placed himself in a fine posture of defence. Catesby entered. The petulant contempt, the snigger of self-reproach for shaken fortitude, were true to nature. Plunging into the thickest of the fight, he performed prodigies of valour; and under a stern and fierce exterior the glimpses which Kean afforded of his internal torment portrayed in vivid colours the chaos of a tempestuous and deeply labouring mind. Anxiety, embarrassment, feverish hurry, secret fear that broke forth into ironical boasting, rage resorted to as a covering from despair, the remembrance of crimes contending with the yet unmitigated fury of evil passions —all these varied concomitants of the closing life of Richard were distinctly and powerfully marked. Pressing fiercely onward, sending before him dismay, flight, and death, and frenzied with the wounds he received in return, he encountered the leader of the opposing army, and as he rushed to the combat with a frightful eagerness and exultation he unconsciously put forth a grandeur that set the heart beating and the blood rushing to one's face. His conception of the death scene was a piece of noble poetry, expressed by action instead of language. The fight was maintained under various vicissitudes, by one of which he was thrown to the earth; on his knee he defended himself, recovered his footing, and pressed his antagonist with renewed fury; his sword was struck from his grasp—he was mortally wounded; disdaining to fall, he fixed his eyes on Richmond with intellectual and heroic power; he expanded his breast with what appeared to be more than human spirit; and with an action which Hazlitt regarded as possessed of a preternatural and terrific grandeur, he extended his arms in motionless despair—in calm but dreadful defiance of his conqueror.   With this magnificent effort the unconquerable soul abandoned its mortal tenement, and he fell to the ground "like the ruin of a state, like a king with his regalia about him." The sublimity of this conception filled all with silent wonder, awe, and admiration; and as the spell was broken by the descent of the curtain, thunders upon thunders of applause swept over the theatre.   " We have felt our eyes gush," writes one of the critics, " on reading a passage of exquisite poetry, we have been ready to leap at sight of a noble picture, but we never felt stronger emotion, more overpowering sensations than were kindled by the novel sublimity of the catastrophe. In matters of mere taste there will be a difference of opinion, but here there was no room to doubt, no

reason could be impudent enough to hesitate.   Every
heart beat an echo responsive to this call of elevated
nature, and yearned with fondness towards the man
who, while he excited admiration for himself, made
also his admirers glow with a warmth of conscious
superiority because they were able to appreciate such
an exalted degree of excellence."

   " Mr. Kean's manner of acting Richard III. has
one peculiar advantage ; it is entirely his own, without any traces of imitation of any other actor.   He
stands upon his own ground, and he stands firm upon
it.   Almost every scene had the stamp and freshness
of nature. . . . . If Mr. Kean does not completely
succeed in concentrating all the lines of the character
as drawn by Shakspeare, he gives an animation,
vigour, and relief to the part which we have never
seen surpassed.   He is more refined than Cooke, more
bold, varied, and original than Kemble in the same
character. . . . . His manner of bidding his friends
good-night, and his pausing with the point of his
sword drawn slowly backwards and forwards on the
ground, received shouts of applause.   He gave to all
the busy scenes of the play the greatest animation
and effect.   The concluding scene, in which he is
killed by Richmond, was the most brilliant.   He

fought like one drunk with wounds, and the attitude
in which he stood with his hands stretched out, after
his sword was taken from him, had a preternatural
and terrific grandeur, as if his will could not be disarmed, and the very phantoms of his despair had a
withering power."— *Morning Chronicle.*

" There is a feeling for which but little credit is
allowed to critics, and which it may be thought great
affectation for us to profess : we shall however venture
to express it in spite of the incredulity of prejudice.
We know, then, no greater pleasure than to hail the
triumph of genius, and to watch over the progress of
a growing fame. A mind of common generosity feels
itself humiliated when it is forced to crush unopposing
weakness; to do execution even on resolute and stout
offenders, though just, is after all but dirty work ;
but to be able to bestow rewards on exalted merit,
seems for the time not only to place us on a level
with the subject of our praise, but even to elevate us
above our ordinary nature. We must not, however,
attempt to explain the feeling too nicely, lest it
should appear rather selfish than benevolent; but be
it selfishness or be it kindness, it was never excited
so strongly in our breast as by the display of the
talents of Mr. Kean.

"In our criticism on his Shylock, we promised to retract our praise, if we saw any reason :—something we do wish to alter in that paper, but not the praise. We said that his voice was disagreeable and his figure insignificant. We did not then know that he was labouring under a severe cold, and the tasteless gaberdine of the old Jew concealed that person which was expanded by the heroism of Richard. Here his soul seemed to enlarge and o'er-inform its tenement, which, under its inspiring influence, became at once impressive and picturesque. Then his fine and somewhat Italian countenance, all intellect and sensibility, excited equally those almost incompatible sensations of high admiration and perfect sympathy. The full force of Shakspeare's mind seems to have been exercised in the portraiture, and we should think that none but a man of kindred intellect could give an adequate image of such a model. This, however, Mr. Kean has done. We cannot recollect any performance—the very finest exhibitions of Mrs. Siddons not excepted—which was so calculated to delight an audience, and to impress it with veneration for the talents of the actor, as the Richard of Mr. Kean."— *Examiner.*

The Times and the *Morning Post* both held that

the long-existing desideratum to the stage — an adequate representation of Richard III.—had been supplied by Mr. Kean. One critic stated that Cooke and Kemble were left at an immeasurable distance; and the *Scots Magazine*, speaking of the fine effects followed by storms of applause, said, "Electricity itself was never more instant or effectual in its operation." The other papers were not less eulogistic. The *Champion* stated that Mr. Kean's assumption had brought his merits to a decisive test, and that paper " warmly congratulated him on gaining all he hazarded, and on establishing himself at the early age of twenty-six, in spite of every disadvantage arising from the effects of severe indisposition, as the first male performer of the day."

But a violent cold and exhaustion were doing their work. While the play-going public were eagerly reading the journalistic notices of the great triumph of the 12th of February, the tragedian lay in bed very ill; and the generous-hearted Committee, sensible of the extraordinary impression which the little man in the capes had produced, sent for Sir Henry Halford, the President of the Royal College of Physicians, to exert his professional skill in the taking care of a life so precious to the public, and to their own interests.

Sir Henry's treatment answered so well, that the tragedian was able to resume Richard III. on the 19th of February, and to sustain the character on that occasion with all his original vigour and effect. Rae, who had declined to recognise Kean before the appearance of the latter, but who now treated him with a respect that was almost servile, came forward to announce the play for the 21st; the audience, however, were unselfish, and cries of "No, no," testified their sense of the impropriety of requiring the repetition of the performance until every disadvantage had been completely removed. Nevertheless, the tragedian did appear on the 21st, and also on the 24th; and a rumour that the Drury-lane Committee were replenishing their empty coffers at the expense of his health, was contradicted (by desire) in the following letter to Arnold:—

"DEAR SIR,

"I have great pleasure in authorizing you to contradict, in the most unequivocal terms, the report to which you allude. You have never pressed me to appear on the stage one day earlier than was perfectly agreeable to my own feelings, and you are aware that I have wanted no other spur to exertion than the gratification of appearing before a public who have conferred on my humble efforts the distinction of so much flattering applause. I am happy to say I am in perfect health, and at the service of the theatre whenever and as often as you think proper to call on me.

"I am, dear Sir, yours sincerely,

"EDMUND KEAN."

"Feb. 26, 1814."

"Just returned from seeing Kean in Richard," writes Byron to Moore, on the night of the 19th of February. "By Jove, he is a soul! Life—nature—truth, without exaggeration or diminution. Kemble's Hamlet is perfect, but Hamlet is not nature. Richard is a man, and Kean is Richard." His lordship's opinion as to the perfectness of Kemble's Hamlet was withdrawn in the course of a month. On the following day he writes, "An invitation to dine at Holland House to meet Kean. He is worth meeting, and I hope, by getting into good society, he will be prevented from falling like Cooke. He is greater now on the stage, and off he should never be less. There is a stupid and underrating criticism upon him in one of the newspapers. I thought that, last night, though great, he rather under-acted more than the first time. This may be the effect of these cavils, but I hope that he has more sense than to mind them. He cannot expect to maintain his present eminence or to advance still higher, without the envy of his green-room fellows or the quibbling of their admirers. But if he don't beat them all, why, then— merit hath no purchase in ' these costermonger days.' " One hope expressed here—that he might " beat them all"—was answered to the very letter; the other, that by getting into good society he might be prevented from falling like Cooke, was scarcely realized.

" They tell me he is like John Bologna," exclaimed John Kemble; " I must go and see him." " Have you not seen him yet, sir ?" inquired a cringing parasite. " No," replied the noble Roman. " He is only a croaker, sir, I assure you," was the sycophantic reassurance. " Indeed !" returned the tragedian, with a contempt of the parasite which, to his credit be it said, he took no pains to conceal; " perhaps his croaking is preferable to some people's acting ;" and he turned away.

On the 12th of March Kean appeared as Hamlet, and represented this matchless compound of fire, fitful passion, filial reverence, indecision, and philosophical

abstraction with a vigour of thought, a tenderness of
feeling, and an acuteness of sensibility which more
than confirmed the reputation acquired by his performances of Shylock and Richard. That the same
warmth of approbation as that evoked by his previous
efforts should attend his representation of the Prince
of Denmark he did not anticipate,—the character
of Hamlet is by no means so intelligible to the
great mob of playgoers as those of Shylock and
Richard; but the stamp of a profound and vigorous
intellect was so deeply impressed upon the sus-
tainment of every scene, the flashes of an understanding as vivid and excursive as the lightning
it resembled so abounded throughout the whole
representation, that it was impossible it could fail
of a correspondent effect. In short, it did not on
the first glance seize immediately on the outward eye,
but it drew out upon it more and more fixedly the
inward observation of the mind, which it awed into a
solemn attention. Disdaining to employ any adventitious aids in his interpretation of the character, he
played it to the understanding, not to the eye; he
never for a moment lost sight of the fact that he was
clothed in the sable garb of a man so deeply immersed
in the soundless depths of a divine philosophy as to

become indifferent to the agitations of the surface, and whose emotions, welling up spontaneously from the heart, could not be faithfully expressed by the dry pedantry and indissoluble hardness which characterized Kemble's performance of the part. In Hamlet, which he was ever inclined to regard as his best character, Kean threw open the flood-gates of his riches, learning, and discrimination; and while his performance displayed the richest hues of imagination and the finest impulses of the human mind, it was interwoven with flowers scattered so profusely about as to become permanently enshrined among the memories of every mind which is dedicated to the reception of the product of undeniable genius, depth, and originality. A rich and fervid imagination, and a quick susceptibility to every form of poetic beauty, imparted to all parts of his performance an untold charm; and thousands have basked in its radiance with an insensibility to all but the delights diffused by a man whose fertile intellect and delicate discrimination enabled him to comprehend the intentions of a mind which he so nobly illustrated and explained. His worship of nature, exhibited more conspicuously in this character than perhaps any other, was ennobling and impressive; everything that was calculated to appeal to finer

sensibilities was adequately felt and fully expressed,
and his understanding fastened by sure, swift instinct
upon any trait or passage which afforded a clue to the
author's ideas.   His conception and execution of the
part—the first regulated by an unerring judgment
and the second by his observance of nature, a graceful
monitress in cases of vigorous thought and deep expression — were in complete consonance with the
spirit of philosophical reflection which pervades the
character; and even in those occasional violences
of feeling which come across that calm and sheltered
mind, like gusts across a lake only to disturb for a
moment its sequestered beauty, and then leave it to
solitude and smoothness as striking and as sudden,
the spirit of the part was never for a moment lost.
His faults, which arose, as in Richard, out of the
plenitude of his riches, were powerless to disturb the
noble impressions received from his performance ; and
his interpretation of Hamlet Prince of Denmark
advanced solid and irresistible claims to be regarded
as one of the most chaste, finished, and beautiful
offerings ever laid at the feet of Melpomene.

Like his Shylock and Richard, his execution of
Hamlet was clothed with the brilliancy of genius. In
the first scene, his deportment, spite of his physical

disadvantages, was eminently graceful, and full of
that native ease which should appear in one described
as the "glass of fashion and the mould of form." The
littleness of his figure had hitherto been unnoticed
under the gaberdine of Shylock or the deformities of
Richard, but in Hamlet it was not to be concealed,
and a momentary feeling of surprise and disappointment swept over the theatre.   His genius, however,
rendered objection impossible.

> "Before such merit all distinctions fly,
>   Pritchard's genteel and Garrick six feet high."

Among the many customs of the stage which precedent had sanctioned, and which were cleared away
by Edmund Kean during his first London season, the
improper manner in which representatives of Hamlet
encountered the Ghost requires a passing mention.
All his predecessors, Betterton excepted, and Garrick
included, had paid more attention in this scene to
attitude than to the spirit of the part; but Kean,
whose mastery and capacity of interpreting the very
essence of the character rendered him independent
of any adventitious aid, endeavoured to become the
Hamlet of Shakspeare, not a student of the strikingness displayed in the sculptural remains of antiquity.

He was not unsuccessful; upon *his* sight the awe-
inspiring shade broke in a manner such as to silence
the voices of the most captious and cavilling; and
throughout the contact all his fervour of feeling and
capability of mind concentrated upon and gave affluence
to the scene and intellectual enjoyment to the spectator.   His sinking on one knee before the solemn
spirit, the filial confidence with which he hastened
to obey its beckoning, the impressive pathos of
his action, and tender vibration of the voice in
addressing it, "I'll call thee Hamlet, Father, Royal
Dane," were pregnant with unsurpassed depth and
solemn   brilliancy.   Originality   of   conception, regulated by a fine and perfect discrimination, was
observable in the treatment of every line ; and the
management of his sword, in which he departed from
the usual erroneous practice of pointing the weapon
towards the shade of his murdered father, but instead
thereof at his friends, in order to protect himself from
their interference, was novel, perceptive, and more
conformable to the character than the conventionalism
referred to. With the tenour of the next scene, where
the ghost reveals the means adopted for his removal
from this "sterile promontory," all that Kean did
was effected in complete and uninterrupted harmony.

The melodious but solemn and impressive tones, the resistless magic of the eye, and those wonderful expressions of feeling "not loud but deep" with which he adorned this scene, were something more than the poet could have dared to wish for, and conferred on the character a sublimity which no other actor could have imparted to a similar extent. The inception of his fixed resolve to fulfil the mission entrusted to him was perfectly and beautifully marked; and the scene where he swore Horatio and Marcellus to secrecy was rendered more than usually prominent by his characteristic vigour and discrimination. The intricacy and difficulty of the character increase with the development of the incident, but like Virgil's Fame—*Vires acquirit eundo*—the actor gathered fresh strength and velocity from the space he cleared, and gained new energies to surmount the difficulties which sprang up in his path. In the lighter scenes with Polonius and Rosencrantz and Guildenstern, he displayed talent unsurpassable, and his manner of taking the two latter one under each arm, under pretence of divulging his secret when he only intended to trifle with them, was a reading praised by Hazlitt as one in complete conformity with the spirit of the character. The critic pays the same tribute to the sup-

pressed tone of irony in which the actor ridiculed
those who gave ducats for his uncle's picture, though
they would "make mouths at him" while his father
lived.   The long soliloquy at the end of the second
act was a fine proof of his perfect comprehension
of Shakspeare, and of the combined excellences of
passion, feeling, and discrimination.   In the soliloquy
on death, he perfectly identified himself with that
chain of reasoning by which Hamlet is induced to
bear his present reverses rather than

" Fly to others that we know not of."

Every look, every tone, every inflexion of his voice
rendered it what it truly is—a series of impassioned
and heart-breaking reflections, and in it might be
seen the philosopher actuated by a desire to seek a
refuge in the grave from the villany and frivolity of
those around him, finding ample causes for the justification of his wish in his abundant sorrow, expe-
riencing a heartfelt regret that he must not yet touch
the forbidden land, but still clinging to his despondency with a tenacity which arises from the depth of
his sorrow.   His scene with Ophelia is to be selected
as the most brilliant of the rich profusion of excellences which adorned his interpretation of the cha-

racter. It was so pathetic, so exquisitely tender, so
rich with colours "dipt from heaven," that those who
could have contemplated it unmoved must have ever
resigned all pretensions to taste and sensibility.
Deviating with unimpeachable propriety from the
conventional coarseness and almost brutal ferocity
with which the scene had been represented, the actor
imparted to it a vein of tenderness which he conceived
it impossible to repress, and so rescued the Dane from
the charge of inflicting undeserved pangs on the
gentle and ingenuous object of his affections. Kean
thought her, as himself, the destined victim of affliction, and, so thinking, expressed for her at once tenderness and severity ; his tenderness arose from a knowledge of her purity and gentleness, and his severity
from a regret that a being so exalted as his grieving
fancy made her should be subject to the common
foibles and accidents of her sex. In accordance with
this conception he spread over the scene an ethereal
fluid too subtle for analysis, which eluded the senses
while it penetrated and fastened on the soul. As
he was about to leave he suddenly turned round ; he
changed countenance, as if struck with the pain he
was inflicting ; and returning from the very extremity
of the stage, he performed an act of tenderness wrung

from him in the fulness of his heart with recollections
of the past sadly contrasting with the present and
the prospective future, and kissed her hand, at
once to reassure her and to vindicate himself. What
a noble touch of nature ! Vigour of thought, acuteness of discrimination, tenderness of feeling, and a
delicate perception of the dignity of manhood were
all developed at one stroke. A soft yet earnest
delight, a transient enchantment, instantly took possession of the mind, and it forgot, or in the gratification of the moment as good as forgot, that what was
before it was the reflection of reality in the mirror of
genius. Hazlitt applauded it as the finest commentary ever made on Shakspeare; Collins held it to be
a fine proof of the actor's genius ; and another critic,
going still further, declared that Mr. Kean had produced in two simple actions, occupying so many
minutes, those noble illustrations of the spirit of
Shakspeare's writings—the dying scene in *Richard III.*
and the parting with Ophelia in *Hamlet*—" which were
worth all the notes, critical and historical, emendatory
and commendatory, declamatory and defamatory, that
ever were written." In the advice to the players the
felicity of tone and action with which he caricatured
those who hold the mirror up to nature by mouthing

the speech, sawing the air with their hand, and
speaking in a manner neither having "the accent of
Christians nor the gait of a Christian, pagan, nor
man," might have been relished as a keen satire
against the prevailing dramatic characteristics of the
time, and as a graceful tribute to his own discrimination by his implicit obedience to the precepts he imparted. Hazlitt doubted whether his
forgetting and recollection of the speech commencing "the rugged Pyrrhus" was in perfect keeping
with the part; but he admits and applauds the ingenuity displayed in the thought. Collins said that
it sided with the parting with Ophelia in proving
Kean to be a man of genius. In this scene of the
play the actor's passion kept pace with the progress
of passing events, and increased with the development
of the plot he had organized. Hazlitt said that the
force and animation given to it could not be too
highly applauded,—that its extreme boldness "bor-
dered on the verge of all we hate," and that the effect
it produced was a test of the extraordinary powers of
"this extraordinary young actor." The closet scene
was highly impressive, and the comparison of the
portraits, as if suggested by the intervention of an
accidental thought, adduced a further evidence of con-

formity of conception and appropriate force of expression. His sudden alteration at the appearance of the spirit from mental disturbance to the awe and solemnity natural to the occasion of such a presence, his constant recurrence to the source of his irritation, the rapid kindling as from time to time he turned to the memorial of the murderer, and the inquiry made at the instance of the spirit,—" How is it with you, lady?"—were beauties which sprang directly from the soul.* The impression created by his "Is it the King?" can never be effaced from the memories of those who experienced it. The graveyard scene comprehended everything that could be wished for, and when he took up the skull he gave the words "Alas! poor Yorick," with a degree of tenderness and feeling which touched every heart. A fine retrospective glance

---

* A letter written in March, 1814, thus adverts to Kean's representation of the closet scene:—" His endeavours to reclaim a parent from guilt, to calm the anguish and terror of a mind appalled with the consciousness of its baseness, and to restore it to a sense of virtue and honour, were marked with the most persuasive emotions of eloquence ; and in the appeal to

'Look here upon this picture and on that,'

in which Hamlet exerts himself to inspire the bosom of his mother with a portion of the indignation with which he is himself inflamed, his acting was admirable, as it also was in his skilful and felicitous transition from admiration of his father to detestation of his uncle."

pervaded his utterance as he dwelt upon the association of the relic with the scenes of his early childhood,—the remembrance of innocent pleasures, of transient happiness, vague indeed and undefined, being recalled to memory in a pristine brightness which rendered its contrast with the present gloom—dark, forlorn, and dreary. Absorbed in a silent grief which benumbed every faculty on learning the death of Ophelia, Kean conceived it inconsistent with the spirit of the character to make up any display in the disclosure of his presence commensurate with the anticipations of those who had been led by precedent to expect a violence of tone and demeanour when springing into the grave; so the disclosure " 'Tis I, Hamlet the Dane !" was delivered with nothing but an unexaggerated expression of the rooted despair which had taken possession of his mind. In the fencing scene he fought with consummate grace and skill. He would have killed the King in a princely manner had it not been for the bungling way in which Powell thought it became a king to fall; but, in spite of the disadvantage, he gave full expression to the terrible resentment which the accumulated wrongs under which he was yielding up his breath were calculated to arouse. His death was a masterpiece of physiological accuracy, impelled to brilliance by the inspiration of genius. It had been usual to show that Hamlet died from the effects of a sword wound, but discriminating with rare intelligence between the manner of death with reference to its cause, Kean conceived that in doing the work of dissolution the rapid agent must have been a powerful mineral, intense internal pain, wandering vision, and distended veins of the temple. His realization of this hypothesis was of an almost awful reality. His eye dilated and then lost its lustre; he gnawed his hand in the vain effort to repress the expression of physical suffering which rose to his countenance; the veins in his forehead swelled and thickened; his limbs shuddered and quivered; his hand dropped from between his stiffening lips, and he uttered a cry of nature so exquisite that it could only be compared to the stifled sob of a fainting woman.

The new readings which Kean introduced into his representation of Hamlet conclusively show that the power which Shakspeare possessed of initiating his hearers into the *thoughts* of his personages belonged to Kean in an eminent degree. As a testimony of the actor's perfect comprehension of the part, and as an illustration of the happy results attained by a close and attentive study, they are scarcely less

valuable than as displaying a felicitous discrimination
between conscientious improvement on the one side,
and the absurd search after variations of accepted
interpretations which distinguished the actors of that
period on the other. In the soliloquy commencing
"Oh, that this too, too solid flesh would melt," the
words "Fie on't! oh, fie!" were, after a short medi-
tative pause, applied to the hasty marriage of his
mother and his uncle, and not, as was customary, to
the subject of the world, "the unweeded garden."
In the description of his father to Horatio, the simple
eulogium,

> " He was a man take him for all in all,
> I shall not look upon his like again,"

was rendered with the following punctuation—

> " He was *a man*.   Take him for all in all
> I shall not look upon his like again."

In the controversy which ensued respecting the propriety of this alteration, it was contended on the one
hand that regarding mankind in an unfavourable light,
Hamlet was not likely to sum up the excellences of
his father in the one word *man ;* but on the other, it
was shown that the aversion which Hamlet entertains towards the whole human race might induce
him to make a particular exception in favour of one

who rose superior to the general standard of humanity. As he laments the degeneracy of human nature, he is all the more likely to appreciate one who realized his notions of what a man should be, and in applying this term to his father he pays him the highest praise which a melancholy founded on distrust of mankind would permit him to bestow. The variation receives another justification from Horatio's preceding words, "He was a goodly king." Kean's variation then implied that this eulogium failed to convey a just idea of the noble qualities of his deceased parent; he was not only a goodly king but *a man*. The words "Very like, very like," were not given as a reply, as they had hitherto been, to Horatio's remark that "the sight would have much amazed him;" but employed as an instrument for the development of the series of those thoughts which the hasty marriage of his mother with Claudius had given rise to. In the recognition of Horatio he substituted an expression which implied that he was willing to exchange the title of friend with him but not that of servant, for the conventional interpretation, "I'll change the name of servant for that of friend." After the disappearance of the ghost he rendered the following passage thus : "There are more things in heaven and earth, Horatio, than are dreamt of in *our* philosophy." What a fine proof of discrimination ! Another varied reading occurred in the scene with Polonius, wherein the words, " For if the sun breeds maggots in a dead dog, being a god kissing carrion," were given as a passage from the book he held in his hand. Abruptly stopping himself he turned to the old courtier and said, " Have you a daughter ?" If the conjecture is well founded that Shakspeare intended to introduce Hamlet in this scene reading the Tenth Satire of Juvenal, the speech in which, commencing " Da spatium vitæ," &c., may be readily reconciled with the description which Hamlet gives of the subject of his contemplation, then the actor's conception was scarcely justifiable ; but in the absence of any conclusive evidence that Shakspeare was acquainted with the Latin poets, we must be content to receive the alteration with a favour increased by the recommendation of the discriminating study in which it arose.

Before entering into any further details of the wonderful results of his genius, it will be advisable to mark the distinction between the different styles of acting, in order that we may understand all the better the permanent and lasting influence which

Kean exercised upon dramatic art. From the earliest development of the drama in this country, acting would appear to have divided itself into two distinct classes or schools—the romantic and the classic. The former relates to that style of acting distinguished by simple truth, fidelity to nature, and passion unfettered by the artificial restraints of the stage; the latter refers to the stilted, the declamatory, and the magniloquent. The first holds the mirror up to nature; the second does exactly the contrary. That acting in the Elizabethan period was of the turgid, pretentious, and premeditated description, there can be little doubt. I have always considered that Hamlet's advice to the players was intended as a keen, lofty satire on contemporary characteristics of the stage,—the mouthing of the speech, the sawing of the air with the hand, and the general disposition on the part of the actors to overstep the modesty of nature. If this surmise is a correct one, the conclusion at which I have arrived is irresistible. In Thomas Betterton, who from 1662 to 1710 maintained against all competitors his position as the greatest actor of his time, the classic and romantic schools, with the more repellant prominences of the former tastefully softened down, met with a not inharmonious union. A discriminating student of nature, Betterton nevertheless sacrificed many beauties of truthful expression to negative objects of mere exterior grace. His successor, Barton Booth, who terminated a highly successful career on the London stage of twenty-three years in 1733, adopted the classical element in Betterton's acting to the exclusion of the natural; and James Quin, who made his first appearance at Drury-lane in 1715, followed in the same wake. In 1741, the classic school, with Quin's faultless elocution to sustain its popularity, stood high in vogue; but a regenerator was at hand. David Garrick appeared at the Theatre in Goodman's Fields on the 19th of October in that year; took the town literally by storm by the power of his genius and fidelity to nature; reduced the most cherished conventionalisms of the stage to disrepute; effected a very undignified collapse of the classic school; and sprang on to the ruins of the fallen temple with nature's banner in his hand. But Garrick did not live for ever. He died in 1779, and on the 30th of September, 1783, John Philip Kemble appeared to undo all the good that his energetic little predecessor had accomplished by re-establishing art on the stage. Kemble's acting was utterly soulless. Possessed of a

noble figure, he aimed exclusively at statuesque effect;
and to the pursuit of this he sacrificed nature, passion,
and the manifold beauties of truth. "He was the
statue of perfect tragedy," writes Hazlitt, "not the
living soul." His acting was studied, not unlaboured;
his utterance was formal and measured, not easy,
familiar, and natural; and in Coriolanus, Penruddock,
and King John these characteristics alone found a
basis upon which he could build up an indestructible
reputation. In Shylock, Othello, Richard III., and
Macbeth he was unequal; and his Hamlet, notwithstanding the fine and impressive exterior perpetuated
by the pencil of Sir Thomas Lawrence, was too stately,
too inflexible to picture Shakspeare's matchless crea-
tion to the mind. Mrs. Siddons also belonged to the
classical school, but there was more truth at times in
her acting than in that of her brother. The principal
feature in her acting was grandeur—grandeur such
that nothing like to it can be conceived; nothing
could have been more noble, nothing more powerful,
nothing more sublime, nothing more awe-inspiring
than her Lady Macbeth. "It seemed as if a being of
a superior order," writes her most ardent critic, "had
dropped from another sphere to awe the world with
the majesty of her appearance." Among the many

imitators of John Kemble, Young deserves to be mentioned. He was a fine declaimer, and his distribution of emphasis exhibited much discrimination; but he had no passion, no energy, no humour, no capability of impressing character on what he undertook. In 1800 the supremacy of the classic school, then in the zenith of its popularity, was challenged by the rough, unstudied, and vigorously natural George Frederick Cooke, who excelled in the humorous, the caustic, and the mentally active, but who failed in characters requiring anything in the way of refined beauty, pathos, or tenderness, such as Hamlet, Othello, or King Lear. "Cooke, indeed, compared to Kean had only the *slang* and *bravado* of tragedy."* Nothing that he ever attempted displayed anything like equality to his Sir Pertinax Macsycophant. He did not, however, succeed in diminishing the repute of the classic school; and Kemble moved on, the acknowledged head of his profession, until 1814. For a quarter of a century antecedent to that period the classic school had reigned supreme; but the Shylock, the Richard, and the Hamlet of Edmund Kean swept it, with its "paw and pause," from the

---

* Hazlitt.

stage, even as Garrick had done seventy-three years before.

This salutary reform was mainly effected by his Hamlet. Pervaded by a fine tone of natural truth, abounding with unpremeditated force, and replete with all the distinctive characteristics of genius, his Shylock and Richard had prepared the public for the important changes that were about to take place ; but his Hamlet!—so natural and exquisitely true was this effort, and so entirely did it harmonize with those healthy feelings and spontaneous impulses which all would desire to cherish, that it at once became evident that all hearts would beat so quickly in response to this elevated call of nature that a regard for its eternal charms would speedily become synonymous with an appreciation of Kean. The disfavour of the Kemble school was inevitable ; and the critics, be it said to their credit, evinced no inclination to withhold honour from him to whom honour was due. The first to hail this restoration of nature to the stage was the *Examiner*. Ever since that paper had been established its conductors had expressed a determined antipathy to the artificial, studied, and imposing elegance of the Kemble school ; and consistently with that course they heartily hailed the advent of Edmund Kean as the regenerator of the stage.   The worthy editor, Mr. Leigh Hunt, was in durance vile for the strictures which had appeared in the *Examiner* on the Prince Regent ; and in his absence the theatrical department of that paper was entrusted to a writer who, holding opinions similar to those of his leader on matters dramatic, rejoiced in the production of an effort not only for the means it afforded of improving the public taste by the purity and power of a style which reproduced nature without affectation, but also for the intellectual enjoyment to be derived from the fine original powers of the new actor.   The critic proclaimed the downfall of the classic school, and the example was contagious.   Other journals censured the acting which deferred to stage effect, while they elevated that of the natural, imaginative, and beautiful ; and the cry was carried along the lines of public opinion with so much energy that nature was speedily re-established on the stage, and a pure, healthful, and invigorating atmosphere introduced into the crowded walks of the drama.   I quote a portion of the *Examiner* criticism as exhibiting the decided contrast between Kemble's and Kean's performances of Hamlet :—

" In his representations of Hamlet Mr. Kemble showed an ignorance of the character which would have been scarcely pardonable in the first stroller picked up at a country fair. Hamlet, whose sensibility is so keenly alive that every trifle administers fresh pangs to its distress, was converted by Mr. Kemble into a dry scholastic personage, uttering wise saws with a sneer, and delivering his ironies with a spruce air and smart tone such as is used by forward girls and boys on their introduction into the world, when they wish to excite attention to their abortive *bon mots* and unfledged sarcasms. Then, in what manner did he treat the gentle Ophelia? What threatening of fists, what ferocity of voice, what stamping of feet, what clattering of doors? Had there been one spark of chivalry left amongst us, the pit and boxes would have sprung on to the stage and dashed to the earth the insolent intruder who could so insult a lovely and harmless woman. But alas! the fashionables in the boxes who hate their wives, and the honest simpletons in the pit who are afraid of theirs, seemed to rejoice in this triumph over the daughter of Polonius as if it had avenged their own particular wrongs. What a striking and amiable contrast was Mr. Kean's management of this encounter. He came on the stage with slow steps, with a fixed sorrow on his countenance, and recited the famous soliloquy on death in a tone of pathos which touched every heart. This beautiful piece, in which the feelings reason as much as the mind, is usually uttered with a solemn declamatory accent like a sermon on a fast-day. Mr. Kean knew better; he was not a stale discourser on a stale general moral, a grim debater of the pro and con. of suicide: he was the man of misery driven by his loathing of life and the villany of those about him to escape all further ills by death. The scene with his mother was managed with equal talent, but not with equal *effect:* his tones told that not his heart but his memory was speaking, but he did not display any of the theatrical tricks which the audience had been used to expect. He did not shake his mother out of her chair, nor wave his handkerchief with a dignified whirl, nor spread his arms like a heron crucified on a barn-door, when he cries, 'Is it the king?' The omission of these singular beauties made many people shake their heads and prophesy that a permanent reputation was beyond the reach of the popular idol. We entreat Mr. Kean, if he should hear of such observations, to disdain them as they deserve; let him abjure low artifices of applause, and act as he has hitherto acted, and we will undertake to promise him that his fame shall last as long as the heart of man shall beat in response to the call of nature."

The most influential journals were equally earnest in their praise. The *Champion* regarded the Hamlet of Edmund Kean as the finest example of the art of acting that had ever been seen on the modern stage, and as indicative of the most acute intellect, the truest notions of art, and of a very poetical imagination. "All his imitations of madness were exquisitely contrived and managed; his scorn of Polonius, his ironical speeches, were given with a master's skill." *The Times* characterized the ghost scene as highly artistic, and the parting with Ophelia both novel and beautiful. Hazlitt, in the columns of the *Morning Chronicle*, recorded that Mr. Kean's Hamlet, spite of the manifold difficulties of the part, had the most brilliant success; and that, high as Mr. Kean stood before in his estimation, he had no hesitation in saying that he stood higher in it, and also that of the public, from the genius displayed in the last effort. "The kissing of Ophelia's hand explained the character at once (as

Shakspeare meant it) as one of disappointed hope, of bitter regret, of affection suspended, not obliterated, by the distractions of the scene around him." Both *The Times* and the *Morning Chronicle* critics occasionally degenerate into hypercriticism. The "singular beauties" satirically referred to in the *Examiner* criticism included "the tumultuous and overpowering effect" which Hazlitt, with a taste not altogether faultless, complained that Mr. Kean did not produce when, springing into the grave, he said "'Tis I, Hamlet the Dane." *The Times*, in objecting to the actor's appearance at court "without his insignia and ornaments," forgot that Kean's sedate, grave, and entirely undecorated garb of black velvet was more consonant with the solemn impressiveness of the character than the tawdry finery with which Kemble was wont to deck himself out when on the stage for Hamlet; and that the Danish order of the Elephant, when worn by a representative of the Dane, is an indisputable anachronism, having been instituted by Christian I. at least five centuries subsequent to the period at which the incidents of the play, which are founded on a story in the chronicle of Saxo Grammaticus, the Danish historian, took place.

The downfall of the Kemble school was surprisingly

rapid. "Never was so entire a revolution," says a
writer in *Blackwood's Magazine*, "wrought in so short
a space of time by one person as that which has just
been effected by Mr. Kean in the art of acting—a
revolution which is the more extraordinary from its
having happened quite unconsciously and unintentionally on the part of its creator, and quite unexpectedly by every one else; and yet one the founda-
tions of which cannot but be laid in the immutable
truth of nature, because it has been instantly and at
once hailed with a universal burst of delight and
sympathy from all sorts and conditions of people—all
except the insignificant few whose petty interests, or
still pettier envies, prevent them from feeling rightly
and from choosing to express their right feelings.
And speaking of this revolution as already brought
about,—for it is so in fact, though not in effect,—the
school of acting which Mr. Kean has established
exists at present in his own person only, but its
practice and principles are now so firmly fixed in the
feelings and understandings of those who are judges
that they cannot, at least in the present generation,
be for ever departed from. Any attempt to supersede
that practice or those principles by such as obtained
seven years ago would be received now just as an

attempt to supersede the plays of Shakspeare would by translations from those of Racine."

The followers of Kemble—"the insignificant few whose petty interests or still pettier envies prevented them from feeling rightly and from choosing to express their right feelings"—did not permit the religion in which they had been brought up to fall into disrepute without a struggle. In this endeavour to counteract the impression produced by the new actor they cannot be blamed; but in the line of action which they adopted to that end they cannot escape without reproach. Proudly disdaining to carry on an honourable rivalry between the two houses, they congregated in the best known resorts of the *corps dramatique*, and enlightened the company with eloquent dissertations on the physical defects of Mr. Kean. "He has not got a good figure." "His voice is positively bad—wanting in compass." "There is no dignity about him." "There is no measure in his speech." "He is not John Kemble." This was all the exception they took, "and this they considered quite enough to prove that he was nothing because he was not something quite different from himself." When the finishing blow was given to the Kemble school by the sibilant shower which subsequently attended its leader's ill-advised attempt to qualify the effect produced by Kean's Sir Giles Overreach, the indiscriminating disciples were comparatively silenced, and after that there was a manifest disposition among several of them to express an exalted admiration of what they had before hypocritically affected to estimate at so low a rate. To refer to this illiberal opposition and its subsequent withdrawal is a less grateful task than to fix our attention upon the animated controversy respecting Kean's merits carried on by a more independent section of the community. Notoriously "food for the critics," there was no end to the topics which he afforded for discussion—for praise and blame. In this marked division of opinion, an unequivocal tribute was paid to the genuineness of his powers. The mediocre and imitative actor encounters no opposition, excites no envy; he may stand out in bold relief from amidst a group of his own stamp, but he exhibits none of that instinctive originality which enables a man of true genius to think and invent for himself. Mistaking toleration for favour, his harmless vanity prevents him from discovering how much higher his powers are in his own estimation than that of the public. But he who, standing firmly on his own ground, gives a new impulse to the public mind, and advances with gigantic strides to the foremost place in the front rank of his profession, has to contend with various obstacles; even those who are disposed to estimate him rightly will cavil at what they term his "singularities" before they declare themselves satisfied with him. This was the spirit in which the coffee-house controversies were carried on for several months after Kean's appearance; but among men of such intellectual stamp as Byron, Hazlitt, and Sheridan the discussion was conducted on a broader and more liberal basis. Such a disposition, and on the part of such men, compensated the actor for the small criticism to which his daring originality and tranquil reliance on himself gave rise; and in the inspiration of genius, judgment, and exquisite taste, he moved grandly on, while the applause of the intellectual world followed him.

Among those who eagerly flocked to do honour to the new actor, was the widow of David Garrick—the beautiful Eva Maria Violetta of fifty years before. After the death of her husband, she almost entirely abandoned herself to seclusion, alternating her residence between Adelphi-terrace and the picturesque villa on the banks of the Thames at Hampton. At the end of the lawn which surrounds the latter,

Garrick built the mausoleum for the reception of Shakspeare's statue and the celebrated chair; and the chief delight of his widow consisted in an enumeration to her female friends of the many learned and distinguished personages who visited the spot during her husband's lifetime. Time had removed all that was beautiful from that once perfect face; time had despoiled her of the activity which formerly lent so great a charm to Eva Maria Violetta; but when speaking of her husband all the old vivacity returned, and for a time she seemed to rise superior to the infirmities of age. Octogenarians may remember the face so faithfully delineated by Mr. Cruikshank appearing in a box at Drury-lane or Covent Garden on the occasion of a new actor's first appearance, the manager prompting her to say that the *"débutant"* reminded her of David in order that the representation might impress itself favourably on the audience; but in the case of Edmund Kean she spoke sincerely, he *did* remind her of Garrick, and resembled him in manner more than any actor she had ever seen. She immediately pronounced him her husband's legitimate successor; sent him fruit from Hampton, and rewarded him for the impression which his Richard produced upon her by presenting him with the Garter,

stage jewels, and various paraphernalia worn by
Garrick in the character. Nor did the respect she
paid to Edmund stop here. When he dined with her
at Adelphi-terrace, she assigned him, with a grave
solemnity of manner, a particular chair for his ac-
commodation. "Why this one in particular?" he
asked, and the old lady in reply informed him that it
was Garrick's favourite chair—"Yes, sir, David's
favourite chair, *his* chair; think of that. You are the
only person I think worthy of sitting in it." A firm
friendship between the old lady and the young actor
speedily took place; and to Mrs. Garrick, who was
often to be seen a welcome visitor at the actor's
house, Kean was wont to communicate his professional troubles. On one occasion he complained to
her of the inaccurate observation of the critics in
their notices of his conceptions, readings, points, and
other peculiarities. "These people," he said, "don't
understand their business; they give me credit where
I don't deserve it, and pass over passages on which
I have bestowed the utmost care and attention.
Because my style is easy and natural they think I
don't study, and talk about the ' sudden impulse of
genius.' There is no such thing as impulsive acting;
all is premeditated and studied beforehand. A man

may act better or worse on a particular night, from particular circumstances; but although the execution may not be so brilliant, the conception is the same. I have done all these things at country theatres, and perhaps better, before I was recognised as a great London actor; but the applause I received never reached as far as London." "You should write your own criticisms," replied the old lady; "*David always did.*" So far from maintaining the authority of his statement that "there was no such thing as impulsive acting," Kean frequently proved exactly the contrary. He studied his characters with the greatest anxiety and care; but he frequently rejected the premeditated course, and played in a manner that even his wife, before whom he constantly rehearsed, had not the least conception of. When asked his reason for so doing, he replied, "I felt that what I did was right. Before I was only rehearsing."

Mrs. Garrick took great interest in Kean's Hamlet, her sole objection to the performance being that Edmund was not so severe with Gertrude in the closet scene as Garrick. For two or three performances Kean suffered himself to be prevailed upon by the old lady to throw more sternness into his reproaches to the queen; but Garrick's severity was not only "cruel" but "unnatural," and Kean speedily returned to his own manner of doing the scene. Hamlet's tongue and soul, as he himself informs us, play the hypocrite in the "speaking daggers" to the queen, and moreover, she is his *mother*.

By this time the doors of the wealthy and the influential had been thrown open to the brilliant and intellectual stranger, and an exalted admiration and respect for his genius were expressed without limit. We have already seen him appear at Holland House in the character of an honoured visitor; and as every facility was being afforded him to enter any class of society from the highest downwards, it was hoped by his well-wishers that he would show his discretion by restricting his communication to persons far above the middle rank. Such hopes, however, were not realized; wherever ceremony or "etiquette" was observed, Kean was not at home. Inured to hardships and privations from his infancy, and reared in an atmosphere rarely penetrated by a refining sun, he contracted a roughness of manner that caused him to feel ill at ease when brought into contact with "that tinsel-covered mass of envy, hatred, and all uncharitableness—polished society." The Coal Hole Tavern, Fountain-court, Adelphi, became his favourite resort; and here, delighting in convivial intercourse, he frequently passed his leisure time. His success did not possess him of any false pride; his manners were as unassuming, his speech as unostentatious, and his dress as simple, as ever. "Do not deck yourself out in any finery," he said to his wife, when they were preparing at Easter to visit Mr. Pascoe Grenfell, at Taplow, " or they will esteem it so much stage tinsel." He never enjoyed himself where he could not feel at ease, and his anxiety lest he should appear to disadvantage when obliged to mix with cultivated society did not escape the notice of Mr. Whitbread, who said to Mrs. Kean, " We don't invite your husband, because we fear that he is somehow made uncomfortable." Kean gave reason good enough for this uncomfortableness. " Your noblemen talk a great deal of what I don't understand—politics and other abstruse matters; but when it comes to plays they talk such infernal nonsense."

The green-room of Drury-lane Theatre had now become a favourite resort of the most distinguished men of the day. Noblemen, artists and literati began to assemble there on a footing of the most social intimacy; a perfect equality between talent, rank, and wealth was strictly maintained; and a tone of refinement, taste,

and good breeding pervaded the conversation of all.
A Boswell might have found in the green-room of
Drury-lane Theatre at this time a favourable scope
for the display of his peculiar powers; Theodore
Hook, writing in 1841, expresses a regret that the
halcyon days of 1814, when some of the most prominent members of the brilliant constellation of talent
which adorned the annals of that period haunted the
first theatre in London, " were gone, never to return."
Constant visitors to the green-room were President
West and James Northcote. The impression which
Kean's Richard left upon the mind of the former was
so deep " that," he says, " it kept me awake all night.
I never saw such expression in any human face
before." West, if not a great painter, was at least a
conscientious one; and with artistic enthusiasm he
introduced the fine Italian countenance of Kean into
one of his pictures. Northcote, I understand, also
attempted a portrait of the actor. Sheridan, although
weighed down with the misfortunes which two years
later laid him on his death-bed, occasionally enlivened
the company in the green-room with what Colman
calls his " savage saturnine wit " and brilliancy of
repartee; Samuel Taylor Coleridge, " logician, me-
taphysician, bard," with some idea of completing a

certain " wild and wondrous " tale entitled *Christabel,* which he had entered upon during his residence at Nether Stowey, Somersetshire, as far back as 1797, may have supplemented Richard Brinsley's enthusiastic declaration that the Richard III. of Mr. Kean was far superior to that of Garrick, by gravely assuring his hearers that "to see the new tragedian act was reading Shakspeare by lightning ;" and Lord Byron was there too, with an ode to Napoleon Bonaparte on the expected fall of his " poor little pagod " looming before his imagination, although his correspondence at this time with Moore abounds with repetitions of a determination expressed in the preface to the *Corsair* in the previous January—viz., to withdraw, at least for some years, from poetry. " No more rhyme for—or rather *from* me." Nevertheless "Napoleon Bonaparte" appeared ; and the expressive action of Kean in drawing figures on the sand with the point of his sword previous to his retirement as Richard III. into his tent suggested to the poet a very fine passage in the ode referred to—

> " Or trace with thine all idle hand
> In loitering mood upon the sand
> That earth is now as free l"

His lordship acknowledged the origin of the passage

in question; and on being asked to write something bearing directly on Kean's Richard, he referred to the lines in the first canto of the *Corsair* as illustrative of the performance :

> " There was a laughing devil in his sneer
> That raised emotions both of rage and fear,
> And where his frown of hatred darkly fell,
> Hope withering fled, and mercy sigh'd farewell !"

Sometimes a favoured few invaded the tragedian's dressing-room, where Arnold watched over him with as much solicitude as if the well-being of a kingdom hung upon his life. Old friends appeared in that dressing-room too, and amongst others Nance Carey turned up to extort 50*l.* a year from her not over-delighted son, to whom she introduced a Henry Darnley, who, to the tragedian's unbounded indignation, and spite of numberless snubs, frowns, and reproaches, *would* call Edmund "dear brother." Although he continued the above-mentioned annuity to Miss Carey up to the day of his death, he never recognised her openly as his parent, nor did he countenance any reports circulated about the theatre that he was the son of Miss Tidswell and the Duke of Norfolk. That hypothesis died a natural death. " Why don't you acknowledge your son ?" asked the Earl of Essex, addressing the

Duke. "My son!—what son? I have no son," returned the latter, inadvertently parodying the passage in *Othello* which the subject of their conversation was shortly to deliver with such inimitable beauty. "Why, Kean," rejoined the Earl: "report speaks of you as his father and Miss Tidswell as his mother." "I am not aware of the fact," replied the hereditary Earl-Marshal; "but I should be very proud to be the father of such a son."

To Miss Tidswell—the "Aunt Tid" of less fortunate days—Kean was invariably kind and attentive. Ascribing his success less to his own perseverance than the instruction which he had received from her in his boyhood, no evidence of gratitude was wanting on his part to prove the high estimation in which he held her kindness, and Miss Tidswell was not forgotten. Once he playfully remarked that he would never forgive her for having dragged him, "tarred and feathered as he was," from the public-house in St. George's Fields to Lisle-street with a rope fastened round him, and for having placed "an infernal brass collar round my neck, as if I had been a dog—never!" How vividly does the street Arab of those days contrast with the great tragedian on that May night of 1814, when, surrounded by a brilliant company, he awaited in the green-room the rising of the curtain on his first appearance in Othello ! Yes, there he stood, surveying himself before the mirror in his Oriental dress, occasionally practising an attitude, the cynosure of all eyes. Some one spoke. " Hush," said Reynolds, holding up a finger to enjoin silence. " Hush ; don't disturb him."

True and beautiful as was his Hamlet, its brilliance was partially obscured by the superior radiance of his Othello, in which, on the 5th of May, he achieved his greatest and most lasting triumph. His representation of the Moor was a masterpiece of genius, and which, had it been sketched as an original, could not have been sustained by any other hand than that of Shakspeare. Definite and vigorous in conception, brilliant and impressive in execution, and abounding with an overpowering energy and pathos which swept the audience along in a stream of perfect sympathy, it formed altogether an exhibition of consummate skill. Nature rose before all in her sacred presence, expanded the mind to an extent which broke through the narrow sphere of its previous cogitations, and looked all into a reverential regard for excellence like hers alone. Kean's delineation of Othello emanated from a mind whose native resources had been nourished to an extraordinary vigour by profound observation and study—from a skill that had a corresponding power of execution with the mind that applied it; and his extensive physiological acquirement assisted in invigorating an expression of intellect still further empowered by a complete and undivided sway over the world of passion. In those principal scenes and solitary pauses where the character is to be laid open, those great intervals in which the poet reposed from the action of the story to mark the birth of a new series of emotions, he fully rose to the conception; and if he occasionally failed in the stately, he had at least a satisfactory apology in those bursts of genius which set discrimination at defiance and formed a being of their own. Tenderness and flexibility, the expression of varying feelings, and the softer strivings of affection, were beautifully delineated; and where that noble, impetuous, and majestic tide of deep accumulating and sustained passion, that is

> " Like to the Pontick Sea,
> Whose icy current and compulsive course
> Ne'er knows retiring ebb,"

was to be stirred, and the whole mind to be turned up like an ocean of stormy troubles, dark thoughts, and irresistible impulses, his acting was above all

praise. With what touching, limpid, and unutterable tenderness he lingered over every mention of
Desdemona's name; with what transcendant power
he abandoned himself to the impulse of his intense
and convulsive passion; with what Laocöonic frenzy
he writhed in the toils of his serpent suspicions!
Every detail, in fine, was so responsive to feelings
and conceptions of nature, so devoid of common-
place, so opposed to mannerism, so awakening to
human sensibilities, and exhibited such a degree of
power, variety, vigour, and combination of talent,
that the spectator could not but come to the conclusion that had Shakspeare excelled as an actor no less
than as a dramatist, he would have presented his
audience with a portraiture similarly replete with the
qualities which constitute the sublime, the grand,
and the powerful in acting—loftiness of conception,
fertility of invention, depth and intensity of feeling,
a facility of imparting all those appearances and incidents in nature which the effort required, and above
all an harmonious and discriminative combination of
the whole. Solicitous not to give undue prominence
to leading traits, the whole performance was governed
by a conception which extended to every point, however small and apparently trivial, in the character;

and the minutiæ, thus invested with proper significance, and tinted with appropriate colouring, went
to the completion of the picture, and served to carry
the general impression of its force, grandeur, and
poetic feeling into the minds of those who saw
it, with an effect at once illustrative of its representative's genius, ardent impulsive discrimination, and
strong sensibility.

The tragedy of *Othello* has been considered by one
of its critics the most finished piece produced by
Shakspeare, and the Moor one of the most difficult
characters to represent out of the noble group which
he has bequeathed to posterity. The first conclusion
is an irresistible one ; with respect to the second we
can with propriety go a little further. . If *Lear* is
more intensely passionate, *Macbeth* more wildly imaginative, *Hamlet* more silently grand, *Othello* is yet
the most refined, complete, and finished of all his
tragedies. How nobly has Shakspeare delineated
with the artistic development of this fine Oriental .
story the fiery, magnanimous, affectionate, and cre-
dulous Othello; the gentle, soft, and exquisite woman-
hood of Desdemona; the social, frank, and good-
natured Cassio; the foolish, improvident, and unfortunate Roderigo, who is a " snipe," but nevertheless

a Venetian gentleman; and lastly, like a dark shadow
falling across a sunlit plain, the silent, subtle, and
serpent-like malevolence of Iago! In my humble
opinion, Othello is by far the most difficult character
in the whole range of English literature to represent
with any degree of success on the stage. In causing
him to repress as much as possible the slightest external indication of the conflicting passion within,
and in working up his noble nature to the very last
extremity that human endurance can be carried,
Shakspeare exhibits a knowledge of nature, an insight
into character, and a consummate art in the application of those resources which cannot be grasped by
the majority of those who "fret and strut their hour
upon the stage." We have had more than one fine
Hamlet, more than one impressive Macbeth, more
than one noble Lear; but we have never had but one
Othello, and that was the Moor of Edmund Kean.
To him alone belongs the honour of an adequate
representation of Othello, for though the character
may be easily traced through all its windings and
shiftings from the first grand principle on which the
part is founded by a reader, the task stands perfectly
isolated in its difficulty for the actor to follow the
poet in the progress of his favourite passion, to em-

body conceptions which none but he could form, and to impersonate those minute differences and delicate shades which constitute the very essence of character and the soul of the Shakspearian drama.

In his performance of Othello, Kean got rid of the difficulty arising from the supposed necessity of blackening the Moor's face, by which much of the play of the countenance on the stage was lost. He regarded it as a gross error to make Othello either a negro or a black, and accordingly altered the conventional black to the light brown which distinguishes the Moors by virtue of their descent from the Caucasian race. Although in the tragedy Othello is called an "old black ram," and described with a minuteness which leaves no doubt that Shakspeare intended him to be black, there is no reason to suppose that the Moors were darker than the generality of Spaniards, who indeed are half Moors, and compared with the Venetians he would even then be black. There is some variety in the colour of the Moors, but it never approaches so deep a hue as to conceal all change of colour. Betterton, Quin, Mossop, Barry, Garrick, and John Kemble all played the part with black faces, and it was reserved for Kean to innovate and Coleridge to justify the attempt to substitute a light brown for the traditional black. The alteration has been sanctioned by subsequent usage.

The conventional aspects of Othello in the senate scene were a quiet ease, a studied polish, purified from all offensive peculiarities, and free from all obtrusive prominences. This manner, however well calculated to repel all possibility of reproach, yet never excited any admiration of the understandings of those who adopted it. Kean's style, on the other hand, was a noble simplicity, springing from conscious dignity of character, from a mind unpolluted by one sordid or ungenerous thought, from a taste chastised from all mixture of offensive and even unpleasant irregularity, from a benevolence delighting in cheerful smiles rather than accomplished obeisances, and all this in some degree corrected and coloured by intercourse with the circles in which his rank and importance in the state entitled him to move. He was "little versed in the soft arts of peace;" *his* eloquence sprang from truth and honour. No graces of oratory or elocution were introduced; all was characterized by a simple manliness equally remote from all formality and from that affected familiarity of treatment which makes even an oration subside into the com-

monplace. His doating fondness for Desdemona, and
the absorption of his faculties into one idea of the
newly-made husband, were beautifully expressed.

> " If it were now to die
> 'Twere now to be most happy; for I fear
> My soul hath her content so absolute,
> That not another comfort like to this
> Succeeds in unknown fate."

In the words, " If it were now to die," in which there
was a soft melodiousness which prepared the audience
for the inexpressible beauty of the " farewell," he
mingled with his heartfelt happiness an expression of
pathos which seemed almost to forebode the misery
that awaited him. The scene where he stopped the
fight between Montano and Cassio was sustained with
consummate skill. Noble was his quiet rebuke of
Cassio's intemperance—" How comes it, Cassio, that
you are thus forgot?" terrific, magnificent, prophetic
was his voice and manner, as, with the stern, inexorable authority of the general, he dismissed the
offender:

> " I love thee, Cassio,
> But never more be officer of mine."

The remainder of his performance uniformly raised
the imagination to the high level of the character;
and among those achievements which delight by

striking upon all those strings of feeling by which
the mind is vehemently moved, those effusions of
intellect which command our admiration by a bright
and beautiful emblazonment of genius—their high
and inventive thoughts—Kean's wonderful embodiment of the high-wrought intensity of passion which
burns throughout the third, fourth, and fifth acts of
Othello was nobly conspicuous.   While it exhibited a
deep penetration into the recesses of the human heart,
and the results of a minute investigation into the
physiological indications of its ebbs and flows, his
acting, allying itself equally to the sublime and the
beautiful, could not fail to enchant the common and
voluptuous as well as the cultivated and delicate
mind.   His power of contrasted intonation in the
expression of feeling can never be forgotten by those
who heard him deliver the memorable passage,

> " Perdition catch my soul but I *do love thee*,
>   And when I love thee *not*, chaos is come again."

In the scene where Iago instilled the poison into his
ear the anxious care with which he endeavoured to
guard against the jealous fears which assailed him
was pregnant with truth and beauty; " ' horror sat
plumed ' on his fixed eyelids" when told to beware of

jealousy; and his reply to the ancient's devilish fear that he was moved, "Not a jot, not a jot," laid open "the very tumult and agony of the soul." Never were the workings of the human heart more successfully disclosed than in the following scene, in which every tone of voice, every movement of feature and body, might be seen labouring under the accumulated agonies of an unbounded love, struggling with, and at last yielding to doubt. He entered with the abrupt and informal step of one to whom the dignity and grace of motion were idle superficialities; he saw in Iago only the immediate instrument of his pain; and raising his head, as the ancient broke the spell with the sound of his voice, he bade him begone with the haughty and authoritative glance of a man accustomed to unquestioned command. He gazed until this, the first burst of passion, recoiled upon himself, and dropping his arms, he relapsed insensibly into a gesture finely indicative of utter exhaustion. As he entered upon the speech commencing "What sense had I of her stolen hours of lust?" the audience, as if by an intuitive impulse, felt that the time had come for some powerful display; and the solemn stillness which prevailed throughout the house was at length broken by the thunder of applause awarded

to his delivery of the line "I found not Cassio's
kisses on her lips," in which, the native fierceness of
his nature predominating, he sprang to his feet, and
threw an infinite volume of expression into a cry of
wild and grinning desperation.   And then came the
quiet despair, the utter sinking of the heart, which
invariably succeeds to the protracted operation of
powerful passion.   The farewell!   No language could
do justice to the soul-subduing pathos which Kean
imparted to that noble passage.   I have heard it
stated that such tones might be imagined to come
forth overloaded with despair from that dread gate
above   which   stands   the   solemn   annunciation,
"Abandon hope, all ye who enter here;" that it was
the voice of desolation broken with utter bitterness;
that the mournful melody of his voice came over the
spirit like the desolate moaning of the blast that
precedes the thunder-storm; that it was like the
hollow and not unmusical murmur of the midnight
sea after the tempest hath "raved itself to rest;"
that his tones sank into the heart like the sighing of
the gentle breeze among the strings of an Æolian
harp, or among the branches of a cypress grove!
Deepening and deepening in their effect like the
tears of a man flowing from sources not often drawn

upon, every word came from the actor with the air of an alienated mind, conscious of his ruined prospects from even the lingering delight with which he pondered on arms, but constrained to yield them up to the weighty and unconquerable depression of an injured love. The lingering fondness with which he dwelt upon each particular circumstance that had endeared his "occupation" to him, and the still despair and combined spirit with which he seemed to anticipate the black misfortune that hung over his head—"It struck on the heart," writes Hazlitt, "like the swelling note of some divine music —like the sound of years of departed happiness." To this calm succeeded a storm of contending passions— rage, hate, intervening doubts; the threat to Iago, "Villain, be sure," and the words he poured out as he continued to grasp the ancient by the throat, could hardly have been surpassed for concentrated force and passionate abandonment; and the fearful contest waged until at length the whole of his already excited energies were yielded up to revenge, when the look and action accompanying the words, "O blood, Iago, blood," cast a thrill over one's frame. Nothing could have been finer than the manner in which he sustained the following scene ; nothing more complete

and impressive than his alternations of suppressed
rage and constrained courtesy in the scene with
Ludovico and Desdemona, in which the contending
feelings were exquisitely contrasted, the delicacy of
portraiture in the one exhibiting the master-passion
in strong relief. Never was a text so nobly handled
as in the great scene with Desdemona in the fourth
act, where love and hate alternately strove for mastery in Othello's soul. With an excess of feeling
which abundantly proved his utter self-abandonment
to the illusion of the scene, his representation of a
mind "perplexed in the extreme" was absolutely
heartrending; and the auditor's mind was almost
tremblingly responsive to the soul of power displayed
in this wonderful expression of smothered passion
as it marked the fixed jaws, the agitated nostrils, the
distended veins of the forehead, the dilated and scin-
tillating eye, and the obstructed respiration. In the
dumb action and mute eloquence with which he described the tumult which raged in his mind the
audience received a proof of his sway over the passions for which they were scarcely prepared. The
gush of heartfelt anguish with which he said to her
in the midst of his stormiest invective, and with the
convulsive agony of a broken love, "Would thou

hadst ne'er been born !" went faithfully home to every
heart ; while the miserable despondency of his " Oh,
Desdemona, away, away !" found echoes responsive in
the sternest breast.   In this last line, the beauty of
which was only to be paralleled by the " Farewell," he
has never been equalled.   " It had in it all that
belongs to love, to grief, to pity.   The very *spirit*
of love, weeping its injuries, and not more than
half reproachful, seemed to hover over him.   His
words sunk, by gentle gradations, from reproof
into compassion, from compassion into a faint and
indistinct sound, which itself gradually expired, like
the sound of a melancholy echo."   The last scene
was pre-eminently beautiful.   Noble was the intensity of passion with which he slew her ; unutterably
expressive was his sudden reflection—" My   wife !
What wife ?   I have no wife !"—with consummate
skill he marked the gradations of passion from the
tumult which raged in his soul when he committed
the murder to the gloomy stillness of despair consequent on the discovery of the shallow artifices by
which he had been duped.   One of the finest instances
of his original conception of the character was in the
utterance of the line, " O fool, fool, fool !"   Booth,
Garrick, Barry, and Kemble raved, tore their hair,

and became convulsed with passion when expressing
these words, but Kean knew better; he felt no agony
at the moment, because neither Shakspeare nor nature
taught him to feel any, " and he repeated the word
quickly, and almost inarticulately, and with a half
smile of wonder at his incredible stupidity in having
been such a ' fool.' " Nevertheless, an overwhelming
conviction of his mistake, the knowledge that he had
smitten down and trampled upon his own happiness,
were fully patent to his mind; but still there was an
indomitable manliness of spirit standing up amidst
the surrounding desolation and rearing its head above
the wreck.   He was again

> " The noble nature
> Whom passion could not shake, whose solid virtue
> The shot of accident, nor dart of chance,
> Could neither graze nor pierce."

The time of the fierce and tumultuous excitement had
passed away; all that rendered life dear to him was
lost, and he determined to escape from the ignominy
of a public execution, or the torture of a lingering
life, by a self-inflicted death.   All was as the dead
calm of a midnight sea; passion seemed to have
"raved itself to rest;" now 'tis happiness to die, for
one bright gleam shot athwart the surrounding dark-

ness—she *did* love him, and all his devoted fondness had not been thrown away. He will die by his own hand ; his address to the officers was an artifice offered without any interest in the tale beyond that of securing its immediate object—that of defeating their precaution ; and he will show them the strength and glory which may be thrown around the fall of a warrior's mind. The temple was to perish, but even in its ruin it was to be distinguished by its pristine grandeur and completeness ; even the foliage which overspread it was to wreath with no unsuited tint and verdure to its superb decay. He entered upon the last speech ; his accent was pervaded with touches of that sadness which incurable misfortune draws over the most heroic spirit ; then, to divert all suspicion, he simulated a pride in his punishment of the turbaned Turk who beat a Venetian and traduced the State ; and as his eyes wandered with searching brilliancy from face to face in order to see whether any suspicion as to his object lurked in their minds, he went through the concluding words with inimitable strength and beauty. " And smote him—*thus !*" and as he spoke the glistening steel entered his breast ; a frozen shudder swept over his frame—every physiological indication of his suffering was faithfully and dis-

tinctly marked; and in the attempt to imprint a last
kiss on the cold, rigid face of his wife, he fell backwards—dead.

Such, as well as I can describe it, was the Othello
of Edmund Kean. The effect which it produced on
the audience has, perhaps, never been equalled. The
hearts of the many thousands that assembled on that
night beat as one man beneath this marvellous exhibition of nature and passion; as all the aspects, conflicts,
and varieties of the latter were struck out and displayed, their emotions and sympathies were so
strongly excited that his noble simulation of suffering
was witnessed with the same tears, compassion, and
pity as if it were a sad, melancholy tragedy in real
life; and the tragedian, conscious of his exercise of
this extraordinary sway over their hearts, might have
said as he did on the 26th of January—"I had them
with me!" The admiration his Othello excited was
one and indivisible; like the gentle Desdemona, no
flaw could be perceived in this matchless delineation,
it was "one entire and perfect chrysolite." Hazlitt
regarded it as the masterpiece of the actor, the highest
effort of genius on the stage, and as fully equal to anything of Mrs. Siddons's. To *The Times* it appeared a
portraiture possible only to the execution of a power-

ful genius.   The *Examiner* wrote :—" There is a delicacy about the taste and feelings of this extraordinary
young actor which must be instinctive.   His genius
in this, as in some other of his characteristics, appears
to bear a striking resemblance to that of Shakspeare
himself.   Their schools have been alike, the green-
room of the theatre ; their book of study alike, their
own hearts.   The blind adorers of Shakspeare, the
praisers of him by rote, will be greatly scandalized at
this bringing their idol in contact with anything
human—still more with an every-day looking person
living and moving among ourselves : not so would
Shakspeare himself have felt had they lived in the
same day ; he would have stretched out his human
hand to Mr. Kean, and have welcomed him with delight as at least a kindred spirit."   I append a few
of the most celebrated criticisms on the performance :—

" Mr. Kean's Othello is, we suppose, the finest piece
of acting in the world.   It is impossible either to
describe or praise it adequately.   We have never seen
any actor so wrought upon—so ' perplexed in the extreme.'   The energy of passion as it expresses itself
in action, is not the most terrific part; it is the agony

of his soul, showing itself in looks and tones of voice. In one part, where he listens in dumb despair to the fiend-like insinuations of Iago, he presented the very face, the marble aspect of Dante's Count Ugolino. On his fixed eyelids 'horror sat plumed.' In another part, where a gleam of hope or of tenderness returns to subdue the tumult of his passion, his voice broke in faltering accents from his overcharged breast. His lips might be said less to utter words than to distil drops of blood gushing from his heart. An instance of this was in his pronunciation of the line, 'of one that loved not wisely but too well.' The whole of this last speech was indeed given with exquisite force and beauty. We only object to the virulence with which he delivers the last line, and with which he stabs himself — a virulence which Othello would neither feel against himself at the moment nor against the 'turbaned Turk' (whom he had slain) at such a distance of time. His exclamation on seeing his wife, 'I cannot think but Desdemona's honest,' was 'the glorious triumph of exceeding love;' a thought flashing conviction on his mind and irradiating his countenance with joy like sudden sunshine. In fact almost every scene or sentence in this extraordinary exhibition is a masterpiece of natural passion. The convulsed motion of the hands and the involuntary swelling of the veins in the forehead, in some of the most painful situations, should not only suggest topics of critical panegyric but might furnish studies to the painter or sculptor."— *Hazlitt.*

" With all our experience of the stage, and with all our scepticism as to the powers of the very best actors in characters from Shakspeare, we never witnessed a performance that struck us so forcibly. It brought back upon us the earnestness and implicit attention of our younger days. We have admired Mrs. Siddons, been infinitely amused with Lewis, been sore with laughing at Munden, been charmed with Mrs. Jordan, but we never saw anything that so completely held us suspended and heart-stricken as Mr. Kean's Othello. In all parts it was as complete as actor can show it,—in the previous composure of its dignity, in its soldier-like repression of common impulse, in the deep agitation of its first jealousy, in the low-voiced and faltering affectation of occasional ease, in the bursts of intolerable anguish, in the consciousness that rage had hurt its dignity and ruined the future completeness of its character, in its consequent

melancholy farewell to its past joys and greatness, in
the desperate savageness of its revenge, in its half-
exhausted reception of the real truth, and lastly, in
the final resumption of a kind of moral attitude and
dignity at the moment when he uses that fine deliberate artifice, and sheaths the dagger in its breast. If
we might venture to point out any part the most
admirable in this performance, it would be the low
and agitated affectation of quiet discourse in which
he first canvasses the subject with Iago, the mild and
tremulous farewell to 'the tranquil mind, the plumed
troop,' &c., in which his voice occasionally uttered
little tones of endearment, his head shook, and his
visage quivered; and thirdly, the still more awfully
mild tones in which he trembles and halts through
the dreadful lines beginning,

> Had it pleased heaven
> To try me with affliction; had he rained
> All kinds of sores and shames on my bare head.

His louder bitterness and his rage were always fine;
but such passages as these, we think, were still finer.
You might fancy you saw the water quivering in his
eyes. And here two things struck us very forcibly;
first, how impossible it is for actor and audience to be
both as they ought to be in such large theatres, since

Mr. Kean's quietest and noblest passages could certainly not have been audible in the galleries; and second, how much an actor's talent might be modified by his own character off the stage—an observation which we reasonably make when it leans to the favourable side; for we conjecture from anecdotes that are before the public that Mr. Kean's temper is hasty and his disposition excellent and generous; and it is of passion and natural generosity that Othello's character is made up. For this reason we can never help being sceptical about Garrick's talents in characters of deep and serious interest, since off the stage he was little better than a quick-eyed trifler, full of phrases of gabbling jargon, and coarse-minded withal. Mr. Kean's Othello is the masterpiece of the living stage."
—*Leigh Hunt.*

" Those who are able to appreciate the best acting of Mr. Kean in Othello, and yet lament that they were born too late to have seen Garrick in the same character, know not what they seek. For our part we are content with one—the one we have. It is to us 'riches fineless.' We could think of it and write about it for ever; for the next best thing to seeing it is to be able to write down our feelings about it unre-

strainedly.   How can we speak of Mr. Kean's
Othello?   Shall we liken his Moor to a royal vessel
tossed hither and thither on a tumultuous ocean—
this moment cast against the clouds—the next plunging headlong into a foaming abyss—emerging thence
only to strike on a hidden rock—breaking, bursting,
sinking, and the roaring waters closing over it for
ever ?   Or shall we compare him to a stricken tiger—
the barbed and poisoned arrow broken into his flesh—
madly tearing up the earth about him with his feet,
or rolling upon it as if to drive the deadly weapon
still deeper in—at last, tearing it out at once with his
blood-stained teeth, and with it, life itself?   These
comparisons may serve to convey some faint idea of
the impressions excited by the more violent parts of
this matchless performance.   But no words can fitly
tell the touching and ineffable beauties of the more
quiet parts :—first, the gentle murmurings and out-
gushings of a heart over-rich in bliss ; then, the
blank but silent despair, at the thought of that bliss
being blasted for ever (the interval between the lightning and the thunder) ; then, still more touching, the
glimpses of reviving hope—the gleams of returning
love—the imaginations of what might have been—
the reminiscences of what had been—the presentiment

of what must be—the immediate feeling of what was; lastly (after the fatal catastrophe), the sudden but vain reflux of love, seeking but finding no entrance in an already death-stricken heart; and the final melting away of the broken and trembling spirit in floods of unavailing tears."—*Anonymous.*

" In regard to Kean's Othello it was surely one of the most consummate pieces of art that the stage has ever presented. The common faults of his acting— the want of massiveness and strict preservation of character—were not observable here. In effect the starts, and turns, and sinuosities of his ordinary life seemed to become a passion, which is itself full of unevenness and change, whose ' numbers unto nought are fixed.' The fluctuation of the story, the overturn, —or rather the uncovering and anatomy of Othello's mind, are fatal to the indifferent actor. He is wrecked on so stormy a strand. But it was otherwise with Kean. He had strength and appetite for the encounter. The transits from anger to pity,—the fall—

> Deeper than ever plummet sounded—

from love into deep despair,—the manly, tender, fiery character of the open-hearted Moor,—the hurry and

violence of the scenes, which whirl us along without
ceasing to the close of this wonderful drama,—were
only so many opportunities of exhibiting his energy,
his pathos, his variety, his resources.   Let no one
presume to deny the merit of Kean in this play.   It
has been acknowledged by many thousand people.
Their tears and sympathy, which are so many attesting
witnesses to his excellence, are not to be impugned or
derided by the opinion or insensibility of any small
knot of men.   The applause which he received was
drawn from all classes, from the busy and the idle,
the learned and the unlettered, the young and the old.
Garrick and Mrs. Siddons drew their plaudits from
the same source, and it has given to *them* imperishable
fame."—*Barry Cornwall.*

" We think the performance (and we speak chiefly of
the third act, though the rest was all in keeping with
it) was, without comparison, the noblest effort of
human genius we have ever witnessed.   It evinced a
kind and degree of talent more rare and more valuable
than any or than all that is to be found in his other
performances, a talent only and not much inferior to
that which was required to write the character.
Never did we witness such vehement and sustained

passion, such pure and touching beauty, such deep and quiet and simple pathos. The performance was worthy to have taken place in Shakspeare's own age—with he himself and Fletcher, and Ford, and Spenser, and Sydney for an audience. We cannot help fancying how they would have acted at the close of it. They would have gone into the green-room, perhaps, —Shakspeare we are sure would—and with a smiling yet serious and earnest delight upon their faces, have held out their hands and thanked him. Think of a shake of the hand from Shakspeare, and of deserving it too!"—*Blackwood.*

His Othello, in short, established his position beyond cavil or dispute the greatest tragedian of modern times. Each successive representation of the character deepened the impression produced by the first, and overflowing audiences continued to ratify with enthusiasm the verdict pronounced as if with one voice on the night of the 5th of May. "I seriously recommend to you to recommend to them," writes Byron to Moore, "the theatre for half an hour, if only to see the third act." John Kemble came with the town to see an effort which press and public were earnestly lauding as one altogether without a

parallel in the annals of the stage ; and it was at once
patent to the older actor that the unpremeditated and
unrestrained manner in which his young and vigorous
rival poured out the noblest touches of nature and
genius resulted from nothing but a pure design to
give truthful expression to the overwhelming tide of
passion which an absorption into himself of the very
essence of the character stirred up in his mind.
Kemble was quick to perceive the advantage which
this faculty possessed over a style invariably characterized by studied elegance and severe propriety ; and
a jealousy of Kean took root in his mind with a
tenacity which refused to allow the young actor any
credit beyond that of " terrible earnestness " and
" brilliancy of execution." He challenged the just-
ness of Edmund's conception, contending that Othello
was a *slow* man !* The jealousy of Kean was not
confined to John Kemble and his disciples. It domi-
nated the hearts and perverted the judgments of

---

* Mrs. Fanny Kemble, referring to John Kemble's notorious
jealousy of Kean, writes:—"I have lived among those whose
theatrical creed would not permit them to acknowledge Kean as a
great actor. He possessed those rare gifts of nature without which
art alone is a dead body. If he was irregular and unartist-like in
his performances, so is Niagara to be compared with the water-
works of Versailles."

more than one member of the Drury-lane company. Dowton, with his characteristic imbecility of ill-nature, saw nothing so extraordinary in the new actor, and in adopting an extremely low estimate of Kean's abilities he felicitously transferred his favourite character of Sir John Lambert's astute deceiver from the boards into the green-room. " *He* play Shylock !" exclaimed the irritated actor to Raymond when the Jew of Edmund Kean was held to be a portrait perfect both in principle and detail ; " why he knows absolutely nothing about it, and so you'll see when *I* go on for it. I'll lessen the size of his name in that character, anyhow." We shall presently see what success attended that attempt; and till then—adieu to William Dowton.

The character of Iago opened the path for the ex-hibition of Kean's talents in additional lustre. " It was the most faultless of his performances, the most consistent and entire. Perhaps the accomplished hypocrite was never so finely, so adroitly portrayed—a gay, light-hearted monster ; a careless, cordial, comfortable villain. The preservation of the cha-racter was so complete, the air and manner were so much of a piece throughout, that the part seemed more like a detached scene or single *trait*, and of shorter duration than it usually does. The ease, familiarity, and tone of nature with which the text was delivered, were quite equal to anything we have seen in the best comic acting. It was the least over-done of all his parts, though full of point, spirit, and brilliancy."* Moreover, he completely separated the character from the conventional errors of its repre-sentation, and, by the originality and fidelity of his conception, imparted probability and consistency to a character which had hitherto formed little better than an enigma to the readers and auditors of Shakspeare.

Very little doubt can be entertained that the light, gay, and careless air which Kean threw over his re-presentation of Iago embodied Shakspeare's views with regard to "mine ancient" with greater fidelity than the preaching solemnity and Saracenic grimness which representatives of the character had hitherto adopted. "Mr. Kean has abstracted the wit of the character," writes Hazlitt, "and makes Iago appear throughout *an excellent good fellow* and lively bottle companion." In so doing, he cannot be said to have misapprehended the peculiar traits which distinguish

---

* Hazlitt.

the Moor's ancient. Iago is a villain who delights in the destruction of his fellow men—in the pursuit of wickedness *con amore ;* and he possesses consummate sagacity, a wonderful activity of intellect, and a varied experience of mankind. These qualities not only point out to him the means most suitable to the accomplishing of his purpose, but also the necessity (always forced upon the hypocrite) to conceal the actual deformity of his character; and he finds it obligatory to *assume a mask* that he never removes save when alone. Kean was the first actor to assume this mask—the first who avoided an obtrusive presentment of patent villany; with Roderigo he was easy, bantering, nonchalant; with Cassio he was social, frank, gay; with Othello he was *honest* Iago,—a rogue with pleasant speech and unwrinkled countenance, who is a soldier and a man of the world, and in whose openness of manner there is a fascination which all but repays for the misery of having been duped. In thus taking leave of the brutal ferocity which had been usually regarded as an important element in the character, Kean did not carry an original and ingenious idea to a paradoxical extreme. Hazlitt endeavoured to show that he did; that Iago, " the very object of whose plot is to keep

his faculties stretched on the rack in a sort of breathless suspense without a moment's interval for repose,"
had no leisure to be gay; and that the hypocrite is
naturally grave, as a reference to Tartuffe, Blifil, and
Joseph Surface would conclusively demonstrate.   Let
us determine the value of these objections.   Iago has
a great stake to play—one that requires his utmost
caution and deliberate skill; but this by no means
argues that he has not any leisure to be gay; on the
contrary, his profound acquaintance with the inmost
features of those with whom he has to deal leads him
to enter the lists with the gay confidence of a general
certain of success because he knows every post and
every movement of the opposition—the shallow intellect of Roderigo, the influence of a stoup of wine over
Cassio, and the capability of Othello of being " as
easily led by the nose as asses are."   The reference to
Tartuffe, Blifil, and Joseph Surface is very much misplaced.   All were pretenders to extraordinary piety
and morality, and gravity was with them an indispensable mask to cover the darkness of their designs—a
necessary instrument to the attainment of their aims
and ends.   Not so with Iago.   He affects no morality,
his conversation is licentious, and no conclusion is de-
ducible from the play that his conduct is more correct

than his language. His friendship is not incompatible with his licentiousness; he assumes the part of an honest, friendly fellow—a man sincere and without guile. Among soldiers this frank and open manner was more likely to pass him for what he represented himself to be than a stiff, formal solemnity. Shakspeare, with true discrimination, saw that politeness partook of the character of insincerity : Iago is consequently blunt, and it is only a gay and cheerful manner that is compatible with bluntness. Moreover, the malice of Iago is personal rather than intellectual. He is actuated less by a native love of mischief than by the more intelligible and direct motive of revenge. He murdered Roderigo because the Venetian "snipe" would call him " to restitution large for the gold and jewels ;" he attempted to murder Cassio because the lieutenant stood in the way of his preferment; he meditated the destruction of Othello because at the hands of the latter he had received a fancied slight, and a fancied injury ; and he murdered his wife under an impulse of desperate and not unusual rage at seeing his whole scheme of villany laid bare when he thought it most secure from discovery. No; Kean was perfectly right when he converted the conventional dark and gloomy monster into a cordial, com-

fortable, easy, humorous villain ; and the most reliable
authorities have borne testimony to its conformity
with the spirit of the part.   Barry Cornwall writes :
—" We saw no longer the undisguised, common-place
assassin and slanderer who had hitherto strutted and
scowled on the stage, but a jocund, elastic villain,
who murdered reputations with a smile, and whose
vivacity and intelligence formed a cloak far more im-
pervious to suspicion than the vulgar, cut-throat aspect which usually disgraces the part, and renders the
jealousy of Othello so supremely ridiculous." Another
writer observes :—" Not merely the confiding Moor,
but the cunningest man on earth must have been
deceived by the manner of a man who was calm,
respectful, and determined, and, at the same time,
while he is torturing his leader with his surmises,
as conversationally easy as if he was relating something not worthy of any particular attention.   This
method of working on the Moor was as original as
it was just and natural.   In general the stage Iago
looks big and solemn, as if he was bursting with some
important secret ; but there is no warrant for this in
Shakspeare, whose Iago does not in the first instance
pretend to any knowledge of Desdemona's criminality,
but merely harrows up his poor victim with hints and

opinions and probabilities of a woman's infidelity under the particular circumstances. Thus, Mr. Kean, in his personation, instead of the usual prologuizing face of pompous mystery, pursued and introduced the subject as almost indifferent chit-chat, and seemed almost unfeignedly astonished when he observed that what he had been saying had made such a dreadful impression on Othello's mind. In our opinion this treatment of the subject made all appear perfectly consistent; Othello must have immediately detected a solemn, preaching rogue, whereas it is not in man to be prepared against an artlessness which showed almost the simplicity of childhood. Mr. Kean appears to be the depository of the very thoughts of Shakspeare."

The Iago of Edmund Kean was a perfect piece of acting—a complete absorption of the man in the character. He seemed to move about the stage like a deadly serpent, fascinating by its external beauty, and carrying death with every spring. A minute and accurate investigation of those sources of information, whether of difficult or easy access, which could in any way elucidate and reveal the distinctive characteristics of the southern blood, gave a reality to the character it had never received before. As in Othello the

richness and volume of his utterance gave peculiar
prominence to the Oriental magnificence and picturesqueness of expression with which Shakspeare, forgetful of nothing, has coloured the impassioned speech
of the lofty-minded Moor, so, in Iago, Kean imparted
a peculiar *Italian* tint to the character of the ancient,
especially in that significant action of silently rubbing
his hands behind him as his plot satisfactorily pro-
gressed.   The contemptuous and condescending manner with which he played on Roderigo was inimitably
fine.   Conscious of his intellectual superiority, he enjoyed a scornful pre-eminence over him.   In his
constant recurrence to the great topic which he so
earnestly desired to cover up and keep separate from
the rest—the "filling up" of the coxcomb's purse, he
avoided the even flexure of voice which had been
usually adopted, and, instead of assuming a manner
so directly calculated to arouse the Venetian's suspicions, he subjected it to a perpetual variation, sometimes urging it with a look, or supporting it with an
argument; sometimes suggesting it as a hint, and
sometimes rendering it with a grave look of one who
was bringing the whole force of his cunning to bear
upon the removal of his companion's hesitation.   The
mingled banter and ridicule in his tone when he re-

called his dupe with "no more of drowning;" and his sneer of triumphant self-complacency when the Venetian announced his intention of selling *all* his land, were fine and perfect touches of nature and genius. So also were the celebrated description of woman, and his reply to Desdemona when she asked him how he would write her praise :

> " O, gentle lady, do not put me to 't,
> For I am nothing if not critical."

In Cassio's drunken scene, the versatility of his talent operated with electrical effect. Iago's song had been, with Cooke, and Henderson, and Kemble, suffered to pass over with comparative neglect; but here Kean rolled out a bold, magnificent flourish, which caught the house at once. The applause was incessant, an encore was called for, and nothing but the manifest indecorum of such a demand could have restrained the general call. His distillation of the poison into Othello's ear was a wonderful exhibition of skill. He watched the Moor with such an earnestness, and at the same time appeared so careless and honestly indifferent about the issue, that the audience found it difficult to persuade themselves that he was really a young man who had put on a soldier's coat to play the villain for an hour or two. His insinua-

tion of female impurity in general; his deviation from
the subject—his venture at last to pronounce the
word "jealousy"—his wandering into vague and in-
definite abstraction on the nature of human reputation—his admissions of a despondency, the cause of
which he could not reveal—the manner in which he
still further excited the curiosity of the Moor by
cautioning him against mistrust of a wife—his vaunt-
ing of the happiness of him who remained in ignorance—his prayer that the souls of all his tribe might
be saved from jealousy—and lastly, the tissue of false-
hood which reduced a noble nature to the verge of
savage ferocity in the intellectual conflict which followed—in all, the actor trod close upon the footsteps
of the genius which had marshalled the way. Fear,
anxiety, sudden exultation, checked by an unconquerable dread of the fierce and turbulent mind he was
deluding; sudden variation of expression and manner
as the eye of the Moor glanced at him with alternate
reliance and hesitation; solemn sincerity when he
adduced the fabricated evidence in support of his
insinuations, and at the close the deep and collected
devotedness with which he knelt and declared his
friend Cassio to be no more for this world, completed
a *tout ensemble* of intellectual and dramatic vigour

which rendered rivalry out of the question, and indicated that the stage was indeed entering upon a new
era of brilliance and prosperity.   The fourth act was
nobly sustained. In the scene where he slew Roderigo
he showed that he never dropped the character for a
moment; that he was ever actively attentive to the
business of the play.   Previous representatives of Iago
did not appear to have remembered that the whole fortune of the ancient hinged upon this event; they
stabbed Roderigo, and then walked away with perfect
ease and satisfaction.   Not so with Kean.   He gave
and repeated the murderous thrust till no life could
be supposed to remain; but feeling this to be too
important a matter to be left in doubt he, though
conversing coolly with those about him, threw his
eye perpetually towards the prostrate body, with an
intensity as if he would pierce its vital recesses to
ascertain the important fact.   Sometimes he walked
by it carelessly, and surveyed it with a glance too
rapid to be observed; sometimes he deliberately approached it and looked at it with his candle as if to
satisfy the spectators that it was the villain who had
attacked his friend Cassio, and thus he continued to
watch and hover over it until he left the stage, his
manner perfectly cool, while his eye expressed the

most restless anxiety. It was by such master-touches as these that Kean evinced a superiority which did not consist in a sounding delivery or picturesque strides, but in a thousand traits which genius and study alone could seize from nature. He was perfectly solemn in the passages where he undertook to murder Cassio and advised Othello to strangle his wife, nor was such solemnity at all inconsistent with the general ease of his demeanour, unless it can be maintained that an open frankness can never, without absurdity, be changed into a serious deportment. When he opened the battle he threw out his insinuations with a quiet artlessness because, like all calculating villains, he never threw away any energy : but as the plot thickened, his honest indifference gave way to earnestness, and he acted as became a friend who "gave up all to wronged Othello's service." The callous levity of his utterance as he asked,—

" How is it, general ?   Have you not hurt your head ?"

when Othello awoke from the trance, was perfectly in character, because Iago is entirely disconnected from the feelings of humanity. Hazlitt took exception to his pointing to the dead body of Desdemona in the last scene as inconsistent with the character of

the part, for, to the critic's idea, it consisted in the
love of mischief, not as an end but as a means, and when
that end was attained, though he might feel no remorse, he would feel no triumph.   This objection is
wholly untenable.   Iago is of a temperament of a cold
and almost lunatic malice; in his haughty resolution
to disclose nothing, even on the rack, he exhibits the
evidence of a mind incurably depraved by ambition
and revenge; and such a man, exulting in the success
of designs the possibility of whose accomplishment
had sustained him so long in the very eye of danger,
would have been impelled by the most obvious springs
of human action to impress his triumph beyond all
doubt.   No; Kean was perfectly right in this; he
turned him full before his victim, and taught him by a
terrific and derisive gesture, before which even the
valiant Othello seemed to shrink, that *nothing* was now
wanting to complete the measure of his revenge.   His
voice and spirit remained unsubdued, and with a
satanic chuckle of satisfaction, and a triumphant survey of his victims, he strode away to his retribution.

   " Was not Iago perfection," writes Byron to Moore
on the following day, " particularly the last look ?   I
was close to him (in the orchestra) and never saw an
English countenance half so expressive."

On the 25th of May Kean signalized his first London benefit by a fine representation of his old character of Luke in Sir John Burgess's alteration of Massinger's *City Madam;* and the announcement met with such an enthusiastic response that the actor cleared 1500*l.* by the proceeds and presents from individuals — the largest sum ever realized by a theatrical benefit. " A large party had been made," writes Moore, " to which we (Lord Byron and the writer) both belonged, but his lordship having also taken a box for the occasion, so anxious was he to enjoy the representation uninterrupted, that, by rather an unsocial arrangement, only himself and I occupied his box during the play, while every other in the house was crowded almost to suffocation ; nor did we join the remainder of our friends till supper." Over that supper the most unqualified admiration of the performance was expressed.

Up to the time when the version of the *City Madam* referred to was produced (1811) the works of Philip Massinger had continued to remain in the unmerited obscurity into which they had fallen under the Puritan prohibition of dramatic representations. The excellence of his versification, the interesting nature of his plots, the terseness of his sentiment, and the

strength with which his characters are drawn, continued unheeded until Sir John Burgess, anxious to
be considered a scholar profoundly versed in black-
letter lore, produced the *City Madam* under a form
entitled *Riches; or, the Wife and Brother*, in which he
removed the objectionable expressions of the Elizabethan period, corrected the obsolete phraseology, and
—omitted several of the most conspicuous beauties.
As a general rule the characters of Massinger are not
founded on some great and instructive trait in the
human mind, but under its most repulsive aspects
and strongest inclinations.   Little that is soft,
gentle, and tender is interwoven with the predominating elements of his plays, a fine command of eloquence
leading him to disregard that refined simplicity in
which the soul of pathos consists; and in the
general management of his characters he exhibits a
disposition to overwhelm the faculties with terror and
astonishment rather than to engage them by purity,
delicacy, and elegance.   This principle adopted, his
Sir Giles Overreach in a *New Way to Pay Old
Debts* constitutes the most vivid picture of terrific
and untameable passions in the whole range of
English literature; and Luke in the *City Madam*
is a delineation of hypocrisy which, rising far

superior to Tartuffe, Blifil, and Joseph Surface, takes rank second only to the Iago of Shakspeare. The character of Luke, moreover, is a grand lesson against the pleasures of prosperity. A man reduced to penury by a freak of fortune might have possessed virtues which his fall would only have served to strengthen; but it did not escape the observation of Massinger that one whose mind had been habitually tainted, and whose vices had reduced him to poverty and dependence, was a being from whose heart the effect could scarcely be supposed to eradicate. Even the abject humility of Luke, therefore, has something vicious in it; and as in adversity he manifests a contempt for all moral obligation, so in his supposed elevation he wholly abandons himself to the gratification of his baser passions, and displays the hitherto partially-revealed deformity in its true and native colours. Both these pictures, with a vivification heightened by the decided contrasts they exhibited, were portrayed by Kean with a skill which, dependent only upon nature as a prototype, gave a vigour and brilliancy to their delineation that had never been imparted before. His dark vivid countenance, the flexibility of his gestures, and his deep undertones where atrocious hypocrisy and mean exultation were engendering within him, gave him eminent advantages in the painting which was to depict the workings of a heart incurably depraved and inflamed with the unexpected power of revenge. The soliloquy in the last act, in which the actor marked with fine and perfect gradations the increasing delirium of Luke in the contemplation of his ill-gotten wealth, was one of the most powerful effects ever witnessed on the stage. The best testimony to the excellence of Kean's Luke, however, is to be sought for in private life rather than in the earnest applause which rewarded his exertions in the character. An old lady admired his acting in Othello so much that she made no secret of her intention to bequeath him a large sum of money, but she was so appalled by the cold-blooded villany of Luke that, attributing the skill of the actor to the inherent possession of the fiendish attributes he so consummately embodied, her regard gave place to suspicion and distrust; and upon her death, which took place shortly afterwards, it was found that the sum originally intended for the actor had been left to a distant relation, of whom she knew nothing but by name. *Riches* was repeated three times that season, which was terminated by Kean on the 16th of July with Richard, and the enthusiastic applause which followed him up to the latest moment carried with it the truest test of genius and power, for nothing else will bear the ordeal of repeated examination, and strike afresh on all hearts with reiterated delight, just like the eternal charms of nature.

The delighted treasurer struck a balance of profit to the theatre amounting to 18,000*l.*, and on the 2nd of September Mr. Whitbread announced a dividend of five per cent. to the proprietors at their annual meeting at the Crown and Anchor. The chairman, in the course of his speech, adverted to Kean in the following terms :—" The extraordinary powers of this eminent actor has, as well may be imagined, drawn forth the criticisms of all theatrical amateurs and judges ; and though there may be some few who do not agree with me in regarding Mr. Kean as the most shining actor that has appeared in the theatrical hemisphere for many years, yet I am happy to find that the general opinion concurs with me in that respect. A combination of all the qualities that are essential to form a complete actor, is found to unite in one man very rarely indeed ; and though objections may be set up to the figure of Mr. Kean, as objections have at all times and in all ages of the world been set up to some one or other of the qualities and proportions of every actor, yet, judging of him in all the great attributes of the art, he is one of those prodigies that occur only once or twice in a century. I have the highest respect for the talents, the erudition, the accomplishments of Mr. Kemble, who is another of those rare instances of superior ability in the histrionic profession; and I have no desire, in speaking of Mr. Kean, to deteriorate from the merit of Mr. Kemble; but it is too much the practice of persons in speaking of an actor to compare him with another, and those who affect to criticize the talents of Mr. Kean most scrupulously, wish always to put him in comparison with Mr. Garrick. Of that great actor I wish to speak with the most marked respect; but who of all those who compare Mr. Kean with Mr. Garrick remember the performances of the latter in his twenty-fifth year? They remember him only after long study and experience had improved and matured all the faculties of his youth; and I am ready also to pay the same compliment to Mr. Kemble, that years of application and study, with a cultivated mind and strong judgment, had acquired him the celebrity he possessed. But in judging of Mr. Kean we must look at him as he is, not the pupil of any school, not a mannerist, but an actor who finds all his resources in nature, who

delineates his passions only from the expression that
the soul gives to the voice and features of a man, not
from the images that have before him been represented by others on the stage. It is from the wonderful truth, energy, and force with which he strikes
out and presents to the eye this natural working of
the passions of the human frame, that he excites the
emotions and engages the sympathy of his spectators
and auditors. It is to him that, after one hundred
and thirty-five nights of continued loss and disappointment, the subscribers are indebted for the success
of the season, and that the public are indebted for the
high treat which they have received by the variety of
characters he has represented."

Such was the lofty position in which the neglected
and despised itinerant actor of six months before found
himself placed. The goal that he had pursued from his
boyhood had been won; a favoured school of acting
had begun to totter before the vigour, originality, and
truth which distinguished his performances; and the
impulse which his fine perception gave to an exalted
appreciation of Shakspeare's genius was so effectual,
"that," writes the celebrated critic of *Blackwood's
Magazine* four years later, " if it had not been for Mr.
Kean we should never have desired to see a play of

Shakspeare's acted again.   We never knew Othello or
Richard till we knew Mr. Kean; and we do not
shrink from confessing that we never felt so much
delight in reading Shakspeare as we have in seeing
Mr. Kean act him."   Onwards he went, reaping imperishable fame and a brilliant harvest; passion and
pleasure hurried him forward

> "From flower to flower,
> A weary chase, a wasted hour.
> *   *   *   *
> A chase of idle hopes and fears,
> Begun in folly, closed in tears;"

onwards he went, the public applause sustaining him
as he ran his splendid race—"a gallant vessel sailing
on the ocean of Shakspeare's genius, its proud waves
bearing him along in triumph to the sound of their
own music.   Now sailing silently in the moonlight
that sleeps along its waves; now scudding before the
breeze in all the glory of sunshine; and now tossed
hither and thither amid storms and darkness; but he
still kept safe above the waters, not presumptuously
scorning the danger, but boldly and magnanimously
subduing it."   If that noble voyage did not come to
so happy a termination as could have been wished,
the voice of censure is dumb.

CHAPTER II.

SECOND SEASON.—1814–1815.

DRURY-LANE opened for the season 1814–15 towards the close of September, and Kean reappeared on the 3rd of October as Richard. During the recess he, fresh from his London triumphs, passed over to Dublin, where, in addition to Shylock, Richard, Hamlet, Othello, Iago, and Luke, he had appeared with great success in Macbeth and Reuben Glenroy. His manager was Frederick Jones, who, it may be remembered, rejected the offer of the strolling player three years before to "do everything" for the very moderate stipend of 2*l.* a week. In the Irish capital Kean speedily acquired the reputation of a "jolly good fellow;" he became the guest of Mr. Grattan, caroused with the whole Irish bar, had an exciting adventure with the watchmen through having appreciated the mountain dew of the country too highly, and then returned to London, leaving the humble recipients of his bounty to exclaim emphatically, " Och, Mr. Kane is

a gintleman !" The expectation excited by his previous
efforts exhibited itself on the night of his reappearance
at Drury-lane in the dense audience which thronged
every part from the opening of the doors; and the
first advance of the tragedian acted as a signal for
warm and protracted acclamations.   His Richard was,
as usual, brilliant, vigorous, and impressive; and the
only instance in which he deviated from his former
manner of doing the character was in the dying scene.
Instead of adopting the magnificent attitude of motionless despair which had produced such electrical
effect in the previous season, he, after being disarmed
and wounded by Richmond, continued to lounge faint
yet deadly-meaning passes with his swordless arm
until he fell.   This conception, which was not perhaps
so striking as the original one, was derived from an
account of the last moments of an officer who fell in
one of the battles in Spain.

Hazlitt did not think the tragedian at all improved
by his Irish expedition.   "His pauses," he writes,
"are twice as long as they were."   These " pauses,"
which afforded a fruitful theme for critical, or rather .
hypercritical, objection on the part of the press, are to
be justified.   A writer in the *Edinburgh Review* stated
that during these intervals, which those who did not

watch the actor's countenance thought tricks, his face underwent a whole series of emotions, filling up, by the finer lights and shades of his ever-expressive and varying features, the character he was identifying. Equally impercipient was the allegation of more than one critic that he was wanting in dignity—a conclusion at which they seem to have arrived because his figure had not been cast in the very mould of classic grace, or because it did not exactly resemble that of Apollo as drawn in the *Feast of the Poets :*—

> "A figure sublimed above mortal degree,
> His limbs the perfection of elegant strength,
> A fine flowing roundness inclining to length,
> A back dropping in, an expansion of chest,
> (For the god, you'll observe, like his statues was drest,)
> His throat like a pillar for smoothness and grace," &c.

"It is a great and a very general mistake," writes the critic of *Blackwood's Magazine,* "to suppose that Mr. Kean's acting is deficient in dignity. So far from this being the case, dignity is perhaps the one quality it exhibits and is distinguished by oftener and more successfully than by any other. Not the dignity resulting from a certain given arrangement of the arms and legs on a certain given occasion according to a code of theatrical bye-laws 'in that case made and provided,' but that real and sustained mental dignity

which springs from lofty and intense feeling, and is
allied to and expressed by spontaneous and highly
picturesque yet perfectly temperate, graceful, and appropriate bodily action.   They must have strange
notions of dignity, even in the most commonplace
sense of the term, who do not find it in Mr. Kean's
manner of dismissing Cassio from his command :—

> I love thee, Cassio
> But never more be officer of mine ;

or in his apostrophe to his name in Richard II. :—

> Arm, arm, my name! a puny subject strikes
> At thy great glory ;

or in his rebuke to Northumberland, in the same
play :—

> No lord of thine, thou haught, insulting man ;

or throughout the whole performance of his Richard III.
They who allege that Mr. Kean's acting is wanting
in dignity would no doubt call the *Beggar's Opera
vulgar.*"

The character of Macbeth, in which Kean appeared
for the first time in London on the 5th of November,
has been the touchstone of many an aspiring actor.
It has never been altogether attainable by any but the
greatest tragedians, such as Burbage, Betterton, and
Garrick; Booth, Quin, Mossop, and Barry failed in

its representation, some altogether, and all in some
great and indispensable requisite.   Henderson's Macbeth was a very fine, impressive performance ; Kemble,
who was excellent in all that there is of stateliness in
the character, "could not forget," writes Leigh Hunt,
" in the more impassioned scenes, those methodistical
artifices of drooped eyes, patient shakes of the head,
and whining preachments which ever injured his attempts at heartfelt nature ;" Elliston gave a noisy
rendering of the Thane's despair in the last scenes,
but wanted all the deep thinking pertaining to the
character in the former ones ; and in avoiding the two
extremes referred to, Young became sombrous, and
Cooke rough and unimpressive.   Kean's Macbeth, notwithstanding one or two assertions to the contrary,
achieved a complete reproduction of this wonderful
portraiture.   The ideal and the preternatural, imagination and human feeling, submissively answered to
his call; consistent in its tone, harmonious in its
parts, vigorous in its interpretation, and uniformly
raising the imagination to the high level of the character, he nobly subdued the difficulties of his task;
and if in the banquet scene he showed that his figure
was not favourable in the assumption of stateliness,
the defect was at most a slight excrescence on a broad

expanse of beauty—a very little wart on a very lovely face. He had thoroughly studied the *nature* of the character; he fathomed all the depths of human nature, discriminated all its metaphysical subtleties, sought out and composed its noble combination of features with complete success. The character of Macbeth, whether regarded from a dramatic, poetic, or metaphysical point of view, constitutes the noblest effort of human genius. It is so subtly diversified, yet with its consistency and truth to nature so tenaciously preserved, that the imagination is bound captive, and the vocabulary of praise impoverished. It is a display of the most inventive fancy and of human knowledge; a combination of the pathetic, the terrible, the argumentative, nay, the descriptive itself, introduced into the midst of passion without injuring one or the other. Why does the character usually produce so poor an impression when placed upon the stage? Because actors in general are incapable of mastering this skilful intricacy; unable to adequately represent it, the predominating aspects are solely brought forward; and as an unmingled, cold, and gloomy murderer, or as the mere subordinate of an ambitious wife, or as a man of high intellectual qualities impelled to the commission of a crime above his nature, we do not experience that almost involuntary disposition to sympathize which a study of the tragedy in the closet excites in our minds. But embodied as it was by Kean, as a marvellous compound of daring and irresolution, ambition and submissiveness, treachery and affection, superstition and neglectfulness of the future, a murderer and a penitent,—the sternest heart was taken captive; and the sympathy awakened by his performance was indicated by the solemn stillness which pervaded the whole house while *he* was before it, and by the earnest and irrepressible acclamations which followed his different exits. Pity predominated over justice; all abhorrence of his crime left their hearts when they contemplated the struggles of his integrity. Both Kemble and Cooke fell short of the requirements of the character in these secondary considerations; they impictured all its ambition, all its remorse, and more than its villany; but the canvas was relieved with none of its irresolution, with none of its gentleness, and with little of its fear.

The scenery was managed with the feeling of a painter. In that part where Macbeth, after his victory over the forces of Macdonald, encounters the witches on the blasted heath, the beauty of the landscape corroborated and corresponded with the vivid imagination of the poet; and every scenic accessory was analogous to the gloomy grandeur and preternatural solemnity of the tragedy. Both the acting and the pictorial illustration were worthy of Shakspeare. The searching look and affectedly careless tone with which, afraid to trust himself to the utterance of his own opinions, Kean sounded Banquo by repeating the prediction of the witches, "Your children shall be kings!" was in the very spirit of Shakspeare; and the same may be said of his start of astonishment and the various workings of his impassioned countenance when invested with the titles of Thane of Cawdor and King of Scotland. In that part where the nobler impulse of Macbeth struggles with the preternatural influences which conspire to overthrow his loyalty and reverse his very nature— who but Shakspeare could have formed and realized such a sublime conception? — Kean's acting was eminently effectual. The soliloquy commencing " If 'twere done when 'tis done" comprised a world of argument; a glance of the eye, an inflexion of the voice expressed volumes; the daring yet dubious mind, the rapid execution of the soldier, the natural visitations of the man, the negligence of the future, the sensitiveness to the voice of human obloquy, the

noble-mindedness which reinforces his eulogy on
Duncan from the "cherubims and sightless couriers
of the air," and enables him to determine not to commit the murder,—these and all the fine alternations
of feeling brought together in the soliloquy were
distinctly and powerfully indicated. Here, and also
in the scene where, amidst other terrible images, the
visionary dagger floated before his imagination,
Kean's powers broke forth in meridian splendour.
He regarded it with a delirious and fascinated gaze;
it grew more and more distinct to his disordered
fancy; and at length he saw this "painting of his
fear" palpable and distinct, imbrued with blood, and
slowly guiding his halting footsteps to the door of
Duncan's chamber. Bewildered, terrified, brain-sick,
he shrank from a belief of its reality, yet returned to
it with a struggling conviction until it obtained full
possession of him; and in the stormy agitation of his
mind, as, with "let me clutch thee," he grasped
nought but "air, thin air," and also when the dagger
again made itself visible to him, "and yet I see
thee still," his acting was above all praise. In this
impassioned soliloquy he gave, there can be no doubt,
the full meaning of his author; and it is equally certain that in his fine denotement of the quick extension

of mental agitation to the senses, physiological and
natural truth were not absent from the performance.
The finest things that Kean had done as yet were the
"farewell" in *Othello*, the parting with Ophelia in
Hamlet, the battle in *Richard III.*, and the scene with
Tubal in Shylock. In witnessing these marvellous
displays—displays of soul-thrilling pathos, poetic
beauty of conception, and resistless, overpowering
passion,—the heart caught the inviolate fire from the
consecrated flame of genius; the powerful springs of
human sensibility were struck upon with the hand of
a master spirit; and the true dignity of nature pervaded the whole. To this list Kean was to add the
scene in *Macbeth* after the murder. No language
could do justice to its excellence. The repentant
agony and sudden subduing of his mind as he pictured the contrast exhibited between the "innocent
sleep" and the fearful watching of the murderer; the
involuntary hesitation which impeded his utterance
as with broken accents he gasped, "I've done the
deed;" the guilty and utter stupefaction of the senses
with which, pale and trembling, he gazed upon his
quivering, blood-stained hands; the tremulous energy
of his voice—the awful fear which governed his soul;
the guilty terrors which grew upon his crime; and

the shuddering agony with which he refused to carry
back the daggers—

> " I'll go no more :
> I am afraid to think what I have done;
> Look on't I dare not;"

—impoverish description.   It was a scene so various,
so portentous,' so magnificent and powerful, as to
gratify all the serious faculties of the mind, and to
fill them with admiration and delight. It accomplished what is never effected save by talents of the
highest order of superiority—it came up to the idea
previously raised by a study of the original.   Those
who saw the scene can never obliterate it from their
recollection; the understanding, the heart, and the
fancy united in fixing it among the fondest treasures
of the memory.

The banquet scene was throughout rich in the
attributes of genius ; but, invariably rational in the
estimate of his own powers, Kean frankly conceded
Kemble's superiority in this part.   It is more than
probable that had Banquo's ghost been dispensed
with, the effect of his acting in the banquet scene
would have been more impressive; for not only was
the interest of the audience divided between Macbeth
and the " horrible mockery," but its introduction de-

prived him of the opportunity of making the presence of the shadow apparent by the force of his feeling, and left him to attitudinize where he might have created, vivified, and appalled. Banquo's ghost is an anomaly; it is unnecessary for dramatic illusion; it throws an impediment in the actor's way which it is difficult to surmount; and it is a heavy and improbable sacrifice to the unintellectuality of those who, being unable to exercise the "mind's eye," make up for the deficiency by a double grossness of the "bodily organ." Notwithstanding these disadvantages, Kean's acting, with a slight exception on the score of a want of stateliness, was very effective. His final encounter with Macduff was second only to that with Richmond in *Richard III.* as a piece of noble poetry. The horror with which he repelled the idea of fighting with the man whom he had so irreparably injured, and the contemptuous superiority both of tone and gesture with which he stopped the contest to tell his antagonist that he bore a charmed life, amounted to an exhibition of extraordinary skill; and nothing could have been more fine than the awful condensation of conflicting passions with which, after all hope is gone, the promises of the witches proved chimerical and illusory, he braced up his energies for the final struggle. With a voice choked and stifled by the various and overwhelming feelings which assailed him, he rushed upon Macduff with terrible impetuosity—an impetuosity and eagerness compounded of a determination to hold out until the last, and a desire to fly for ever from the development of those supernatural mysteries which open one after the other to distract and destroy him. As he received his death-blow, there was a fine contrast of fierceness and feebleness—the energy of his soul resisting the destruction of the body; his strong volition kept him standing for some moments; and as the expiring flame burnt up brightly at the last, he aimed a final blow at his antagonist, and then fell forward on his face, "as if to cover the shame of his defeat." This falling forward on the face was suggested to the actor by the figure of a soldier on Sir Ralph Abercrombie's monument in St. Paul's Cathedral.

Kean's faculty of individualizing each character in which he appeared showed that his intellectual energies were eminently adapted to the interpretation of an author whose works are characterized by a distinctiveness preserved not only in characters opposing a direct contrast to each other, but in those which approach a near resemblance in their general fea-

tures, governing principles, and more obvious appearances. "He individualized every character," writes
Dr. Francis; "we saw not Mr. Kean." It was in
this faculty, among others, that he towered so much
above his histrionic contemporaries. They were alike
in every character; but Kean individualized his
Othello, Richard, Shylock, Hamlet, Iago, and Macbeth with all due completeness, and without the
slightest appearance of effort. In criticizing his
Macbeth, however, Hazlitt contended that he did not
distinguish the Scottish chieftain from his Richard so
completely as he might have done; and after drawing
an ingenious and elaborate contrast between the two
characters,—showing that Macbeth is impelled to
crime by necessity and accidental circumstances, while
Richard plunges into the dark abyss of guilt with a
restless love of mischief, a gaiety in the prospect of
his villanies, and a disregard of everything but his
own ends and the means by which to accomplish
them,—he takes exception to a certain "compactness
and tenseness of fibre" in Kean's Macbeth which he
held to be more appropriate to the crookback tyrant
than to the murderer of Duncan, "whose soul is
subject to all the skyey influences, and the agitation
of whose mind resembles the rolling of the sea in a

storm." Now, or I am very much mistaken, this objection is not to be sustained. Both Richard and Macbeth have qualities which nothing but a certain compactness and tenseness of fibre can illustrate—the former in his indomitable courage and implicit self-reliance, the latter in the energetic manliness of soul which leads him to resist the preternatural influences which attack his loyalty and integrity, to superinduce an acute sensitiveness to the voice of his fellow men raised in execration against him, to expose him to the burning pulses of remorse for the murder of Duncan, and to render him easily accessible to feelings of pity, sympathy, and uxoriousness. Acting upon this conception, Kean followed the spirit of the part in the most faithful manner; and, so far from intro-ducing anything incongruous into the performance, the compactness and tenseness of fibre in question were nothing but a well-illustrated phase in the diversified character of Macbeth.

Praise of the actor's fresh effort was liberally be-stowed on all hands. *The Times* and the *Morning Post* were earnest in their eulogy, the latter merely object-ing to Mr. Kean's substitution of the word " golden " for that of " gory" when he described the appearance of the corpse to Macduff and Lennox. Hazlitt did

not see that Kean was unable to impart melodious retrospective tones to the soliloquy, "My way of life,"
&c., in consequence of hoarseness, neither could he
appreciate the agility of the actor's movements when
contrasted with Kemble's stately strides ; but his
critique is not without some marks of perception.
"As a lesson of common humanity," he writes,
"the murder scene was heartrending. The hesitation, the bewildered look, the coming to himself
when he sees his hands bloody, the manner in which
his voice clung to his throat and choked his utterance, his agony and tears, the force of nature overcome by passion—beggared description. It was a
scene which no one who saw it can ever efface from
his recollection."

Mrs. Richard Trench, writing to Lady Fanny
Proby, Nov. 16, 1814, says: "I took my boys to see
Macbeth last night, but found that, though they read
Shakspeare, they did not readily catch the language
of the scene. They understood Kean well, his tones
are so natural; but the raised voice and declamatory
style in which most others pronounce tragedy, renders
it, I see, nearly unintelligible to children. I was
astonished by Mr. Kean's talents in all that followed
the murder, highly as I before thought of them. I

suppose remorse was never more finely expressed, and I quitted the house with more admiration of him, and even of Shakspeare, than ever I had felt before."

For the first time in the annals of the English stage the witches were exhibited on this occasion in the light of solemn instead of comic characters—as the engines of terror rather than of laughter. This is an honour which should never be omitted in any mention of Edmund Kean's representation of Macbeth. By this salutary reform an epoch in the history of the tragedy was marked which every admirer of Shakspeare hailed with earnest gratification; for it may be remembered that the witches are incarnations of mischief and malice—the organs of "the numbing spell." The idea that the witches were to be regarded from a grotesque point of view appears to have prevailed from the time of the Restoration; when *Macbeth* was produced at Davenant's theatre, the weird sisters were assigned to the low comedians of the company, the utmost licence in the way of grimace and buffoonery being granted. Dressed according to the popular conception of the witch—in tall conical hats, mufflers under their chins, high-heeled boots and scarlet kirtles, and the traditional crossing-sweeper's broom in their hands — they formed the very beau ideal of the Mother Bunch and the Mother Goose of the children's books. In the course of the play, they delighted the galleries by certain comic dances, and leapt over their brooms at intervals in such a droll manner as to provoke general hilarity.   Kemble, convinced that the effect of the tragedy itself was weakened, if not destroyed, by pleasantries of this description, endeavoured to suppress them; but he only succeeded in softening down the more obtrusive prominences of the repulsive interpolation—the "gods" *would* have the dance and the broom business; and it was reserved for Kean to put a final stop to it.   "I'll have the witches played properly," he said; "the rubbish shall be cleared away, I'll have none of it."   Dowton, who was by no means disinclined to obtain a round of gallery applause at the expense of good-taste, was compelled to obey the mandate, and, to his credit be it said, wound up the charm with awful solemnity.

Kean's improvements in the representation of Macbeth were not confined to the new light in which the witches were introduced on the stage. He redeemed the costume of the character from the incongruities which his predecessors had tolerated;

having examined several sources of information relating to the subject, he deposed the inappropriate dresses which Garrick and Kemble had adopted, in favour of a costume in every respect identical with that of a Scottish chieftain of the eleventh century. It is to be regretted that his improvements did not extend to the removal of Banquo's ghost.

The accession of Miss O'Neill to Covent-garden on the 14th of October, obtained for that theatre a counterpoise against the overwhelming attraction of Kean at Old Drury, gave a fresh impulse to the obstinate controversy respecting his merit which had been carried on since the previous February, and confirmed the hold which nature had laid upon the stage with his appearance. Miss O'Neill had graduated in Ireland for three years, having made her first appearance on the boards at the Crow-street Theatre in 1811, as the Widow Cheerly in *The Soldier's Daughter*. The circumstances attendant upon her first start into fame are curious enough. In the summer of 1814, Miss Walstein, the "star" actress at the Dublin Theatre, demanded an increase—a very exorbitant increase—in her salary, threatening in the event of a refusal to immediately withdraw; but Manager Jones, much to the lady's astonishment, quietly accepted the alternative, and, acting upon the counsel of a trusty adviser, substituted Miss O'Neill, then an obscure and unknown actress, in her place. The experiment proved a very fortunate one; the treasury overflowed; and Miss O'Neill passed over to London to renew her Dublin triumphs at Covent-garden. The impression created by her Juliet was very great; even Byron has left on record that he never saw her, having made and kept a determination to see nothing that should divide or disturb his recollection of Siddons. Eminent as were Miss O'Neill's external advantages, she was indebted for her success wholly and entirely to her internal powers. Her figure, " though not in the first order of fine forms," was far from inelegant; her features were ennobled by a feminine and lovely delicacy; her voice was deep, clear, and full of tenderness ; her manner was marked by a graceful simplicity and impressiveness ; and altogether she seemed " moulded by nature for the sensibilities of private life." Her style of acting was eminently natural. Like Kean, she rejected the pride, pomp, and circumstance of the Kemble school ; in *her* acting there were none of Mrs. H. Johnston's creaking cadences, none of Mrs. Powell's sombre monotony and shrill peacock-like screams of passion, none of the dryasdust pedantry and mock sublimity of Mrs. Bartley. No; Miss O'Neill proved herself a representative of human and not of unnatural passions; her weapons were melting tones and tender smiles and sobs and tears; and never was this irresistible artillery more skilfully or beautifully worked. She was a worthy rival of Kean, her merits were of the same genuine stamp, and that stamp nature's. She was not equal to him in energy of understanding, but in the expression of love or grief she found her way to the heart with equal certainty. It was next to impossible to hear her sob of sorrow or the gentle pathos of her voice without being moved; and every heart susceptible to beauty and truth yearned towards her. Her acting struck directly on the heart without waiting for the decisions of the head; like the presence of a person dear to us, it captivated instantaneously. But it did not leave a permanent impression on the mind—it passed away with the momentary illusion of the scene. In this she opposed a direct contrast to Kean. His bursts of genius and passion at once became interwoven with the finely-wrought texture of sensibility and thought; like impressions of friendship, they existed in the mind for ever after in all their pristine freshness and beauty. Miss O'Neill's acting commanded praise; Kean's afforded a never failing source of observation and discussion.

Towards the close of November, Miss Walstein, the actress who had so unconsciously assisted the advancement of Miss O'Neill at Dublin, obtained an engagement at Drury-lane, where for some months she sought to divide the applause awarded to her more talented rival. She withdrew from the unequal contest at the close of the season, and left Miss O'Neill to pursue her brilliant path without a rival. To exterior attributes of the highest class, Miss Walstein brought a degree of intelligence, an acuteness of sensibility, a fine education, and a variety of talents that could not do otherwise than adorn her interesting art; but the attractiveness and value of these qualities were detracted from by an injudicious adoption of the heirlooms of tragedy from time immemorial—the solemn stare, the measured strut, the affected tone, and the austerity and even insolence of demeanour which belong to the artifices of the stage. This pride, pomp, and circumstance had become too firmly implanted to admit of rectification; but in those parts in which singing is introduced—as for instance, Ophelia in *Hamlet,* and Blanche in *The Lady of the Lake*—she rose far superior to Miss O'Neill. Overshadowed by the superior brilliance of the other, she returned to her native stage, and there pursued and closed her career.

While *Macbeth* at Drury-lane and *Romeo and Juliet* at Covent-garden engaged the attention of the play-going public, the latter tragedy was in rehearsal at the first-named house, Kean, at the instigation of the Committee, but strongly against his own inclination, consenting to appear in the character of Romeo. "They have actually persuaded me to come out in Romeo," he said to his wife when he returned home one day, "but I'll disappoint them in it, damned if I don't." This determination merely referred to the balcony scene, and he kept his word. He appeared in the character on the 2nd of January. With none of the seductive fervour and silver-toned eloquence of Barry, with none of the passionate earnestness of Garrick, he stood like a statue of lead in the balcony scene. There is no doubt that he could have easily surrendered himself, had he chosen, to the ardent enthusiasm and the voluptuous tenderness of the character in this scene, as his parting with Ophelia in *Hamlet* and his "If 'twere now to die," and several other passages in *Othello* conclusively showed; but for some reason that does not appear he determined to have nothing of the lover in his performance, and consequently played it in the most unimpassioned and unimpressive manner possible. But if his acting in the balcony scene disappointed the expectations of the audience, the deficiency was more than redeemed by the surpassing excellence of the scene with Friar Lawrence and the last one (that of the death). In the former he struck with unerring instinct the true key of nature; and as he presented Romeo under the influence of the passion with which the character is invested, his energy became electric, it touched every fibre of the large assembly in front, and for a time even the spectator who was wrapped up in the traditions of the Garrick-Barry era could not, under the influence of the perfect sympathy with which the performance filled him, think of anything else but what he now saw. Kean's representation of the scene with the friar abounded with true pathos, eloquent passion, and unaffected simplicity. His impatient rejection of the consolation which the old friar endeavoured to pour into his wounded soul, and the tone in which he gave the words—

" Thou can'st not speak of what thou dost not feel,"

were very expressive. " In the midst of the extravagant and irresistible expression of Romeo's grief,"

writes Hazlitt, " at being banished from the object of
his love, his voice suddenly stops and falters, and is
choked with sobs of tenderness when he comes to
Juliet's name. Those persons must be made of
stronger stuff than ourselves who are proof against
Mr. Kean's acting both in this scene and the dying
convulsion at the close. His repetition of the word
banished is one of the finest pieces of acting the
modern stage can boast. He treads close indeed
upon the genius of Shakspeare." The concluding
scene, in which he died in Juliet's arms, was the most
brilliant. The preparative of the disclosure of having
taken poison ; the absorption of all lower thoughts in
his delight at Juliet's recovery ; the workings of the
poison, indicated by the writhing of his countenance,
averted from her gaze, giving indications of what he
would not utter ; the rising of the effort as his torment became more trying ; the fine instance of conduct in the struggle with which he soothed his
wife and concealed his own agony ; and then—the
sharpening of bodily pain into delirium, the floating
of visions before his eyes, and the eventual aberration
of reason ;—in all this there was such truth, such
power, such an assurance that the waters of nature's
pure and sparkling fountain had been exhausted, that

the feelings of the audience appeared to be wrought up to the highest pitch. His vigour slowly relapsed, and he faded almost imperceptibly away; his voice sank into a scarcely distinguishable whisper; he dropped lifeless from her arms; and the applause which followed was a tribute due from intellect to intellect,—a lawful tax for a noble and powerful display.*

---

* Garrick's version of *Romeo and Juliet*, which has held possession of the stage up to the present time, was published by Tonson in 1758. Its deviations from the original, especially in the last act, are very great; and as a piece of barefaced impudence, it is only to be paralleled by Colley Cibber's alteration of *Richard III.*, or Nahum Tate's ridiculous version of *King Lear.* Garrick, in his preface to *Romeo and Juliet, with Alterations and an additional Scene*, states that his principal design was to "clear the original as much as possible from the jingle and quibble which were always the objections to the reviving it," and announces that a part of the play had been altered in deference to an opinion that the sudden transition of Romeo's love from Rosaline to Juliet constituted a blemish in his character! Adding injury to insult, Garrick proceeded to insert the additional scene. Shakspeare, as is well known, derived the incident of *Romeo and Juliet* from the Italian novellist Bandello, who caused Juliet to awake before the death of Romeo, which circumstance Shakspeare omitted; and Garrick, unable to reconcile himself to the sacrifice of such a material contribution to stage effect, furbished up a scene which bore a suspicious resemblance to a similar one in Otway's *Caius Marius*, and hoped, as he expresses it in the preface, that his attempt to *redeem the deficiency* of so great a master would not be deemed arrogant, or the employment of two or three of his introductory lines be accounted a plagiarism.

After twelve representations, and not to the over-regret of the apparently unloverlike tragedian, *Romeo and Juliet* gave place to a revival of Morton's comedy of *Town and Country*, in which Kean represented Reuben Glenroy with a success that has permanently associated his name with the interpretation of the character. In the performance of Reuben Glenroy the actor encounters in its inconsistency a stumbling-block which nothing short of the highest skill can surmount. The play itself is, moreover, in its general features insignificant; the incidents wild and improbable; and the dialogue of a description such as may be said to derive an isolated charm from the pureness of its insipidity. The character of the hero, which might be drawn without any particular manifestation of talent by a man accustomed to breathe the air of fashionable life, is saddled with a heavy incongruity; and so far from embodying the high-minded youth which it is intended to represent, the whole conception and execution of the character tend to exclude him from the domain of English life. Yet with these strong and offensive improbabilities to overwhelm the interest, the character rose in Kean's representation into no slight occasional vigour. With an intensity of feeling which smoothed over the unpleasant prominences of the character, he seized upon all that could be reduced to natural feeling with a consuming influence which revealed itself in a series of striking and impressive pictures. In the early scenes of the play, where, rambling about the Welsh mountains, he rescued travellers lost in the storm, and assisted the neighbouring peasantry, his acting was singularly beautiful; and the interview with his brother in the gaming-house, in which he developed his love-story to the supposed seducer of his mistress, was a striking display of that high-wrought intensity of feeling which throughout his career formed the great charm of his expressive delineation of the moody mountaineer. " Had Mr. Kean never played more than these two scenes in his life," writes the critic of the *Morning Post*, " we should feel no hesitation to pronounce him one of the greatest expounders of human passions on the stage."

The carpings and cavils of the Kemble school had been in some measure silenced by the fidelity with which the public and the more independent critics stood by the new actor; and the expiring flame only acquired something of its former brightness when he performed Richard II. on the 9th of March. In the beginning of 1815, this fine historical play was altogether unknown through the medium of the stage. It had slept in peace upon the shelf for two centuries; Betterton, Booth, Quin, Garrick, and Kemble had passed it over as unworthy of their talents, and it was reserved for the sympathetic susceptibility of Kean to its striking beauties, its historical truth, and its strong and well-drawn character to show that as a very noble and effective stage play it advanced sterling claims to our admiration. It cannot be said that it was presented under a very desirable form. Wroughton, to whom the task of "adapting it to the stage" had been entrusted by the intelligent Committee, produced a version of *Richard II.* in which one part was curtailed, the characters of the Duchess of Gloucester and Duchess of York left out, and the deficiency made up by assigning the omitted dialogue to the Queen and Bolingbroke. Remembering the complete individuality with which Shakspeare has separated his characters one from another, it is far from difficult to form an idea of the incongruity which distinguished Mr. Wroughton's version of the play; and it is not very gratifying to the admirers of the genius of Hazlitt to find that, under these circumstances, he should have been so destitute of perception as to praise the version in question as "the best that has been attempted, having consisted entirely of omissions." In his conception of Richard II. Kean was obviously at fault. With regard to the general out-line it was a splendid misrepresentation. Hazlitt very properly pointed out that the actor made it a character of passion, that is, of feeling combined with energy; whereas it is a character of pathos, that is to say, of feeling combined with weakness. As an instance of this he refers to the scene with Hereford, where, instead of helplessly letting the glass fall from his hands, Kean dashed it to the ground with all his might: and again, in the expostulation with Boling-broke, the actor's fierce and heroic delivery of the speech, " Why on thy knee thus low?" &c., which should have been sad, thoughtful, and melancholy. In other respects Kean's performance was inimitably fine. It was full of the most varied and brilliant de-clamation, the most pure and simple pathos, the most lofty and temperate dignity. " His loftiness in pros-perity, his confidence in his fancied strength, his despondency at finding it vanished, his alternate bursts of despair and hope when he now sinks under and now resolves to grapple with his fate, his struggle with his pride, his forced humility and resignation when he divests himself of the majesty of kings, and the desperate valour with which he encounters his

assailants at his death were given with all the energy
of truth.   His tones, his gestures, and, above all, the
varied changes of his countenance, revealed all the
conflicting emotions of his soul ; and when mortally
wounded he sank to the ground, and amidst the
agonies of death, hearing the voice of his queen, extended his arms towards the sound, as though to steal
a moment from fate and expire in her embrace : both
the action and the anguish mixed with hope depicted
in his face awoke all the sympathy, and might be
called the sublime of sensibility."*

Moore and Byron were constant visitors to the
theatre at this time.   " We have seen," writes the
former, " how enthusiastically his lordship expressed
himself on the subject of Mr. Kean's acting, and it
was frequently my good fortune during this season to
share in his enjoyment of it, the orchestra being more
than once the place where, for a nearer view of the
actor's countenance, we took our station." Yes, there
the two friends were often to be seen, Byron almost invariably witnessing the performance in the attentive
attitude so well depicted by Westall in 1814, and
Moore sitting by his side, a warm and earnest ad-

---

* *Morning Post.*

mirer of the fine talents of " this extraordinary phenomenon." The author of *Lalla Rookh* had no
patience with Hazlitt's captious and frivolous objections to part of Kean's acting. " Poor Mr. Kean,"
he writes in his correspondence, " is now in the
honeymoon of criticism. Next to the pleasure of
writing a man down, your critics enjoy the vanity of
writing him up; but when *once up* and fixed there, he
is a mark for their arrows ever after."

The production of a new play entitled *Ina*, written
by Mrs. Wilmot, afterwards Lady Dacre, and to
which Moore had contributed an epilogue, was a result
of the acquaintance which ensued between the actor
and the diminutive poet. *Ina*, however, which was
performed for the first and last time on the 22nd of
April, and in which Kean sustained the principal
character, proved totally unsuccessful. The authoress,
who was stated to be a near relative to Mrs. Sheridan,
had selected the incidents of her play from a by no
means uninteresting period of Anglo-Saxon history;
but, disqualified in the most important respects for
conducting her labours to a fruitful issue, a tragedy
had been written so sketchy in its construction, and
so unequivocally indicative of a hopeless deficiency in
dramatic skill, that its fate was sealed long before the

performance had been half got through. Kean, who
was not over-delighted on finding that the pains he
had taken with the character of Egbert had been
expended to no purpose, entertained a sanguine hope
to redeem the failure of *Ina* by his representation of
Penruddock in Cumberland's comedy *The Wheel of
Fortune,*—in many respects an injudicious choice. The
character had been written for Kemble; his powers,
habits, and physical and moral peculiarities had been
taken into consideration; and in consequence his
very defects blended with his excellences to the completeness and unity of the picture—" the studious
and important precision, which was affectation in all
Kemble's other parts, contributed to the strength, to
the nature of Penruddock." Kean could not so far
divest himself of his characteristic restlessness of
energy as to fall into the measured step, gradual
action, fixed gaze, formal address, and ponderous
deportment which, in the keeping of Kemble, invariably conformed to the spirit of the author with
truth, harmony, and feeling; and in courting a comparison with what the most competent judges were
inclined to consider as Kemble's finest impersonation,
he cannot be said to have been well advised. It is
true that in a few detached portions of the character,

and in a few situations which afforded a more direct scope for the display of his peculiar powers, Kean equalled, not to say surpassed, his rival: as for instance, his dialogues with Henry Woodville; the trying interview with the mother; his magnificent reply to Sydenham in the third scene of the third act, " Do you know that? I know it too," a passage in the finest and most touching sense of the passion to which it referred; the eager emotion with which he gazed on the countenance which reminded him of Arabella; the subsequent scene where the same feeling occurred to him and interrupted his speech; the words, " You bear a strong resemblance to your mother," which furnished one of the most exquisite pictures of the pathetic ever witnessed on the stage. In the display of grief or violence or tenderness or contempt vehemently enforced, delicately chastened, or ingeniously complicated with the collateral emotions of the scene, he was equally brilliant and impressive; but in the ordinary demeanour of Penruddock, where he subsides away into his pensive melancholy, his acting wanted all the beauty of Kemble's representation to complete the delineation—the exquisite rounding, the mellowing of philosophy, the calm of solitude, the incrustation of time.

All was redeemed, all transient deficiencies lost to view amidst the overwhelming splendour of his Zanga, in which at one stroke he deposed Mossop from his traditional supremacy, and deprived Kemble of one of his oldest and most valued possessions. Kean appeared in this character, together with that of Abel Drugger, for his benefit on the 24th of May; and the public expectation ran so high that a party of the most distinguished patrons of the drama were glad to secure seats in the upper boxes. *The Revenge* is, in its predominant aspects, an obvious transposition of the two principal characters in *Othello*, with this exception, that Zanga is invested with a nobility of soul and an intensity of purpose which oppose a direct contrast with the light, gay, comfortable, cordial villany of Iago. The ancient reveals an ignoble origin in all his sentiments, but Zanga is of a cast of intellect which redeems him from an utter alienation of sympathy. His motives are, at least to

" Souls made of fire, and children of the sun,"

strongly founded; the modes, however insidious and repulsive by which he effects his purpose, are strictly acted to the end; and the gratification of his chief, and, indeed, his only passion, is never out of the

author's view. The implacable spirit of vengeance
may be modified, but there does not occur a single
sentence from the commencement to the conclusion
in which it does not commingle more or less with
the life-blood of Zanga, and communicate itself to
every motion, look, and gesture. The limited few
who have succeeded in imparting to the character in
dramatic representation that gloomy, vigorous, and
majestic colouring so admirably supplied by Dr.
Young, consist of Frederick Mossop, John Kemble,
and above both, Edmund Kean. Since the time of
the first-named actor, who was much celebrated for
his representation of the character in the middle of
the eighteenth century, *The Revenge* slept in peace
upon the prompter's shelf, or had been only roused
from its slumbers to incur partial degradation in the
hands of some ambitious aspirant, until it was
restored to genuine lustre by the talents of John
Kemble. Although wanting in the varied, intense,
and burning energy demanded in the performance of
Zanga, Kemble's captive Moor advanced sterling
claims to distinction; and it was not until Kean
undertook the part, and invested it with a radiance
altogether new to the public experience of its representation, that he finally abandoned a rôle which he

could no longer fill with entire credit to himself, or
to the complete satisfaction of his most ardent
admirers.   To state that Kean's conception of the
character was perfect, will not be saying much for
his power of understanding, for the outline is traced
with so much distinctness, and the various tints of
passion filled in with so much truth and richness, as
to place even an unintelligent performer in the full
possession of the author's sense.   But with the
execution of the part it is another matter.   The
genius of the painter is not so much shown in the
design as in the filling in of the picture.   " We have
seen Mr. Kean in no part," writes Hazlitt, " to which
his general style of acting is so adapted as to Zanga,
or to which he has given greater spirit and effect.
He had all the wild impetuosity of barbarous revenge,
the glowing energy of the untamed children of the sun,
whose blood drinks up the radiance of fiercer skies.
He was like a man stung with rage and bursting with
stifled passions.   His hurried movements had the
restlessness of the panther's ; his wily caution, his
cruel eye, his quivering visage, his violent gestures,
his hollow pauses, his abrupt transitions were all in
character."   In the first four acts the spirit of vengeance, animated to action by the death of a father—

slavery—a blow—were smothered to the very moment when, in the gratification of his revenge, the vital beam of joy played around his heart, and burst forth with an intensity proportionate to the calamities into which his subtlety had involved his master. The first suggestion of the plot which he afterwards executed; his words, " Then lose her!" the whole scene where he renders Alonzo jealous of his wife; his delivery of the lines—

> " If you forgive her the world will think you wise,
> If you forget the world will think you good,
> But if you take her to your arms again
> The world will think you very, very kind ;"

the passage where he incited Alonzo to eclipse the Grecian and the Roman fame by the immolation of Leonora; the natural expression which attended his interruption of the relation to his victim—" I know you could not bear it ;" the native majesty which impresses Alonzo with " awe of one above him ;"—in all these parts the effect of his wonderful acting was, to employ the prescriptive phrase of dramatic critics, " electrical." But all was cast into the shade by the unspeakable grandeur of his avowal of the terrible success attendant upon those stratagems which had turned the hydra of calamities—jealousy—to his dire intent—

" Born for use, I live but to oblige you ;
    Know, then, '*twas I*."

His eye lit up with a preternatural brilliance; the
long-smothered hate blazed forth with fearful intensity ; as Alonzo fell he majestically extended his
arms over the fainting Spaniard; towering over the
prostrate body with terrific energy and power, he
trampled upon it in an attitude which Hazlitt regarded as not the less dreadful from its being perfectly
beautiful. The effect was appalling; the fiery soul
flashed out with a look and gesture which imparted a
corresponding dignity to the body; Rae (Alonzo),
although by far the larger man, seemed to wither—
shrink into half his size and appear smaller than
Kean ; and as Barry Cornwall contemplated the dark
and exulting Moor standing over his victim with his
flashing eyes and arms thrown upwards (" as though
he would lay open his very heart to view") he thought
that he had never beheld anything so like the " Arch-
angel ruined." He was recalling to mind the line
descriptive of the " sail-broad vans" of the great
spirit of Milton when, by an extraordinary coincidence
of idea, he heard Southey exclaim to a companion,
" By God ! he looks like the devil."

The expectation excited by the announcement of

Kean's appearance in *The Tobacconist* met with no alloy in his characteristic interpretation of Abel Drugger.   Exhibiting a comic versatility which was praised by more than one veteran playgoer as equal to that of Garrick, it showed that his powers were by no means confined to the workings of the soul, the intensity of passion, the solemnity of situation, and the deeper scenes of tragedy.   His unctuous and persuasive humour was nothing less than an effectual weapon in the hands of a master—of one who could stir to laughter as well as to enthusiasm or tears. "Mr. Kean's Abel Drugger," writes Hazlitt, whose opinions with respect to the performance were confirmed by other journals, especially the *Morning Post*, "was an exquisite piece of ludicrous naïveté.   The first word he uttered, 'Sure,' drew bursts of laughter and applause.   The mixture of simplicity and cunning in the character could not have been given with a more whimsical effect.   First there was the wonder of the poor tobacconist when he is told by the conjuror that his name was Abel, and that he was born on a Wednesday; then the conflict between his apprehensions and his cupidity as he becomes more convinced that Subtle is a person who has dealings with the devil; and lastly, his contrivances to get all

the information he can without paying for it.   His
distress is at the height when the two-guinea pocket-
piece is found upon him : ' He had received it from
his grandmother, and would fain save it for his
grandchildren.'   The battle between him and Face
(Oxberry) was irresistible ; and he went off after he
had got well through it, strutting and fluttering his
cloak about much in the same manner that a game-
cock flaps his wings after a victory.   We wish Mr.
Kean would do it again !"

Mrs. Garrick and the press were at issue respecting the merits of Kean's Abel Drugger.   Her brief,
laconic note to the actor—" Dear Sir,—You can't play
Abel Drugger, Yours &c., EVA GARRICK," and his
courteous reply—" Dear Madam,—I know it, Yours,
EDMUND KEAN,"—constitute one of the most interesting traditions of the stage.   When Mrs. Garrick next
saw him she counselled him to lay aside the character
without loss of time ; but Kean, who by no means
wished to abandon it so readily, but who out of respect
to the old lady resolved to act upon her advice, was
determined not to let Abel fall out of his repertory
without a retort.   " Could David sing ?" he asked.
" Sing !—no," replied the old lady.   " Well, then,"
retorted the actor, " I have one advantage over him at

least, for I can." .The wish expressed by Hazlitt was gratified by two more representations of the character ; and *The Tobacconist* then disappeared from the bills.

On or about the 5th of May, 1815, the Coal Hole Tavern, Fountain-court, Adelphi, was dedicated to sublimer uses than usual. The Wolf Club, the motives attendant upon the formation of which subsequently became the subject matter of so much controversy in the theatrical world, was inaugurated by Kean. The actual design and principles of the club may be gathered from the following address, which the tragedian, as chairman, delivered at the first meeting :—

"GENTLEMEN,—If we look to traditions, our arts and sciences, our laws and government in embryo were uncertain, disputable, and vague ; to accomplish perfection in any degree has been, and will remain, the work of years and constant perseverance. I am therefore aware of the difficulties we have to encounter in bringing our little society from its formation to an extensive circle of adherents ; but in spite of all opposition that may occur, my vain mind brings a figure to my imagination ' that it is the morning gleam from a chaotic mass' that will hereafter glow in full splendour on good fellowship and harmony. Gentlemen, there is one precept I am sorry to say too much neglected in this world of more false pride than talent, which I cannot express better than in the language of Terence,

" Homo sum; humani nihil à me alienum puto."

When men consider they were created for each other, not only for themselves, the interests of mankind must be blended with individual speculation, and in everyone that bears the human form each man must be a brother; and it is my wish to instil these sentiments into the minds of our little community, that no insignificant distinctions shall have weight when we can (with personal convenience) serve a fellow creature; or worldly exaltation prevent us from mixing with worthy men, whom I must conceive the great Author of all being intended for equality : no one, I hope, will enter this circle of good fellows without a pride that ranks him with the courtier, or philosophy that levels him with the peasant. These sentiments preserved, the convivial board will be enjoyed with feelings of philanthropy, and retrospective delight follow the feast of reason. Courage, the only distinction our ancestors were acquainted with, must be one of the first principles of our body, and to what better end can we employ that magnificent ingredient in defence of our friends against the foes of a general cause? It is my hope that every Wolf oppressed with worldly grievance, unmerited contumely, or unjust persecutions, with a heart glowing with defiance may exclaim, ' I'll to my brothers; there I shall find ears attentive to my tale of sorrow, hands open to relieve and closed for my defence.' Not to fatigue my hearers longer with prolix rhetoric, I conclude with my sincere hope and prayer for the successful increase of honourable members to this (as yet) imperfect society; and that every brother may feel health, prosperity, and happiness will ever be the wish of its founder, and study to promote, as far as his duty in this club extends."

The Wolf Club was composed chiefly of men whose principal object was to enjoy themselves in each other's society, preference being given at the election of members to those who seldom visited the theatre, or who took little or no interest in dramatic matters. Conviviality was at all meetings the order of the night, and Fountain-court not unfrequently re-echoed the jubilant roars that issued from the interior of the Coal Hole. In society like this, Kean found a congenial element. His many estimable and endearing qualities as a man; his love of social and convivial

x 2

intercourse; the superior description of his conversa-
tional powers; his inexhaustible fund of anecdote
and reminiscence; the vigour and pointedness of his
satire; his occasional felicity of repartee; and, above
all, the entire separation of his manner from anything
suggestive of false pride, arrogance, or ostentation,
rendered him a delightful companion; and quickly
earned for the Wolf Club a reputation as a sort of
rendezvous of sociableness, conviviality, and good
fellowship.   At first, the disposition to admit no one
into the newly-formed club who was interested,
directly or indirectly, in theatrical matters, was strictly
adhered to; but in the course of a few months it gave
way, and the room set apart for the meetings of the
members frequently presented a good assemblage of
celebrity and talent.   Honest, good-humoured Jack
Bannister, with his deep, sonorous voice, round, full face,
and sparkling eyes, presided on one occasion over the
convivialities; Oxberry, for whom Kean entertained a
strong regard, not having forgotten the glass of
brandy-and-water on the night of the 26th of January,
1814, is there, a welcome member; Frederick Reynolds,
author of *The Dramatist*, and who is serving Covent-
garden in what he terms the capacity of a " thinker,"
or, in less ambiguous language, the performer of all

literary labour required in that establishment, gives the company an excellent illustration of what lively conversation is; Elliston, who is a fervent admirer of the bottle, and who sometimes induces the company to pass an hour away at whist, enlivens them with his vivacity and humour; Liston, in the production of whose risibility stirring-features Thalia must have intrigued with Momus, sets the table in a roar; John Pritt Harley, who has recently made a highly-successful first appearance at the Lyceum, and who is recognised on all hands as Jack Bannister's legitimate successor, is present; and, amongst several others, Messrs. Robert Palmer, Bartley, Pope, Rae, Knight, Braham, Powell, Wallack, Wewitzer, and Thomas Dibdin, now and then put in an appearance. Rank, as may be supposed, was rarely seen at the meetings of the Wolf Club. Lord Byron once made his head visible from behind the door, and hypocritically turned his eyes upwards and shook his head as he contemplated the convivialities going on within. The conversation never flagged. The news of the day, which principally related to Napoleon, was animatedly commented upon; the dramatic criticisms in the newspapers dissected and laughed at in a manner that would not have brought a smile to the faces of the

writers had they been present; and no members of
the club enjoyed the following *jeu d'esprit*, which
is capital in its way, more than Liston and
Reynolds :—

"*The Case of Mr. John Bull set forth by the Covent-
garden Physicians.*

" It so happened that during the last two seasons
Mr. John Bull was suddenly attacked by a species
of madness, which, for want of a better name, we, the
proprietors of Covent-garden Theatre, thought proper
to term the Kean mania.   As sole physicians to the
said Mr. Bull, we were under the necessity of attending to his disorder, but as much slander has been attached to us in the discharge of this duty, we now
think proper to favour the public with a full statement of our practice on this occasion.   It is to be observed, that we have treated this disorder according
to the most approved modern practice, applying our
remedies both to the mind and body.   In the beginning of his disorder, Dr. F. Reynolds applied his
famous pilula abusiva, or abusive pill, which he administered publicly every morning at Hookham's
Library in Bond-street.   Mr. Bull, however, did not
seem to relish this pill in the then weak state of his

stomach, but the doctor persisted in the use of it, and, we think, with some effect. The ingredients were as follows :—

" Mr. Kean's shortness.

" Mr. Kean's hoarse voice.

" Mr. Kean's differing from all that went before him.

" This, with a quantum sufficit of Joe Miller, composed the pill; and surely nothing more innocent can be imagined, although it has been slanderously averred that Dr. Reynolds had destroyed the patient's palate.

" The patient's health not improving so rapidly as we could wish, Dr. Farley was called in, who was of opinion that the disease being solely a disease of the mind, the remedies ought to be purely mental. In support of this he observed that the patient in all other respects was healthy, that his pulse beat temperately, nay, that he even conversed upon his disorder with some degree of reason; he therefore proposed some kind of amusement, the more foolish the entertainment the better. For this purpose horses were brought from Astley's; Dr. Pocock* in-

---

* Pocock, an author of melodramatic plays. Hazlitt writes of him, in 1822: "Mr. Pocock lives; and while he lives, never let the lovers of melodrama despair."

sisted upon our trying his melodramatic draught, and, though a great quack, being ably supported by his claims, he was permitted to make a trial of his skill. Mr. Liston officiated as the apothecary, and so infinitely delighted the patient by his grimaces that he not only took the medicine quietly, but wished Mr. Liston to leave trade, and very generously promised him his protection if he chose to turn Merry Andrew.

" Mr. Bull had now been under our hands several months, but it was not observed that he grew better. Dr. Harris, considering the disease to originate in nervous irritation, prescribed the haustus soporificus Kemblianus, or Kemble soporific ; but this, though it often sent the patient to sleep, produced no further advantage. The moment this effect had ceased, the patient became as Kean mad as ever.

" Finding the disorder not in the least abated, we had recourse to an old but very powerful remedy, the linimentum newsparianum, or newspaper liniment ; a composition of dull lies, dull jokes, and false criticisms, distilled in the alembic of an editorial skull, and carefully poured into the patient's ear every morning at his breakfast. Sometimes this remedy was repeated in the afternoon.

" This efficacious medicine has not as yet been

attended with any very favourable results, but at the same time we have great hopes that in the course of a few months the cure will be accomplished; for it really is a grievous pity that so fine a gentleman as Mr. Bull should be so seriously indisposed. In consequence, we have to hope that this plain statement will satisfy the minds of the public, and convince them that we have been actuated by no sinister views of profit, but by a laudable desire of doing good to our fellow-creatures.

(Signed) " HENRY HARRIS,* M.D., and A.S.S.

     CHARLES FARLEY, M.D., and Member of the most honourable the Society of Wise Men.

     ISAAC POCOCK, M.D., and A.S.S.

     FREDERICK REYNOLDS, M.D., and D.U.N.C.E.

     JOHN LISTON, Apothecary, and Vice-President of the Merry Andrews."

In short, a spirit of heartiness and goodwill pervaded every meeting of the Wolf Club, and it soon became understood that the drama had fixed her social head-quarters at the Coal Hole. This understanding

---

* Manager of Covent-garden Theatre.

gave rise to the misapprehension which prevailed as to
the objects with which the club was formed, to which
reference will be presently made.

Kean's appearance as Leon in Beaumont and
Fletcher's comedy of *Rule a Wife and Have a Wife*, on
the 20th of June, showed that although Abel Drugger
had been relinquished, he was not about to abandon
the range of action to which that character belongs.
The strength of Leon, however, is not laid in its exhibitions of low comedy, for as the play draws to a conclusion with the transition from his original passive
acquiescence to the gravity of an indignant and determined spirit, he takes leave of his former laxity and
humour, and is invested with a manner that almost
approximates to tragedy.   Nevertheless, the qualities
of the character are not so mixed and interwoven as
to afford scope for the display of any especial finesse
and dexterity in its representation, its points being
confined to the mimicry and simplicity in the earlier
scenes, and the subsequent vindication of a husband's
rights.   Kean's performance commanded high praise.
His somewhat saturnine manner was eminently
adapted to that degree of comic versatility which,
however trifling, is still a necessary ingredient in the
character; and his clownish guise and assumed pas-

sive submissiveness in the earlier scenes were humo-
rously eloquent in his favour.   His strict adherence to
the author's sense was, however, attended with equivocal results.   Kemble had toned down the more
offensive prominences of the part by the contrast exhibited between the assumed character and the noble-
ness of his presence, but Kean both acted and looked
it too well.   " At the same time," writes Hazlitt, " we
must do justice to the admirable comic talents displayed
by Mr. Kean on this occasion.   The house was in a
roar.   His alarm on being first introduced to his
mistress, his profession of being " very loving," his
shame after first saluting the lady, and his chuckling
half triumph on the repetition of the ceremony, were
complete acting.   Above all, we admired the careless,
self-complacent idiocy with which he marched in carrying his wife's fan and holding up her hand.   It was
the triumph of folly.   Even Mr. Liston, with all his
inimitable graces that way, could not have bettered it."

The ranks of his critics now received an important
addition.   Leigh Hunt, released from the imprison-
ment to which he had been sentenced for having
inserted in the *Examiner* what the sensitive Regent
regarded as libels upon his fair fame and character,
resumed the editorship of that newspaper, more espe-

cially the theatrical department, and exhibited a
tasteful sensibility to those exquisite touches in
Kean's acting which in the very midst of tragedy
introduced a noble and natural familiarity utterly
unknown to the mere declaimer. He applauded the
actor's gestures and turns of countenance as tending
in a very happy manner to unite common life with
tragedy, " which," he says, " is the great stage desideratum ;" he regarded him to be equal at all times
to the best actors in vogue, and to going far beyond
them in particular passages ; and makes up for a few
hypercritical objections (subsequently withdrawn)
with the grand avowal that Mr. Kean's performances
never interfered with his conception of the character,
but that, on the contrary, he uniformly raised his
imagination of the part he acted. Behind the scenes
the appreciation of his talent took a more substantial
form. Wroughton gave him the beautiful tippet of
point lace worn by Garrick in the fifth act of
Richard III. ; Sir George Beaumont gave him a handsome Spanish cloak, and with good-humoured satire,
a portrait of Garrick in Abel Drugger ; Lord Byron
gave him a gold box, having a boar-hunt on the top
wrought in mosaic, accompanied by the lines prefixed
to this volume ; and finally, Sir Edward Tucker gave

him a lion. The majestic quadruped, which often figured in the stern of the tragedian's boat as he rowed up the river, was, luckily for a visitor who once unexpectedly made his appearance in the actor's drawing-room, and found it couchant on the hearth-rug, of an American race, tame, docile, and inoffensive. Kean accepted these presents with a better grace than that with which he received the persistent and fawning servility of his ancient enemy Raymond, who had contemptuously told the little man in the capes that his innovations in Shylock "would not do." One evening the studied compliments of the stage-manager proved too much for the tragedian's endurance, and in a fit of indignation he deluged the unfortunate Raymond with the contents of a bowl of punch. He handsomely afforded his antagonist an opportunity of satisfaction, but Raymond was not accessible to this mode of argument, and fearing that the bowl itself might follow, he beat a precipitate retreat.

On the 4th of July, in aid of the Theatrical Fund Benefit, Kean appeared as Octavian, in Colman's impressive play of *The Mountaineers*, and depicted the various passions by which the unhappy victim to despair and disappointed love is assailed with a truth, a force, and a richness such as to sensibly affect the audience.

His delineation was inexpressibly touching and pathetic; and the rapid transitions from frenzy to comfortless despair, from melancholy to the wild excess of joy, were described with a subtle power which, spreading itself over a broad expanse of beauty in molten brilliance, rendered the spectator unable to detect the slightest blemish in the performance. " In the cottage scene, both before and after the entrance of Floranthe, he exhibited a fearful picture of insanity struggling with the return of reason. Nothing in art could be finer than the alternate light and shadow that played upon his face, like the fitful blazings of a fire, flashing up for a moment, to sink again into utter darkness. There was a painful consciousness of the truth expressed in every feature, a wavering between reason and insanity, till the fit again came on him in all its strength, and then it seemed to plough up his very soul. There was an irresistible and sweeping grandeur in his passion that made him in form like a giant; it was a visible emanation of the mind, fresh and flowing from the fountain; and the expression of superior intellect, whatever was its character, can never be called little."* Some years later Hazlitt

---

* *The London Magazine*, June, 1822.

willingly conceded his superiority over Kemble in the representation of Octavian, nor was he alone in the conviction of Kean's pre-eminent excellence in the character.   One critic writes that, in addition to the boldness and beauty of its outlines, there was a quiet grandeur in Kemble's performance that gave it all the effect of a marble statue, but that it wanted colour and that pliability of mind and face which constituted the highest excellence of Kean, and perhaps of all acting. And another wrote, " There is a grandeur in stillness, awful and unapproachable,—this is Kean's.   It may be truly said of him, his speechlessness speaks for him.   The whole of his Octavian is of this soul-sub-duing character; it is a performance to be witnessed in silence and applauded but by tears."

In Octavian and Abel Drugger—his third and last performance of the latter—Kean brought his second season to a close on the 6th of July, having throughout concentrated a degree of interest on his performances which no actor ever before was able to boast.

Upon Jack Bannister—the staunch and hearty " Wolf," the curtain descended for the last time on the 1st of June.   The comedy of *The World*, and the afterpiece of the *Children in the Wood*, were represented

on the occasion, and naturally wishing, with Dryden's
Sebastian, that " the setting sun should leave a track
of glory in the skies," Bannister was that night superior to himself, whether in the mute wretchedness of
Master Walter, or the mingled simplicity, good
nature, and affectation of Echo. As an actor he possessed a fine capability of assuming distinct characters.
For instance, the varied traits of Colonel Feignwell in
A Bold Stroke for a Wife were by him represented
with such individual distinctness, that one unacquainted with the play would have supposed that it
was not one but several persons who successively
assumed the different characters. Bannister's joviality,
generosity, and good temper were notorious. He was
never known to lose the latter but once, and that
was when a malicious critic, writing upon a performance that never took place, censured him for acting
ill when he was too ill to act at all; and bringing
an action against the newspaper, he succeeded in
recovering damages. Bannister, who saw the brilliant and meteoric career of Edmund Kean to its
melancholy close, enjoyed his retirement for twenty
years, dying at his residence in Gower-street, on
the 7th of November, 1835. Six years before his
death Sir George Rose celebrated his attainment

to the ripe old age of seventy, in the following
epigram :—

> " With seventy years upon his back,
>   Still is my honest friend Young Jack;
> Nor spirits checked, nor fancy slacked,
>   But fresh as any daisy ;
> Though time has knocked his stumps about,
> He cannot bowl his temper out,
> And all the Bannister is stout,
>   Although the steps are crazy."

CHAPTER III.

THIRD SEASON.—1815-1816.

DURING the recess Kean fulfilled, amongst others, an engagement at Portsmouth, where a highly characteristic incident occurred. One morning he accepted an invitation to lunch with the manager and a few friends at one of the principal inns; and for such a visitor as the great Mr. Kean the landlord could do no less than wait upon the party in person. Kean no sooner caught sight of the worthy Boniface than his manner altered instantly, and he exclaimed, " Stay ! is not your name —— ?" The landlord, not a little astonished at the way in which the tragedian spoke to him, replied in the affirmative. " Then, sir, I will not eat or drink in your house. Eight years ago I went into your coffee-room and modestly requested a glass of ale. I was then a strolling player, ill-clad and poor in pocket. You surveyed me from top to toe; and, having done so, I heard you give some directions to your waiter, who looked at me suspiciously, and then presented to me the glass with one hand, holding out the other for the money. I paid it, and he gave me the glass. I am better dressed now—I can drink Madeira—I am waited on by the landlord in person—but am I not the same Edmund Kean as I was then, and had Edmund Kean the same feelings then as he has now?" The landlord stammered out an apology. "Apology!" cried the tragedian, scornfully; "away with you, sir; I will have none of your wine." With this he hurried out of the house.

The town of Portsmouth was by no means unknown to Kean. We have seen how, when but a mere child, he shipped himself here as cabin-boy on board a vessel bound to Madeira; how, on his return thence, he electrified those who carried the supposed invalid from the ship by a sudden and vigorous execution of the college hornpipe; how, five years later, when his search for Ann Carey proved unsuccessful, he defrayed his expenses back to London by the proceeds of a tavern entertainment; and how, a few months subsequent to the close of his Haymarket engagement, in 1806, he visited Portsmouth as a strolling player. On the last occasion but one, "Master Carey, from the Theatre Royal, Drury-lane," had received much

kindness at the hands of the proprietor of the tavern
where the entertainment was given; and that kindness was extended to him in the most liberal manner
when he became an itinerant actor on his own
account. After his fine rebuke of the servile innkeeper, he, accompanied by his friends, sought out
this old benefactor. To his great regret, he found
that the latter was dead, the house tenanted by a
stranger; but there was a sort of half-waiter, half-
potman, who had grown grey in the service of the
man for whom the tragedian inquired. Kean listened
with great interest to an account of his friend's last
moments; and when about to leave, he asked what
time it was. The waiter ran to look at the clock.
"Have you not a watch?" "No, sir." "Then,"
said Kean, putting five pounds into the hand
of the astonished attendant, "take that, buy one,
and, whenever you look at it, think of your late
master."

It was in this, as well as in numberless other
instances of magnanimous and almost extravagant
generosity, that Edmund illustrated his natural goodness of heart, and exhibited a superiority to the silly
vanity of wishing to bury his antecedents in oblivion. The spirit which prompted Napoleon to as-

tonish the crowned heads at Dresden by adverting
to something which happened "when he was a lieutenant in the regiment of La Fêre," and Goldsmith
to startle a brilliant circle at Bennet Langton's by
referring to something which occurred "when he
lived among the beggars in Axe-lane," distinguished
the great tragedian of fifty years ago in an eminent
degree.   A hatred of anything savouring of false
pride he ever displayed; he delighted in rewarding
those who had shown him kindness during the period
of his humbler fortunes; and he was ever ready to
play gratuitously for needy managers, to open his
hand to the necessitous, and to lend his encouragement and assistance to struggling merit.   Let me
relate two or three anecdotes by way of illustration.
Shortly after his first appearance in London, he found
a strolling company at Sevenoaks in anything but a
flourishing condition.   He had known the manager
and a few of the actors in his early days; and he,
now the great Mr. Kean, played Shylock in a barn
for their benefit.   The rush was very great, and a
large majority were obliged to content themselves
with the sound of his voice outside the improvised
temple of Melpomene.   After the performance he
invited all the *corps dramatique* to sup with him at

the principal tavern; and when he departed from
Sevenoaks on the following morning, he left a well-
filled purse to be divided among the company. In
1817 he played gratuitously for the benefit of two or
three actors at Brighton. One of them pressed him
at least to allow them to defray his travelling expenses, but his reply was very characteristic: "My
dear sir, a friend does you a very little favour in
making you a present of a hare when he puts you to
the expense of carriage and porterage." A few nights
later he played for the benefit of the manager; and
when the latter tendered half the receipts, Kean,
learning that he had a large family, gently pushed
them back. "I'll have none of it; for you have nine
children, and I have only one." On another occasion
he met an old histrionic acquaintance in very reduced
circumstances. The child of the latter played the
younger prince to Kean's Richard III., and after he
had been smothered by Glocester's orders, the actor
slipped a packet which subsequently proved to con-
tain ten guineas into his hand, telling the recipient
not to give it to his father until they went to bed.
But of all instances of his generosity, that exhibited
to Butler, manager of the Northallerton company, is
the most grateful to our recollection. It may be

remembered that when Kean obtained his engagement at the Haymarket in 1806, Butler provided him with the means of travelling to London by the stage-coach, in order that he might reach the metropolis within the required time, and that, on leaving Northallerton, the youthful actor assured the generous manager that if fortune ever smiled on his efforts he would not forget him. Shortly after Kean's departure Butler died, and, in the absence of his managerial tact and skill, the company, reduced to disorganization, would have dispersed itself in various directions had it not been for the liberality of Miss Lawrence, a member of the De Grey family, who reorganized the company, and secured them from absolute want by a yearly allowance of twenty-five guineas. The management then devolved upon Butler's son; and when, shortly after his London triumphs in 1814, Kean paid a professional visit to Northallerton, he found the company in a very prosperous condition, and Butler's son the proprietor of the theatre in that town. Unrecognised by his ancient colleagues, Kean opened a short engagement in Richard III., and stirred the usually quiet town to a ferment of enthusiasm. On the following day Butler, acting in accordance with the terms of the engagement, waited upon Kean with

80*l.*—half the receipts of the night's performance. He was proceeding to satisfy the tragedian in a business-like way that it "was all right," when the latter stopped him by a wave of the hand. "My dear sir, oblige me by putting that money into your pocket." The worthy manager, thoroughly mystified, asked him what he meant. "When a boy of nineteen, and an obscure strolling player," answered the tragedian, "I joined your father's troupe,"—a ray of recognition broke over Butler's face—"and while in the troupe I got engaged for the Haymarket, and if I did not reach London in a certain given time I was to miss the chance; and when I found it impossible to tramp it, your father paid for an outside seat on the coach for me, and I told him that if ever I became a great actor I would not forget him. And now, old fellow," he continued, advancing and shaking the manager heartily by the hand, "pick up that money, and let me redeem the promise to the father by rewarding the son. Man alive! don't you remember young Ted, who played Harlequin to your Goose when we first produced *Mother Goose* here? And don't you remember the boys of the town calling after you, 'Goose—goose?'" The manager replied in the affirmative, and returned the grip with interest.

"And where's old George ?" asked the tragedian ;
"I have a surprise in store for him." Behind the
scenes of the Northallerton theatre they found the old
actor, whose hair had now grown white with age. "Do
you recollect me, George ?" Kean asked. "I can't
say that I do, sir," was the reply. "Last night, when
I saw you going through that wonderful performance
of yours, there was something in your eye that made
me think I had seen you before ; and I tried to
recollect you, but my memory is not so good as it
once was, and I couldn't, try all I could." "Well,
then, I am the Master Ted who used to sleep with
you, and of whom you often predicted good things,
and you see that you are a sort of conjuror." And
the noble-hearted tragedian, who enjoyed the utter
bewilderment of old George, slipped 20*l.* into his
hand. A story told in the *Champion* shortly after
Edmund's first appearance in London may be
related in further illustration of his willingness to
recognise his old associates. Just after he had gone
off the stage in one of the scenes of *Richard III.*,
and "while the thundering applause of the house was
rushing after him like an overwhelming torrent," he
caught sight of a subordinate performer, dressed as a
menial in the play of which he was the hero. "Do

you not remember me, my friend?" "No, sir,"
returned the man, somewhat startled at such an
unexpected interrogatory; "I fear that I cannot
claim the honour of having ever been known to you."
"You mistake. Don't you recollect when you played
the part of —— at Drury-lane, that a little boy
bore up your train?—I was that little boy." The
story of the man who claimed to be a brother actor
with Garrick, saying, "When you played Hamlet I
played the Cock," is precisely the reverse of this.

Injury or insult, or slight, sunk deeply into Kean's
heart, and lay there ever after. The fine manner in
which he could rebuke the servility of those who had
contemned him in the strolling player has been illustrated by his repulsion of the Portsmouth innkeeper;
but his desire to revenge himself upon those who had
scorned him in adversity and then bowed down before
him in prosperity was not unfrequently overlaid and
put to flight by the natural generosity of his disposition. An instance of this is related by Mr. Leman
Rede in his *Recollections.* About two years after Kean's
appearance in London he performed in the circuit of
a man who had pitilessly insulted him in his poverty.
Mr. Manager, finding that the strolling player had
become a great man, evinced an inclination to let

bygones be bygones; but Kean sedulously avoided him. Years rolled on, and in 1827 the manager found himself reduced to abject poverty. He applied to Kean, who chanced to be playing there at the time, to perform Richard III. for his benefit; and the tragedian, acting upon his usual impulse, immediately consented to do what was asked of him. On the night previous to the performance Kean and a large party of actors were seated in a tavern parlour when the *ci-devant* manager, thinking the remembrance of the ancient indignity buried, made a speech allusive to Kean's generosity, and informed the company that the great tragedian, who had known him in his prosperity, was not averse to prove himself a friend in adversity. This was too much for Kean's patience. He rose to his feet, and, darting a look—oh, such a look!—at the manager, said to him " Don't let us misunderstand one another; I am bound to you by no ties of former acquaintance; I don't play for you because you were once *my* manager or *a* manager. If ever man deserved his destiny, it is you; if ever there was a family of tyrants, it is yours; I do not play for you from former friendship, but I play for you because you are a *fallen man*." He sat down; the sometime manager pocketed the affront—and the splendid receipts of the performance on the following day. "I am sorry I forgot myself," said Kean, when affording some explanation of his conduct, "but when I and mine were starving, that fellow refused to let a subscription for me be entertained in the theatre."

Upon the commencement of his third season, we find Kean occupying the house formerly tenanted by Lady Rycroft, in Clarges-street, Piccadilly. The house in Cecil-street, in which Kean had exchanged the comfortless garret for more cheerful apartments, had been abandoned at the instance of Mrs. Kean, whose tastes were altogether at variance with those of her husband. The lady wished to divest her new station of the slightest colouring of less exalted associations, and delighted in entertaining company at Clarges-street, persons of " distinction" finding especial favour in her eyes; Edmund had no affection for such an atmosphere, and sought more congenial society at the Coal Hole, where he contributed a little to the duty upon brandy, and enjoyed his favourite repast of a rumpsteak the more because it was not served up in the " style" insisted upon by Mrs. Kean in Clarges-street. Nevertheless, his industry was as indefatigable as ever. His studies were prosecuted with unwearied zeal; new characters derived the benefits of a close and earnest consideration; and he would sometimes remain up all night before the pier-glass, endeavour-ing to realize by modulation, gesture, and action, the conception at which he had arrived. At other times, he would rehearse scene after scene before his wife, who was herself not unfrequently affected by the vigour of his conceptions and the resistless force of his execution; and if he suspected that his rendering of any particular passage was not in character, he never with-drew his attention from it until both were satisfied that the true vein had been struck. In the routine of his daily life all regularity was set at defiance. As a tra-gedian he was, as Hazlitt subsequently remarked, "one of those wandering fires whose orbit is not calculable by any known rules of criticism," and this constituted one of his most prominent characteristics, publicly and privately. After returning from the theatre, hot, jaded, and panting, he would mount his coal-black steed Shylock, ride away into the darkness of the night, display his skill in equestrianism by clearing turnpike gates in the most magnificent style, take infinite delight in the unutterable bewilderment of their drowsy custodians, make rustics believe that Shylock, silently proceeding with muffled feet along the road, bore upon his back a certain cloven-footed personage of whom they had heard so much, and return home about eight o'clock in the morning, not wanting any breakfast, as he had already enjoyed that meal and some home-brewed ale with an honest farmer! In the afternoon he might be found indulging his aquatic proclivities by rowing up the river, the stern of the boat being occupied by his lion; and in the evening there he was on the stage, the cynosure of all eyes, stirring them to ecstasy or subduing them to tears at his will.

It was about this time that he turned his attention to the study of music. His love of harmony was a passion; it would have been strange indeed if *he* had remained insensible to its eternal charms. A friend of mine tells me that on one occasion, when he and Kean together heard some magnificent strains, he saw the blood rush to the tragedian's face; and with such a taste there can be little doubt that, during his sorrowful career as a strolling player, he must have deeply felt the want of the time and means by which he could have cultivated it. Now all such obstacles were removed, and in a very short space of time he, assisted by a fine ear and intuitive appreciation of melody, rendered himself able to touch the piano and other instruments with a degree of skill that would not have disgraced a professor.

On the 16th of October Kean opened his third season in *Richard III.*, and for the first time gave the concluding speech of the tyrant, as written and interpolated by Cibber. He now grandly depicted the state to which the crookbacked monarch was reduced, a state resembling the stupor of intoxication; he fell from exhaustion, and as loss of blood might be presumed to have cooled his frame and restored his sanity, so did he grow calmer and calmer through the dying speech till his mighty heart was hushed for ever. On the 6th of November he appeared as Bajazet in Rowe's tragedy of *Tamerlane.* The character of the captive chieftain is one which is solely adapted to an actor whose powers reside in an aptitude for noisy declamation—for the display of physical passion and external energy. It is violent, fierce, turbulent, noisy, and blasphemous—"full of sound and fury, signifying nothing." Destitute of that calm and indomitable courage which constitutes the perfection of heroic character, he shows all the impotence of despair, but none of the energy of fortitude. An epitome of all that is revolting in Iago, Richard, and Zanga, and destitute of the relief supplied in the wit of the first, the gaiety of the second, and the high-mindedness of the third, he raises no mingled emotions in the minds of the audience. Kean elevated the character into something of dignity by a truth of nature and passion which carried everything before it. Genius, like the sun, irradiates everything around it, however unworthy of laying fine resources under contribution. "A viper never darted with more fierceness and rapidity on the person who has just trod upon it than he turned upon Tamerlane in the height of his fury. An unslaked thirst of vengeance and blood seemed to take possession of every faculty, like the savage rage of the hyæna when run to bay by hunters; and in the description of his defeat, the fiery soul of barbarous revenge, stung to madness by repeated shame and disappointment, was embodied with transcendant power and force." Two individual beauties may be referred to— the striking sentiment where he defended ambition as the hunger of noble minds, and when, in reply to Tamerlane's sneer,

> " The world, 'twould be too little for thy pride,
>   Thou would'st scale heaven ?"

he said, with insolent and blighting scorn,

> "I would—away !—my soul disdains the conference."

Throughout he towered above all; the victorious monarch appeared no better than a bundle of rags covered in ermine; Aspasia moaned in vain; Moneses roared out his wrongs disregarded; all interest centred in the principal actor, upon whom the yellow-brown tinge of the Tartar chieftain lay with an effect most picturesque. *Tamerlane* commanded but six representations. The success of his Aranza (December 5) was, to say the least, equivocal. The light and evanescent humour, the smooth and undisturbed ripple of the mind, and the highly-polished style pertaining to the character constituted an element of ordinary life in which he did not feel a congenial glow; and his Aranza on the stage at Drury-lane was not dignified by that felicitous expression which he had formerly given to the commanding spirit of the duke, the mixture of stern and authoritative admonition, the playfulness of manner which does not result from levity but a consciousness of his own inflexible will, and the noble sentiments which break from him in such refined and beautiful language. The performance was, however, not without some attractions, from which we may select his graceful and elegant dancing and the temperate yet kind and touching dignity with which he delivered the well-known sentiment as to the character of the man who lays his hand in anger upon a woman. "Well, Tom, how did you like the Aranza?" was the question addressed by one playgoer to another. "Fine," was the answer; "Kean's dancing is glorious itself, by Jove."

To the taste and discrimination of Kean the public were indebted for the revival of a series of Elizabethan plays during his third, fourth, and fifth seasons. Although at first sight the works of a race of dramatists so comparatively unknown, either through the medium of the closet or that of the stage, might have been presumed to promise little of a nature to interest the cultivated auditor of nobler and more energetic plays, a further consideration of circumstances tended to show that much which was calculated for effective representation might spring from the very causes that led the actor at first to distrust the possibility of adequate attraction. Massinger's plays of *A New Way to Pay Old Debts*, and *The Duke of Milan;* Marlow's tragedy of *The Jew of Malta;* Ben Jonson's chef d'œuvre, *Every Man in his Humour;* and Beaumont and Fletcher's comedy of *The Merchant of Bruges*, were found on examination to possess points of excellence which could not fail to arrest and sustain the interest of a discriminative audience. *A New Way to Pay Old Debts* was the only play of the group about to be revived which had retained a hold of the stage; but the representatives of Sir Giles Overreach had been so utterly unequal to the task that the audience, ascribing the evident debility to the play rather than to the actor, caused that hold to remain far from secure or assured. It was, consequently, reserved for Kean to show that *A New Way to Pay Old Debts* is the finest play out of the Shaksperian range which adorns the pages of English literature. *Every Man in his Humour*, notwithstanding the excellence of Cooke's Kitely, was all but unknown to the playgoers of that period. As the sun communicates light and heat to the attendant planets, so must the dramatists of the Elizabethan period have derived additional inspiration and brilliance from the presence of Shakspeare; and, thanks to the discriminative researches of Charles Lamb and Mr. Collier, the early English drama is found to yield flowers which, although obscured to some extent by the rank and untended weeds which occasionally surround them, cannot fail, when laid open to view, to prove attractive to a cultivated taste, whether perused in the closet or represented on the stage. Invited by these qualities, which it is just to say he was one of the very first to detect, Kean conceived the design of reviving the above-mentioned monuments to the genius of their authors; and he exhibited so great a taste and delicacy in their reproduction, that for the first time the performance of an old English play was attended by women with a sense of security from the objectionable expressions common to the age in which they were written. The design was not formally announced, neither did the tragedian's name appear as the promoter; but as soon as the news of the revivals was bruited abroad, considerable interest was excited in the intellectual world relative to the success which might or might not attend the enterprising experiment.

Beaumont and Fletcher's comedy of *The Merchant of Bruges* was produced on the 14th of December. In the necessary alterations of this play Kean was assisted by the Hon. Douglas Kinnaird. Contrary to green-room expectations, it answered completely. In this comedy, which is certainly one of the best constructed its authors ever produced, the fortunes of the principal character are traced through a variety of interesting circumstances, from his outset as the wealthy and liberal-minded merchant to his multiplied dangers, distresses, and embarrassments, until their final union with those of the mendicant monarch embrace and re-establish those of the nation itself. Kean's interpretation of Godwin was in every way worthy of its representative; and the electric fire which irradiated his performance wholly effaced the recollection of his imperfect success in Aranza. The celebrated scene where his enemies come to exult in his anticipated reduction to poverty was sustained with a Timon-like bitterness which derived additional strength from the unmoved quietude of manner which accompanied its cutting severity. His other excellences, as noticed by Hazlitt, consisted in his vindication of his character as a merchant, and his love for Gertrude, against the arrogant assumptions of her uncle, and the disarming the latter in the fight; the full justice he gave to the poets' heroic spirit and magnanimity of conception where, after depriving his antagonist of his sword, he says to his mistress, " Within these arms thou art safe as in a wall of brass ;" and afterwards, rising in his extravagant importunity, " Come, say before all these, say that thou lovest me ;" and the force and feeling which he gave to the scene where he is in a manner distracted between his losses and his love. "We have seen him do much the same thing before. There is a very fine pulsation in the veins of his forehead on these occasions, an expression of nature which we do not remember in any other actor. One of the last scenes, in which Clause brings in the money-bags to the creditors, and Kean bends forward pointing to them, —and Munden after him, repeating the same attitude but caricaturing it—was a perfect *coup de théâtre*. The last scene rather disappointed our expectations; but the whole together went off admirably, and every one went away satisfied."

Dowton did not neglect his promise to come forward in Shylock to prove that Kean did not know how to play the character. Public expectation was not raised very high on this occasion, and it was not disappointed. The envious actor inverted Kean's fine, original conception of the character, and, reproducing the conventional manner of its performance, transformed Shylock into a snarling, grinning, growling old man, "bent with age, warped by prejudice and passion, and grinning deadly malice." The great point of novelty consisted in the introduction of some Jewish friends into the court, and when, on being told that one of the conditions of his release was his becoming a

Christian, he fell fainting in their arms, and in this state carried off, the tittering which had been excited from the scene with Tubal in the third act was exchanged for roars of laughter.   Dowton was deeply mortified, and anathematized Kean, Shylock, and the audience with all the vigour of a " good hater." He never boasted of his Shylock again !

Sir Giles Overreach ! If the old ballad of Chevy Chase had that in it which stirred the soul of Sir Philip Sidney like the effect of a trumpet, how thrilling must be the sound of Edmund Kean's name in association with that of Sir Giles Overreach, in which, from the force of his soul - absorbed and terrible intensity, he drove women from the theatre in hysterics, sent the greatest poet of that or any other age into a convulsive fit, and established by his wild energy and intense passion a fame so great, a triumph so perfect, that all London may be said to have looked on and envied him.   The character of Sir Giles is, without exception or reservation but in favour of Shakspeare, the most grand, resistless, and effective portrait of villany in the whole range of English literature.   It has little variety, little relief ; but as a picture of terrific and untameable passions leading to the commission of the most odious crimes it stands without a rival. The wonderful compound into which it has been wrought could only have been accomplished by a mind profoundly conversant with the intricacies of human nature, and endowed with the extraordinary faculty of combining and generalizing the results of its observation. Throughout his representation of this character Kean imparted to it a complexion of the blackest hue. It was the very demon of extortion. He seemed to revel amidst the turbulent passion of the part as though there were a fiend in him. The subtle, malevolent, and ironical oppressor; the hardy bravo who maintains by his sword the wrong he offers; the miser loaded with the spoils of triumphant avarice dressing up to himself a second idol in ambition that he may be refreshed by the acquisition of a double stimulus to the accomplishment of further crimes; the contrast between the spirit of evil which governs his soul and his indomitable courage and manliness—his nobler qualities perverted —were struck out and presented to the eye with such marvellous force and vigour that the mind felt upon it the fresh and spirit-stirring atmosphere of genius; it partook of a profound and almost reverent wonder; it banqueted on the terrible and the grand From the moment that he appeared on the stage the audience felt that he was at home in the part—his eye told them so. His occasional relaxation into an assumed and designing levity was not the least instance of the power which he here exercised to such wonderful effect, and which was in dreadful harmony with the villanies he contemplated and the fiercer passions he but half concealed. The tone of severe though almost involuntary sarcasm with which he never failed to utter the title of " Lord," or the epithet " Right Honourable," had in it something strikingly suggestive of a spirit that mocked the puerility of its own ambition. His finest scenes were the first communication to his daughter of her intended marriage with Lovell; his avowal to that nobleman of his contempt for every upright principle and moral obligation; and the last, in which the parchment that conveyed to him half the fruits of his oppression was obliterated, his villanies detected, his schemes disappointed, and his daughter married under the authority of his own signature to Allworth. His rage at the destruction of the parchment was powerfully expressed; his voice choked itself, his livid lips quivered, and his whole body seemed to totter from a temporary deprivation of the senses. The storm of murderous passion with which he offered to slay his daughter, shook his frame like a strong oak in the blast.*　The tempest of rage and vengeance swept over his soul with tremendous force, and produced a despair so terrible, a torpor so fixed and shocking, that the look which accompanied his removal from the stage bore not the most remote resemblance to anything ever seen except the expression which sometimes rests upon the human countenance when a violent death has imprinted there the image of its final agonies.　Scream after scream reverberated through the solemn stillness of the house—a stillness now broken by the confusion caused by the removal of hysterical women; Lord Byron was seized with a sort of convulsive fit; the pit rose *en masse ;* all parts of the house followed its example; and as hats and handkerchiefs were waved with unparalleled enthusiasm, thunders on thunders of applause swept over the theatre.　But the effect of the actor's intensity was not confined to the audience; it had the extraordinary and unprecedented effect of communicating itself to the actors

---

* In the Royal Academy Exhibition of 1820 an attempt was made by Mr. Clint, in his picture of *The Last Scene in A New Way to Pay Old Debts,* to reproduce the physiognomical expression of Kean as he offered to slay his daughter, but with equivocal success.

themselves. Mrs. Glover, an actress who, from her powerful intellect and long experience, might have been supposed proof against any species of dramatic illusion, fainted outright on the stage; Mrs. Horn staggered to a chair and wept aloud at the appalling sight; and Munden, who sustained Marall in a manner worthy of his leader, stood so transfixed with astonishment and terror, that he was taken off by the arm-pits, his legs trailing and his eyes riveted with a species of fascination on Kean's convulsed and blackened countenance. Once behind the scenes, however, and recalled to himself, the old comedian recovered. " My God!" he murmured to Harley, "is it possible ?"

With much of the trembling excitement with which, two years before, he hastened to the humble garret in Cecil-street to announce to his anxious wife the tidings of his first London success, Kean now ran from Drury-lane to Clarges-street, and, in panting, breathless accents, told her of the reception awarded to his Sir Giles Overreach. " Well, Edmund," said Mrs. Kean, " and what did Lord Essex say of it?" " Damn Lord Essex, Mary," retorted the tragedian with impulsive contempt, and then came the burst of enthusiasm, " *the pit rose at me !*"

All praises from distinguished quarters were valueless in his estimation to that signal mark of honour—the "rising" of what Shakspeare and Ben Jonson have termed the "groundlings." He did not, like Kemble and Mrs. Siddons, invariably convert his performance into an appeal to the equivocal discrimination of the galleries; he played to the pit, "for sir," said he, "the only judges of acting *I* care about congregate in the pit—doctors, lawyers, artists, critics, and literary men." He never sought to astonish and delight the galleries by displays effected at the expense of making the judicious grieve at his want either of the taste to know what was good, or of the firmness to confine himself to it. He regarded such exhibitions as offensive, because needless perversions of talent. "The applause of the galleries," he remarked on one occasion, "is a harlot ever at variance with sound principle and reputation."

"We cannot conceive of any one doing Mr. Kean's part of Sir Giles Overreach so well as himself. We have seen others in the part, superior in the look and costume, in hardened, clownish, rustic insensibility; but in the soul and spirit, no one equal to him. He is a truly great actor. This is one of his very best parts. He was not at a single fault. The passages which we remarked as particularly striking and original were those where he expresses his surprise at his nephew's answers, ' His fortune swells him. 'Tis rank, he's married !' and again where, after the exposure of his villanies, he calls to his accomplice, Marall, in a half-wheedling, half-terrific tone, ' Come hither, Marall, come hither.' Though the speech itself is absurd and out of character, his manner of stopping when he is running at his foes, ' I'm feeble— some widow's curse hangs on my sword,' was exactly as if his arm had been suddenly withered, and his powers shrivelled up on the instant. The conclusion was quite overwhelming. . . . . We have heard an objection to Mr. Kean's manner of pronouncing the words ' Lord—right honourable lord,' which he uniformly does in a drawling tone, with a mixture of fawning servility and sarcastic contempt. This has been thought inconsistent with the part, and with the desire which Sir Giles has to ennoble his family by alliance with ' A lord, a right honourable lord.' We think Mr. Kean never showed more genius than in pronouncing this single word *lord*. It is a complete exposure (produced by the violence of the character) of the elementary feelings which make up the common respect excited by mere rank. This is nothing

but a cringing to power and opinion with a view to
turn them to our advantage with the world. Sir
Giles is one of those knaves who 'do themselves
homage.' He makes use of Lord Lovell merely as
the stalking-horse of his ambition. In other respects
he has the greatest contempt for him, and the necessity he is under of paying court to him for his own
purposes infuses a double portion of gall and bitterness into the expression of his self-conscious superiority. No; Mr. Kean was perfectly right in this.
He spoke the word 'lord' *con amore*. His praise of
the kiss, 'It came twanging off—I like it,' was one of
his happiest passages. It would perhaps be as well
if in the concluding scene he would contrive not to
frighten the ladies into hysterics; but the whole together is admirable."—*Examiner.*

"Sir Giles Overreach, if not the greatest, is certainly the most perfect of all Mr. Kean's performances.
It is quite faultless. The character of Sir Giles
Overreach is drawn with great force and originality.
It seems to have begun in avarice—blind and reckless avarice—which at the period of the play is become merged and lost in intense personal vanity. He
has glutted himself with wealth till his very wishes
can compass no more, and then, by dint of gazing at

himself as the creator of his boundless stores, avarice changes into self-admiration, and he henceforth lavishes as eagerly to feed the former passion as he has amassed to gratify the old one. In delineating this latter part of the character the author has, by an admirable subtlety of invention and a deep knowledge of human nature, made Sir Giles build up an idol in the person of his child, in which, by a self-deceit common to vulgar minds (for his mind *is* a vulgar one, notwithstanding its strength) he worships his only god—himself. He is pleased to see her shining in gold and jewels because she is *his* child ; he lures decayed gentry to do the menial offices of his house because she is *his* child; nay, he even anticipates with delight the moment when he shall have raised her to such a rank that even *he* will be compelled to bow down before her; for, by an inconsistency which is not uncommon in real life, while he regards titles *in others* as empty names, *in her* they will appear to be substantial realities, because she is *his* child.

"Mr. Kean plays the first part of this character with a mixture of gloom and vulgarity that is admirably original and characteristic. And though we did not intend to have mentioned any particular parts of the performance, we cannot help noticing the manner in which he pronounces the titles of the person whom he wishes his daughter to marry. It is always in a tone of derision and contempt, which is but half concealed, even when he speaks to 'the lord.' At first sight it might appear inconsistent that Sir Giles should feel contempt for rank and titles, and yet make them confessedly the end and object of his toils. 'My ends—my ends are compassed, I am all over joy,' he exclaims, when he thinks that he has finally arranged his daughter's marriage with 'the lord.' But on reflection it will be found to be one of the most refined parts of the performance. We have before said that part of Sir Giles's character is a propensity to worship that *in himself* which *in others* he cannot help despising, and this half-contemptuous tone, when speaking of that which is the object of all his wishes, springs from the natural part of his character predominating over the artificial.

"The last act of Mr. Kean's performance of Sir Giles Overreach is without doubt the most terrific exhibition of human passion that has been witnessed on the modern stage. When his plans are frustrated, and his plots laid open, all the restraints of society are thrown aside at once, and a torrent of hatred and revenge bursts from his breaking heart, like water from a cleft rock, or like a raging and devouring fire, that, while it consumes the body and soul on which it feeds, darts forth its tongues of flame in all directions, threatening destruction to everything within its reach. The whole of the last act exhibits a vehe- mence and rapidity, both of conception and execution, that perhaps cannot be surpassed."— *Blackwood's Magazine.*

There were softer and less obtrusive beauties in his performance of Sir Giles Overreach that demand no less consideration than those which created so extraordinary an impression, and enabled the audience to bask in the very sunshine of intellect. I have given a passing mention to the scene in which he expressed to Lovell his contempt for every upright principle and moral obligation, and I waived a de- tailed account in order to introduce a piece of very eloquent writing by Dr. Doran. Overreach expresses his firm, inflexible resistance to the consequences of his oppression in one of Massinger's most picturesque passages :—

> " *Lovell.* Are you not frighted with imprecations
> And curses of whole families, made wretched
> By your sinister practices ?
> *Over.* Yes, as rocks are

When foamy billows split themselves against
Their flinty ribs ; or as the moon is moved
When wolves with hunger pined howl at her brightness."

" I seem still to hear the words and the voice as I pen
this passage ; now composed, now grand as the foamy
billows; so flute-like on the word ' moon,' creating
a scene with the sound; and anon sharp, harsh,
fierce in the last line, with a look upward from those
matchless eyes, that rendered the troop visible and
their howl perceptible to the ear ;—the whole serenity
of the man, and the solidity of his temper, being illustrated less by the assurance in the succeeding words
than the exquisite music of the tone with which he
uttered the word ' brightness.' "   And then his walk
round his daughter, previous to her introduction to
Lovell !   He scrutinized her dress and ornaments—
his eyes glistened like a serpent's at the prospect of
an alliance with " a lord," and he proceeded to enforce
his equivocal instruction as to her behaviour when
Lovell began to woo—"and if he kiss you, kiss
again."   But even the savage and unprincipled Overreach could not but recognise the beauty of female
modesty, and, moreover, that he was speaking to his
own child ; the last words, therefore, were delivered
with hesitation, smothering at the same time the

grossness of the instruction with a hurried whisper. What a fine proof of discrimination!

The Sir Giles Overreach of Edmund Kean was attended with two remarkable results; firstly it served to give palpable form to the disrelish with which his acting had been for some time regarded by the refined appetites of the upper circles, and secondly it gave the crowning blow to the popularity of the Kemble school. Invariably rejecting the superficial in favour of the natural, his acting had in every performance been found to be *too true;* human nature was exhibited in all its naked reality, and in consequence vanity sustained a shock and pride a mortification. The boxes and dress circles were " so thoroughly wrapped up in themselves, so fortified against any impression of what was passing on the stage, and so completely weaned from all superstitious belief in dramatic illusion," that it was not seen from those elevated spheres that in casting the superficialities of artificial acting far into the intellectual background of admiration and praise the tragedian showed himself capable of enriching, adorning, and honouring human nature. A similar disadvantage was encountered by Garrick through the raciness and originality which distinguished his acting; " the court

dresses, the drawing-room strut, and the sing-song
declamation which he banished from the stage were
thought much more dignified and imposing." What
Byron endeavoured to effect as a poet, Kean endeavoured to effect as an actor. "He sought to wield
the power of Mephistopheles over the scenes and
passions of human life and society," disclosing their
hidden machinery, stripping them of all conventional
allurements and disguises, and laying bare the pri-
mary anatomy of the soul. Holding the mirror up
to nature thus, and exhibiting a richness, warmth,
and sensibility which arose exclusively from an implicit obedience to the dictates of truth, the treasure of
the characters which he embodied with such noble completeness became thoroughly manifest; whereas had
he suffered his characteristic independence of thought
to be restricted and cabined by a regard for the decorous appetites of antiquated dowagers and brain-
less fops, his discrimination and judgment would
have been impugned but too fatally by the intellectual
and right thinking, and his genius reduced to a level
which could raise no claim to an honourable and permanent reputation.

Fortunately, no such opportunity of destroying his
reputation occurred ; and to the powerful ebullitions

of passion and sweeping vigour in his Sir Giles Overreach, which so rudely shocked the delicate sensibilities of the upper circles, the final collapse of the
Kemble school is to be ascribed. For the last two
years the cold antique had struggled with natural
truth for the mastery, but without success; art could
no longer impose upon the mind—the testimony of
common sense became too strong, too cogent to allow
any one to indulge in such extravagance of fiction.
Quodcunque ostendis mihi sic, incredulus odi. In Kean's
Sir Giles Overreach the very soul of acting was to be
found ;—the abandonment to the unpremeditated impulse of the situation, the leaving precision to shift
for itself, and the reliance upon genius and an instinctive sense of power to rescue him from all disadvantage. This genuineness—the very life-blood of
dramatic art—enabled him to gain one of the most
remarkable victories that the annals of the stage can
instance. John Kemble, as if to challenge comparison
with Kean in the character, appeared as Sir Giles
Overreach ; the audience at first marked their sense of
the ill-advisedness of the attempt by maintaining a
cold silence ; they could not place good acting in a monotony however dignified, or in a feebleness of muscular expression, however disguised ; they thought of

Kean—of the lightning which flashed from *all* corners of his mind and face, and of the thunder which followed such flashes, and such only; and the comparison was so fatal to the older actor that it provoked a circular discharge of hisses from the back of the pit. Kemble's friends endeavoured to counteract the mortifying sibilation, but the hisses came "full volley home." The actor felt it deeply, and as he went off the stage murmured "It is time that I should retire." He there and then expressed his determination to withdraw from the stage at the close of the following season.

" We never saw signs of greater poverty, greater imbecility and decrepitude in Mr. Kemble, or in any other actor: it was Sir Giles in his dotage. It was all ' Well, well,' and ' If you like it, have it so,' an indifference and disdain of what was to happen, a nicety about his means, a coldness as to his ends, much gentility and little nature. Was this Sir Giles Overreach? Nothing could be more quaint and out-of-the-way. Mr. Kemble wanted the part to come to him, for he would not go out of his way to the part. He is, in fact, as shy of committing himself with nature as a maid is of committing herself with a lover. All the proper forms and ceremonies must be dispensed with before ' they two can be made one flesh.' Mr. Kemble sacrifices too much to decorum. He is chiefly afraid of being contaminated by too close an identity with the character he represents. This is the greatest vice in an actor, who ought never to *bilk* his part. He endeavours to raise nature to the dignity of his own person and demeanour, and declines with a graceful smile and a wave of the hand the ordinary services she might do him. We would advise him by all means to shake hands, to hug her close and be friends, if we did not suspect it was too late—that the lady, owing to this coyness, had eloped, and is now in the situation of Dame Hellenore among the Satyrs.

" The outrageousness of the conduct of Sir Giles is only to be excused by the violence of his passions and the turbulence of the character. Mr. Kemble inverted this conception, and attempted to reconcile the character by softening down the action. He aggravated the part so that he would seem like any sucking dove. For example, nothing could exceed the coolness and *sang froid* with which he raps Marall on the head with his cane, or spits at Lord Lovell: Lord Foppington himself never did any common-place indecency more insipidly. The only passage that pleased us, or that really called forth the

powers of the actor, was his reproach to Justice
Greedy :—'There is some fury in the *gut.*' The indignity of the word called up all the dignity of the
actor to meet it, and he guaranteed the word, though
'a word of naught,' according to the letter and spirit
of the convention between them, with a good grace,
in the true old English way. Either we mistake all
Mr. Kemble's excellences or they all disqualify him
for this part. Sir Giles *hath a devil;* Mr. Kemble
has none. Sir Giles is in a passion; Mr. Kemble is
not. Sir Giles has no regard for appearances; Mr.
Kemble has. It has been said of the Venus de
Medicis, 'so stands the statue that enchants the
world;' the same might have been said of Mr.
Kemble. He is the very still life and statuary of the
stage; a perfect figure of a man; a petrifaction of
sentiment that heaves no sigh and sheds no tear; an
icicle on the bust of Tragedy. With all his faults,
he has powers and faculties which no one else on the
stage has; why, then, does he not avail himself of
them, instead of throwing himself upon the charity
of criticism? Mr. Kemble has given the public great,
incalculable pleasure; and does he know so little of
the gratitude of the world as to trust to its generosity?"—*Examiner.*

Crowned as Massinger had been of late by the masterly efforts of one who might have boasted with Warwick that " he had made his favourite reign," his repute as an effective and original dramatist was extended by the production on the 8th of March of the tragedy of the *Duke of Milan.*   The character of Sforza, which was represented by Kean, is by no means so grand, so broad, and so resistless as that of Sir Giles.   Its predominant characteristic is an inherent selfishness ; obedient to impulse, the creature of circumstances, Sforza acknowledges no other principle than his own imperious will, no better object than the unlimited indulgence of his own pleasures. His breach of faith to Eugenia, his cruel love for Marcelia, and his determination to destroy the latter rather than that she should survive him, are all illustrative of the disposition referred to.   Kean's performance of the Duke was pregnant with all the interest of which the character is susceptible ; but "it is too much at cross purposes with itself, and before the actor has time to give full effect to any impulse of passion, it is interrupted and broken off by some caprice and change of object."   The affectionate softness which pervaded his first scene with Marcelia ; the exquisite beauty of his acting

when, in turning towards his wife with a perfect
expression of mingled love and sadness, he beautifully
relieved his despondency by the sparklings and flashes
of tenderness which broke over his features and eyes;
his first intimation to Francisco of his dark purpose—
his exclamation, " I am not jealous;" the fine effect
given to the passage, " Silence that harsh music,"
through the contrast displayed between the mournful
melody of his voice and the pretty air which made
itself heard from behind the scenes; the depth of
feeling in his acting where, enumerating the excellences of Marcelia, he gave the lines beginning
" Add, too, her goodness;" his watching over her
dead body when he thought she was but sleeping,
and his rapid transition in the words " I am hushed!"
—these may be selected from the rich profusion of
gems which he scattered over the representation.
The death of the duke was provided for in a manner
altogether at variance with, and inferior to, the
original arrangement.

With the production of the *Duke of Milan*, Kean's
endeavours to redeem the works of Massinger from
the obscurity in which they had hitherto been allowed
to remain, terminated. Other plays suggested themselves to him for revival, but he desisted from the

undertaking, feeling sure that in *A New Way to Pay Old Debts* he had opened to view the fruitful mine which Massinger's plays afford.   In the meantime an interesting comedy was enacted by the actor in private life.   On the morning of the 26th of March he was passing through Deptford when he recognised in a pale, attenuated individual standing at one of the tavern doors a fiddler named Smith, whom he had known in the country.   The recognition was mutual, and Kean, happy to meet one of his old associates, took the fiddler into the tavern, regaled him to an immoderate extent, promised him that he should be speedily installed in the orchestra of Drury-lane Theatre, and finally gave him a purse of money.   The unfortunate man, exhilarated by so sudden and un-expected a brightening of his prospects, became fear-fully intoxicated, and on the way home got drowned in the Thames near Southwark Bridge.   Unaware of the melancholy fate of his *protégé*, the tragedian sat down to dinner with some boon companions of his early days.   He was announced to appear in the *Duke of Milan* that evening, and had set out from Clarges-street with every intention of returning to fulfil his duties.   In the excitement of the bottle, however, he forgot all about Massinger, Sforza, and

the duties they entailed upon him, and—overstayed
his time. His friends, convinced that it would be
impossible for him to reach Drury-lane in time for
the performance, despatched his servant and the
empty chariot with an elaborately prepared tale to
the effect that, while returning at a very quick pace
to London, the horses had taken fright by the
cackling of some geese in the roadway; that the carriage had overturned; and that the unfortunate tragedian, thrown with considerable violence from the
vehicle, had sustained a dislocation of the shoulder.
The story was repeated from the stage by Rae, who
came forward

> " With rueful face,
> Long as a courtier's out of place,
> Portending some disaster."

The audience, who had negatived the substitution of
Douglas for *The Duke of Milan*, suffering the entertainment to begin with a farce in hopes that the
absentee might yet turn up, were filled with alarm;
and their rising dissatisfaction immediately gave
place to regretful sympathy when they learnt that
the tragedian had been very much stunned and
bruised "through his anxiety to keep his engagement
at the theatre." On the following morning Kean's

embarrassment on finding the equivocal position in which he stood was scarcely alleviated when an attendant entered his room to inform him that several gentlemen had arrived to see him. "Who are they?" "Lord Byron, Sir Francis Burdett, and Mr. Kinnaird," was the reply. The tragedian, filled with consternation, jumped out of bed, and there, sure enough, in front of the house waited the carriages of the distinguished individuals referred to. What was to be done? Mr. Horn came to the rescue, and prevailed upon the tragedian to suffer his face to be whitened, and his arm bandaged and placed in a sling. He was then placed in bed, the room darkened, and a neighbouring apothecary bribed to countenance the hoax. The disciple of Esculapius played his part inimitably well. "Mr. Kean," he said to the visitors as they were admitted, "has sustained a great shaking, and any excitement must be avoided." The commiserating trio condoled, well wished, and departed. To Mr. Horn was entrusted the task of breaking the melancholy news to Mrs. Kean. The latter, to the unutterable dismay of the informant, immediately announced her intention to go to her husband. Mr. Horn pleaded in vain; the lady's resolution was not to be shaken; and accompanied by a clergyman and Mr. Anthony White, surgeon, of Parliament-street, she proceeded to Deptford. They sought out his chamber, and there, ghastly, moaning, and stretched at full length on the pallet, was Mr. Edmund Kean, of the Theatre Royal, Drury-lane. After the patient had replied to his wife's anxious inquiries with laconic evasiveness, he was tenderly carried from the bed to his carriage, and there propped up with pillows in order that his dislocated arm might not be injured by the jolting of the conveyance. In this manner the journey from Deptford to Clarges-street was performed. Arrived home, he was deposited in his arm-chair, and advised to go to bed without loss of time. Mrs. Kean was in the act of tenderly relieving him of his coat, when the garment flew off " as if by magic," and the injured arm flourished about in all directions. The wife, with mingled alarm and incredulity, stared at him with all her might. The comedian, as we are told, then gave way to the man. " Are you really not hurt?" " Not a bit," he replied, bursting into a hearty laugh; and removing a formidable and pretentious-looking plaster from his shoulder, the Deptford tragedy, comedy, farce, or whatever the reader may please to call it, terminated.

A certain grave morning paper was pleased to be facetious on this accident. It observed that this was a very *serious* accident; that actors in general were liable to *serious* accidents; that the late Mr. Cooke used to meet with *serious* accidents; that it was a sad thing to be in the way of such accidents; and that it was to be hoped that Mr. Kean would meet with no more *serious* accidents. This ill-timed pleasantry called forth an indignant defence by Hazlitt, who, after expressing a sincere hope that Mr. Kean would not meet with any more serious accidents, and that the public would not be treated with any such profound observations upon them if they should happen, characterized it as an instance of that "hateful cant of criticism which slurs over an actor's character with a half-witted jest, and only to be equalled by that spirit of bigotry which in a neighbouring country would deny them Christian burial after death !"

Kean reappeared on the 1st of April in Shylock; determined, for the sake of "my reputation," to lose no opportunity of convincing the world that he really had suffered from the effects of an "accident," he chose the character, as it required, he said, less bodily exertion than his others. When he appeared, the welcoming applause was not altogether unqualified with signs of disapprobation. He immediately advanced to the front, and addressed himself personally to a London audience for the first time :—" Ladies and gentlemen,—For the first time in my life I have disappointed the expectations of a London audience; for the first time in this theatre, out of 269 nights, as the public will acknowledge and the managers will attest. To your favour I am indebted for the reputation which I enjoy, and I throw myself on your candour as a shield against unworthy prejudices." This neat and short apology at once turned the scales entirely in his favour. It would have been unjust had the reception been otherwise; and if certain beadles and whippers-in of morality take exception to what they term a piece of " hypocrisy," let them also recollect, that when a reputation stood in danger of being damaged it was not time to be particular as to the means of preserving it in its pristine completeness, especially when the means adopted were not amenable to any grave censure. Moreover, it was no disinclination to play that caused him to disappoint the audience on the night of the 26th of March. It was a fact characteristic of the man that his exertions in his profession had been unremitted and indefatigable; that he had never missed a single rehearsal, and had always been ready to go on for his part at the appointed time.

On the 9th of May the world witnessed the rare phenomenon of a new and successful tragedy in the celebrated *Bertram* of Maturin. This play had been submitted to the committee some time before, and was on the point of being rejected when Byron's intuitive perception of poetic beauty saved the world from the deprivation of a rare source of intellectual enjoyment, the subject of these memoirs a permanent and legitimate success, and the author of the *House of Montorio* one of the firmest pillars of his reputation. Kean no sooner read the play than he expressed an ardent wish to appear in the principal character, and the address of the author having been discovered (he had sent in the tragedy without it), the noble bard sent him a favourable answer, together with something more substantial. In rescuing this play from impending oblivion Byron's conduct was marked by the same unvarying susceptibility to the claims of the beautiful which distinguished him during the time he held a membership of the Drury-lane Committee. Exerting every endeavour to restore the legitimate drama, he attempted to effect the revival of Joanna Baillie's *De Montfort* and Sotheby's *Ivan,*

but in vain—Kean emphatically refused to appear in
the latter; he also tried to wake Coleridge to write
a tragedy, but Samuel Taylor seemed perfectly content to rest his reputation as a dramatic poet on his
fine tragedy of *Remorse,* produced at Drury-lane towards the close of 1813.   Even the latter, replete as
it is with the author's finest poetry and wildest
imagination, united to a romantic plot which commands unwearied interest, shared the same fate—the
shelf; Proctor, Haynes, and Knowles had not yet
appeared in the field; and as tragedy sank, melodrama, hitherto all but unknown, rose in the estimation of the public, who, deprived of a legitimate
source of attraction by the indecisive and non-enter-
prising Committee, were not slow to hail the advent
of a class of entertainment which, from its realistic
action and adventitious colouring, was calculated to
create a marked impression in the absence of any
counteractive element in the tragic department.
Melodrama thus took its first root in the histrionic
soil; modern tragedy was manifestly at a low ebb;
intellectual vigour was wanting to retrieve the losses
it had sustained; and precisely at the right moment
Charles Robert Maturin stepped in with his tragedy
of *Bertram.*

The plot of this play, without anything of peculiar complication and diversity, was obviously one which gave room for much delicate development of character and dexterity of authorship. The author availed himself of the latter opportunity with so much licence that a number of essential requisites of an acting play were sacrificed to the pursuit of literary excellence, and the beauties of *Bertram* are consequently rather "those of language and sentiment than action or situation." The interest frequently flagged; the character, however delicately delineated, is not free from the charge of superfluity; there was an imperfect adjustment of cause and effect; but *Bertram* achieved a complete and well-merited success. The plot was constructed on the German model, and several characteristics of the Kotzebue school were imported into the play with equivocal results; but *Bertram* is not amenable to the objections which a regard for moral influences must ever make to the *Stranger* and *Pizarro*. Immediately prior to that fine passage where Bertram is represented as spurred to the commission of his crimes by the direct agency of a supernatural and malevolent being, the author had in the first instance introduced Satan on the stage in order to render his intention more intelligible to the

audience ; but this return to the characteristics of the
early miracle plays of the Elizabethan period would have
proved by no means suitable to the tastes of modern
playgoers, and Byron removed the arch-fiend from the
scene without injury to the play, or causing any
mystification as to the influences which governed the
destiny of Bertram. Hazlitt quoted several passages
as specimens of very beautiful and affecting writing,
and Sir Walter Scott eulogizes the tragedy as grand
and powerful in the highest degree, the language as
full of animation and poetry, and the characters
sketched with a masterly enthusiasm. By the publication and performance of *Bertram* the author realized
upwards of 1000*l*.

The success which Kean achieved in the character of
the outlawed count was not ephemeral, for in addition
to it forming one of the most attractive features in
his repertoire, his name is exclusively associated with
the part. He has never been "doubled" in it, and
he was, to employ an Italian phrase, the "creator" of
the character. Although he had entered upon the
study of Bertram *con amore*, he never entertained a
very high opinion of it. "It does very well for relief
from Othello, Richard, and Sir Giles," he remarked
on one occasion ; "it is 'all sound and fury, signifying

nothing.'"   But there were portions of his performance which could raise no appeal to a superior
excellence.   His acting was absolutely sublime when,
as the unconscious penitent, he raised his fervent eye
upwards in prayer.   I have heard the transition
spoken of as beautiful, when, roused by the Prior, his
features resumed their cherished ferocity, and despair
shook off the pious tear that glistened on his cadave-
rous cheek.   Revenge flooded from his soul with
fiend-like gall—here he realized " the champion of
guilty desperation."   His scene with Imogine in the
solitary walk, and his dreadful curse when he discovered that she was the wife of Aldobrand, were
worked up with wonderful force of genius and intensity of passion; but all was surpassed, even his
noble delivery of the speech, "The wretched have no
country," by the unspeakable tenderness and feeling
with which he pronounced the blessing upon the
child.   He had determined to avenge his wrongs by
killing it, but its innocent helplessness caused his
resolution to fail him, and he caught it up in his arms,
and gazed intently upon its face, and broke into the
affecting prayer, delivered with such exquisite pathos
that many and many a tearful eye bore witness to his
power, " God bless the child!"   That power and

pathos had been acquired at home through having repeated the words over and over again as he looked upon his sleeping boy Charles; and we must agree with Dr. Doran that "a prettier incident in the life of this impulsive actor is not to be found."

But to Sir Giles and Bertram were not confined Kean's triumphs in this memorable season. He appeared as Kitely on the 5th of June, and immediately showed that in this character he had nothing in the shape of a rival on the stage. The excellence of *Every Man in His Humour*, upon which the reputation of rare Ben Jonson almost exclusively yet firmly relies, consists not so much in any natural or ingenious construction of the plot as in the vigour of its language and its accurate portraiture of contemporary character. The fatuitous jealousy which arises in the diseased mind of Kitely is of so incongruous and contradictory a character, that, constituting as it does the master-key which governs the incidents of the play, the effect of the general management is to a certain extent destroyed; the secondary parts — Brainworm, Bobadil, Matthew, Stephen—each of which approaches a complete delineation of character, neither assist in the development of the story nor correct the impotence of the principal personage; and the pathos pertaining to Kitely is, to quote an opinion expressed in *A View of the English Stage*, " as dry as the remainder biscuit after a voyage." On the other hand, there is a certain logic of passion and knowledge of human nature expended on the delineation of the character which offer peculiar advantages for representation ; and when freed from the obsolete terms and quaint phraseology of the Elizabethan age, the play will be found to act much better than it reads. Kean's delineation of Kitely was very fine. From all other representatives of the part he stands out in bold relief. He literally verified the remark made by Garrick in the prologue to his revival of the comedy during his management of Drury-lane:

" Nature was nature then—and still survives,
    The garb may alter, but the substance lives."

All the peculiar and diversified features of the character were represented with a force and feeling which entitle Kitely to rank with his happiest efforts in comedy. The waverings, suspicions, and various transitions of his jealousy in its less turbid and destructive state were depictured with inimitable skill, and in the scene with Cash, where Kitely would fain disclose his secret to the steward, but fearful lest his confidence should be betrayed, his interpretation of the workings and perturbations of jealousy comprehended a finished picture of emotions varying with fears and hesitations, and the alternate revival and extinction of confidence and apprehension. His agitation in the fourth act was very forcibly depicted. "The reconciliation scene with his wife," writes Hazlitt, "had great spirit where he told her, to show his confidence, that 'she may sing, may go to balls, may dance,' and the interruption to this sudden tide of concession with the restriction—'though I had rather you did not do all this'—was a master stroke. It was perhaps the first time a parenthesis was ever spoken on the stage as it ought to be. Mr. Kean certainly often repeats this artifice of abrupt transition in the tones in which he expresses different passions, and still it always pleases,—we suppose because it is natural. This gentleman is not only a fine actor in himself, but he is the cause of good acting in others. The whole play was got up very effectively."

Kean, curiously enough, never considered his Kitely a successful performance. There was nothing in his delineation which justified the poor opinion he entertained of his efficiency in the character; but from some misapprehension or another he thought otherwise, and everything failed to remove his conviction that he was, to use his own words, "a damned bad Kitely."

One of his finest rebukes of servile sycophancy, preserved by Mr. Leman Rede, is associated with his appearance in this character. He was told on one occasion by some fawning flatterers that his Kitely was
one of the greatest things in nature; that Robert
Palmer had adjudged it superior to Garrick's; and
that all shortcomings were due to the fact that Ben
Jonson had in *Every Man in His Humour* sacrificed
passion to a portraiture of contemporary character.
Kean arose; his eyes quivered with a peculiar nervous
excitement; and, patting his son Charles on the head
(the incident occurred in his drawing·room at Clarges-
street) he muttered—

> " They flattered me like a dog;
> They told me I was everything;
> 'Tis false : I am not Kitely proof."

At this time Miss O'Neill resided in an opposite
house. Since her first appearance at Covent-garden
in October, 1814, she had made rapid progress in
public favour; her Belvidera, Isabella, Elwina,
Monimia, Calista, and Mrs. Haller were in the first
order of histrionic superiority ; her Lady Teazle and
Widow Cheerly were decided and unequivocal failures.
She is to delight the playgoing public but three years
longer, for in 1819 she will become Lady Beecher,

and retire from the stage without any formal leave-
taking.   On the morning subsequent to her unsuccessful impersonation of the Widow Cheerly, she
passed down Clarges-street with a very dejected air.
This was remarked to Kean, who, with what Mr.
Leman Rede describes as "a quaintness that was
really irresistible," replied, "Ay, poor soul, she can't
play Kitely."

The Drury-lane Committee, adopting a suggestion
made by Oxberry, resolved to mark their sense of
Kean's matchless power in Sir Giles Overreach by
presenting him with a cup, modelled after the celebrated Warwick Vase, and at a cost of three hundred
guineas.   With the exception of Munden and Dowton,
every member of the Drury-lane Committee subscribed
to the testimonial.   The former, with his characteristic parsimony, excused his subscription; and
Dowton, who was still smarting under the ridicule
heaped upon him for having attempted to divide the
honours with Kean in Shylock, replied to Oxberry's
application with the savage sneer, "You can *cup* Mr.
Kean if you like, but you don't *bleed* me.   Joe
Munden deserves the testimonial more, for his
Marall."   This opinion was, however, limited to Mr.
Dowton, who did not succeed in prevailing over any

one to coincide in his views; and on the 25th of June, a brilliant assemblage thronged the green-room to witness the presentation. The cup bore the following inscription:—

TO

EDMUND KEAN,

This Vase was presented on the 25th day of June, 1816,

by

ROBERT PALMER,

Father of the Drury-lane Company,
in the names of

Right Hon. Lord Byron, Hon. Douglas Kinnaird, Right Hon. George Lamb,
Chandos Leigh, Esq., S. Davies, Esq.,

Alex. Pope,	J. S. Smith,	J. Smith,	R. Peak,
Alex. Rae,	H. Coveney,	J. Wallack,	R. Wewitzer,
Benj. Wyatt,	H. Burgess,	Miss A. Smith,	S. Penley, jun.,
Mrs. Brereton,	H. Smart,	Miss C. Tidswell,	S. Spring,
Mrs. Billington,	J. Braham,	Mrs. Orger,	S. V. Elrington,
Mrs. Bland,	J. Byrne,	Mrs. Mardyn,	T. Dibdin,
Ch. W. Ward,	T. Cook,	Mrs. M. Horn,	T. Greenwood,
Edw. Knight,	J. Hughes,	Miss S. Boyce,	W. Dunn,
Edw. Warren,	J. Kent,	Miss Poole,	W. Linley,
Miss F. M. Kelly,	J. P. Barnard,	Mrs. Sparks,	W. Maddocks,
Miss L. Kelly,	J. P. Harley,	Mad. Storace,	W. Oxberry,
J. Price,	J. Powell,	J. Whittaker,	W. Penley, sen.,
J. Rorauer,	J. Pyne,	R. Chatterley,	R. Palmer,

In testimony of their admiration of his transcendant talents,
and more especially to commemorate
his first representation of the character of

Sir Giles Overreach,

On the 12th of January, 1816,

When, in common with an astonished public, overcome with the irresistible power of his genius, they received a lasting impression of excellence which 26 successive representations have served but to confirm.

Above were heads of Shakspeare and Massinger, and the masques of Tragedy and Comedy.   To the former was attached—

> " Out of his self-drawing web he gives us note,
>   The force of his own merit makes its way ;"

and to the latter—

> " But to speak the least part to the height
>   Would ask an angel's tongue, and yet then end
>   In silent admiration."

Beneath the masques of Melpomene and Thalia appeared—

> " All the world's a stage."

The inscription and the names of the subscribers were engraved on the lower part of the vase and on its pedestal.

Mr. Robert Palmer presented Kean with the vase in a few brief and appropriate words, and the tragedian replied in the following terms :—" If ever I lamented a want of eloquence it is on the present occasion, when I feel how incapable I am to reply to my friends in the glowing and brilliant language they have used.   I cannot but lament my deficiency, and express my pleasurable feelings in the dictates of my heart.   Gentlemen, it is not hyperbole when I declare that this moment is the proudest of my existence.

In public favour there has been, there is, there will
be, those that hold an equal, perhaps superior, share ;
but the superiority I have gained in the attachment
of my brother professionals I will resign to no one.
It has ever been my study to maintain their good
opinion, and this token of regard I proudly conceive
a testimony of the success of my endeavours. As
true feeling I consider can be expressed in a few
words, I shall endeavour to be as brief as possible ;
but I must be deemed insensible if I did not express
how fully I appreciate the honour conferred on me in
the presence now, and past attentions of, Mr. Robert
Palmer, the father of the stage. A certain prejudice
generally exists in favour of early impressions, particularly with the veteran who can remember the old and
acknowledged superior school; the respect they owe
the memories of a Garrick, a Barry, and a Henderson
makes them consider them always alive and present;
consequently I must say, the approbation of a man
who has trod the boards with those whose fame must
live for ever is the *ne plus ultra* of dramatic com-
mendation. Still, I say, I should receive this truly
valuable donation with diffidence did not my heart
whisper me that my professional success but gratifies
me so far as it procures me the means of serving

those who may not be equally fortunate; nor can envy, however violent against me, confute a bold asseveration, *exulto non mutando*. I conclude, gentlemen, by offering you individually and all my sincere thanks; assuring you that it shall always be my study to preserve your good wishes, and that the remembrance of this hour is indelibly engraven on my heart."

On the following day he concluded his third season with Bertram. He proceeded immediately to Bath, where he appeared on the 29th as Richard. Subsequently he played Sir Giles, Hamlet, Othello, Luke, and Abel Drugger, being received on each occasion with enthusiasm. "When Kean was carried off in the last scene of the play," Geneste, speaking of Kean's second performance of Sir Giles in Bath, writes, "the audience called out for the curtain to fall, and the piece was accordingly terminated there and then, which was the more improper, as on the 2nd of July, Stanley (Wellborn) had spoken the last speech particularly well." From Bath Kean proceeded to Edinburgh, where the natural truth and originality of his style provoked some animated controversies respecting his superiority to his predecessors. Here is the *Edinburgh Courant* criticism upon

his Richard, Shylock, and Sir Giles.   After some
introductory remarks, the writer proceeds :—

"Similar causes seem to have produced the same
effects upon Mr. Kean's reception here.   The school
of Kemble, meaning by that phrase the school of
grandeur, grace, and elegance—not certainly at variance with natural emotions, but always connected
with and accompanying them—had not only formed
a numerous and highly-gifted race of pupils, but had
also contributed to give a certain tone to popular taste
and criticism.   Upon the soundness or rectitude of
this taste, we do not presume to decide; but, in so far
as it operated at all, it must have operated against
Mr. Kean, whose powers are all of the grandest moral
and intellectual nature, but whose person and deportment have no manner of alliance with external grace
or dignity.   During the greater part of the first three
acts, accordingly, the prevailing feeling of the audience, if we may judge from the calmness of their
attention, seemed to be that of disappointment: and
it was not till Richard had cast off the serpent's skin,
and assumed the tone and bearing of the hero, that
the spectators were aroused to the full perception of
his excellence.   It was here that, like his illustrious
predecessor, he bore down and triumphed over every

feeling of doubt or hesitation. The fire and rapidity of his action—the quickness of his transition from passion to passion—the whirling atmosphere of bustle and exertion in which he involved himself—made every spectator's heart beat and leap with his own; and when, at the catastrophe, losing his sword, and dumb with rage and despair, he made impotent thrusts with his disarmed and failing hand at his adversary, the emotions excited by this new and hazardous experiment burst forth in torrents of admiration. The energy of the soul, recovering for a few moments the exhaustion of its mortal companion, was displayed in gestures of increasing fury and revenge; till, at length, the rageful spirit sunk in the conflict. The glare of malice, which fastened upon his adversary while one atom of consciousness remained, had an effect most deeply terrific, and here the feelings of the audience found vent in the loudest exclamations of delight.

" The greatest defect of Mr. Kean is unquestionably his voice, yet this must be explained ; for no proposition was ever farther from truth, than that Mr. Kean has a bad voice : it is, strictly and accurately speaking, merely defective. When limited to level discourse, or displayed in the tones of persuasion, entreaty, or love, it is eminently beautiful and melodious; but being defective in power, and singularly confined in extent, it is a most inadequate crater for those bursting turbillions of passion which often rend his mortal machine. Yet such is the resistless fire and brilliancy of his action, so true, so vigorous, and original his conception, so rapid and so decisive the flashes of his eye, that the soul is hurried along almost without the agency of the ear; and the same storm of passion which almost robs the actor of the power of speech, absorbs the auditor in a conflict of emotions which render him insensible of his loss.

" Admirable as his delineation of Richard was, his Shylock, which was exhibited on Tuesday evening, struck us as being a still more masterly display of genius. Of the representatives of Shylock belonging to the present day Cooke approached nearest, till now, to that mental image which every reader forms for himself of the stubborn and savage Jew; but there is not one feature of the character, as represented by Kean, besides its infinitely stronger impression of general truth, in which the delineation of Cooke does not fall short of his successor. The colouring of Cooke was always just and always strong; but it was also coarse and broad and general. That of Kean, on the

contrary, while it is equally true, and yet more powerful, is various, changeful, multiplied in its tints, now
deepening, now mellowing, exhibiting, by fitful and
shifting glances, every shade and nicety of hue that
belongs to the actual painting of nature. This infinite
variety is one of the strongest charms, as well as one
of the highest distinctions, of this remarkable man's
art; and, in this power, we question whether he has
ever been equalled but by Garrick, whom we should
suppose him strongly to resemble.

"But both these representations fall far short of
the delineation of Sir Giles Overreach, which was
given to us last night. It was in this tremendous
display of the blackest and most savage workings of
the soul that the splendour of Mr. Kean's genius
shone forth, out-dazzling competition, and baffling
every attempt at rivalry; and it is here that we are
forced to relinquish even the effort to give any idea
of his excellence, for while the language that aimed
to describe it adequately would perhaps be charged
with exaggeration, it would fall far below the truth.
We really have not the courage to cope with the attempt. It is a hideous character, and Kean aggra-
vates every frightful lineament belonging to it. In
the catastrophe, where all the pride and malice of the

fiend are lapsed in the unmitigated bitterness of his
rage and despair, he seemed to borrow his colouring
from the nether world—so frenzied and demoniacal
were his ravings, so much more appalling was the
terror of his silence.   The acmé of his frightful sufferings struck the ghastliness of dismay through the
house.   It will be recollected that his last words
are—

> " ——Shall I thus fall
> Ingloriously, and yield ?   No : spite of fate,
> I will be forced to hell like to myself ;
> Though you were legions of accursed spirits,
> Thus would I fly among you !"

" In delivering these words, Kean attempts to draw
his sword, and rushes madly among his enemies ; but
he has miscalculated the strength which his temporary
energy had given him, and falls exhausted and insensible on the ground.   Recovering from their amazement and horror, the by-standers order him to be
carried off, and his servants accordingly betake themselves to the performance of that office.   At the
moment when they are bearing him away, his senses
slowly return—he slowly recovers his recollection,
and with it all the demoniac fury of his remorseless
nature.   Its expression is confined, however, to his
countenance, for every limb is chained up in impotence.

His eyes kindle with renewed rancour, and he seems on the point of springing upon his victims; but at this moment of horrible interest, when fate and vengeance are glaring in his eyes, his physical powers utterly and at once forsake him, and his head drops lifeless on his chest. He is carried off.

"The applause of the house here broke out into shouts and hurrahs. They were too highly wrought to bear more, and the curtain was ordered to fall, leaving the play unfinished. Mr. Kean's triumph was complete."

Kean was now to lose one of his very best friends. Lord Byron, separated from his wife, loaded with newspaper abuse, and filled with a bitter antipathy to English society, departed for the continent—

"Once more upon the waters, yet once more!"

We have already seen how the friendship which arose between the poet and Edmund was strengthened by the similitude in one sense of their early culture; how great was the admiration which his lordship entertained for Kean's brilliant talents; how manifest was the interest which he took in the endeavour to maintain the tragedian in that rank of society to which his genius had raised him; and how he showed that his regard for the man was altogether independent of his high estimation of the actor. In one respect they exhibited a decided contrast. The one was the brilliant poet of *Childe Harold*, moving in polished circles with inimitable ease and grace; the other was the unapproachable expositor of Shakspeare, rough and unrefined in his manner, and finding no congenial element in the smokeless atmosphere of St. James's. To this he preferred the unhealthy odours of the Antelope in White Horse-yard, and the Coal Hole in Fountain-court; and it was in vain that his lordship attempted to convince him that his celebrity required him to reject these lowly associations, and to mingle exclusively with rank, wealth, and refinement. Kean was obdurate and unpersuasible; and we now arrive at an incident which strongly illustrates his unalterable devotion to his humbler friends, and his utter contempt for those classes of society in which ceremony and etiquette were religiously observed.

The "evenings at the Kinnairds'" are familiar to every reader of Moore's *Life of Byron.* "Not the least agreeable," writes the poet-biographer, "were those evenings we passed together at the house of his banker, Mr. Douglas Kinnaird, where music, followed by its accustomed sequel of supper, brandy-and-water, and not a little laughter, kept us together usually till rather a late hour." There it was that his lordship displayed a perfect familiarity with the annals of the prize-ring, and his thorough initiation into "the most recondite phraseology of *the fancy ;*" there it was, as he himself informs us above, that the author of the charming *Irish Melodies* passed away an evening or two in an agreeable manner ; and there it was that the little, restless, Italian-faced, brilliant-eyed man who exercised such a magical influence over the sensibilities of crowded audiences in Drury-lane Theatre occasionally put in an appearance. With music, supper, brandy-and-water, not a little laughter, and with such a *bon vivant* as Lord Byron, Kean was very far from not being "at home ;" but when studied gentility and refinement invaded the room, he was rendered uncomfortable. It was here that, one evening in 1815, a dinner was given to Lord Kinnaird on his return from Greece, and amongst the many distinguished individuals invited to be present was Mr. Kean. Now it so happened that the night in question had been long since set apart for a meeting of Incledon's friends at Cribbs's in Panton-street, Haymarket, over which Kean, out of respect to his old friend, had promised to preside; and the actor, in whose eyes the Kinnaird supper was absolutely charmless aside of the fondly-anticipated carouse at Cribbs's, pleaded to his lordship a previous engagement. The noble bard, however, was peremptory in his refusal to accept any excuse; and at the time when the company at Cribbs's were anxiously awaiting his appearance, Kean, who had not informed his lordship what the "previous engagement" was, sat upon thorns at the Kinnairds'. The dinner proceeded in the most stately and ceremonious manner; Kean was fidgety, evasive, and evidently ill at ease; the dinner concluded, the cloth was removed, and—the great tragedian's chair was found to be empty. No one had noticed him leave; and upon inquiry it transpired that his carriage had been ordered directly after dinner. His lordship whispered something in the ear of Douglas Kinnaird, who replied by a nod of intelligence; and having begged to be excused for a short time, they sallied forth in search of the incorrigible runaway. The two friends went to the Coal Hole and several other favourite resorts of the actor, but of course without succeeding in finding him; and, as a sort of forlorn hope, they determined to try Cribbs's celebrated house in Panton-street. To

Cribbs's they accordingly proceeded, and came upon the absentee at the moment when, surrounded by an approving and uproarious group, he was raising a goblet to his lips, and damning lords with all the vigour of a " good hater." His lordship felt this apparent slight of himself so severely that he held aloof from Kean for some time, nor was it until he saw the tragedian's Sir Giles Overreach that his resentment disappeared. As Edmund was carried off the stage in the last scene, he felt once more the pressure of Byron's friendly grasp as the noble bard exclaimed, " Great! great! By Jove, that *was* acting. But, hang it, you should not have treated me so scurvily by running off from the Kinnairds' to such a place as Cribbs's." Kean explained to the poet his early obligations to Incledon, and his lordship pardoned the offence when he learnt the motives by which the other had been influenced. On the following day he sent to him a valuable Damascus blade in token of their reconciliation.

This was not the only occasion on which the steadfastness and sincerity of Kean's friendship for Incledon were subjected to a very decisive test. One morning he received a note from the Earl of Essex, who had ever manifested an active interest in his welfare, requesting him to favour his lordship with a call at his earliest convenience. On entering his lordship's library, the Earl, after a few preliminary observations, said, " It is scarcely necessary for me to say that I am an earnest admirer of your great talents, and that I esteem you highly. Now from the distinction which those talents have acquired for you, and from your reception in the highest circles, I am sure you must feel how anxious I and all your friends are that you should maintain that position in society to which your merits have elevated you ; but I have just heard with much concern a circumstance which will interfere with all our intentions and views in this respect, and I have sent for you in the hope that you will enable me to give an immediate contradiction to the report, which is, that you have been seen walking in Bond-street arm-in-arm with Mr. Incledon. Now although Mr. Incledon enjoyed considerable celebrity as a vocalist, yet as he never did belong to our set, and as his popularity is now quite *passée*, it is a duty which I conceive I owe to you as well as to myself and our friends, to say that your continued intimacy with him may militate against your own reception in the circles in which you have hitherto been a most welcome guest." Maginn, who related the anecdote in *Fraser's Magazine*, states that Kean's reply was as prompt as it was ingenuous and manly. "My lord, Mr. Incledon was my friend in the strictest sense of the word when I had scarcely another friend in the world; and if I should now desert him in the decline of his popularity or the fall of his fortunes, I should little deserve the friendship of any man, and be quite unworthy of the favourable opinion your lordship has done me the honour to entertain for me." And so saying he rose from his seat, and, making a profound bow to the earl, left the room.

With this inveterate hatred of "lords," there was not a little pardonable pride mixed up. When the Duke of Wellington returned to England from the Waterloo campaign, a certain countess held a levee of the most distinguished *haut ton* of the day, and applied to Kean to entertain the company with a few recitations. He refused without a moment's hesitation. He was told that the duke's numerous engagements, &c., precluded a visit to the theatre, but like his grace's eminent coadjutor, the late immovable Sir Thomas Picton, Kean was one of those men who, having once arrived at a determination, could never be induced to cancel it. When asked his reason for refusing the application, his reply was very characteristic. "I am asked by these people," he said, with a dash of mingled anger and bitterness in his tone, "not as their equal—not as a gentleman—scarcely as a man of talent—but as a wild beast, to be stared at." He was "proud, in his way."

CHAPTER IV.

THE opening of Drury-lane for the season 1816–
1817, on the 7th of September, was signalized
by the production of Byron's monody on the death of
Sheridan—a noble and feeling tribute to the genius of
the departed dramatist, orator, and wit.   Kean reappeared as Richard on the 24th, and trod his ancient
footsteps with unabated energy and brilliance.   His
production of *Timon of Athens*, on the 28th, showed
that the fervent admiration which he had always expressed for the innumerable beauties of this play was
not overlaid by considerations of its unsuitableness to
the stage.   *Timon of Athens* is essentially undramatic.
No one but Shakspeare, whose intellect was magnanimous in the extreme, could have had the courage to
unite such scanty material into a whole; little ingenuity is expended upon the construction of the incidents, few passions brought into activity which form
the most conspicuous agents of real life.   Yet, in

spite of these difficulties, Kean's representation of the principal character in this play, which is to be enjoyed rather in the closet than on the stage, was attended with the most fine and perfect results. The sustained force of his Shylock, and the caustic vigour of his Richard, might have been accepted as a reliable presage of the excellence with which he embodied the Timon of Shakspeare. His acting throughout was deep in feeling, intense, varied, and powerful. The earlier dialogues passed off with a degree of languor from which the finest acting could not redeem them; but as the play advanced, admiration of Kean's talent excited a deep solicitude; and the energy with which he gave the execrations of Timon, the intense thought which he infused into every word of his parting address to Athens, his altercation with the rugged and philosophical Apemantus, and his encouragement of the thieves in their warfare upon mankind, were unexceptionably admirable. His burst of impatience, "Give me breath," and the manner in which he reprobated the guests at the empty feast, were electrical; and nothing could have been more beautiful, or in closer conformity with the spirit of the part, than the grim and savage fury which possessed him throughout his different encounters with those who disturbed his soli-

tude in the woods. Mr. Harry Stoe Van Dyk writes
in an unpublished letter that Kean breathed the very
soul of melancholy and tenderness in those impressive
words :—

> "But myself,
> Who had the world as my confectionery;
> The mouths, the tongues, the eyes and hearts of men
> At duty, more than I could frame employment,
> That numberless upon me stuck, as leaves
> Do on the oak, have, with one winter's brush,
> Fell from their boughs, and left me open, bare
> For every storm that blows."

"The finest scene in the whole performance," writes
Leigh Hunt, "was the one with Alcibiades. We
never remember the force of contrast to have been
more truly pathetic. Timon, digging in the woods
with his spade, hears the approach of military music;
he starts, waits its approach silently, and at last in
comes the gallant Alcibiades with a train of splendid
soldiery. Never was scene more effectively managed.
First you heard a sprightly quick march playing in
the distance,—Kean started, listened, and leaned in a
fixed and angry manner on his spade, with frowning
eyes and lips full of the truest feeling, compressed but
not too much so; he seemed as if resolved not to be
deceived, even by the charm of a thing inanimate ;—
the audience were silent; the march threw forth its

gallant notes nearer and nearer, the Athenian stan-
dards appear, then the soldiers come treading on the
scene with that air of confident progress which is produced by the accompaniment of music; and at last,
while the squalid misanthrope still maintains his posture and keeps his back to the strangers, in steps, the
young and splendid Alcibiades, in the flush of victorious expectation.   It is the encounter of hope with
despair."

The classic school had sunk into disrepute; the
final performances of John Kemble were announced:
and the appearance on the scene of William Charles
Macready, who at first seemed disposed to become an
adherent to the now unpopular style, could not avert
its destruction.   Mr. Macready was born on the 3rd
of March, 1793, in Charles-street, Fitzroy-square, where
his father, at that time a member of the Covent-garden
company, then resided.   He was educated at Rugby
for the church, but having when a boy evinced a
strong predilection for the drama, his father, influenced
by a favourable prediction of Mrs. Siddons's, permitted him to pursue the bent of his own inclination,
and at the age of seventeen he made his first appearance on the stage as Romeo at Birmingham.
Having for a period of six years devoted himself

to the assiduous cultivation of every acquirement
necessary to the stage, he made his "*début*" on the
London stage at Covent-garden on the 16th of September, 1816, the character selected for the occasion
being that of Orestes in the *Distressed Mother* (Am-
brose Philips's version of Racine's *Andromaque*). From
the restricted nature of the part it was difficult to determine the full extent of the powers of the new candidate, but he acquitted himself of his unthankful
task in such a manner that the audience were sensibly
impressed in his favour.   Hazlitt was convinced that
he was by far the best tragic actor that had come out
within his remembrance, with the exception of Mr.
Kean ; and Edmund himself, who was present on the
occasion, honestly avowed that he had never seen
such a complete representation of the character.   Mr.
Macready's second part was Mentevole, in Jephson's
forgotten play of *The Italian Lover*, in which he confirmed but failed to extend the repute which he had
won in the previous effort.   Courting a direct contrast
with Kean, he played Othello to Young's Iago.   The
venture was not a fortunate one.   He failed to elec-
trify the audience with bursts of passionate emotion
so sudden and so overwhelming, or subdue them so
often by unlooked-for pathos, as Kean, whose marvel-

lous skill and energy in the character were indelibly
impressed upon the public mind; but Mr. Macready's
Othello was still a very excellent performance, abounding with individual traits of grandeur and beauty, and
forming altogether a consistent and harmonious whole.
One of the critics very accurately summed up the relative merits of Kean and Macready in this character
when he said that "we go to see Mr. Macready in
Othello; we go to see Othello in Mr. Kean." In
Sheil's tragedies, written expressly for Miss O'Neill,
Young, Charles Kemble, and himself, Mr. Macready
laid a solid foundation of future celebrity; and by the
success which he achieved in Gambia and Rob Roy
he so completely associated himself with the rise of
melodramatic representation in this country that he
regarded his reputation as an expositor of Shakspeare
and the poetical drama utterly ruined thereby. Fortunately his fears were not altogether realized; for
Knowles's *Virginius* had yet to be placed upon the
stage.

Timon of Athens was withdrawn from the Drury-lane
bills on the 18th of November, and on the 23rd Kean
appeared as Sir Edward Mortimer. *The Iron Chest*,
Colman's dramatized version of Godwin's fine novel,
Caleb Williams, is in itself undeniably weak, the scope

for the display of dramatic talent limited to a few powerful and interesting situations, and those situations being only interesting to those to whom they happened to be new. Originally produced in 1796, *The Iron Chest* was emphatically damned the first night, and the author, in the most insulting of prefaces, attributed the ill success of the play to an alleged wilful negligence on the part of John Kemble, who filled the rôle of Sir Edward Mortimer. The reason of its failure, however, is to be sought for in the very unsuitableness of Kemble's powers to a part invested with such motives and passions as the Falkland of Godwin's novel. " Give Kemble only the *man* to play, why he is nothing; give him the paraphernalia of greatness, and he is great. He ' wears his heart in compliment extern.' He is the statue on the pedestal, that cannot come down without danger of shaming its worshippers; a figure that tells well with appropriate scenery and dresses, but not otherwise. He contributes his own person to a tragedy— but only that. The poet must furnish all the rest, and make the other parts equally dignified and graceful, or Mr. Kemble will not help him out. He will not lend dignity to the mean, spirit to the familiar; he will not impart life and motion, passion and imagination to all around him, for he has neither life nor motion, passion nor imagination, in himself." Moreover, on the first night of *The Iron Chest* Kemble was too ill to act at all. For some years the tragedy lay on the shelf, till the fine voice and graceful demeanour of Elliston recalled it into popularity as a sort of melodrama scarcely definable between pantomime and opera. It remained in Elliston's possession up to the present time, when the public were startled to find Kean on a sudden converting the text which had been almost valueless from the lips of his predecessors into the means, point after point and scene after scene, of paralysing and electrifying his audiences. As the character admits of singular energy in its representation, there were few parts better adapted to Kean's peculiar conformation of powers. In the delineation of this wretched victim to a mistaken and deluded sense of honour, who worships the shadow of Nature while he violates her laws, he displayed more skill, because more variety, than he did in any character out of Shakspeare. The contrast between the original gentleness and benevolence of Mortimer and the incidental fits of terrified frenzy superinduced by circumstances, or provoked by some casual expression of those about him bearing ever so

remotely on the crime he had perpetrated, was marked
with matchless traits of truth and beauty; while his
description of the state of mind in which he slew his
oppressor, and his detail of the injuries which urged
him to the commission of the crime, left nothing to
be desired in the way of absorbing fervour and passionate intensity.   There was a terrific grandeur in
his abrupt and startling avowal to Wilford—

> " I stabbed him to the heart,
> And my gigantic oppressor rolled
> Lifeless at my feet;"

and the audience could only find relief from the
attendant impression by repeated rounds of applause.
In the concluding scene, in the execution of which
George Colman appears to have laid his best resources under contribution, Kean's acting was so fear-
fully impressive that doubts were expressed whether
the effect which he produced was not even greater
than that created by his representation of the final
scene of *A New Way to Pay Old Debts*;—a perfectly
natural doubt, for while his Sir Giles moved us to
terror his Sir Edward touched the finest springs of
human sensibility.   As Overreach he was altogether
alienated from the sympathies of his audience; as
Mortimer his broken heart was viewed with irre-

pressible sentiments of sorrow and compassion. In every part he was equal to himself. Nothing could have been more callous and hardened than his hypocrisy on the trial; nothing fiercer than the persecution which he relentlessly advanced; nothing more vivid, high wrought and terribly intense than the torpitude of his despair when the parchment was discovered, and the blood-imbrued dagger fell from within it. Nor had the audience been often more deeply moved than by the humbled and repentant tenderness which seemed to dissolve his worn-out spirit when he threw himself into Wilford's arms and besought his forgiveness. Hazlitt writes: " In the picturesque expression of outward passion by external action Mr. Kean is unrivalled. The transitions in this play from calmness to deep despair, from concealed suspicion to open rage, from smooth, decorous indifference to the convulsive agonies of remorse, gave Mr. Kean frequent opportunities for the display of his peculiar talents. The mixture of common-place familiarity and solemn injunction in his speeches to Wilford, when in the presence of others, was what no other actor could give with the same felicity and force. The last scene of all—his coming to life again after his swooning at the fatal discovery of his guilt, and then falling back after a ghastly struggle, like a man waked from the tomb into despair and death, in the arms of his mistress, was one of those consummations of the art which those who have not seen and not felt them in this actor may be assured that they have never seen or felt anything in their lives, and never will to the end of them." And Barry Cornwall says: "He looked — as no one ever looked before or since. The tones of his voice, trembling with remorse, penetrated your heart; and in the trial scene, where he sat silent and death pale, his fingers grasping the arm-chair in which he sate, till you thought that the strong oak must crumble into powder—who has ever done the like?"

The admiration of the audience was so great, that when Wallack came forward to announce the entertainments for the ensuing week, they insisted, as if with one voice, that *The Iron Chest* should take precedence of all others. Wallack retired to consult the actor, and found him in his dressing-room. He repeated the demand of the audience. "They want you to play Mortimer on your nights next week. I have prepared Richard for Monday, and Sir Giles for Wednesday. What's to be done?" "Anything you like," was the reply. "I'll play Mortimer on Monday, Wednesday, and Friday, it don't matter to me." This colloquy recalls to memory one that occurred some years later. "If you please, sir," said the call-boy, entering the dressing-room, "Mr. Elliston's compliments, and would like to know what you will play to-morrow night?" "Tell Mr. Elliston to suit his own convenience," was the answer. Intimate acquaintances of Kean will tell you that it was nothing unusual for the tragedian to arrive at the theatre unaware what character he was to appear in that evening. He was ever ready to undertake any of his parts at a moment's notice.

While *The Iron Chest* was in the full blow of its success at Drury-lane, Kean was studying to realize his high-piled conception of the beauty and impressiveness expended upon the character of Oroonoko, in Southerne's tragedy of the *African Prince*. Upon first considerations it might have been deemed that the character of Oroonoko, which shows a spirit shrinking within the measure of its chains, was not exactly adapted to the talents of an actor who had exhibited faculties more suited to a disposition to burst them asunder, and whose powers for the most part resided in the delineation of those conflicts of

passion which wayward circumstances enkindle. All
such anticipations were disappointed, for Oroonoko
proved one of his very best parts. The task was not
without some heavy responsibilities and difficulties.
The whole weight of the play rested upon his
shoulders, the interest of the *African Prince* centring
almost exclusively in the principal character; and the
subserviency of the author's fancy to his heart, which
renders his plays more feeling than poetical, invests
the pictures of slavery pertaining to the play with so
much truth that nothing short of absolute talent can
operate to sustain an audience under this impression.
Kean, however, passed safely through the ordeal. His
Oroonoko, while it achieved the end to which we
have referred, afforded another proof that he was as
successful in the deep, involuntary, heartfelt workings
of passion as in its more violent and muscular expression, in energy of action, discrimination of character,
and every variety of breadth, force, and grandeur. As
his Shylock and Richard III. might have presaged
the excellence with which he gave the causticness of
Timon, so innumerable passages in his Othello,
Hamlet, Richard II., and Octavian might have given
warning of the matchless beauty of his Oroonoko.
It was throughout highly impressive; and the un-

looked for strokes of passion which seemed to well up
spontaneously from his heart moved the audience to
tears.   Of this kind was the passage where his agonies
and his apprehensions at the supposed dishonourable
treatment of his wife were dispelled by Imoinda herself, and as he fell upon her neck with sobs of joy and
broken laughter, the social affections of the audience
sympathized with the actor in a way very rarely
witnessed.   His magnanimity in his slavery, the
relation of his marriage with the white man's daughter, the impassioned grandeur which pervaded his
sufferings, the preservation of his honour among the
dishonourable, his rebuke of the Christians for their
inhuman traffic—disdaining, however, to curse, "for
if any God had taught them to break His word he
need not curse them more;" his rooted and undying
love for Imoinda, and the comparison of his recollected greatness with his present ignominy, developed
talent of the very highest order.   The first glance he
gave to the long-lost loved one, where indeed

" His soul stole from his body through his eyes,"

was eloquently suggestive of the breathless eagerness,
surprise, astonishment, and distrusted conviction of
sight which crowded upon him; and in his fine

transition to tenderness and love the feelings of
Oroonoko, as conveyed by Edmund Kean, seemed to
gush from his heart, as if its inmost veins had been
laid open.   When Aboam suggested that if they
remained where they were Imoinda would become the
mother, and himself, an African Prince, the father of
a race of slaves, his ejaculation " Hah!" resembled,
writes Hazlitt, " the first sound that breaks from a
thunder cloud, or the hollow roar of a wild beast,
roused from its lair by hunger and the scent of blood."
Southerne, both in Oroonoko and Isabella, has often
" beguiled us of our tears."   The loves of the prince
and Imoinda in the former are the most tender,
the most pure, and the most exalted that have been
depicted since the days of Shakspeare.   He died at
the age of eighty-five, in 1746. ˙ Gray, the poet,
speaks thus of him in a letter dated from Burnham,
in Buckinghamshire, 1737 : " We have here old Mr.
Southerne at a gentleman's house a little way off: he
is now seventy-seven years old, and has almost wholly
lost his memory : but is as agreeable as an old man
can be : at least I persuade myself so when I look at
him and think of Isabella and Oroonoko."

Notwithstanding the combined attractions of the
Kembles, Young, Macready, and Miss O'Neill, Covent-

garden was gradually sinking in its competition with the single power of Kean at Drury-lane; and, finding that a figure of Apollo-like symmetry and proportions no longer constituted the *ne plus ultra* of dramatic renown, the managers employed a phalanx of agents to scour the country theatres and barns in search of an actor whose personal appearance might resemble that of Mr. Kean, or who, at all events, could so dress for Richard as to seem "to the manner born." This measure resulted in the introduction of Junius Brutus Booth, who made his first appearance in London at Covent-garden Theatre, as Richard III., on the 12th of February, 1817. Having had many opportunities of familiarizing himself with Kean's acting in the character, Booth, who was admirable as an imitator, found himself able to copy it with remarkable fidelity; and, "borrowing his predecessor's coat and feathers to appear in on the first and trying occasion," he exhibited an ingenious, perfect, and at the same time successful piece of plagiarism. Now the prime merit of an actor results from originality of thought and the selection of Nature as his model. If he does this, and succeeds, he is entitled to advance to the very front rank of his profession. But he who imitates the manner of others, however skilful and close the imitation, has but a poor ambition, and will never acquire eminence. Booth was an instance of this. He could do no more than catch the manner of his prototype; the soul which gave life and spirit and brilliance to that manner was beyond his reach, or of any other actor. " The faults of original genius are so easily outdone; its graces are so hard to catch." The success of Booth as an actor was, to say the least, equivocal. John Kemble was out of town, and, to quote Hazlitt's fine satire, " the managers of Covent-garden Theatre, after having announced in the bills that Mr. Booth's Richard the Third had met with a success unprecedented in the annals of histrionic fame (which to do them justice was not the case), very disinterestedly declined engaging him at more than two pounds a week." Now Booth (to borrow a simile from Hazlitt) had one property of the cameleon—that of reflecting all objects which he confronted; but not another—that of living upon air. He was not disposed to make himself hoarse three times a week for a pitiful stipend, and accordingly closed with an offer of the Drury-lane Committee to play second to Kean for a salary of ten guineas a week. On the 21st of February, *Othello* was played: the Moor by Kean;

Iago by Booth. The latter, if possible, was a still more ingenious and skilful imitation of Kean than of his Richard. He adhered to the copy in the most trifling minutiæ, and was not a bit deterred when, in the celebrated description of woman, he accidentally caught the eye of the noble Moor glancing at him with mingled curiosity and astonishment from one of the wings. He went through the part with firmness and decision, and Kean, standing at the wing, seemed to be preparing himself for a tremendous effort. We are told by Mr. Procter that on this occasion there was a greater firmness in his tread and general deportment, and that the tones of his voice were (beyond their wont) clear, rapid, and decisive; like those of a man conscious of his strength, and resolved to scatter aside by a single blow the vexations which an inferior antagonist had thrown in his way. At the commencement of the third act, Booth seemed for a moment to shrink from the contest, but he recovered his self-possession and proceeded. "But Kean!— no sooner did the interest of the story begin, and the passion of the part justify his fervour, than he seemed to expand from the small, quick, resolute figure which had previously been moving about the stage and to assume the vigour and dimensions of a giant. He glared down on the now diminutive Iago; he seized and tossed him aside with frightful and irresistible vehemence. Till then we had seen Othello and Iago as it were together; now the Moor seemed to occupy the stage alone. Up and down, to and fro he went, pacing about like the chafed lion who has received his fatal hurt, but whose strength is still undiminished. The fury and whirlwind of the passions seemed to have endowed him with supernatural strength. His eye was glittering and bloodshot; his veins were swollen, and his whole figure restless and violent. It seemed dangerous to cross his path and death to assault him. There is no doubt that Kean was excited on this occasion, as much as though he had been maddened with wine. The impression which he made on the audience has, perhaps, never been equalled in theatrical annals. One comedian, a veteran of forty years' standing, told us that when Kean rushed off the stage in the third act, he (our narrator) felt all his face deluged with tears, 'a thing, I give you my word, sir, that has never happened since I was a crack— thus high.' "*

That night stands out in bold relief and proudly distinguished from all others. It disclosed the im-

---

* Barry Cornwall.

portant secret that he could play better than he had ever played before. Two events only can be recurred to with anything like an approach to the pleasure of this recollection of Kean; firstly, his performance of the Moor on that November night in 1822 when Young played Iago; and secondly, the sight of the Kemble family in *Henry VIII.* Those who witnessed these matchless performances (and they are few now), recur to and reflect upon them with a sense of pleasure so unmingled that not only would they have made considerable sacrifices rather than have missed them, but they unconsciously cherish a little feeling of individual merit when they are referred to by persons who speak of the occasions by report only. To them it seems for the moment that the glory of the events in a degree reflects upon themselves, because—to use the French idiom—they " assisted" at the ceremonies. "I remember nothing of my old master" (Garrick), said honest John Bannister, the value of whose praise was enhanced by the fact that when he played with David, he had all a boy's tender susceptibility to histrionic excellence, while now he was " hardened in his art"—"I remember nothing of my old master which affected me so much as Kean's Othello, when Booth played Iago to him."

"Mine ancient" quickly discovered that he had
made a most unlucky move on the theatrical chess-
board. The contact had proved fatal to him. One
alternative presented itself; and, as the drowning
man grasps at a willow branch, he immediately
adopted it. Having been threatened with a legal
process by the officials who so disinterestedly fixed
his salary at two pounds a week, he induced the
Committee of Drury-lane to cancel the engagement
into which he had entered with them, and, like a
prodigal son, went back to Covent-garden, where he
encountered an opposition only to be paralleled in its
violence by the celebrated O. P. riots of 1809. He
might have said with angry Ned—"A plague on
both your houses." The opposition was eventually
silenced, partly by an apology from Booth, in which
he "threw himself upon the mercy of the house,"
partly—Hazlitt is pursuing his vein of keen satire—
"by the administration of club law to all those persons who thought they had a right to express their
disapproval as well as approbation of the behaviour
of an actor or the managers of a theatre towards
them; and partly by the aid of those enlightened
and impartial judges and distinguishers between
right and wrong, their watermen and firemen, who

were ordered to suspend the habeas corpus during the good pleasure of the powers that be."

The proprietors of Covent-garden Theatre were pleased to consider themselves sorely aggrieved over this matter. They regarded it as an unpardonable breach of propriety that Mr. Kean, acting upon a conviction that Mr. Booth's talents deserved a better recognition than they had obtained at their hands, should have interfered with what did not concern him by inducing the new actor to pass over to Drury-lane; and, smarting under the discredit which Mr. Kean's course of conduct had served to draw upon them, they deemed it expedient in their own interests, and also those of Mr. Booth, to circulate a false and malicious report on and concerning the gentleman to whom the agitation which now prevailed was entirely due. " The proprietors of Covent-garden Theatre" —so ran a placard which appeared two days subsequent to Booth's reappearance on that stage—" have received an intimation from a person, who states that he was at a place called the 'Coal Hole,' on Sunday last, where a club called the 'Wolves' are accustomed to assemble, and that he heard the whole party pledge themselves to drive Mr. Booth from the stage. They very properly discredited the person's evidence,

although he gave them a list of the names of the
club, and he has offered to identify their persons.
Such a dreadful combination surely never could exist;
the severest punishment that the law could inflict
would be too lenient for such conspirators against an
unprotected and inexperienced youth." Now it fortunately happened that this terrible design to damn
an inexperienced young man wanted one important
feature—*truth*. The Wolf Club had ceased to exist
upwards of nine months; and in order that the above
statement may be appreciated at its proper value, it is
necessary to refer to the circumstances under which
it was broken up. In the *Examiner* of April 28, 1816,
there appeared a letter, signed with the somewhat
plebeian name of John Brown, stating that a combination was in existence to crush if possible every
actor that appeared in any of Mr. Kean's characters;
that a club called the "Wolf Club," of which Mr.
Kean was president, had pledged themselves by oath
to damn every effort to rival him; and that this
laudable undertaking, which was supported by some
few of high rank in life, might, if made public, check
the infamous design, and leave to merit a fair chance.
The fact that the letter was written with the view of
mitigating the severity of the disapprobation ex-

pressed towards Cobham, a "ranting, roaring, periwig-pated ruffian" who had recently made an unsuccessful attempt to play Richard, and who, Mr. Brown alleged, had been hissed down by the "Wolves," gave rise to the necessary impression that the letter indirectly emanated from the Covent-garden authorities, who had the best reasons for wishing to expose Kean in an unfavourable light to the public—an impression participated in by Mr. Leigh Hunt, who, convinced that such a combination as that described by Mr. Brown was an impossibility, and aware that several members of the Covent-garden company belonged to the club, candidly told the writer that he did not believe a word of his allegation. Kean, in short, was acquitted by general consent from the motives which had been imputed to him ; but as there are a set of persons who, although shown that certain scandals are without foundation, persist against all appearances to believe that "there is something in it," he determined that the Wolf Club should be broken up. This determination was immediately carried into effect; but, with the view of catching his uninformed enemies tripping, he contrived that the dissolution should be kept a strict secret. A secret it was kept, and kept so faithfully that no one knew but what the Coal Hole in Fountain-court continued to remain the social head-quarters of the drama; and in endeavouring to allay the ferment against Booth by stating that the Wolf combination had determined to crush him, the Covent-garden authorities walked unsuspectingly into the trap which the tragedian had prepared for them, and by which he showed that envy, hatred, and all uncharitableness constituted the non-existent individual "from whom intimation had been received."

END OF THE FIRST VOLUME.

www.ingramcontent.com/pod-product-compliance
Lightning Source LLC
Chambersburg PA
CBHW030943110726
47900CB00004B/1106